Kiss Me Like You Mean It

Laura Wood is an author and an academic. Her debut adult novel, *Under Your Spell*, has sold into eighteen languages. She is also a bestselling and acclaimed author of children's and young adult novels. Laura has a PhD in nineteenth century literature, and lives in Warwickshire with her husband and their dog, Bea. You can visit lauraclarewood.com and follow her on Instagram @lauracwood.

Also by Laura Wood

Under Your Spell
Let's Make a Scene

LAURA WOOD

Kiss Me Like You Mean It

SIMON & SCHUSTER

London · New York · Amsterdam/Antwerp · Sydney/Melbourne · Toronto · New Delhi

First published in Great Britain by Simon & Schuster UK Ltd, 2026

1 3 5 7 9 10 8 6 4 2

Simon & Schuster UK Ltd, 7th Floor,
199 Bishopsgate, London, EC2M 3TY

Simon & Schuster Australia, Sydney
Simon & Schuster India, New Delhi

www.simonandschuster.co.uk
www.simonandschuster.com.au
www.simonandschuster.co.in

The authorised representative in the EEA is Simon & Schuster Netherlands BV, Herculesplein 96, 3584 AA Utrecht, Netherlands. info@simonandschuster.nl

A CIP catalogue record for this book is available from the British Library

Paperback ISBN: 978-1-3985-6300-1
eBook ISBN: 978-1-3985-6301-8
Audio ISBN: 978-1-3985-6302-5

Typeset in Bembo by M Rules
Printed and Bound in the UK using 100% Renewable Electricity at CPI Group (UK) Ltd

FSC www.fsc.org
MIX
Paper | Supporting responsible forestry
FSC® C013604

This book is dedicated to screwball comedies, and Dolly Parton, and autumn leaves, and pink squirrel cocktails, and book groups, and excellent dogs and a very specific maple oat latte I drank in Camden, Maine. I am grateful to all of these things for reminding me that there is delight to be found even in tough times.

PART ONE
Las Vegas

Chapter One

Lee

I wonder if the designer who selected this crushed velvet, leopard-print bar stool imagined it would one day be occupied by an accountant having an existential crisis.

Probably not. A luxury, five-star casino in Las Vegas isn't really an existential crisis sort of place. As far as I can tell the whole point of Vegas is to overstimulate you to the point where it's impossible to worry about anything at all.

But, hey, I've always enjoyed a challenge.

'Gin martini with a twist,' Jake, the handsome bartender, says, setting the glass in front of me with a smile. 'You sure I can't get you anything to eat?'

I shake my head. It's 5 p.m. on a Friday and I'm already regretting grabbing a drink at the bar, instead of heading up to my room, ordering room service and watching home improvement shows in my pyjamas. But I *am* under strict instructions to 'live a little' on my last night.

'Just the drink, thanks.' I slip some cash across the top of the bar, and he holds his hands up like I've pointed a gun at him.

'No way,' he says. 'Boss's orders. But anything you need tonight, you let me know.'

There's something in the way he says this. Is it possible that this man is flirting with me? Let's not get ahead of ourselves ... the Americans do take their customer service very seriously. I sip my drink, eyeing him over the top of my glass as he spins a cocktail shaker with large, capable hands.

This bar is certainly not my normal habitat. Between the deep, claret red walls, the splashy modern art and the enormous chandelier that looms overhead, strung with over 300,000 sparkling crystals (I've seen the itemised invoice to prove it), there is absolutely nothing subtle about it.

A neon sign glows above the bar in a scrawl of red light: SINNERS WELCOME.

I wonder how they feel about neurotic rule-followers.

My eyes dart towards Jake again.

What if he *was* flirting with me? Would I ever have the guts to do something about it? Would flirting back count as 'living a little'? And how, I ponder, tapping my fingers against my glass, would someone go about such a thing?

I pull out my phone and type *How do you flirt with a bartender?* into Google. The results are something of a minefield. The first two answers are *be conversational*, and *be reserved*.

See, *this* is why people are so hard.

I keep scrolling and there are suggestions of smiling, dropping compliments and a post about doing something anatomically improbable with your tongue and a cherry stem.

Taking a deep breath, I send Jake a smile across the bar. I have no idea if it seemed flirtatious, but he does come straight over.

'Something I can get you, Lee?'

I'm not totally sure how to respond. How do you do reserved conversation? And I don't have a cherry.

'I like your name badge,' I blurt.

Jake's eyebrows lift. Okay. I will admit it wasn't the sexiest compliment, but it was *something*, right?

'Thank you,' Jake replies after a moment.

'Where did you get it?' I ask breathlessly. Maybe the breathless thing is coming off as sexy? Either that or I sound like I'm about to have an asthma attack.

'Um . . . it came with the uniform,' he says. 'But I can ask someone if you like?'

'Sure,' I nod, trying to look casual while my palms are sweating. 'That would be great.'

He leans forward, his forearms resting on the bar. They're good arms. 'Anything for my favourite customer,' he says with a wink.

A wink! And a lean! He *is* flirting! Or maybe bartenders in Vegas wink at people all the time? God, this is torture. I'm probably supposed to say something. Maybe he's winking so that I can . . . what? Buy him a drink? Pick him up? Engage in a night of passionate lovemaking?

I need more gin as that thought settles.

A one night stand? I mean, it would be *dramatically* out of character for me, but then, I am in Las Vegas. Sin City. The place where people come to act out of character. I could be someone different here. I could be a little wild. Just for one night.

There's only one thing to do. I grab a napkin and a pen from my bag and set about making a pros and cons list. I scrawl 'One Night Stand?' across the top, draw a line down the middle and in the 'pros' column I write:

Haven't had sex for four months. Then I consider it for a moment, cross out *four* and write *five.*

I eye the words as I reach for my glass. It's a pretty compelling argument actually.

'Daisy? Is that you?'

I choke on my drink.

The familiar gravelly voice hits my system harder than the gin.

There's only one person in the whole world who calls me Daisy. And there's no way he's here.

Slowly, I spin around on my stool. My eyes are fixed on the floor, as I take a deep, steadying breath, so that the first thing I see is a pair of scuffed leather boots.

My heart is dancing an Irish jig in my chest.

I let my gaze travel up, over the jeans, over the hard, muscular body, the broad shoulders in the battered leather jacket. It feels like everything has slowed down, like time is stretching out between us as I take him in, cataloguing every feature.

The firm jaw, darkened by a day or two of scruff; the laughing mouth, with the tiny scar above his top lip; the deadly pair of cheekbones that he inherited from his professionally attractive mother; the suntanned skin of someone who is permanently outdoors; the carelessly tousled dark curls, longer than the last time I saw him; and the gleam of gold from the tiny hoop in his ear.

I register all of it in rapid, high-definition snapshots, before my eyes meet his – dark, crinkled at the corners as he looks at me, surprised and delighted.

'Nico,' I manage, his name little more than a whisper.

I wonder then if this is a mirage, the way a man who's dying of thirst in the desert might hallucinate a shady oasis with clear, running water.

I just see Nico.

Yeah, that tracks.

'Lee!' he exclaims. 'What the fuck are you doing in Vegas?'

Before I can answer, he's hauling me off the bar stool, and wrapping his arms around me, wrapping his whole body around me, and my cheek is pressed against the soft leather of his jacket.

Not a mirage then. Mirages don't smell this good. They don't feel this good, this strong and safe and thrilling at the same time. All of my muscles relax as I melt into him. I think I might . . . moan? Please, please, please let that sound have been in my head.

Then his hands are on my shoulders and he pulls back from me, holding me steady. Which is good, because the combination of gin and Nico is a potent one and my knees are a bit shaky.

'You're here?' I say, and even though I'm ninety-nine per cent certain I haven't hallucinated him, the words still sound like a question.

'For work,' he confirms. 'You look great.'

I glance down and try not to wince. I'm wearing black, high-waisted trousers and a white silk blouse done all the way up to my throat. God, couldn't I even loosen a couple of buttons? I was in the middle of flirting – or attempting to flirt – with a handsome bartender. At the very least, I should have been flashing some clavicle. In fact, why didn't I get changed before heading to the bar?

I almost laugh out loud at that thought, one that implies I have a suitcase full of seductive ensembles to choose from, rather than what I actually packed: four variations on this outfit and a pair of pyjamas. And not sexy pyjamas either, but stretched out, comfy ones covered in pictures of little pineapples wearing sunglasses.

All of this runs through my head, but when I open my mouth, what comes out is a slightly croaky, 'Thanks, so do you.'

'So,' he lifts a brow, 'don't keep me in suspense. What's a nice girl like you doing drinking alone in a bar in Las Vegas?'

'Oh,' I wave my hand in a dismissive gesture, 'I'm here for work, too.'

Nico nods. 'Is there a convention or something?' He glances around the bar as if he expects to see an army of calculator-wielding accountants.

'No—' I start, but he's already pulled out the seat next to mine, and he's leaning over, trying to catch Jake's attention.

My stomach lurches when I spot the napkin with my barely started pros and cons list on it next to his elbow, and I think I pull a muscle snatching it away and stuffing it in my pocket.

The bartender makes his way over, and when he looks at me, his smile has dimmed. I can't blame him – most men take one glance at Nico and know they can't compete, even if in this case any competition would be purely theoretical.

I might have been in love with Nico since I was five years old, but if you ask him he'll tell you I'm the little sister he never had. It is, in fact, the great tragedy of my life: hopelessly pining over Nico Hart, my brother's best friend, for twenty-six years and counting.

'What are you drinking?' Nico asks me.

'I'll have another martini, please, Jake,' I say. 'And a bottle of Corona with lime if you have it. Would you add it to my tab?'

'Of course, Lee,' he smiles.

When I turn back to Nico, he's grinning. 'Well, well, well,' he says. 'I didn't realise I was going to be cramping your style. Do you want me to leave?'

'No!' I blurt, way too earnestly. 'You're not cramping anything.'

We're interrupted when Jake places our drinks in front of us, and I watch him leave without a single pang of regret. Nico appearing is like a message from the universe: stay in your lane, Ophelia Turner-Jones. No wild one night stands for you.

Nico holds his bottle towards me in a silent toast and I tap it with my glass.

'Thanks for the drink,' he says. 'And for remembering my order.'

I try not to watch too closely as he lifts the bottle to his mouth. I should be more careful about giving myself away. I shouldn't know what his favourite beer is. I shouldn't know the ten thousand other tiny facts I know about him like the way he loves raspberry-flavoured things but hates actual raspberries, how he does jigsaw puzzles working from the inside out (the lunatic), or how he got that scar on his lip trying to do a wheelie on his bicycle to impress Tansy Bennet when he was thirteen. I shouldn't jealously hoard these scraps of information like a magpie with an eye for something shiny.

'Sorry. Did you want a cocktail or something?' I'm flustered and I hate it. I wasn't ready for him, I wasn't prepared for his Nico-ness, not here and now.

'It's perfect.' He puts the bottle back down on the bar and scrubs both hands over his face. 'Just what I need after a long day.'

'You said you've been working?'

'If you can call it that. Spent a few days hiking in the Grand Canyon with a couple of friends. Had to get away from all the drama.'

'What drama?'

Nico rolls his eyes. 'All the legal stuff that comes with Dad's death. Honestly, I don't even understand half of it but it seems to involve an entire army of lawyers and everyone wants their pound of flesh.'

I wince. Nico's father was a duke – yes, an *actual* duke – but Nico's mum Claudia was his second wife and the two of them had a pretty acrimonious divorce. His dad passed away a few months ago and Nico's half-brother Ward, from his father's first marriage, inherited the title and the estate. As far as I know, Nico doesn't speak to that side of his family at all.

'I'm sorry,' I say hesitantly. 'I should have said right away. I know how strange it must have been for you. Your relationship was complicated.'

He laughs then, though it holds no humour. 'That's a polite word for it. Anyway, this trip has been just what I needed, and I got some great shots of the condors. It was beautiful, but after all that peaceful communing with nature I felt the itch for some noise, bright lights and a decent meal, so I headed here.' His eyes meet mine and an electric zing runs through my whole body. 'And look at how that's worked out. Serendipity.'

'I can't believe you're really here.' I shake my head. 'It seems like ages since I last saw you.'

'It's got to be about a year, right?' Nico looks thoughtful. 'At your mum and dad's house with Jack and Cynthie?'

The first time my brother had brought his fiancée Cynthie home to meet the family. It had been as fraught as most interactions are with my parents. Thankfully, Nico was there to smooth the way. The peacemaker. It's a role he's played often over the years.

'Right,' I agree now. 'At least a year. And Gran was *very* upset that she missed you.'

'Oh, don't worry, I know. I got a proper telling off.'

It's my turn to grin. My parents, Max Jones and Caroline Turner, were two of the biggest stage and screen stars in their day, and their relationship makes Burton and Taylor's look like a Disney movie. Gran was the one in charge of us kids. With all the time Nico spent at our house growing up there's a running joke in our family that he's her favourite grandchild. It should be noted that neither of them have ever denied this.

'Did she make you feel like a worm?'

'What do you think?' He tilts his head, mischief dancing in his eyes. 'How's she doing, anyway?'

'Gran? She's great. She's taken up Taekwondo because, and I quote, "*we're two vulnerable women living alone and if anyone ever broke in you'd be about as much help as some limp spaghetti*." Which is ridiculous,' I huff, 'because – first off – I'm surprisingly scrappy, and secondly, no one's getting past the security system Jack insisted on having installed at our place. It'd be like breaking into the Pentagon.'

Nico chuckles. 'Still, good to know you'll be living with Jason Bourne should shit hit the fan.'

'Yeah, maybe give her a few more weeks before she's ready to roundhouse kick potential intruders. It seems to be mostly about bowing and breathing at the moment, which is a relief. I do worry that she's not slowing down *at all*,' I confess. 'The woman *is* eighty-two. She's terrible at remembering to take all her pills and she ignores everything the doctor says about her diet. I'll bet you any amount of money she's spent the last few days consuming nothing but foie gras, posh crisps and vodka.' My fingers tap a nervous tattoo on the bar.

'I know her better than to take that bet.' Nico takes my hand in his and squeezes my fingers. His touch is warm and steadying. (If something that makes your entire body sing can be described as steadying.) 'I also know you worry about her. We all do, but she's an adult, Lee. She's in better shape at eighty-two than most people are at fifty. Some fancy pâté isn't going to bring her down.'

I exhale a slow breath. 'You're right. I just can't imagine . . .' I trail off, and Nico lets go of my hand in favour of slinging an arm around my shoulder so that I can lean into him.

He understands why I'm anxious. Gran is a force of nature and even thinking about a world without her makes me want to curl up in a small ball.

'Come on,' Nico says, 'let's go and sit in one of those shadowy booths so that you can fill me in on all your gossip. It's getting noisy in here, and I want you to myself.'

YOU CAN HAVE ME!!!! my brain shrieks, but thankfully, my mouth manages a casual, 'Sure.'

Nico slides from his seat, catching Jake's attention and gesturing to our drinks before hooking his thumb towards one of the cosy booths that line the side of the room. Jake nods, and I gather my handbag and the black Temperley jacket hung over my seat. Nico takes my hand, tugging me along after him.

I don't come from a touchy-feely family. Even Gran isn't big on physical affection, but Nico has always been incredibly tactile, and as usual it's a kind of delicious torture every time he touches me.

Wedging himself into the corner of the booth, Nico's long legs sprawl under the table, and his arm rests along the top of the banquette. I resist the urge to draw closer to him and focus on asking questions about the hike he's just done.

'And how long are you in Vegas for?' I ask eventually.

'Until tomorrow.' His fingertips toy with my hair, which is pulled back in a mermaid braid. I didn't previously think that hair had nerve endings, but try telling that to the rest of my body, which is lighting up like a Christmas tree. 'I'm actually heading to LA to catch up with Jack and Cyn for a few days.' He gives my plait a teasing tug. 'You should come along.'

'I have to work,' I say. *And I wasn't invited*, I add mentally, while trying not to show that it hurts, that my brother rarely seems to remember that I exist.

At that moment, a woman struts by our table. She's absolutely gorgeous, her curves poured into a tight, short dress. Tossing her hair, she flashes Nico a seductive smile over her shoulder, her red lips curving in invitation. Clearly, this woman realises I'm no threat at all. If I wasn't here killing the vibe, I'm sure he'd be half way up to her room already. As it is, Nico's too polite to do more than return her smile before his attention is back on me.

'Speaking of work, stop distracting me with questions and tell me what you're doing here,' Nico says.

'Oh, well, actually—' I start, but I'm cut off when Nico leans forward.

'Holy shit!' he murmurs, and his hand drops to my leg under the table, which means his next words take a long moment to reach me. 'Sorry to interrupt but . . . I think Frankie Martelli just walked in.'

'I—' I start again, still thrown by the feeling of his fingers lightly pressing against my thigh. 'Frankie Martelli?' I repeat, dazed.

Nico nods, and his expression is elated. 'He owns this place. He doesn't bother coming down to the floor much these days, the guy's got to be almost ninety. He's a *legend*. Oh, shit, I wish I had my camera. Look at that face.' His fingers tense, squeezing my flesh, and I inhale sharply, but fortunately he doesn't seem to notice. 'He's coming this way,' he practically squeals. '*Be cool*.'

I turn my head to watch as the hotel owner approaches, wearing a broad grin. Nico's right, he's got a great face. Heavily lined, and full of character. He stops beside us and beams down from behind a pair of oversized glasses. He's dressed in a snappy dark red suit and he looks every inch the owner of one of Las Vegas's biggest casinos.

'Sweet Ophelia!' he booms.

Nico makes a small, sharp sound of surprise as I reply:

'Hey, Frankie.'

Chapter Two

Nico

'Hey, Frankie,' Lee says. Then she nudges me so she can slip out from the booth and Frankie 'The Shark' Martelli kisses her enthusiastically on both cheeks.

'I see you took my advice about visiting the bar,' he beams at her.

'Was it advice?' Lee asks dryly. 'It felt more like an order.'

'A beautiful woman like you really classes up the place. It's good for business.'

I think my head is going to explode. Lee, as usual, looks utterly unruffled. It's as if ageing mobsters fawn over her all the time. Maybe they do. Lee's life is a bit of a mystery to me, and to be honest I've tried to keep it that way.

It's not a good look to be too interested in your best friend's little sister. Especially when that sister is Lee – insanely bright, funny and – sure, I have eyes – extremely beautiful.

That poor dope behind the bar was practically drooling over her when I showed up. Not that I could blame him. She made quite the picture, sitting alone, one leg swung over the other, the red soles of her dangerously high heels peeking out from under her black trousers, her honey-gold hair pulled back in a long, soft braid. She looked so put-together and elegant, all buttoned up in a silky white shirt, like a gift waiting to be unwrapped. Slowly.

At least that's what I assume that Jake character was thinking. *I* was very careful not to think things like that. I'd been careful in that direction for years. I *definitely* didn't feel the wild, momentary urge to punch that guy right in the mouth.

'Frankie, this is my old friend, Nico Hart,' Lee says now, making the introductions. 'Nico, this is Frankie Martelli. He owns the hotel.'

Yeah, along with half the strip.

I keep my expression neutral as I lean over to shake his hand. Frankie's grip is firm, and there's a paternal glint in his eye as he looks between me and Lee. His hand tightens briefly around mine before he lets go, and I understand the warning. *Hurt her and I'll break your legs.*

With Frankie Martelli it's not an idle threat.

'This your guy, Lee?' Frankie asks, still watching me from behind the enormous glasses that magnify his eyes, but Lee only laughs.

'No, Nico is Jack's best friend. We actually grew up next door to each other.'

'Is that so?' Frankie still doesn't exactly look friendly, but his posture relaxes slightly. 'Well, any friend of Lee's is a friend of ours here at the Coliseum. Anything you want, consider it comped.'

'That's very kind of you, sir,' I reply, still bemused.

'Not with all the money this one saved me this week.' Frankie turns to Lee, and the tough guy pose melts away entirely. 'I came to ask if you'd join me and the boys for poker again, but I can see you're busy.'

What. The. Fuck?

'Oh,' a small line appears between Lee's brows, 'well, maybe Nico can join us? He and Jack are actually the ones who taught me to play poker.'

I smile at the memory. 'Yeah, you were nine and you absolutely hustled us.'

Frankie exhales a wheezy laugh. 'You played her recently?'

'Not for years.'

Amusement glimmers in his eyes. 'Come along then, it'd be nice to watch her fleece someone who isn't a frail old man.'

'Frankie!' Lee actually gives the fucking *Shark* a little shove. 'First of all, you and that motley crew are hardly frail old men.'

Frankie pulls a leather case from the breast pocket of his jacket and extracts a cigar, clamping it between his teeth. 'We're a virile bunch,' he agrees, around the sides of the unlit cigar.

'And I don't *fleece* people,' Lee continues primly, as if he hasn't spoken. 'If you don't want to risk losing then you shouldn't play.'

I stare at her, this tiny blonde woman scolding the one-time leader of the Martelli crime family. And he's beaming down at her like he loves it.

Lee darts a look at me, and takes a deep breath before turning back to Frankie. 'Do you think it would be okay . . . if Nico took some pictures of the game?'

My spine straightens and I try to hide my surprise.

'Pictures?' Frankie frowns.

'Nico's an *amazing* photographer,' Lee says earnestly, and then she's fishing her phone out of her handbag and showing Frankie some of my work, which she apparently has saved for easy access. I watch as she murmurs something about the photographs she pulls up, and I catch her name-dropping various publications I've worked with.

Whatever she's saying has Frankie looking grudgingly impressed, but he's still hesitant. 'I don't know, Lee, the fellas might not like it . . .'

'You know they'll say yes if you do,' Lee insists. Her smile turns sly. 'And Nico already told me you have a *great* face.'

'This old mug?' Those magnified eyes swing towards me again.

I shrug, trying not to look too invested in the outcome. 'It's true. Plus, in my experience, interesting subjects make interesting photographs.'

'Hmmm,' Frankie sniffs, but I can tell he's on the hook. 'You got your camera with you?'

'Not right this second but it's in my room.'

'Bring it along and we'll see.' He turns his attention back to Lee. 'We're meeting in the back room at seven.'

'We'll see you there,' Lee nods, and then the two of us watch in silence as Frankie leaves, calling out greetings to people as he goes.

'That was Frankie Martelli!' I exclaim when he's out of earshot. 'You just got *Frankie Martelli* to agree to a photo shoot.'

'I know. I told you, he owns the hotel.'

'He's a mobster, Lee.'

She laughs. 'Frankie? He's a sweetheart.'

'He used to be the head of the Martelli crime family until he "retired" a couple of decades ago and his son took over.' I keep my voice low. 'He's a proper, old-school gangster. He practically ran Las Vegas in the late Sixties. *He shook hands with Sinatra!*' I finish a little desperately.

'He has no criminal convictions,' Lee frowns. 'Nothing that was flagged in background. I think you're wrong. Well, except about the Sinatra thing, Frankie told me that himself. He has some great stories.' She smiles at this, the rare, wide smile that makes twin dimples appear in her cheeks.

I laugh. 'I'm not wrong. Although he's cleaned up his image a lot. Gone legit.'

'Oh, well then,' Lee shrugs, spectacularly unworried by this information. 'I suppose that makes sense. He's a very astute businessman, you know.'

'Yeah, I bet,' I manage. 'So, are you going to tell me how the hell you've become poker buddies with the guy?'

'I met Frankie at a work event a couple of years ago and we hit it off. We stayed in touch and he hired me to take care of some business for him.'

'You're his accountant?' I say in disbelief. '*You*,' I point at her, 'are *Frankie Martelli's* accountant?'

'I wish you'd stop saying his name like that,' Lee huffs. 'Whatever he did in the past, now he's a respected member of the community.'

'Sorry.' I try to keep the laughter out of my voice and appear properly chastised. 'So. You're his accountant?' I say again, and I keep my tone carefully neutral this time.

'I'm *one* of his accountants,' Lee says vaguely.

'You've been – what – helping him with his taxes?' I prod, thinking about the comment Frankie made about her saving him money.

Lee looks wary now, and picks an invisible fleck from her trousers. 'I'm not that type of accountant.'

That gives me pause. I've never thought much about Lee's job, which I now realise makes me a pretty shitty friend. 'What type of accountant are you?'

'I'm a freelance forensic accountant.' Seeing my blank look at this, she adds, 'I investigate potential financial crimes.'

'So you're investigating Frankie?'

'No!' She rolls her eyes. 'When he ran into a problem, he asked me to go over his accounts and look out for any . . . anomalies.'

'Holy shit,' I breathe, leaning forward. 'Don't tell me someone was stupid enough to try and steal from The Shark?'

Lee purses her lips. 'Client confidentiality prevents me from answering that question.'

'So that's a yes, then. I can't believe anyone thought they'd get away with it.'

'*Hypothetically*,' Lee says, 'as Frankie heads an enormous business operation, it would be possible for a person to help themselves to relatively small amounts over long periods of time that would fail to raise any red flags. If they were careful and very, very clever.'

'Not clever enough apparently.' I eye her with appreciation. 'So you've uncovered the thief and handed them over to Frankie. I don't like their chances.'

'Don't be ridiculous, Nicolas,' Lee says, and she sounds so much like her grandmother that it makes me grin. 'Naturally, I have passed on all the relevant materials to the authorities myself. Frankie knew that was one of my conditions when he contracted me.'

'Why on earth would he agree to that?'

'Because I'm extremely good at my job, and Frankie only hires the best.' She pauses. 'And because he's not the criminal mastermind you seem determined to paint him as. You'll see tonight when he's showing you pictures of his grandchildren and reminiscing with his friends.'

'Yeah, yeah, and tell me, do his friends all have names like Freddie-Four-Fingers and Billy the Fish?'

Her dimples quiver. 'One of them is called Spuds, for reasons I have yet to determine.'

'He probably used to beat people to death with a potato.'

'Or he enjoys a nice plate of chips.'

'Or that.' I lean back. 'Either way, I can't believe we're going to spend tonight playing poker with Frankie Martelli, and I get to take pictures of it. What a story! We'll be telling the grandkids about this one.'

Lee gives a little huff of laughter. 'Grandkids? Chance would be a fine thing.'

'No future Mr Lee Turner-Jones on the horizon?'

'My romantic life is a bit of a wasteland at the moment.' She fiddles with her shirt cuff.

'You'll meet someone,' I say, and I don't have to fake my

confidence. Lee is absolutely the sort of woman you marry. If you're the sort of person who gets married, that is.

'I'm thirty-one,' Lee sighs. 'I've been thinking I need to get a move on.'

'Yes, I didn't like to say anything but you're giving off real aged spinster vibes. You've no money and no prospects, you're already a burden to your parents . . . and you're frightened.'

She laughs, and some of the tension leaves her eyes. 'Please, Nico. You know better. We only recognise the 1995 *Pride and Prejudice* adaptation in my family.'

'But, Lee,' I counter, 'what about the hand flex?'

Her eyebrows arch. 'I'll give you the hand flex, but that is all the ground I'll concede. And you'd be wise to accept that as the final word on the subject if you ever want to binge the entire BBC box set with Gran and me again.'

'Fair enough.'

'Anyway,' Lee continues. 'The point is I haven't been in a relationship for ages and I live with my eighty-two-year-old grandmother. Most of the time I'd rather hang out with her than drag myself out on a date with anyone.'

'That makes perfect sense. I'd rather hang out with Gran than go on a date, too. Besides,' I continue, 'we're here in Las Vegas, at one of the most exclusive hotels in the world, and we can have anything we want, free of charge. Now isn't the time to be moping.'

'You're right.' Lee straightens in her seat, a funny look of determination settling on her face. 'I can let loose for once. I can . . . live a little. What's the harm? We've got forty minutes before the poker game. What do you want to do?'

I glance over at the bar and then I turn back to her and smile.

'Which do you think is their most expensive bottle of champagne?'

Chapter Three

Nico

When I prise my eyes open, the throbbing in my head has me biting back a groan. As the scene in front of me dips and weaves I wonder, dimly, at what point I got on a boat. I close my eyes again. The world seems to steady, and this time, when I open them, I realise I'm not on a boat. I'm in bed.

And I'm not alone.

It takes me a long time to organise the facts. My arm is wrapped around someone, pulling her back against me. She's pressed, all warm, soft curves, against my front. Sunlight streams over us, and I don't care for it, but it does highlight the spill of gold hair across the pillow beside me. Whoever it is, she smells good – sweet and a little smoky. I realise I'm not wearing a shirt, but I am still wearing my jeans.

What am I doing in bed in my jeans?

Especially when there's someone else in the bed with me. Drowsily, I stroke the blonde hair back, revealing the line of her neck, and she moves against me in her sleep, rocking her hips back against mine. Even with the pounding headache I can appreciate that.

'Nico,' the woman murmurs huskily, and that is the moment I go rock hard.

It's also the moment I realise I'm in bed with Lee.

I freeze as she shifts again, but after several tense seconds tick by I know she's still asleep, and it's time to take stock of the situation.

What the ever living fuck happened last night? My brain gropes for memories that don't seem to be there. Plus, thinking too hard seems only to intensify the blinding pain in my skull. Let's start with something easier. *Where am I?*

Lifting my head is a Herculean task, but I manage it for long enough to take in my surroundings. This definitely isn't my hotel room. This is an enormous, ridiculous suite – the kind that costs an astronomical amount of money, the kind they put Beyoncé up in. All the hideous daylight that is offending my abused corneas pours in from the huge windows that take up one whole wall of the bedroom. I can see the entire strip laid out below us like a children's toy, a stream of tiny Matchbox cars marching along the busy streets.

The bed we're in is the size of a small, private island, but that hasn't made much difference because Lee and I are wrapped tightly around each other in the middle of it.

Lee.

Fuck, fuck, fuck.

I wince again, trying to pull gently away from her. My hand is resting on her stomach, and I can feel the warm silk of her skin under my fingertips, but there's fabric, too, the soft cotton of a waistband. She's wearing pyjamas.

Okay, she's wearing pyjamas and I'm wearing my jeans. This could be perfectly innocent.

But try telling that to my dick, which doesn't seem to have received the message that the body it's responding to belongs to my best friend's extraordinarily off-limits sister with whom I have a strictly platonic relationship.

I carefully untangle myself from Lee, and roll so that there are several inches of expensive, ten-thousand-thread-count sheet between us.

After that effort I need a bit of a rest again. Several minutes tick by as I screw my eyes shut and keep my body as still as possible. I remember the poker game in Frankie's 'back room', which turned out to be a cushy private den, all mahogany and red silk and cigar smoke. I remember the way Lee sat serenely gathering in everyone's chips and the way five retired gangsters grinned in approval. I remember the raucous storytelling, the drinks being passed around. So. Many. Drinks. I remember Lee and I heading to a different bar afterwards, and there being shots involved . . . shots that were on fire, maybe? And after that it's pretty much a blank.

Just as I'm psyching myself up for an attempt to move, Lee sends me careening towards cardiac arrest by sitting straight up in the bed like a fucking vampire.

'Nico?' she whispers, blinking down at me as she clutches the sheets to her chest. She looks dazed, and there are panda smudges of mascara under her indigo blue eyes.

'Oh my god,' I rasp, my hand pressed over my heart, which seems to be trying to beat its way out of my chest. 'Do you always wake up like that? I think I'm having palpitations. I might need medical attention.'

'You're here,' she says as if I haven't spoken. 'You're . . . in my bed.' Her eyes widen. 'Did we . . .' Her gaze drops to my bare chest, where it lingers for a long moment. Her lips part in shock.

'No!' I say firmly, then I pull the sheets back to reveal my denim-clad legs. 'I slept in my jeans. *Like a gentleman.*'

Lee doesn't need to know that I spent the night wrapped around her like a fucking vine. That was sleeping Nico, I can't be responsible for sleeping Nico. *Awake* Nico thinks of Lee purely as a friend. Awake Nico is very respectful. And very, very hungover.

'Okay,' Lee murmurs, and she looks down at her pyjamas, which I now see are covered in weirdly cheerful tropical fruits. She seems, somehow, to have buttoned herself into the top half back to front. Her hand goes to the backwards collar that threatens to strangle her. 'Okay,' she says again.

I rub my hands over my face. 'I think I died,' I croak finally. 'I think I am dead right now. My whole body hurts.'

'If you hurt, you're probably not dead,' Lee points out distantly. Her brow is creased as if she's deep in thought.

'Oh, yeah. Well, that's good news, at least. Then again the cool embrace of the infinite void sounds pretty inviting right now.'

'It's too early for existential dread.' Lee sinks back against the pillow, her face pale. 'Or is it? What time is it?'

'I have no idea.'

'What *happened* last night?' she asks after a moment.

'It's a bit . . . hazy,' I admit.

'Yeah.' Lee nods, and then winces as if the movement was painful. 'There was the champagne. And the cocktails. And the shots—' she cuts herself off abruptly. 'Oh god,' she moans, before stumbling from the bed and in the direction of a door that I'm guessing leads to the bathroom. It slams shut behind her.

With a groan I roll over onto my side and then slowly, *slowly* pull myself up to a sitting position. My feet hit the floor and I hiss out a long breath. The clock on the bedside table says 12:34 and I stare at it for a moment, trying to remember what numbers are and how time works. I haul myself to my feet and shuffle towards the bathroom like an elderly man.

I'm thirty-eight years old. I should not be waking up this hungover in Vegas. These are lessons I learned many years ago when I was young and full of vigour. Then, I would have laughed this off and suggested we go for a morning hand of Blackjack and a cheeseburger. Now, a hangover like this one could end up putting me out of action for a week. I have to catch a flight in only a few hours, and the thought is monstrous.

'Lee?' I say, knocking on the door.

'Go away,' comes the miserable response, followed by the unmistakable sound of someone throwing up. Lee says something that my brain can't make sense of.

'Are you . . . speaking Japanese?'

'It wasn't me,' her voice is forlorn. 'It was the toilet.'

'The . . . toilet?'

'It shouts at you in Japanese,' she mumbles. 'I think it said something about warming the seat for me.'

'You speak Japanese?'

'Nico, is this really the time to get into my CV?' she asks, and then there's more retching.

'Daisy, let me come in and hold your hair for you,' I try.

'Nico Hart, if you come in here right now, I will *murder* you.'

I rest my forehead against the cool, cool door for a moment. 'Fair enough.' Making my way (slowly) back to the bed, I lift the phone on the bedside table to call room service.

'Coffee,' I beg. 'Please. All the coffee. And dry toast. And ibuprofen.'

'Certainly, Mr Turner-Jones.' The voice on the other end of the phone is unfathomably perky. 'Can I also interest you in a couple of our vitamin blast smoothies? They're just the thing if you're feeling . . . under the weather.'

'Sure,' I reply wearily, too exhausted to correct her on the name thing. 'Whatever you'd recommend to raise the dead. Thank you.'

I hang up the phone, managing to get it back in the cradle on my third attempt. There's something dangling from the lamp beside it, and my fingers close around the scrap of shell pink lace, untangling it.

It's a bra, the silk slipping cool as water between my fingers. I close my eyes. I could definitely live without the knowledge that my best friend's little sister wears expensive French underwear.

The door to the bathroom opens, and I jump guiltily, throwing the bra up in the air.

Smooth, Nico. Really fucking smooth.

Lee's face is clean of any makeup, and that tangle of gold hair has been ruthlessly subdued and coiled on top of her head. She's still bleached of colour, but she looks back in control. She gestures for me to use the bathroom, which I do as quickly as possible, basically sticking my entire head under the cold tap in an attempt to clear it, and when I emerge she's still standing in the same place, looking pained.

'I can't get out of this,' she says, and it takes me a minute to realise she means the flannel pyjama top that's trying to throttle her.

'Right.' I clear my throat. 'Turn around.'

Lee spins and I stand behind her. She smells of soap and toothpaste and I start to undo the line of buttons running down her spine. As each button is released it reveals another inch of skin. There is a constellation of small, dark freckles on her back. With a sinking heart, I realise that she could hardly have put herself into this shirt backwards, and from the rigid way she's standing it's a conclusion she's probably already reached.

Finally, the last button is undone, and she turns, holding the fabric to her front, even though the sleeves mean it's not going anywhere. 'I'm going to shower,' she says. 'And then we can . . . talk.'

'Great,' I agree as she snatches the bra up from the floor where I've thrown it. There's a touch of pink in her cheeks and she avoids meeting my eye as she heads back to the bathroom, turning the lock with a click.

I've made her uncomfortable, and a generous dash of self-loathing is added in to the potent cocktail of regrets rushing through my system.

I've known Lee since she was five years old and she's the most by-the-book, rule-following, straight-laced person you can imagine – there's no way this night of hard drinking was her idea. *I'm* the wild one, I'm the one who gets blackout drunk in Vegas, the one who wakes up hungover in strangers' beds. (Admittedly, that hasn't happened recently, but let's say I've got form.)

Lee is the one who makes pros and cons lists about having a one night stand. She thinks I missed that one last night, but I didn't. The words *five months* float through my mind, but I shove them away. Lee's sex life is absolutely none of my business.

What *is* my business is this mess. She's the most unflappable person I know, and one night with me has her hiding in the bathroom, embarrassed.

Jack would kill me for putting his sister in this position. Forget Jack, Gran is the real threat – even before she started doing Taekwondo. Hell, I want to kick my own ass.

I take a deep breath. I can fix this. First thing's first: I'm going to put on a shirt. Then I'm going to make sure Lee has breakfast. I'm going to crush any weird physical responses I have that are not those of an old, loyal friend. I am basically about to go full emotional support animal on her. She will feel nothing but safe and comfortable.

I pick up the phone again with renewed determination.

'Hi, I'd like to add a couple of things to our room service order.'

Chapter Four

Lee

Wiping some of the steam off the bathroom mirror, I eye my reflection sternly.

'You can do this. Just be cool.'

I have literally never been cool in my life, but maybe now, when I have woken up in bed with the man I've been in love with for as long as I can remember, when I have no clue how I got there, and when I'm nursing the hangover to end all hangovers, is the moment I'll pull it off.

Seems unlikely.

I close my eyes and, unbidden, the image of a shirtless Nico appears. I'll probably be haunted by his perfect, sculpted torso for the rest of my days. That picture of him might be tattooed permanently inside my eyelids and I just have to live with that now – with the knowledge of the hard planes of muscle, of the black ink that decorates his upper arms, of the deep v-lines where his obliques meet his transversus abdominis and the dusting of hair heading down towards . . .

Nope.

My eyes spring open. My cheeks are flushed, a vibrant wash of pink against the deathly pallor of my skin. I think again about the fact that he slept in his jeans. That information, coupled with the pineapple-patterned strait-jacket he had clearly bundled me into, makes it mortifyingly plausible that I could have thrown myself at him last night. There's every possibility that he had to fight off my advances.

Oh, god.

Live a little, I said. *What could be the harm?* I said.

This. This is the harm. What if I *told* him? What if I confessed all of my pathetic lovelorn feelings? What if I unleashed twenty-six years of pining all over him last night? I know I said I wanted to shake things up, to step out of my comfort zone, but I don't think there's any way to recover from this. I grip the side of the beautiful marble sink and force myself to take several deep breaths.

When I finally summon up the courage to leave the bathroom, the bedroom is empty. The sheets have been pulled back into some sort of order, my clothes – which had been strewn across the floor – are neatly folded.

Has Nico gone? Has he actually *run away*? Before I can start to spiral about that too much, I catch the sound of someone moving around in the next room. He hasn't run away, he's giving me some privacy after being forced to listen to me throw my guts up in the fancy Japanese toilet.

'Are you okay in there?' Nico calls from somewhere near the door.

'Fine!' I reply brightly. 'Totally fine, just . . . fine!'

It's possible that the three 'fines' in a row have made me sound, in fact, very *not fine*.

Making short work of ditching my giant, fluffy white bathrobe, I tug on a pair of trousers and a soft, grey shirt. My clothes feel like a layer of armour, and in the mirror, I look like the unruffled professional I've tricked everyone into thinking I am. Everything is neatly pressed, there's not a single hair out of place. I even slip my feet into a pair of heels.

It was my mother who had been intent on teaching me to walk in four-inch heels as a young teenager. ('It's no use clomping around like an elephant or whingeing about blisters,' she'd said, her tone very drill-sergeant-at-a-military-academy. 'Beauty is pain, Ophelia, but it's also power. You need to know how to wield it.')

I guess deportment classes are a weird mother–daughter bonding tradition, but it's as close as we ever got. Thanks to Caroline Turner, I probably have nerve damage in my feet, but I could also do the hundred metre sprint in these Louboutins if I had to. These days I wear them so often for the boost of courage they give me, that I think at some point I'll take them off and find I stay up on my tiptoes like a Barbie doll.

I look down at the shiny shoes, gleaming black as midnight, sharp as a knife. *These are not the shoes of a woman on the verge of a nervous breakdown*, I tell myself. *These are the shoes of a powerful badass.*

Drawing my shoulders back, I make my way to the doors that open into the enormous living area.

Nico is sprawled on the L-shaped sofa, looking out through another wall of glass that frames incredible views of the city. He appears a little shell-shocked by his surroundings and I can't blame him. When Frankie insisted on putting me up in the hotel's most ludicrous suite for the week, I told him it was unnecessary, but I'd be lying if I said I hadn't enjoyed living in such luxury.

Speaking of too much . . . the six-seater dining table is practically groaning under the weight of the food Nico has ordered. There are plates of gently steaming bacon, scrambled eggs, sausages, a pile of pastries, a basket full of toast. There are platters of fruit, mile-high stacks of pancakes and an actual pyramid of glazed donuts.

My stomach gives an uncertain lurch, but I'm not sure it's totally down to the breakfast buffet.

Nico looks over and smiles.

'Hey,' he says, jumping up and grabbing a glass off the coffee table in front of him. 'The hotel's surefire hangover cure. I didn't enquire about the ingredients. They said something about vitamins, but it tastes like rocket fuel. Did the trick, though. I only feel ninety per cent like giving up on life now.'

He's so relaxed, so absolutely un-self-conscious. I wonder if he's already realised that this giant suite has another bedroom, that despite that fact we still woke up in bed together.

And what, exactly, does *that* mean? I know I didn't imagine the feeling of his arms around me this morning, the way his body was pressed against mine. I was mostly asleep, but I can still feel the ghost of all those muscles encircling me, can still feel the way his breath stirred against my neck.

'Painkillers, too,' Nico follows up, holding them out and breaking into my reverie. His face gives nothing away.

'Thanks.' I take the pills from him and knock them down with the bright yellow drink. Instantly, my mouth is on fire, my eyes sting, and I come perilously close to throwing up on Nico's feet. Then, against all odds, my body does some sort of abrupt U-turn, the clouds in my head part, and I feel significantly better.

'Huh,' I murmur, looking down into the glass in my hand.

'I know, right?' Nico turns and pulls out a chair for me at the dining table. 'Now sit down and eat some carbohydrates.'

I pick up a donut and nibble cautiously. It tastes great, and I take a bigger bite, suddenly starving. 'I don't think I've been this hungover . . .' I cast around for a comparison, 'ever.'

Nico frowns, but turns his attention to pouring me a cup of coffee. 'I wish I could say the same.' He keeps the words light. 'But I'll admit it's been a long time. There was this one trip to Bali . . . I still can't even stand a sniff of arak.' He shudders.

I take a long, slow sip of coffee and the caffeine hits my bloodstream like a defibrillator. 'You should have known better than to drink something called an Arak Attack.'

'I forget that you know all my secrets,' he muses, then he pulls out a seat across from me and stretches his legs out. 'So, about last night . . .'

'Right,' I wince, but I'm determined to be as unfazed as he is. 'Well, I remember the poker game.'

'Yeah.' Nico runs a hand across his stubbled jaw. 'Frankie wasn't kidding about you being a hustler.'

'Being good at something doesn't make me a hustler.'

He scoffs. 'I still don't know how you did it . . . You're like a human lie detector.'

I only smile enigmatically into my coffee. There's no need for him to know that I've spent over twenty years studying his face like a besotted weirdo.

'I think things started to go downhill when Frankie pulled out the good whisky,' I murmur, changing the subject.

It's Nico's turn to look a bit green around the edges. 'Right, the whisky. And the cigars.'

'Which were disgusting by the way,' I put in.

'No one *made* you try one.'

'But everyone else was smoking them,' I protest.

'Oh, Daisy.' Nico shakes his head sorrowfully. 'Giving in to peer pressure. Didn't you ever have a school assembly about this stuff? Honestly, just because the cool kids are doing it . . .'

'Okay, *cool kid*. It wasn't peer pressure. I didn't like it that you all *assumed* I wouldn't want one because I'm a delicate little woman.'

'Hey, I don't think you're delicate or little,' he says, then his mouth pulls up at one corner. 'Well, you are actually very short but you have the energy of a much taller person.'

'I have tall person energy?'

He nods sagely. 'It's why you had a room full of retired gangsters wrapped around your little finger.'

'*Alleged* gangsters.'

Nico gives me a pitying look, making sure I know he's humouring me when he says, '*Alleged*, sure. All those stories about the Rat Pack, though ... the people they hung out with. Do you think Frankie had something going on with Marilyn Monroe at one point?'

'Frankie's too much of a gentleman to say either way.'

'Obviously I was a bit dubious at first, but I have to admit I get it now. He's a likeable guy. And I got some *great* shots last night. Before it all got a bit ... cloudy.'

'Oh, the photos!' I exclaim, immediately regretting that burst of enthusiasm when my headache screams behind my eyes. 'Maybe you've got some pictures of the rest of the night?'

He perks up. 'Good idea, Nancy Drew.' He gets to his feet, but after taking a couple of steps, he comes to a sudden halt. 'Shit.' He looks around the room. 'I've got no idea where my camera is.'

You don't need to be an expert in Nico's micro-expressions to see that panic is close at hand.

'You check in here and I'll check the bedroom,' I suggest.

Ten frantic minutes later, there's no sign of his camera anywhere, and we turn the place upside down looking. My handbag is also missing.

'Okay,' I say soothingly. 'I'm going to ring Frankie. Don't worry, the chances are you left it with him.'

Nico paces the floor as I make the call, watching me like a parent whose child has been kidnapped and is forced to sit by as the cops make contact about the ransom demand.

'Lee, baby!' Frankie booms in my ear.

'Hi, Frankie.' I try not to wince at the volume of his greeting. Clearly, *he* isn't feeling the effects of last night. 'Sorry to interrupt, but I needed to check ... do you have Nico's camera?'

'Sure,' Frankie says. 'He left it with me when the two of you headed out. I'll have someone bring it to his room.'

I give Nico the thumbs up gesture. He falls back into the sofa, the picture of relief. 'Nico's here with me,' I say absently.

'Oh yeah?' Frankie yells, delighted.

'It's not—' I start, casting an anxious look at Nico and turning away from him, my shoulders hunched.

Frankie doesn't let me finish. 'You know, I like him for you,' he's already musing loudly in my ear. Do these phones have a volume control? I begin frantically smashing buttons as Frankie continues shouting. 'He's a good boy. Talented, too. Those pictures he took of me and the guys?' Frankie gives a low whistle. 'I'm gonna have them framed in the hotel lobby.'

'They—' I try to cut in again but it's like facing down a steamroller.

'At first I wasn't sure,' Frankie admits, unwittingly echoing Nico's own opinion of him. 'But now I got a good feeling about him. I mean the kid's practically part of the royal family.'

I freeze. 'Did he tell you that?' I ask in a low voice.

Frankie makes a dismissive noise. 'I had my people check him out. Full background. Wanted to make sure he's good enough for you.'

I cast another look over my shoulder at Nico, but thankfully he's busy scrolling through his phone, not paying attention. Nico's dad is – for obvious reasons – a touchy subject.

'The two of you make a great couple,' Frankie continues to wax lyrical. 'Classy, y'know? Like something out of *Downton Abbey*.' I forgot about Frankie's unlikely obsession with *Downton Abbey*, and there's no stopping him now. 'Does he know King Charles? Does he play polo? If you had a kid, would it be a lord?'

'Frankie, it's not like that,' I whisper firmly, cutting him off. Knowing Frankie, he's already picturing himself at a shooting party on the duke's estate. I bet he's been internet shopping for tweeds all morning. The man loves a snazzy outfit.

Frankie only laughs. 'It sure looked like that last night.'

What the hell does that mean?

'About last night,' I murmur, steering him away from the royal wedding he's planning. 'It's all a bit blurry. Do you know where we went after the poker game?'

'You left around ten,' Frankie says. 'And you headed back down to the bar. Last I heard you were trying to talk Nico into flaming sambucas.'

'Flaming sambucas?' I whisper, and my stomach practically moans in protest.

He's laughing again. 'What the pair of you got up to after that, I can't possibly say.' His tone is arch, the meaning clear.

'Well, it wasn't what *you're* thinking.' I rub my forehead, trying to gather my thoughts. 'Did I leave my handbag with you as well? I can't find it.'

'No, you had that when you left,' Frankie replies. 'I know because I told you to be careful throwing all your winnings from the game in it. You walked away with a bundle last night.'

There's a knock on the door and Nico goes to answer it.

'The camera's here,' I say. 'Thanks, Frankie. I'll come and say goodbye before I leave.'

'Well,' Nico says, coming to stand beside me and pressing at the buttons on his camera, 'if we left this with Frankie then there aren't going to be any clues about the rest of the night on here.' His face relaxes into an expression of pleasure. 'But I did get some great shots.'

I lean over his shoulder to have a look, and even on the small screen it's easy to see he's right. There's one of Frankie, a cigar clamped between his grinning teeth, a winning hand of cards fanned on the table in front of him. The light is diffused through a cloud of cigar smoke, and every expressive line of his face is perfectly captured.

'That's gorgeous,' I say. 'I want a copy.'

'I'll send you one,' Nico promises, flicking through image after image. 'I wish I'd shot some on film,' he adds absently.

'Frankie's pretty sure we headed off for flaming sambucas after poker,' I say, moving over to the sofa and grabbing my jacket off the back of it.

'Yeah,' Nico rubs his eyes, 'that tracks.'

'Mmm,' I murmur in agreement, running my hands over the fabric and checking the pockets for any other clues. 'He also said I had my handbag when I left so it looks like that might be lost. Apparently it was stuffed full of my poker winnings.'

Nico grimaces. 'Shit.'

'At least my phone wasn't in it,' I say, trying to sound philosophical while the thought of cancelling all my cards in my current condition makes me want to lie down on the floor and weep.

I pull a receipt out of my pocket and smooth it out. 'Okay, seems we left the hotel and headed out on the strip,' I say, handing him the piece of paper, which is a bar bill for an astronomical amount of money.

'And now we know where your poker winnings went.' He points to the bottom. 'You paid cash.'

I eye the lengthy bill. 'I must have been buying a round for everyone there, right? There's no way we drank that much. I mean, I know we feel bad now, but surely we'd have *died*.'

'Unless you think we drank fourteen appletinis, that's my guess,' he replies, scanning the itemised receipt.

'Wait, this is ringing a bell. Didn't we run into a hen party?'

'Okay, yes.' Nico's forehead furrows as he stares into the middle distance. 'I'm definitely having flashbacks to sashes and ... penis straws?' He looks slightly haunted. As well he might – I don't need a clear memory to know that Nico would be catnip to a bunch of drunk women on a hen do.

'What's this?' A small square of cardboard is slipped deep into my pocket and I ease it out. It's a Polaroid photograph and I flip it over. 'Oh. My. God,' I breathe.

'What?' Nico ranges himself over my shoulder.

All I can do is stare at the photo.

My voice sounds very far away when I say, 'I think we ... *got married*?'

Chapter Five

Lee

The picture clutched in my trembling hand is a group shot. We're surrounded by a pack of women who are smiling wide and wearing bejewelled denim jackets with bright pink BRIDESMAID sashes. Two of them are enthusiastically embracing a man with a very orange spray tan, who has donned a rhinestone-studded Elvis jumpsuit, slashed down to his belly button, and a pair of giant sunglasses.

In the centre of the picture Nico has swept me up into his arms and is laughing down at me. My hair has totally escaped its braid. I'm wearing a veil and a white sash emblazoned with the word BRIDE over the top of my suit, and I'm beaming up at Nico like he's the best thing I've ever seen.

Behind us there's a neon sign that reads: LITTLE CHAPEL OF LOVE.

'Oh my god,' I manage again.

I try desperately to remember anything about this, certain that I couldn't forget *getting married*, but it really is like my mind is reaching for something that isn't there. I stare at the Elvis impersonator, and maybe he does look familiar . . . I'm having misty visions of curled lips and lots of '*thank you very much*' and enthusiastic hip thrusts, each one followed by high-pitched squealing, presumably from the gaggle of bachelorettes we'd collected along the way.

Over my shoulder, Nico starts laughing. 'Have those women got tiny pink penises bedazzled all over their jackets?'

'What are you *talking* about?' Panic has my voice climbing breathlessly high. 'How can you be *laughing about penises at a time like this*?'

'Daisy.' Nico reaches out and holds onto both my elbows, steadying me. 'Take a breath. We didn't get married.'

'We didn't?' I whisper, and I sound humiliatingly disappointed while I blink up into his face.

I'm far, far too hungover for this emotional rollercoaster. My pathetic jelly-like limbs are about to collapse. Maybe I'll give in entirely, slide down onto the floor and dissolve there into a sad puddle of sambuca and confusion. Honestly, that sounds pretty good right now.

Nico shakes his head again. 'Even in Las Vegas you can't just *get married* . . . whatever the movies say about it. You have to have paperwork, a wedding licence.' He pulls out his phone and starts tapping away before turning the screen to show me.

He's right. I eye the millions of search results that reassure me of the fact.

'Okay,' I say, a bit steadier. 'So what's with the picture?'

He shrugs. 'A photo opportunity. It *is* Las Vegas, and they love this stuff. I bet they charged us a fortune to pose with Elvis.'

'Right,' I reply with a nod, trying to get my frantically hammering heartbeat under control. 'Of course. Sorry, I – it was a bit of a shock.'

'Well, yeah.' Nico has the audacity to laugh again. 'God, can you imagine the two of us getting married!'

'Mmm,' I murmur. 'Imagine.'

As if five-year-old me hadn't announced over dinner that she was going to marry Nico Hart one day. Nope, it had never occurred to me.

Nico sighs, breaking into my fun little stroll down memory lane, and treating me to a long, measuring look before rubbing a tired hand over his eyes. 'Daisy, I'm sorry that I dragged you down with me last night. Believe it or not, I've been partying way less than I used to.'

He sounds a bit desperate, like he thinks I won't believe him, but that's not actually the part I'm hung up on.

'What do you mean "dragged" me down with you?'

'Just that the state we got in with the drinking, the way we're both feeling this morning and the memory gaps . . . I'm sorry you got pulled into it.' He sounds so serious. 'I can be a self-destructive bastard, and the absolute last thing I'd ever want to do is put you in a bad situation.'

I blink. Why do I feel so insulted by this? 'Nico, I'm not some pure virgin sacrifice that you've sullied . . .'

His face loses all colour and he rears back like I've struck him. 'Christ, Lee, I promise you – *nothing* happened last night. I would *never* have let it,' he adds, in a low, deeply earnest voice. 'Absolutely no way.'

Okay, now I definitely feel insulted. And mortified.

Clearly, my feelings for Nico aren't reciprocated, but *wow*. Does he have to go all pale and shaky at the mere suggestion?

'Obviously, nothing happened,' I say stiffly. 'I didn't mean it that way, but you're acting like you took advantage of me, when I'm perfectly capable of making my own choices.'

Nico looks uncomfortable. 'I know you are. But I feel . . . you know, responsible for you.'

My face heats. I struggle for some poise. 'Responsible for me? I'm not a *child*, Nico.'

'Of course not.' Nico pushes his hair back from his face. 'It's just, you're Jack's little sister. You're not—'

'Not what?' I ask, even though I can finish his sentence for him just fine. Not adventurous like him. Not someone he sees as a grown woman. Not someone he sees at all. I'm only *Jack's sister.* In the end that's all I'll ever be to him.

It hurts. It hurts so much more than it should. I feel so stupid then, so small and inconsequential.

It's obvious Nico knows he's said the wrong thing; the stricken look on his face makes me want to scream. (I won't, of course, I'd never scream at anyone.) Instead, I do what I always do and I shut it all down, lock everything up tight.

'I don't need you to take responsibility for me,' I say, the picture of calm. 'I'm fine and so are you. Like you said, nothing happened except we had a few too many drinks. Let's not make more of it than it is.'

There, that sounded sufficiently cool and collected. There's no need to let him see all the emotion roiling inside me. I smooth my face out into a mask of bland indifference. No hurt feelings here. No feelings at all.

He shifts uncomfortably on his feet. 'Sure,' he says. 'You're probably right. No big deal.'

There's a beat of tense silence.

'So,' Nico says finally. 'What time are you leaving?'

'I have a couple of loose ends to tie up with Frankie. My car's booked for six.'

He makes a humming sound in the back of his throat. 'I guess I'd better head back to my room and get my shit together. I've got a flight to catch.' He looks at his watch and winces. 'Shit. I really had better get a move on.'

'Of course,' I murmur, and my own voice sounds distant. 'Give Jack and Cynthie my love.'

'I will. Give mine to Gran and tell her I'll call next week.'

I am struck by the sudden urge to cry. It feels like something's been ruined between us, and I don't know in this moment how to make it right. I'm so frozen with embarrassment.

The bits of last night that I do remember were good – happy, fun, maybe even a little flirty – and this morning we even woke up in bed together. But in the cold hard light of day, Nico couldn't make it any clearer: he sees me as nothing more than his best friend's kid sister. Not even a friend, but a *responsibility*. Anything more I might have imagined is precisely that: a fantasy, pure fiction.

'Bye, Lee,' he says, heading for the door. 'It really was good to see you.' He turns and looks over his shoulder, flashing me that quick, easy Nico grin, but I know his face better than I know my own – it's a smile that doesn't reach his eyes.

'Bye,' I manage, but he's already gone, the door closing heavily behind him with a click.

I stand, frozen for a long moment, staring down at the photograph that I'm still holding in my hand. How humiliating to look at it and still feel a little thrill. Now, I'm forced to confront the mortifying fact that a small, stubborn part of me always dreamed that Nico would finally see me the way that I see him. Clearly that's never going to happen.

This ridiculous crush has gone on long enough. It's lucky I didn't make an even bigger fool of myself last night. Taking a deep breath, I tear the picture in half, throwing the pieces in the bin.

An hour later, I'm busy finishing up my packing when my phone rings. My traitorous heart leaps when – for a brief, shining moment – I think it's Nico, wanting to clear the air between us, but instead it's an unknown number.

'Is this Ophelia Turner-Jones?' an unfamiliar male voice asks.

'It is.' Something in his deep, official tone already has my stomach twisting.

'This is Dr Clarke at the Princess Grace Hospital in London,' he continues. 'I have you listed as the emergency contact for Mrs Bridget Turner, is that correct?'

'She's my grandmother,' I force the words out, my mouth dry.

'I'm afraid I have some bad news . . .'

PART TWO

One Year Later

Chapter Six

Lee

'I'm back!' I call, closing the front door behind me. There's no reply and I realise Gran must be out again. I set my bag down and wander along the hall, through to the light and airy kitchen, where I spy her note, pinned to the door by a magnet that says FRIES BEFORE GUYS:

> Darling!
>
> Out for lunch with Peter then a night on the town. Expect a great debauching so see you . . . tomorrow? If you haven't heard from me in a week, send out a search party with electrolytes.
>
> Xo Gran

With a sigh, I check her pill organiser to make sure that she's at least taken all her tablets today – which she has – and head for the stairs, sliding my shoes off on the way.

The townhouse where Gran and I have lived for the last five years is in a quiet, leafy part of London, and her rooms are on the ground floor, overlooking the pocket-sized garden ('Just enough space for us to sit and have a gin and tonic,' Gran had said approvingly when we viewed the place. 'I couldn't bear becoming one of those garden obsessives. It seems to me you hit a certain age and suddenly your brain is full of nothing but dahlias.' I actually thought that sounded quite nice, but I wasn't about to argue with her when this was the seventeenth property we had looked at.)

While my octogenarian grandmother would have absolutely no problem navigating the stairs, she conceded the top half of the house to me in an effort to give me 'the sort of privacy that a young, single woman needs'.

I accepted with enthusiasm, which briefly bolstered Gran's faith in me, but she was sorely disappointed when she realised that my dreams for my own 'private space' consisted of an extremely tidy home office and – in an act of total decadence – a small home library complete with floor-to-ceiling shelves (though tragically no ladder to roll around on).

'Lee,' she huffed on seeing it all completed. 'I swear, being young and gorgeous is utterly wasted on you. A *library*? And an *office*? This could be one of those kinky Christian Grey type dungeons full of interesting . . . paddles and whatnot.'

'*Paddles?*'

'A sex swing!' she exclaimed. 'That's what you need. Not more calculators.'

Now, I let my toes sink into the plush carpet as I pad from room to room, organising my notes from the meeting I've been trapped in all day, laying out the findings of my latest investigation. It's the part of the job I like the least. The part with all the people.

On the plus side, it seems there's plenty of financial crime to keep me busy in the UK. I've pretty much stopped taking jobs abroad because – despite what she has to say on the subject – I don't like to leave Gran alone.

After her *very mild* heart attack last year (her words) I've been trying hard to get her to stick to the lifestyle changes that the doctor suggested. Predictably, it hasn't gone well. Her blood pressure is still too high, and her cholesterol is as well. She might be an expert in the art of hedonism, but she's *not* good at taking care of herself. As evidenced by the note she left on the fridge door as soon as I was out of the way.

I'm sorting my clothes out to be taken to the dry cleaners, when my phone rings. Adrian's name flashes across the screen.

'Hi,' his deep voice rings out. 'You managed to escape at a reasonable hour then?'

'Yes.' I put the phone on speaker and place it on top of the bed as I carry on sorting. 'It was all relatively straightforward in the end.'

'I'm glad . . . you've really been putting the hours in lately,' Adrian says sympathetically.

We've been seeing each other for about three months now and I think it's going well. He's a partner in a law firm with his own busy life and he's exactly the sort of man I *should* be dating – steady, reliable, a proper grown up. So far we've kept things very casual, and it suits both of us.

'It's been a lot of work,' I agree. I've ducked out on more than one date in the last couple of weeks in favour of wrestling with the numbers involved.

'Now, about tonight . . .'

'Sorry, I don't think I can make dinner. I don't want to leave Gran on her own at the moment.' It's only a little white lie. Sometimes people don't respond well to the truth: that I've spent too much time out in the world, and I need quiet and alone time to recharge my battery. I know it can sound like a brush off, even when it's not.

'Oh. Okay,' Adrian says, but the sympathy is gone and he sounds almost sulky.

'How was your week?' I ask, changing the subject, and he embarks on a lengthy description of some obscure piece of contract law that requires little input from me – the occasional hum of agreement or 'Oh, really?' – so I can carry on sorting through my laundry.

Eventually, he says he needs to go and jump on a Zoom call with a client in New York.

'I'll see you at the weekend?' he asks.

'Yes, please. If the weather's nice we could go for a walk?' I try to sound conciliatory, making an effort. 'Pub lunch?'

'Perfect.'

By the time we hang up I've pretty much finished with my tidying and I'm at a blissfully loose end. I stretch my arms over my head and roll my shoulders, allowing some of the tension to run out of me. When I log on to the computer in my office I find an email waiting for me from Tara and I grin at the subject line: SMUTTY MC SMUTFEST.

Tara is probably my closest friend, and despite the fact she only lives a four-hour drive away in York, we've never actually met in person. We were first introduced in an online book club during the pandemic when we both hated the chosen – deeply misogynistic – book with the fire of a thousand suns. While everyone else was raving about the powerful imagery, I felt like I must have totally missed the point.

Tara got into a heated debate with another reader, and when he started in on his derision for the entire romance genre, I actually felt annoyed enough to chime in for the first time (camera off, naturally). This only fired Tara up further, culminating in her telling the man he could 'suck it'. At that point things unravelled somewhat, and Tara and I were ejected from the meeting.

Afterwards, Tara messaged me asking if I wanted to start a new book group with her – one where we read books that were actually fun.

And so the 'Reading Between the Wines' book club was born, and it didn't take long for my friendship with Tara to spill over from the monthly meetings. Now it's rare for a day to go by without us messaging or calling each other.

I click through to her most recent email and after a lengthy – and very funny – account of her latest online dating disaster there's a list of suggestions for our next book group read.

> Sal has suggested again that we try a monster romance, and I know you don't think it's going to be your cup of tea, but I say we give it a go FOR SCIENCE. I can tell them to pick something without too many tentacles or whatever. Monster light?

I grin and dash off a quick reply, commiserating on the terrible date and including a link to an article I read recently about how single women live longer.

> Re monster romance – let's go for it, I add at the bottom, and tell Sal they're free to choose what they like. If we're going to do it, let's COMMIT. All the sexy tentacles!

I scan through the rest of my emails. Mixed in with the usual stuff there are a couple of work enquiries that have somehow found their way to my personal account, and one with the subject line HAPPY ANNIVERSARY!

I frown and click through. For the second time in my life, the photo knocks all the air out of my lungs.

Above the picture of me in Nico's arms, there's a flashing banner that reads:

> HAPPY ONE YEAR ANNIVERSARY!!!!!!!!

And below it there's a voucher code for a discount on merch. For only $29.99 I can own a mug with the photograph on it. There's also the option of T-shirts, socks, tote bags and a mouse mat, all with my stupid, beaming face on them.

My stomach twists.

Nico and I haven't spoken since that deeply awkward morning in Vegas. He was already with Jack and Cynthie in LA by the time I got hold of my brother to tell him about Gran's heart attack. The three of them flew into London together, but I managed to dodge seeing Nico at all on his brief visit. Avoiding confrontation is a particular skill of mine, honed over decades, and it was simple enough to make sure my visits home to sleep and shower just happened to coincide with Nico turning up at the hospital. A military operation couldn't have run more smoothly.

Jack didn't seem to realise Nico and I had bumped into each other in Vegas, and almost immediately it felt too late to mention it without it being a big deal. The whole thing was suddenly a secret that the two of us were keeping, which only added to the strange illicit thrill, swirling in with all the humiliation.

I've spent the last year ruthlessly quelling the urge to even *think* about Nico. That night was a lesson learned about the consequences of letting my guard down. Well, no danger of that now . . . with my focus firmly on taking care of my grandmother, my life for the last twelve months has been the picture of safe, steady respectability.

Which is probably why the sight of the photograph leaves me feeling winded.

Unhappily, I hit reply on the email and write out a brief message, informing the administrator at littlechapeloflove.com that I've been sent their message in error, that I only partook of a photo opportunity, and that I'd like to be removed from their mailing list. I certainly don't need this popping up once a year for the rest of my life. An annual haunting courtesy of my childhood crush . . . no thank you.

I'm surprised to receive a response almost immediately.

Dear Ms Turner-Jones

I'm afraid there seems to have been some misunderstanding! Here at the Little Chapel of Love, photography comes only as part of our exclusive range of wedding packages. Our records indicate that you and MR NICOLAS HART purchased our HUNK OF BURNING LOVE package for $329, which includes two song performances by one of our ordained Elvis impersonators, a fresh rose boutonniere, the photograph, a witness (if necessary), the admittance of up to eighteen guests, and – of course – the ceremony itself, officiated by an impersonator officially licensed by Elvis Presley Enterprises. Following the ceremony you were presented with your signed and recorded marriage licence. If you have misplaced this then a copy should be available to you for a fee via the Las Vegas Marriage Licence Bureau, and I have copied their details below.

I hope this clears things up for you!

Have a love-filled day!

Jaime Miller

Customer Care Operator

It takes a moment for the words to settle on the screen. I blink several times as the letters dance around in front of my eyes. I read the email again. Then I read it six or seven more times, just to make sure I understand. Because what I'm reading seems to heavily imply that Nico and I *actually got married* in Las Vegas.

And that's ridiculous.

Right?

Chapter Seven

Lee

After several minutes of serious freaking out, which – because I am me – occurs in the sort of absolute, unmoving silence that you might expect to find on a frozen tundra, I attempt to pull myself together.

It *is* ridiculous. It's also not possible. You *can't* get married without the proper paperwork.

I snatch up my phone and dial the number for the Las Vegas Marriage Licence Bureau, navigating the automated menu to try and reach an actual human. When the plinky-plinky hold music (an instrumentalised Elvis medley, naturally) is finally interrupted and someone does pick up, it's a perky-sounding woman who introduces herself as Megan.

'I'm looking for information about a wedding licence,' I say, then I hesitate. 'Or I suppose I'm looking for information about the non-existence of a wedding licence.'

'You want me to do a search to make sure a wedding licence *isn't* on our system?'

'That's right,' I agree. 'I've been getting some spam mail from a local wedding chapel and I want to make sure—'

'Say no more,' Megan breaks in, her tone still upbeat. 'We get a lot of this sort of stuff here.'

'Oh,' I say weakly, not sure if that makes me feel better or worse. One night of hedonism and I have become the ultimate Las Vegas cliché.

'So what are the names?'

I give her our details and the seconds that pass as I hear her clacking away at her keyboard feel like they're stretching out into years.

'Okay,' Megan says finally, 'got you. The marriage licence was registered on October 12 last year. Oh! Happy anniversary!'

I drop the phone.

'Ms Turner-Jones?' Megan's voice calls out tinnily as I crawl about on the floor to retrieve it.

'I – yes – hello,' I croak, clamping the phone to my ear as I remain sprawled on the carpet. 'Sorry, so there . . . *is* a wedding licence?'

'That's right, ma'am!'

Now the chirpiness is starting to grate.

'I'm terribly sorry,' I say again, becoming increasingly polite as I get more agitated and I'm aware that this is probably the most British I've ever been. At this point my accent is so intense I sound like a member of the royal family. 'I don't mean to be a nuisance, but I think there must be some mistake. I don't see how there can be a marriage licence when we didn't fill one in.'

'I have forms here filled out by both you and Mr Nicolas Hart,' Megan says as she continues to tap. 'The birth dates you gave me match up, too.'

'No. It can't . . . it was late!' I exclaim desperately. 'It must have been past midnight when we went to the chapel. So, you see, it's not *possible* that we got a wedding licence without knowing about it. I was working that day. This must be some kind of bizarre fraud thing—'

'We're open from 8 a.m. until midnight, seven days a week,' Megan says cheerfully, bursting my bubble completely. 'Actually, those late night hours can be some of our busiest.'

'I can't believe this . . .' I manage, dazed.

'Oh, hey!' Megan exclaims, and she sounds even happier than she did a minute ago, the absolute psychopath. 'I've pulled up the scans of your IDs and I remember you!'

'You . . . do?'

She makes a noise of agreement. 'I wouldn't usually . . . you know, we have a lot of people come through here. But I remember you because you complimented me on my pen and we had a great chat about stationery.'

Shit. That does sound worryingly plausible.

'You had all the forms organised perfectly. I made a joke about you being my dream customer. I think you'd even put little sticky labels where everyone needed to sign. You had a bunch of them in your handbag.'

Yep, this has a definite ring of authenticity about it.

'And,' Megan continues, her voice dropping conspiratorially, 'I hope you won't mind me saying, but that husband of yours was really something. He definitely sticks in the mind, you know?'

'Yes,' I say mechanically. 'My husband. My husband. Nico Hart. My husband. I'm his wife. Nico is my husband.'

'Are you okay?' Megan asks, which is understandable because I definitely sound like I'm malfunctioning.

'I'm not sure,' I reply honestly. I wonder if I should put the phone down and call an ambulance. Perhaps I'm having a stroke.

'So do you want me to email a copy of the paperwork over to you?' she asks. 'There's a fee but I can take payment over the phone.'

'I – yes, that would be fine. Thank you.'

Ten minutes later my inbox pings with digital copies of my marriage licence, marriage certificate and the proof of marriage for foreign citizens. (This, I understand, is only necessary on my part, because Nico has dual citizenship. What good news that I was organised enough to ensure that the marriage was official on an INTERNATIONAL SCALE.)

It's all there. Ophelia Turner-Jones and Nicolas Hart are married. The wedding took place at the Little Chapel of Love, 1700 Las Vegas Blvd on 12 October, and it was witnessed by a woman called Tifanii who dots the three improbable I's in her name with little hearts. Presumably the original paperwork was in the handbag that I lost that night.

It would appear that even when absolutely hammered, my meticulous organisational skills are still up to arranging a legal ceremony complete with paperwork. I have been brought down by my own efficiency, laid low by a love of sticky tabs. And I've taken Nico with me.

Nico.

For a whole year I've tried not to even think about Nico Hart. I've been very, very careful not to ask Jack about him at all, and any time anyone mentioned him in passing I quickly changed the subject. It's totally hypocritical but it hurts that he never reached out to me either. From bits and pieces I've caught along the way, I've gleaned that he's in a relationship, a pretty serious one. I think he might even be living with someone, which is a first, and I've told myself, firmly, that I don't care.

My head fills with white noise as I realise I now have to tell Nico that we're married. That we've been married *for a year.* My mind flashes to Adrian. Oh my god! I've been sleeping with another man while being a married woman! I'm an adulteress! I can't imagine Nico's live-in girlfriend is going to be too thrilled either.

Okay. I make an effort to steady myself. Deep breath. I'm a pragmatic, sensible person and I can take care of this. So we accidentally got married, it's not the end of the world. We can get a divorce. Or . . . an annulment, maybe? The only context I have for this is a dim memory of my school history lessons when we learned about Henry VIII trying to marry every woman who crossed his path. Isn't an annulment something you can get when the marriage has never been consummated?

An image of Nico shirtless in bed beside me flashes across my brain and I remind myself very firmly that *nothing happened*. Unfortunately, it seems unlikely that we'll be able to get either a divorce or an annulment without me actually *telling* Nico about it and the thought of that makes me want to die.

I have his number in my phone – unless he's changed it – and my finger hovers for a moment over the dial button, but I can't bring myself to press it. It's too much after all this time . . . the thought of hearing his voice is too hard. Instead, I'll draw on the introvert's friend – the email. All I need to do is to draft a message with the perfect amount of exclamation marks. I am breezy! I am poised! I am not unhinged at all!!!

I drag myself back up to my desk and try to find the right words to describe the situation we're in.

> Hi Nico!
>
> Sorry to contact you out of the blue like this, but I've received some ~~troubling~~ interesting news~~!!!~~. It seems that the wedding ceremony we took part in in Las Vegas was more legitimate than either of us realised! Of course I was ~~disturbed shocked agggggggggg!!!~~ concerned by this development, but I hope we can resolve the matter quickly. I can consult a lawyer here if you agree that's easiest. ~~Although probably not my boyfriend ha ha ha!!!~~ I've attached the relevant paperwork for you to look over so please let me know how you'd like to proceed.
>
> I hope you are well, otherwise.
>
> ~~Love~~
>
> ~~Yours~~
>
> Best wishes,
>
> Lee ~~x xxx x~~

Exhausted, I hit send and then collapse back in my chair, my eyes closed, trying to picture Nico's face when he reads it. I always dreamed of marrying Nico Hart one day and now it's really happened. Then again I imagined it pretty differently. I thought he'd know about it, for a start.

'Lee?' Gran's voice drifts up, breaking through my misery. 'Are you home?'

My head snaps up. What is she doing back? She's never left a party early in her life. The bit in her note about disappearing for a week was no exaggeration, it's been known to happen.

Should I tell her about what's going on? She'll never let me live it down, but she might be able to offer some advice. Then again Nico should probably be the first to hear about it. What if *he* doesn't want people to know? I'll play it cool. Relaxed.

'Hello,' I greet my grandmother from the stairs, and my voice sounds like it belongs to a cartoon chipmunk. I'm not sure what to do with my arms. 'What are you doing back? I thought the great debauching was under way.'

I lean against the wall and fold my arms across my chest. I'm trying to look casual but I think it's coming off more awkward-'90s-boyband photo shoot.

Gran looks up at me, her mouth a pout of perfectly applied red lipstick.

Bridget Turner is a small, elegant woman with a crop of dark hair for which she pays her hairdresser a great deal of money. She has the same wide, indigo blue eyes that I see in the mirror every morning, and looks a good twenty years younger than her eighty-three years. (Admittedly, helped along by the Botox she claims she's never touched.)

'Well, I was supposed to be,' she says, unwinding a Chanel scarf from around her neck. 'But Peter is on a health kick and so the debauching was off the cards. I was rather put out to discover that the majority of his personality was owed to a stiff whisky and soda – without one in his hand the man turned out to be a dead bore. I had to hear far too much about the benefits of a diet that consists – from what I could tell – largely of cabbage.' She shudders. 'Can you imagine? Only think of the *odours*.'

'I think it's good that he's looking after his health,' I say pointedly.

She ignores this completely, drifting through to the kitchen, and I follow as she opens the fridge and starts fixing us both a martini. 'The tiniest splash of gin,' she says when she catches me looking disapproving. 'And you can have most of it.'

'I need it.' I sit on one of the bar stools at the kitchen island and pull the biscuit tin that lives there towards me. Prising off the lid I dip my fingers in and grab one of Gran's lemon shortbread biscuits.

Gran is a phenomenal baker, a fact that takes most people by surprise as it *is* tricky to imagine her in an apron. (She doesn't actually wear one when she bakes: 'Aprons are for children and morticians, darling.')

Now, Gran looks up, sympathetic. 'Did your meeting run long?'

'Er, yes,' I agree quickly. 'Very long.'

'Those government types are so dreary,' she sighs, dropping a perfect curl of lemon peel into my glass and sliding it over to me. 'I don't suppose you actually get to meet any of the real spies do you? All a load of pencil pushers.'

'You know I can't talk about my work.'

Gran pouts again. 'What's the use of having a granddaughter who consults for the intelligence services if I don't get to meet James Bond?'

'I'll be sure to raise that issue next time,' I smile. 'Although, apparently Jack's in the running to play the next Bond so you could be hanging out with him sooner than you think.'

'Well, your brother does look marvellous in a tuxedo,' Gran

muses. 'And I could teach him some of my Taekwondo. I'm a yellow belt now.'

'I thought you were stopping the Taekwondo,' I frown.

'The doctor said exercise was good for me,' Gran huffs. 'If it were up to you, I'd spend all day locked in this house doing nothing. Speaking of which, why aren't you out somewhere enjoying your youth?'

'I was supposed to be going for dinner with Adrian, but I'm too tired.'

The thought of Adrian brings the events of the last hour thundering back with such violence that I feel breathless. Adrian, my boyfriend. Who doesn't know I'm married to someone else. Does it make it any better that I didn't know either? He's very even-tempered but I can't imagine he's going to be thrilled.

'Hmmm.' Gran looks down into her glass.

My spine stiffens. 'What does *hmmm* mean?'

'Nothing, nothing. I'm sure a romantic dinner with Adrian would have been ... very exciting.' The tiny snort she gives at the end of this sentence makes it clear she doesn't believe anything of the sort.

Normally, I would ignore Gran's little dig at my boyfriend, but today – for obvious reasons – I'm feeling a little defensive about my love life.

'Not all relationships need to be full of high drama,' I say firmly. 'You've never liked Adrian and I don't know why. He's a very nice man.'

Gran sets her drink down with a clink. 'He's perfectly nice, Lee,' she agrees. 'But he's *so* dull! Last time he was here he talked at me for thirty minutes about some legal wrangling with the council that I neither understood nor cared about. You're too young to be settling down with someone so ... staid. I know you, darling, you need someone who will challenge you, push you out of your comfort zone.'

'I *like* my comfort zone.'

'And what about *passion*?' She throws the word out like she's starring in a daytime soap opera.

I shift uncomfortably in my seat. 'I know very well what too much passion looks like and I have no interest in it. I'm *happy* with nice. He's not staid, he's steady. There are no surprises, we never argue.'

Gran's expression softens and she leans across the island, reaching for my hand, a rare display of physical intimacy. 'Lee, your parents . . . that's not . . .' She struggles for the words. 'It doesn't have to be that way.'

I shrug, taking a sip of my drink, and the burn of the gin in my throat is a welcome heat, a lick of flame settling in my chest.

'I'm just saying, you have barely any social life,' she continues stubbornly. 'You're stuck in this tepid relationship with a man who has all the personality of a glass of skimmed milk.'

'Now, that's not true,' I protest. 'Adrian is intelligent and thoughtful. We have a nice time together.'

Far from appeasing my grandmother, this only brings more colour to her face. I watch anxiously – a red face may be a sign of high blood pressure. Perhaps I should get her monitor, to be safe.

'A *nice time*,' Gran repeats, as I head to the incredibly well-stocked medicine cabinet I created in the kitchen. When I showed photos of it to Dr Clarke he'd been deeply impressed. (Or, at least, I choose to believe that's what he meant by his comment that if they ran out of anything at the hospital they could just pop over to our place.)

'There's that word again,' Gran continues. '*Nice.* What I think of the man wouldn't matter a bit if I thought you actually cared about him. It's been months and you're drifting along. And it's wrong – for both of you – to drag out a relationship that you know in your heart is going absolutely nowhere. It's *cruel*, Ophelia.'

Cruel? The word stops me in my tracks. Have I been cruel?

Gran continues in this vein, getting more and more heated, and the whole time she talks there's an empty feeling in my chest; my stomach is hollow. There's enough truth in what she says to make me wince, but I don't want to look at that right now. I have more than enough going on. She sounds genuinely frustrated with me, like I've made her unhappy. I don't understand how we've ended up in this situation. We never argue.

'I know you've always been quiet, self-contained,' she's saying now, 'but this last year it's like you've shut yourself off completely . . .'

'I'm not like you,' I manage. 'I don't need to live the kind of life you do.'

Gran huffs, a sound of exasperation. 'I know that but you're not acting like *you*. I raised you, Lee. I know when something isn't right. I don't know what's happening, if it's because of *me*, but you're so distant all the time. Cancelling all your trips, no socialising with friends, this business with Adrian. You're so unfeeling, so . . . cold.'

Cold. It's not the first time I've been called that. I know my painfully introverted nature can be misread as being aloof or unfeeling, but it hurts to hear *Gran* say that. To feel so misunderstood by the person who has always known me best in the world. The irony is that her words have left something boiling inside me, something hot and messy, something that makes me feel out of control. I swallow it down, fight for control, knowing as I do that I'm only proving her point.

'I'm not *cold*,' I say, trying to keep the hurt from my words.

'I didn't—' she starts, but she cuts herself off, takes a breath. 'I just think you're playing it too safe,' Gran continues stubbornly. 'You're burying yourself in work. You're travelling less—'

'Because I need to be here with you!' I point out, exasperated.

Her lips flatten into a firm line. 'No, you don't, Lee! I'm an adult and I don't need a babysitter. You act like you have to put your life on hold for me, but I never asked you to!' She glances at the blood pressure monitor clutched in my hand with obvious distaste. 'I don't need you . . . *hovering* over me and fussing all the time.'

'You had a heart attack!'

She scoffs. 'Barely. And everyone made such a fuss over it.'

'You had surgery.' I try to keep my voice level. 'You can't just keep pretending it didn't happen.'

'The doctor says I'm perfectly fine and I'm sick of you using me as an excuse not to live your life, for turning into some sort of robot!'

She sounds angry now, properly angry, and my stomach dips; my heart is hammering in my chest. Every fibre of my being wants to get out of here.

'It's been a long day,' I say, getting to my feet. 'I'm tired. I think I'm going to go and lie down.'

'Lee, I'm trying to have an important conversation with you,' she snaps, nettled. 'Stop running away from me. You're being ridiculous.'

'I'm not running away. I told you. I'm tired.'

With that I leave the room, hoping she won't notice the way my hands are shaking. I go back upstairs and get ready for bed. It's not even that late, but all I want to do is pull my duvet over my head and forget this day even happened.

As I'm about to turn out the light, my phone buzzes.

I have a new email. And it's from Nico. I steel myself for whatever he has to say about our situation, but when I finally open the email nothing has prepared me for his response.

Hi Lee!

Wow, that is a shock! I'm in the States right now. Why don't you come out here so that we can talk about all of this in person? I'd love to see you. As soon as possible.

Lol

Nico x

#YOLO

Attached to this email is a plane ticket. To Portland, Maine. Leaving London tomorrow.

I blink at the screen, read the words again. He's just found out we're married and he'd *love to see me*? As soon as possible? We haven't spoken for a year and he's sent me a plane ticket? What does that *mean*? Doesn't he realise I can't drop everything and fly to Maine? That would be reckless, impulsive.

That would be nothing like me.

My breath catches. The argument with Gran is too close to the surface, my heart is still tender from her words. She doesn't need me here. She said as much. She thinks I'm not living my own life and I'm obsessing over hers instead.

She thinks I'm cold and closed off. A robot.

Is she right?

I get out of bed, my legs shaking as I pull out my suitcase and start throwing clothes inside. (By which I mean carefully folding them and packing them into my well-labelled packing cubes.)

When that is done I stand, still flooded with adrenaline. There's something else I need to do. Something I can't put off. Gran might have been wrong about a lot of things, but she was right about this.

I pull out my phone.

'Hi, Adrian. We need to talk.'

Chapter Eight

Lee

Less than twenty-four hours later I'm in Maine, and no one is more surprised about that than I am.

The scenery that rolls along outside the window is gorgeous. Slender-trunked trees line the wide road, the foliage is changing, amber and gold fire licking at the touch-paper edges of their leaves. It's after 6 p.m. local time, and the sun is starting to set, the light growing heavy. I try very hard to convince myself that this was a good idea as I settle back in the seat of the cab.

Although perhaps *cab* is the wrong word. The battered, sunshine yellow VW Beetle *does* have the words BUD'S TAXI painted on the side of it in peeling red paint, but on the other side of the car, BUD'S FUNERAL SERVICES is written in a more sombre black, and while I'm a great supporter of the side hustle, I have to admit it doesn't inspire a lot of confidence.

Bud himself is an enormous bear of a man with a rough red beard, who was waiting at the airport for me, holding a sign with my name on. The sign was on pink cardboard and the individual letters of my name had been cut out of magazines and surrounded with a border of purple glitter. I think it was supposed to be festive but it looked like something Barbie might create, if Barbie was a serial killer.

'Wow,' I murmured, eyeing it – and Bud – with a good deal of suspicion.

'I didn't make it,' Bud grumbled, thrusting the sign at me and reaching out for my cases with a hand the size of a dinner plate. 'Phoebe did.'

'Oh,' I nodded, and the name rang a faint bell, though I wasn't sure why. When no further information was provided I asked, 'Is Phoebe your . . . daughter?'

Bud looked at me, and I could have sworn that for a moment his face took on a panicked expression. 'No,' he replied finally.

'Ah,' I said, none the wiser. 'And Nico sent you?'

'You got his email about it.'

That was true. He'd also described the man exactly and that was the *only* reason that I got into the back of the potential murder-mobile that, Bud informed me with a hint of pride, was the only taxi in Roseport, the town where I'm apparently meeting Nico.

Those were the last words we exchanged and we have now been driving for over an hour in total silence. If I wasn't still slightly worried about Bud plotting my untimely demise (and then efficiently arranging my funeral afterwards, I guess), I would be very happy about it. There's nothing worse than small talk.

Ten minutes later we drive past a sign that says WELCOME TO ROSEPORT in swirling calligraphy. Underneath this greeting is the information that I am also entering the HOME OF THE WORLD'S SECOND LARGEST POTATO.

Bizarre potato pride aside, I feel my shoulders relax. Okay, perhaps Bud is not driving me to an abandoned pig farm to bring about my grisly end, and now all I have to worry about is seeing Nico. Then again, maybe the pig farm doesn't sound *so* bad?

I clutch my handbag, which has all the information on divorce and annulment options that I managed to gather when I couldn't sleep last night.

I rub my tired eyes. How is it even possible that it's been little more than a whole day since I found out Nico and I were married? What am I now doing on the other side of the world, having blown up my perfectly nice relationship? Am I having some sort of mental health crisis?

Gran and I haven't talked since our argument. I left her a brief note explaining that I'd been called on a last minute work trip to the States and arranged for our next door neighbour – a very sweet retired GP with a massive crush on Gran – to check in on her while I'm away.

I text her now. Not a long message like I'd usually send – we even exchange voice notes fairly regularly – but a curt Arrived safely.

Her response is immediate and just as brief. Okay.

It seems I'm not the only one with hurt feelings about how we left things.

Thankfully, I'm distracted from my worrying by Bud, who exhales a grunt that seems designed to get my attention.

'Downtown,' he says with a gesture of his hand.

This appears to be the extent of the tour.

Clearly, we've hit the middle of Roseport now and I exhale a little huff of surprise. What on earth is Nico doing here?

In the dim twilight, it looks exactly like the kind of small American town you see in Hallmark movies. I press my fingers to the glass, a smile pulling at my lips.

'Oh, it's *lovely*,' I say, which garners another grunt – this one of approval, I think.

We pass a white clapboard church with a single tall steeple, set behind a picket fence, facing the town square. A bandstand, which is currently lit with candles and lanterns, is occupied by a group of older people in brightly coloured Lycra doing a yoga class. At least I assume that's what they're doing as they all move into Eagle pose with various levels of success. More than one of them lifts a hand to wave at Bud as we pass (only further compromising their balance).

He rolls the window down to stick his burly arm out and return the greeting and I'm sure I hear a distant blast of Nirvana's 'Smells Like Teen Spirit' coming from the speakers on the bandstand.

'Hey, Bud!' one big voice yells. 'You owe me fifty dollars. Patriots suck!'

'Fuck you, Ern,' Bud growls, and his friendly hand gesture rapidly transforms to a middle-fingered salute as we crawl past.

'Namaste,' the yoga class chorus.

We drive along the main street, where a higgledy-piggledy arrangement of buildings line the sidewalks, all pushed up against each other with signs offering ice cream and yogurt and taffy and oysters (thankfully not all from the same place). The odd window is lit, but it's mostly quiet, with very few people around. Old-fashioned black, iron lampposts spill small pools of gold light over the pavements. Bud has left the window down and the air is cool and sweet. I can't believe this is real; it's like being on a film set tour. I half expect the buildings to be totally flat, propped up by wooden joists.

After a moment, we turn off onto a long, curved street. Here the houses are big and more private, set back from the road by well-tended lawns, hidden behind high hedges. We drive for a few more minutes and eventually we come to a building that is perched slightly away from the rest. There's a stone wall with a sign built into the corner with a light above it, proclaiming THE HUMMINGBIRD INN in slightly tarnished gilded letters. Underneath is another, hand-painted sign: UNDER RENOVATION.

As we pull off onto the drive, the view opens up and Bud's headlights throw out an arc of light, briefly illuminating the building. Three storeys tall, white clapboard, blue shutters at the windows, a wide porch and some sort of climbing plant around the door.

It looks lovely, but it's quite clearly closed. There are huddled shapes on the porch that must be covered furniture, several of the windows are boarded up, and there's a tall ladder propped up against one wall; a work bench sits out on the front lawn.

'Er, sorry, Bud, are you sure this is the right place?' I ask, but he's already out of the car, heaving my giant suitcase out the boot. I cling to the handle of my carry-on.

A groan sounds from behind me and I turn, realising it's the front door being wedged open. A woman appears, sweeping a torch over us. She's in her early sixties perhaps, tall and angular with bright red hair. She wears a purple silk kimono over a brightly clashing floral jumpsuit and she gives me a thorough once over.

'Oh, honey, you're *gorgeous*!' she exclaims, delighted, coming towards me with her fingers outstretched. She keeps the torch trained on me, momentarily dazzling, so that I feel suddenly like I'm under interrogation at a black-ops site. 'And your energy is so bright!'

'Um, thank you?' I manage, blinking and taking her hand, which is warm and soft. Rather than shaking it, she pulls me in for a lavender-scented hug.

'I'm Magda,' she says when she lets me go, and I try not to look too flustered, smoothing down my shirt.

'Nice to meet you,' I say, still unsure who she is or what's going on. 'I'm Lee.'

'Thanks, Bud,' Magda calls over my shoulder, giving the taxi driver/funeral director a broad wink. 'You did good. We'll see you tomorrow.'

'Later, Magda,' Bud grunts, pouring himself back into the car and pulling away in a spray of gravel.

This is when I notice a girl standing behind Magda. I don't spend a lot of time with children so I have no idea how old she is, but she's quite small. Her fair hair hangs in two long plaits, and there's a smattering of freckles across her nose. She observes me steadily through brown eyes, magnified behind her glasses.

'This is Phoebe,' Magda says brightly.

'Oh, you're the one who made the sign for the airport.' I try a smile.

Phoebe treats me to another long, measuring look. 'You don't look much like a wicked stepmother,' she says finally. 'Except for the shoes.'

I glance down at my heels, currently sinking into the gravel driveway. Probably not the most practical choice, but if ever I needed my emotional support footwear it's today. 'Um, thank you?' I say again. I know I'm not the most socially aware person in the world, but it definitely feels like the greetings I'm getting from people in this town are . . . weird?

'Phoebe, honey,' Magda says, shooting her a look. Some sort of silent communication seems to happen between the two of them. 'Why don't we go inside?'

I glance at the building. 'I don't think I can stay here,' I say. 'Isn't it closed?' All of a sudden it seems *very* dark. The ghoulish glow from Magda's torch is the only light as the sky has rapidly deepened to a sombre navy, the first stars blinking awake.

'Oh, you're not staying here,' Magda beams. 'Ordinarily we'd love to have you of course, but the whole place is getting spruced up right now. It's long overdue!'

'Right,' I nod. 'So . . . sorry, I'm a bit confused. Is Nico here? Nico Hart? I'm supposed to be meeting him.'

'He'll be here soon,' Magda says, and now the brightness seems forced. Something fishy is definitely going on. Have I escaped Bud's clutches unscathed, only to be kidnapped by this unlikely duo? Suddenly the big empty house looks more menacing than magical. I try to remember the self-defence moves Gran showed me. The little one doesn't look like much of a threat, but perhaps she's a biter. I eye them both warily, taking a step back.

'Okay, I think I should maybe go and find my hotel—'

'There isn't another hotel,' Phoebe says. 'You're staying with me. Me and my dad.'

A strangled laugh escapes me. 'That's kind of you, but no, thank you,' I take another step back. 'I think there's been some sort of misunderstanding. I'm looking for my friend. I'm just going to . . .'

I grab the handles on my cases and hastily turn to walk away, but as I do, my heel sinks further into the gravel, and my ankle twists. I let out a hiss of pain, and stumble forward, my knee buckling. Throwing my hands out, I close my eyes, bracing for the impact of hitting the ground.

This is going to hurt.

Before that can happen, a pair of strong hands wrap around my upper arms. Instead of falling onto the gravel driveway, I hit the warm, firm planes of someone big and male. There's a smell I know, a gorgeous, spicy smell mixed in with sawdust, and I peel my eyes open, exhaling a huff of relief.

'Nico,' I breathe.

His fingers tighten on my arms and he looks down at me. In the light from the torch his profile is gilded, beautiful.

'Lee?' Nico's eyes widen. 'What the hell are you doing here?'

Chapter Nine

Nico

Lee blinks up at me, a dazed expression on her face. 'Was I supposed to be somewhere else?' she asks. 'This is where Bud dropped me off.'

'Bud?' I repeat blankly. I realise that I'm still cradling her against my chest, and I ease her back, putting several inches of clear air between us. It's more for my sake than for hers. Catching her had been an instinct, but the smell of her perfume – smoke and honey – hits my system like a drug, my mind going hazy.

I have no idea what she's doing here, and I'm not sure how I feel about that sharp shock of gladness I experienced when I realised who had tumbled into my arms.

'He picked me up from the airport,' Lee says slowly. 'Like you arranged?'

'Like I—' I break off, my gaze moving over her shoulder to where Magda and Phoebe are standing. Magda looks guilty and Phoebe looks the picture of innocence, which means she is *also* guilty of something.

'What's going on?' I ask slowly.

'Let's go and sit down inside,' Magda says, clearly flustered. 'We weren't expecting you back yet and there are a few things we need to discuss . . .'

'What type of things?' I look at Phoebe now, because whatever harebrained scheme this is, she's probably the ringleader. 'Phoebe?' I lift an eyebrow.

She smiles back winsomely – only further evidence that she's been up to no good. She's never winsome.

'Daaaad,' she begins, her singsong voice cajoling, and Lee's sharp inhale has me looking back at her.

'*Dad?*' Lee murmurs.

I want to wince, but I'm careful not to, not in front of Phoebe. *Shit.*

'Lee, this is my daughter, Phoebe.' I turn back to Phoebe. 'This is my friend, Lee.'

'I know who she is.' Phoebe rolls her eyes.

'You have a daughter?' Even in the dim light from Magda's torch, Lee looks totally stunned, and when her gaze meets mine I'm surprised by the hurt mingled with the shock there.

'I do,' I confirm quietly, feeling like a dick that she didn't hear it months ago from me. We haven't spoken for about a year, and while it's not unusual for us to go a long time without contact, I have to admit that I thought about calling her more than once. The desire to do so caught me by surprise, and so I pushed it down. Way down.

Besides, what could I even say? The last time I saw her had been messy. And awkward as fuck. I didn't even get the chance to apologise during my fleeting trip to London after Gran's heart attack. I got the feeling she was avoiding me, which made me feel like even more of a piece of shit about how we'd left things. I'd obviously embarrassed her, put her into an awkward situation and she wanted nothing to do with me. If she wanted to talk, she'd reach out, I reasoned. I was surprised by how much it hurt that she never did.

'I think you and I have a lot to catch up on,' I say carefully now.

'Yes.' It's Lee's turn to look flustered. 'Of course, and then with the wedding and everything—'

'What wedding?'

She frowns. 'Our wedding. Not that it was really a wedding. Of course, *legally* it was a wedding. That's the whole problem.' She's rambling, her cheeks pink, her eyes darting between me and Phoebe. I've never seen Lee so ruffled before and it's enough of a novelty that it takes several long seconds for me to register what she's saying.

'Wait.' I hold up my hand. 'Are you talking about Las Vegas?'

The line between her brows deepens. 'Yes. What else would I be talking about?'

Lee takes a step towards me, clearly concerned by the look on my face, which I can only imagine is the look of a man suffering some sort of medical disaster.

'Are you saying that we're . . . that you and I . . .' I trail off.

Phoebe makes an impatient sound. 'She's saying you're married, Dad. Lee is your wife. Isn't that great? You really needed a wife and now you have one!'

My daughter beams at me; Magda offers her own smile. Lee looks as bewildered as I feel.

'You didn't know?' she asks, her face pale. 'But what . . . The emails? The ticket?'

'I really think now would be a good time for us to go inside and have a nice glass of my homemade lavender lemonade,' Magda interrupts, and she takes Lee by the arm, guiding her up the steps towards the front door, muttering something soothing as though Lee has been involved in an accident. It's not that much of a stretch – personally, I do feel like I've been hit by a metaphorical truck.

'Come on, Dad.' Phoebe tugs at my hand.

'What the f—' I cut myself off, just in time. 'What *exactly* have you two been up to?'

My daughter only smiles, showing off the gap where she lost a tooth last week. 'We're going to explain everything,' she says. 'Come inside and sit down.'

Following the arc of Magda's torch, I allow myself to be pulled through the entrance hall, which is currently a mess of building materials, and into the sitting room, which is in no better state. Someone has dragged a crate into the middle of the room and spread it with a floral tablecloth. There's a pitcher of lemonade and a plate of cookies arranged on top, along with a small glass vase of daisies. Lee's eyes linger on the flowers for a moment before meeting mine. She looks away.

There are candles on the table, too, which Magda lights, giving the whole scene a bizarrely romantic atmosphere.

'Why don't we sit down?' Magda gestures to the folding chairs that have been put out.

'This is very civilised,' I say, trying to hold onto my temper as I take a seat. 'But the pair of you had better start talking, right now.'

Phoebe helps herself to a cookie. 'It started when Lee emailed you.'

'Phoebe . . . intercepted the email,' Magda adds.

'You *hacked* my email?' I ask.

Again, Phoebe rolls her eyes. She's eight years old and I'm already terrified by the prospect of her teenage years. 'I didn't need to hack anything. The passcode on your phone is 0000. I was actually watching a video about female serial killers on it. Did you know that approximately sixteen per cent of serial killers in the United States since 1820 have been women?' She turns to Lee, who looks dazed.

'I didn't know that, no,' Lee says, clutching the glass of lemonade that Magda has poured for her.

I briefly close my eyes and make a mental note that I need to do something about setting up better parental controls on my phone. Do I also need to have a talk with my daughter about female serial killers? Is that some sort of milestone I have missed? I wonder if there's anything in my various parenting books about that . . .

'Anyway, the notification popped up about the email and I read it,' Phoebe continues completely without shame. 'And then *she* said that she was married to you.' She gestures towards Lee with her half-eaten cookie. 'So I thought that could be a good thing because *you* said that you really needed a wife.'

I close my eyes, hissing out a long breath.

'That was not . . .' I start hopelessly. 'That wasn't . . .' I turn to Magda. 'How the hell did you end up getting wrapped up in this?'

'Now, Nico.' Magda's face is lit with mischief. She's enjoying this. It's not difficult to see where her granddaughter gets her outrageous streak from. 'When Phoebe came to me with Lee's email of *course* I said we should tell you about it, but then the more I thought about it, the more it felt like destiny, you know? Here you are, in this predicament, and the universe offers up a bride! It's so romantic!'

'Fucking hell, Magda.' I drop my face into my hands.

'That's another dollar for cursing.' Phoebe pulls a pencil and a small notebook from her pocket, and runs her finger over the neatly accounted figures there, before making a note. 'Looks like me and Taco are getting ice cream.'

Lee, I can't help but notice, observes the book with interest and something approaching approval. I'm glad that my failures as a parent are giving the accountants something to bond over.

'We thought if we could get Lee out here then she'd be willing to—'

'Magda, that is deranged,' my voice is sharp as I try to rein in my temper. 'I know you're worried about . . . things, but I don't understand how you think this could be the answer. Having Lee fly out here like this, *lying* to her.'

I look at Lee, but I have no idea what she's thinking. Her expression is almost totally blank.

'Yes, I did feel a bit guilty about that part,' Magda looks chagrined for a moment, 'but in the end I thought the two of you needed to talk about all this face to face anyway. And Nico . . . did you know?' Magda's in raptures again. 'She's an accountant! An actual *accountant*!'

'People aren't usually so excited about that.' Lee's voice is dry. Her expression remains calm but her toe is tapping against the floor. There's an uncomfortable pause and I try to unscramble my thoughts.

Lee gets there first. 'Let me get things straight: are you saying that Nico never saw my email? It was you and Phoebe who replied? You sent me the plane ticket, and Nico had no idea?'

Magda nods.

'You sent her a *plane ticket*?' I have to try very hard to keep my voice level as I face my daughter.

'We wanted to get her here as soon as possible.'

'And how did you pay for that?'

'I used your credit card of course,' Phoebe answers, as if I am being especially dim-witted just to annoy her.

'That is . . .' I reach for the words, 'a *crime*! Phoebe, that is an actual against-the-law crime!'

'Pffft.' Phoebe waves a dismissive hand. 'It was an investment. You gotta spend money to make money.'

'Where are you getting this stuff?' I ask wearily.

'You know . . . around.' Phoebe keeps her answer vague, pushing her glasses up her nose. 'I think you and me need to have a talk about your crypto wallet.'

'I don't have a crypto wallet.'

'You don't *have* a crypto wallet?' She echoes me in disbelief before turning to Lee and making a face like *can you believe this guy?*

Lee makes a choking sound that could be a laugh.

'And where were you when my daughter was committing grand larceny?' I ask Magda, who has the decency to look guilty.

'Phoebe did that without me knowing,' she admits, 'and I told her it was wrong. But the ticket was non-refundable so there was no point in *not* sending it to Lee. Plus,' she adds gently, 'she is *your* wife, Nico.'

My wife.

My *wife*.

The words echo in my head, and I can't even begin to sort through the way they make me feel. I clear my throat. 'How did you hide all this from me?' I ask gruffly.

'I deleted the emails afterwards,' Phoebe shrugs, before taking a noisy slurp of her lemonade. 'They're probably in your trash folder.'

I pull my phone out, scroll through and find the entire exchange that 'I' apparently had with Lee. First, there's her brisk, efficient laying out of the facts. Lee clearly kept a cooler head over this whole debacle than I did. Then there's a reply from me.

'Hashtag YOLO?' I exhale a shaky sound somewhere between a laugh and a groan.

Magda looks proud. 'Didn't I do a great job getting into character? Throwing in some young person speak and all.'

Phoebe leans against me, reading the email over my shoulder and wrinkles her nose. 'I tried to tell her that young people don't say YOLO. And that she used 'lol' wrong.'

'Lots of love!' Magda insists.

'Right.' I rub my temple. I can definitely feel a stress headache coming on.

'*And* I told her that trying to sound young was a dumb plan anyway because you're actually really, really old,' my daughter adds with devastating candour.

'We were going to talk to Lee before you got back from Portland,' Magda says. 'Explain everything about—'

I get abruptly to my feet.

'That's enough. That's . . .' I trail off and take a deep breath.

Okay. So this is really happening. My daughter and her grandmother have basically kidnapped my best friend's little sister and delivered her to me like some sort of mail order bride, and I am going to have to untangle this whole situation as best I can.

And also get a divorce, I suppose.

That is when we are interrupted by the frenzied sound of barking coming from the next room.

'Oh, yeah. Suzy dropped Taco off,' Phoebe announces unnecessarily, going over to open the door. 'She says he tried to eat three of her socks and a plastic water bottle and he might be untrainable.'

The moment the doors open a small, sturdy whirlwind of fur erupts, heading straight for Lee.

'Is that . . . a dog?' Lee asks doubtfully.

Taco is, in fact, a dog – though one of indeterminate breed – who I adopted as part of a series of ill-advised parenting bribes about six months ago. He has a scruffy black and white coat, stubby legs and a long, barrel-shaped body. He also possesses oversized floppy ears, slightly bulging eyes and a squashed face. No one could describe him as an attractive creature, he has abominable manners, and zero respect for me.

I would lay down my life for him.

'Get down,' I say, trying and failing to sound stern.

Taco ignores this request, homing in on Lee who stands, taking a step back behind her chair. They never had pets in her house growing up, and Lee eyes Taco like he's an alien species, which – to be fair – I have occasionally suspected.

'Oh no,' she says, taking another step back. 'These trousers are dry-clean only.'

The dog is unmoved by this argument and throws himself up against her legs until she surrenders and rubs his head.

'Sit?' she suggests, and I'm surprised when Taco's bum hits the ground, his stumpy tail wagging furiously.

'Huh.' I try not to be put out by the fact that Taco-the-untrainable actually listened to Lee and is now looking at her with giant heart eyes. That traitor. *I* was the one mopping up his vomit at 4 a.m. after he broke into his treat tin again.

'Look,' Magda interjects, 'Lee's here now and there's plenty of time for us to talk about the details later, but I'm sure she must be exhausted from all her travel so why don't you take her home?'

I feel my heart seize.

'Home,' I say slowly.

'Well, of course,' Magda laughs. 'Lee will be staying with you, won't she?'

'I *told* you that you were staying with me and my dad,' Phoebe turns to Lee.

'I know you did,' Lee murmurs, and she sounds distant. 'But at the time I thought you might be a very small serial killer.'

'Oh.' Phoebe looks pleased, pushing her glasses up her nose. 'Cool.'

'Of course I didn't realise that was so statistically unlikely.'

'Still *possible*, though,' Phoebe points out.

Then nobody says anything.

'Maybe I should check in to a hotel,' Lee says finally. 'I don't want to impose.'

'Don't be ridiculous!' Magda chuckles. 'First of all there isn't another hotel in town, and you can hardly stay in this building site with no electricity or running water. Plus you and Nico are friends, aren't you? I don't know how they do things in England but here in Roseport we don't let our friends stay with *strangers*.' She looks at me expectantly.

'Right,' I say, shaking my head to clear it. 'Yes, sorry, obviously you'll stay with us.'

Lee still looks uncertain. 'If you're sure . . .'

'Of course I'm sure,' I say with way more certainty than I feel. After all, it's my fault she's in this mess in the first place. 'It will be fun.'

I treat Magda to a dark look. 'We can discuss this more tomorrow.' I hope that I sound suitably ominous, but Magda doesn't seem at all put out.

'Perfect,' she agrees. 'We need to discuss the finer details of the plan, anyway.'

I definitely don't want to know what that means.

'And you and I will also be having a conversation,' I say to Phoebe. 'About how grounded you are.'

'How grounded am I?' Phoebe asks, interested.

Fuck. I am so bad at this stuff.

'Six . . .' I start confidently, and then I end up flailing a bit. 'Weeks?' I finish, and I know it's not great that it sounds like a question.

Phoebe considers this. 'Okay. As long as I can still see Maya and Jamie, and go to Rose's birthday party.'

'I—We'll discuss it later,' I manage.

Resigned, I grab Lee's suitcase, and Phoebe – supremely unbothered by my attempts at discipline – clips on Taco's hot pink lead. After saying goodbye to Magda, she leads the way around the side of the building to where I've parked my battered, blue pickup truck. Phoebe and Taco jump in the back, and I check they're in properly before I load Lee's cases.

'I really am sorry about this, Daisy,' I say softly, opening the passenger door for her.

'It's fine,' she replies, climbing up.

'The seatbelt is a bit . . .' I reach up by her shoulder and give the seatbelt two sharp tugs, then I pull it across and clip it into place.

My arm is pressed against her body, one hand at her hip, the other braced against the headrest. Our faces are so close together that I can practically count every one of her long eyelashes. My gaze drops to her mouth, lingering for a moment on her lips. My senses are unexpectedly swimming in her: the feel of her silk shirt against my bare forearm, the warmth coming from her body, the dizzying scent of her perfume.

'Sorry,' I mutter, forcing a smile. 'I guess I'm used to buckling people in these days.' I pull myself away, standing with my hand wrapped around the top corner of the door.

'No problem,' she replies, and I wonder how she looks so neat and tidy after a long day of travelling. I wonder why that tidiness has heat running through my body, a sensation that it takes me a moment to identify as lust.

Shit. This is not good. As if things aren't complicated enough, without adding my sexually frustrated hormones into the mix. Single fatherhood hasn't exactly done wonders for my love life.

'Okay then,' I say, closing her door. 'Let's go home.'

And as I make my way around to the driver's side I have a stern word with myself.

The absolute last thing this situation needs is me lusting after my wife.

Chapter Ten

Lee

The drive to Nico and Phoebe's house takes less than ten minutes and there's no conversation, just the gentle hum of country music from the radio.

It's not even close to enough time for me to unscramble my thoughts. Nico is a *father*. He has a daughter. And it seems like he's living with her in this picture-postcard small town in America. On its own, this would be plenty to process, but there's clearly something else going on that I don't know about. Why on earth would Magda and Phoebe smuggle me out here?

Dealing with this when I am jetlagged beyond belief and my brain feels like it might start leaking out my ears is not my only problem, because my body continues in its attempts to betray me. If I ever had any hope that a year away from him would diminish my physical reaction to Nico, that dream has been ruthlessly crushed.

The man put my seatbelt on for me and I thought I was going to combust.

It's even *worse* than last time I saw him. I want to touch him so badly it's making me feel dizzy. I clasp my hands tightly together in my lap, just to make sure my fingers don't reach out of their own accord to stroke along the edge of his jaw. I feel like my insides are *on fire*. I worry that I might spontaneously combust, become a living, breathing column of flame and the subject of one of those 'world's weirdest disasters' TV shows.

We bump off the road and along a short track. 'Here we are,' Nico says as we emerge from the trees.

'Oh,' I manage. Once again I've been ambushed, ruthlessly charmed without warning. The light from Nico's headlights sweeps over a little bungalow clad in wooden slats, painted a warm, buttery yellow. A covered porch runs the length of the building and there's an actual porch swing, with lights wrapped around the sides. The front door is picture-book apple red. The house sits in a clearing, surrounded by tall trees, and it feels like something from a fairytale.

When Nico turns off the headlights, only the lights on the swing and the small lamp on the porch struggle against the darkness. I jump out of the truck and tip my head back, looking up at a spangled sky, thick with stardust.

Phoebe clatters up the steps to the front door, with Taco yapping happily behind her.

'Okay?' Nico asks at my side.

I nod, find myself struggling with a tangle of emotions. 'It's lovely,' I reply. 'It's not . . . somewhere I would have pictured you living.'

If I'd thought about him staying in one place at all, I guess I'd imagined an apartment somewhere, high up, looking out over the lights of a big city.

Nico huffs out a soft laugh. 'Yeah.' He lifts a hand to rub the back of his neck, looking at the house, the front door now hanging open, lights popping on in the windows, marking Phoebe's path through the rooms inside. 'I—' he starts, and then he shakes his head. 'Let's get you set up inside. You must be exhausted.'

I pick my way up the wide wooden steps, avoiding a chewed-up tennis ball and a pair of small purple trainers. There are two bikes propped up against the wooden railings. I don't know why the sight of those bikes – one adult sized, and one child sized – brings a lump to my throat, but it does. Clearly, the jetlag really is catching up with me.

A thought occurs to me then, one that should have occurred to me much sooner. 'Phoebe,' I say out loud. 'You live with Phoebe.'

Nico slides me a puzzled look. 'Yes,' he agrees.

'I just—' I begin, then bite my lip. 'Sorry. I knew you were living with someone, I assumed it was a partner . . .'

'Ah.' Nico ducks his chin in understanding. 'No. It's just the two of us.'

I try to ignore the euphoric rush of relief that thrashes through my whole body at that piece of information.

When I step tentatively through the front door I find myself in a surprisingly big open plan living space. An L-shaped kitchen runs along one side, and there's a round dining table with four chairs in front of a large window at the back of the house. It's too dark to see what's out there, but it's easy to imagine how light and sunny it would be in the mornings. A comfortable sofa and an armchair are arranged around a coffee table in front of the wall-mounted television.

There is a lot of *stuff* around. The house doesn't look messy – not exactly – but lived in. There's a pile of shoes by the door, empty coffee mugs on the kitchen counter alongside a couple of abandoned cereal bowls. The table is covered in papers, scattered with felt-tip pens. There's a pile of half-folded laundry on the sofa, the fridge bristles with paperwork and a wipe-clean calendar, held in place by bright plastic magnets. A dog bed sits in the corner and Taco trots over, curling up and gnawing enthusiastically on something that looks like an antler.

'Er, not sure we're really ready for company,' Nico says from over my shoulder, his tone apologetic. 'Phoebe!' he yells. 'Come and clear your homework off the table.'

'In a minute!' the answer comes from behind the door next to the kitchen.

Nico only sighs and moves to the right, opening a door next to the living area. 'Your room is through here,' he says, and I follow him as he carries my suitcase inside.

I hesitate in the doorway because one thing becomes immediately clear. This isn't *my* room. This is Nico's room. His books are on the bedside table, his watch is on the dresser, his hoodie is thrown over the back of a chair.

He obviously takes in my expression because he clears his throat. 'There are only two bedrooms,' his voice holds a note of apology again, 'but I can sleep out on the sofa.'

'No, no.' I take a step back. 'I can sleep on the sofa. I can't take your room.'

'Lee,' Nico says quietly, and he moves towards me, hooking his fingers under the strap of my handbag, which is currently resting on my shoulder. I try not to shudder as he gently slides the bag down my arm and then carries it over to the bed, setting it on top of the sheets.

His bed. *His* sheets.

'Obviously you're not sleeping on the sofa,' he says firmly. 'You know I was raised better than that. You were *there*. My mother would be horrified.'

I let out a small croak of laughter, and his mouth lifts at one corner.

'Now, the good news is that this was one of the inn's holiday cottages, so you have your own bathroom through there.' He nods towards a door at the back of the room. 'I'll share with Phoebe.' He casts an eye over the room. 'The sheets are clean, and if you give me a couple of minutes I'll clear some of my stuff out for you.'

'You don't—' I start, but he cuts me off with a stern look.

'Go and sit down, grab yourself a drink. Even better, make my delinquent daughter grab one for you. Phoebe!' he yells again.

Phoebe appears in the doorway. She's holding a bag of sweets that look like chewy red shoelaces.

'Want one?' she asks, holding them out to me.

'No, thank you.'

'I take it your grandmother has fed you some vegetables this evening?' Nico asks.

'Broccoli,' Phoebe wrinkles her nose, '*and* carrots.'

'Right, well, don't eat the entire bag of Twizzlers.' Nico looks pained. 'None of us need the extra trip to the dentist. Will you get Lee a drink, please, while I straighten out this room?'

'Yeah.' Phoebe turns and I follow her. 'Do you want a cocktail?' she asks. 'Jamie's mom drinks these things called a fuzzy navel. I looked it up on the internet and it sounds disgusting.'

'Just some water would be great,' I reply faintly.

'Do you want to see my room?' Phoebe asks after she hands me the glass, but I guess it's a rhetorical question because she's already leading the way to a door on the other side of the kitchen, at the opposite end of the house to Nico's.

I don't know what I'm expecting, but it's not whatever this is. Three of the walls and the ceiling have been painted midnight blue. Above the bed there's a mural of the solar system, and the ceiling is covered in glow-in-the-dark plastic stars. There's a bookcase along one wall, absolutely heaving with books – everything from old, battered picture books to *Percy Jackson* and a huge amount of non-fiction, mostly about space.

'I'm probably going to be an astrophysicist,' Phoebe says when she catches me looking at them. 'And maybe an astronaut, too. Like Rosemary Coogan. Or a history teacher. Or a mortician. I haven't decided.' She gets up on her bed and gestures at the mural. 'My dad painted this, and I like it even though he got the number of rings around Saturn wrong, and he included Pluto, which is only a dwarf planet.'

'It'll always be a full planet to me,' I say.

'That's what Dad says.' Behind her glasses, Phoebe fixes me with a withering look. 'It's been twenty years. Get over it.'

'Wow,' I whisper.

Phoebe only blinks.

'What about this?' I ask, pointing to the fourth wall, which has been painted in blackboard chalk.

Phoebe shrugs. 'Me and my best friend Maya like making lists.'

I can't help but notice that the one that has GRUDGES written at the top is quite long, several names on it ominously crossed out.

'I like making lists too,' I volunteer. I don't have a huge amount of experience with talking to children and I worry that I sound like I'm trying *too hard* but Phoebe nods. It's hardly a ringing endorsement, but I'll take it.

There's a knock against the doorframe, and Nico stands there. 'Okay, little Bee,' he says to his daughter. 'Time to get ready for bed. No reading past eight-thirty, please.'

While Nico and Phoebe enter into bedtime negotiations (that I'm not certain Nico will win) I slip quietly out of the room. After a moment's hesitation, I sit on the sofa, which has been cleared of laundry, next to Taco, who has curled up on one of the cushions. He lifts his head and places it on my knee with a happy sigh. Tentatively, I pat his head and he closes his eyes. He starts drooling on my trousers and when I try to move away he grumbles low in his throat.

I look at my phone and find I have messages waiting. A bunch of them are from Tara, who had been asking about book club when I abruptly hit her with the news I was getting on a plane.

WAIT. What do you mean you
ACCIDENTALLY GOT MARRIED?????

And you're GOING TO AMERICA???

To talk to your HUSBAND???????

Call me when you can. I want to know EVERYTHING. 🍿🍿🍿

This is interspersed with a frankly irresponsible number of gifs of people screaming.

There's also a message from Adrian, which is unexpected and makes me feel a pang of guilt. He took our breakup well, but asked if we could stay friends.

I reply to both of them, telling Tara I'll call tomorrow and telling Adrian I'm fine and away on business.

Finally, Nico reappears looking like he's been put through the wringer. I get the impression that raising an eight-year-old is not a walk in the park. He looks down at me and his drooling dog, and smiles.

'Time for a real drink?' he asks.

'Honestly, I already feel half-drunk on jetlag,' I say. 'Maybe a tea?'

'Fortunately, I get proper teabags online,' Nico moves around to the kitchen behind me and I hear the tap running. 'Do you want something to eat? I can throw some pasta together or order a pizza?'

I yawn. 'I'm fine. I think I'll have an early night.'

He places two cups of tea on the coffee table in front of me and takes a seat in the empty chair. He leans forward, his forearms resting on his knees, and lets out a long breath. The silence stretches between us.

'I don't even know where to start,' he admits.

'Yeah,' I agree. 'There's quite a bit to unpack.'

Nico's gaze slides away from mine. 'The last time we saw each other—'

'Let's just forget about it,' I say quickly.

His lips press together. 'I didn't like how we left things. It was my fault we ended up in that situation in the first place.' His frown deepens. 'It's my fault we're here at all. You wouldn't even be in this mess if it wasn't for me. I'm sorry.'

'You don't have anything to apologise for,' I insist, fighting the urge to wring my hands. Nico still seems determined to take the blame for our wild night out, and now instead of frustration I feel ashamed. I can't bring myself to confess that if anyone was responsible for the impromptu wedding it was probably me: after all, I've dreamed of marrying Nico for most of my life.

'And now you've been dragged half way across the world by my lunatic family,' he continues, oblivious to my inner struggle.

'I like your lunatic family. I like this house,' I say, looking around.

Nico sits back. 'I was lucky that Magda agreed to rent it to me long term.'

'How long have you been here?' I ask.

'About eleven months,' he replies.

I try to keep the shock from my face, but it's clear that I fail because he frowns.

'I'm sorry, Daisy. I didn't realise ... I thought you'd know. I thought—'

'You thought Jack would tell me. Or Gran.'

He shrugs and the gesture is so like Phoebe's it's a bit unnerving. 'I guess I shouldn't have assumed I was such a big topic of conversation in your house. Clearly, my ego is overinflated.'

'No, I heard them talking about Phoebe,' I say. 'They probably both assumed I knew, but I misunderstood. I thought you'd moved in with a girlfriend.'

How can I tell him that I've spent a year avoiding any mention of him, carefully steering the conversation away any time his name came up? I now realise why Phoebe's name sounded familiar when Bud said it; I just hadn't made the connection because I'd assumed Phoebe was a grown woman. 'Phoebe finally moved in with Nico!' I remember hearing Gran tell Jack on the phone, jubilant, as I felt my heart sink.

I can't explain to him that after the last time we saw each other, I felt like I had to cut him completely out of my life, like an addict going cold turkey.

I don't know how to tell him that as hypocritical as it is, despite those choices, *my* choices, it still hurts that I didn't know. I just sip my tea, careful not to meet his eye.

'So you found out about Phoebe almost a year ago?' I ask after a moment.

He nods. 'Last November.'

'I'd imagine that was . . . quite a surprise.'

He huffs out a laugh. 'Yeah, you could say that.'

'How did you find out?'

'Magda called me.' He looks down into his own mug now. 'It wasn't long after I was in London visiting Gran. She told me about Phoebe and I flew straight out. The second I saw her . . . I don't know how to explain it. It's like something cracked open inside me.' He lifts his hand to his chest and rubs his fingers absently over his sternum. 'Magda insisted on doing a DNA test, for my peace of mind, but I honestly didn't need it. I knew she was mine. I looked at her and I knew.'

'She has your eyes,' I agree.

'Do you think?' he asks, clearly pleased.

I nod. 'And what about . . . Phoebe's mother?'

'Stacie,' Nico says softly, putting his mug down on the table. 'She and I had a brief thing nine years ago. I met her when I was doing some work in South America. She was on a trip with some friends. It was casual . . . for both of us,' he adds quickly. 'A holiday fling. We spent a couple of days together and then that was it, I never saw or heard from her again. I didn't even know her last name. Honestly, my memories of her are hazy at best, which is . . . pretty fucked up. I can't blame her for not reaching out. She hardly knew me and what she did know wouldn't exactly make her think I was good father material.'

He thinks he's hiding it, but I can feel the pain behind his words as sharply as if it were my own. I stay quiet, waiting for the rest.

'She passed away not long after Phoebe was born,' he carries on, and he looks tired. 'It was sudden, an undiagnosed heart condition. And her parents – Magda and Tom – took over raising Phoebe. Stacie had tracked down my information when she found out she was pregnant – my job made me easy enough to find online – but she hadn't wanted to contact me. Magda and Tom decided it was best to respect her wishes.'

I swallow. 'It sounds like there were no easy choices,' I say carefully after a moment.

'No. They'd just lost their daughter. I can't imagine . . .' His gaze moves to Phoebe's door and his mouth presses into a firm line. 'And they didn't know me. I could have been anyone. Could have tried to take Phoebe away.'

'So how did you end up here?'

Nico's expression remains grim. 'Tom died in a car accident. Magda was the only family Phoebe had left and in the end she thought she should reach out. It was a very difficult time for her, and you're right – a hard decision to make alone.' He sighs. 'Magda's been nothing but great to me. And for the last eleven months – with her help – I've been navigating how to be a good dad to a now eight-year-old girl.'

'That's . . . a lot,' I say finally.

'Phoebe is the best thing that's ever happened to me.' Nico smiles. 'But, yeah. It's been a fairly steep learning curve.'

'I can imagine. Still, the two of you seem to be doing really well.'

He makes a noise that's half laugh, half groan. 'I wouldn't say *really* well. I still feel like I don't have a fucking clue what I'm doing most of the time. I'm a total pushover and she knows it. It took a long time for her to even start to really talk to me.' His words come out fast, falling over each other as he unburdens himself.

'It was six months before she moved in here permanently. Right around the same time she started calling me Dad. Before that it was *Nicolas*.' His smile is rueful. 'I'm more than ninety per cent certain she finally decided to move in because she wanted to live with Taco. It's been . . . inch by inch and I know there's still a long way to go.'

I battle the urge to reach over and take his hand. 'I'd say you're doing better than you think.' I try to keep my tone light. 'You've made a real home here. I saw her room. You made that space for her because you wanted her to feel seen. It's perfect and she loves it. Even if you did include Pluto on her mural.'

Nico looks outraged. 'You can't just downgrade a whole planet!'

I hold up my hands in mock surrender. 'Hey, you're preaching to the converted, I told Phoebe the same thing.'

'And what did she say?'

'She told me it had been twenty years and I should get over it.'

Nico barks out a laugh. 'Brutal.'

'Devastating, honestly,' I agree, unable to hold back my own grin. It feels good to make him laugh, to feel some of the tension in the room leach away. Still, I can't help remembering why I'm here in the first place.

'So you've been going through all this, and now I've brought a mess to your door.'

'No,' he replies quickly. 'I told you, *you* haven't. We can sort everything out. I'll contact a lawyer and take care of it. I'm sorry;

Phoebe and Magda meant well, but they should never have tricked you into coming out here.'

There's a beat, a pause.

'Why did they do it?' I ask and this time I do lean over, this time I do touch him, my fingers brushing across his knuckles. It's the lightest touch, but his hand turns over, his palm settling underneath mine, and after a second our fingers lace together. Something warm and golden races up my arm and settles deep in my chest. I worry that I might be glowing like a nightlight.

'Nico,' my heart is jumping, 'why did Phoebe say you needed a wife?'

Nico looks at our hands, and his jaw tightens.

'It's nothing,' he says abruptly, pulling away. 'A misunderstanding.' He gets to his feet. 'I shouldn't be keeping you up like this when you're exhausted. Is there anything else you need?'

'No,' I say and I stand up, too, feeling thrown off-balance by his sudden shift. 'I have everything I need.'

Everything except answers. Judging by Nico's frown, I don't think I've done a good job at hiding how hurt I am by his withdrawal. I wonder why it feels like he just shut a door in my face.

We stand awkwardly for another moment.

'Well, goodnight,' I say with a weak smile, heading for the bedroom.

'Goodnight.' His voice drifts towards me. 'I'm sure we can get this all sorted in the morning.'

Chapter Eleven

Lee

The next morning I wake up late in Nico's bed, tangled in sheets that smell like him.

It's so easy to imagine him here, sprawled across the mattress, to imagine waking up beside him, his arm around my waist, my mouth pressed against his neck, his hand tangling in my hair, my fingers trailing down his chest . . .

My brain pulls the emergency brake and I sit up, pushing the sheets off me like they're on fire.

That is quite enough of that.

I have a long, hot shower, resting my forehead against the tiles as the water pours over me, and tell myself that it's time to get a grip, that I need to do what I came here to do: discuss legally ending my marriage and then get back to my life.

Nico has made it clear that he doesn't want to talk about whatever is going on with him, and I will respect that. I can be calm and clear-headed. All business.

But when I leave my bedroom I find Phoebe and Nico in the kitchen, bickering.

'Everyone knows the first pancake has to go in the bin,' Nico grumbles, his voice still rough with sleep. 'You need to get into the zone.'

A worn grey T-shirt hugs his torso. He's wearing a pair of pyjama bottoms and his feet are bare; his hair sticks up at the back in dark curls and whorls. His face is unshaven, shadowed with stubble.

He looks delicious.

Which is more than can be said for whatever he's cooking.

'This pancake needs to be buried in the backyard.' Phoebe's nose wrinkles as she pokes at the plate. She is wearing a long, fluffy black hoodie, and the hood, which is pulled up, has cat's ears on top of it. 'Why is it green in between the black bits?'

'I put spinach in the batter,' Nico says defensively. 'I found the recipe online. Apparently you can't taste it and I'm trying to get some vitamins into you.'

'Do donuts have vitamins?' Phoebe asks.

That's when Nico spots me and he smiles. He has a smudge of flour on his cheek. My heart rolls over in my chest.

'Morning,' he says.

'Lee, my dad is trying to poison us.' Phoebe slumps, the picture of desolation, against the kitchen counter. 'Do *you* know how to make pancakes?'

'No, I'm afraid I don't.' I approach the kitchen, which is heavily splattered in green batter that I'll admit looks troublingly like nuclear waste, but I sense that Nico needs a parenting win. 'But I think spinach pancakes sound delicious.'

I am rewarded when Nico beams. 'Right? And the woman I follow on TikTok says that the flax seed totally covers the taste.'

I try not to blanch while Phoebe looks accusingly at me and mouths the words *flax seed* like a dark curse.

'Great,' I say weakly.

'Do you always dress so fancy?' Phoebe asks then, giving me a once over.

I glance down at my cream-coloured shift dress, and then uncertainly towards Nico, who swats at his daughter with his spatula, sending more drops of green batter flying. Thankfully I am outside the line of fire.

'You look lovely, Daisy,' he says and his eyes run over my dress and down my legs, where they seem to linger for a moment. He swallows and turns back to the stove. 'Phoebe's just not used to seeing clothes without creases in them.'

'Oh,' I mull this over. 'I brought a travel steamer with me. You can borrow it if you like?'

Phoebe snorts as Nico huffs out a deep chuckle so I'll take that as a no. Joke's on them because a good travel steamer is the key to creating a perfectly formed capsule wardrobe that accounts for all the variable weather that October brings.

We sit around the table and I try really hard to eat the disgusting grey-green abominations Nico serves up, while Phoebe makes loud retching sounds and drops them on the floor for Taco.

The dog takes one sniff and lets out a distressed howl before running off to the other side of the room, cowering with his tail tucked between his legs.

'Okay,' Nico says, 'that feels a *touch* overdramatic. I've seen that dog literally eat rocks.'

'Rocks would taste better than this.' Phoebe takes a deep gulp of orange juice, swilling it around her mouth.

'Daisy?' Nico looks at me hopefully.

'It's a really . . . unique flavour.'

Nico's head sinks into his hands.

It's a perfect, sunny Saturday, and light filters through the big picture window in front of us. Tall trees fill the view and I think how lovely it must be, watching the seasons change. Right now it's a bonfire of red and gold.

In the light of day, I can see that the back door opens onto a small deck and fenced yard cut into the trees. I sip the coffee Nico made – delicious and spinach free – and can't help thinking how nice this is. *A family breakfast.* I've never had that before. Even as a kid, the closest I got was mornings with Gran, but it was rare she'd take the time to sit and eat breakfast with me.

It reminds me of walking around the neighbourhood where I grew up. In the winter, when people put the lights on in their front windows, I'd peek into those cosy domestic scenes and imagine that I lived inside them. Long tables full of noisy relatives, lines of stockings hung over the fireplace at Christmas, people curled up on the sofa together, lit by the glow from the TV. Simple things that filled me with longing.

For a moment – with the sunshine and the pancakes and the pyjamas – I can almost pretend that I belong, here in this house, here in this family.

'Why *do* you call Lee "Daisy"?' Phoebe asks her dad, interrupting my daydreams.

Nico is lifting his coffee cup to his lips and he hesitates. 'It's been so long I don't even remember,' he says, but his eyes meet mine and I know that he does remember, he just doesn't know if I want to talk about it.

'It was the very first time I met your dad,' I say, picking up the bottle of maple syrup and drowning my pancakes in it, hoping it might cover the awful taste. 'I was five and he was twelve and he'd just moved into the house next door to ours. My mum and dad were having a . . . disagreement,' I continue diplomatically. My parents' volatile relationship was not easy to live with and this particular 'disagreement' featured a soundtrack of screaming, crying and smashing porcelain as my mum threw an entire set of Wedgwood china at my dad's head. I wish I could say it had been out of the ordinary, but the truth is it was pretty much a weekly occurrence.

'I was by myself, hiding out in the back garden, waiting for them to . . . finish. And then this boy suddenly appeared out of nowhere. Like magic.' I smile.

Nico takes up the story. 'I found a gap in the fence. And there was this little girl sitting in the middle of the lawn by herself.' He looks at me and a frown passes over his face at the memory.

'He sat on the grass with me and showed me how to make a daisy chain,' I cut in, taking a sip of my coffee. 'He made me a crown.' I don't say that I still have it, pressed between the pages of an old book, faded and fragile. A reminder of that boy with the wide smile and the kind eyes who had spoken gently, and made me laugh until the shouting inside stopped and the world got quiet again.

'Then he disappeared, back into his own garden and I didn't see him again for almost a week. I thought I'd made him up, like an imaginary friend.'

Nico chuckles. 'You never told me that.'

I nod. 'Oh, yeah. I had a few of them back then. You fitted in great.'

'I've never had an imaginary friend,' Phoebe looks put out.

'Probably because you have plenty of real ones,' I say lightly. 'I bet you and Maya have been best friends for a long time.'

'Since I was a baby,' Phoebe agrees.

'There you go then. I didn't have a lot of friends growing up, so I suppose I invented them.' It's only as I say it aloud that I realise quite how pathetic that sounds.

'Why didn't you have a lot of friends?' Phoebe asks, and the question is blunt and careless, as if it's not something that needs exploring delicately over several years with a qualified therapist.

'I was shy,' I shrug. 'Quiet. I found people difficult ... still do sometimes. And then I skipped a year of school so I didn't really fit in.'

'I forgot about that,' Nico says, and he's frowning again. 'You were really little when that happened, right? How did that work? Did you go to secondary school early? University?'

I nod. 'I started uni when I'd just turned seventeen.' The

academic bit had been easy enough but the rest of it was pretty miserable. I don't like to think about it.

'So you're really smart then?' Phoebe asks.

'She's brilliant.' Nico's voice is firm. He throws his arm around the back of my chair, and I can feel the warmth of his skin through my dress.

'I don't know about brilliant, but above average. Anyway, it turned out that I hadn't made Nico up after all, because my big brother Jack brought him home with him a few days later. Your dad looked at me, and said "Hi, Daisy girl".'

'And eventually "Daisy girl" became just Daisy,' Nico finishes. The frown has softened and a smile crinkles the corner of his eyes. His arm has stayed where it was, not quite touching me, but still *there.*

His gaze tangles with mine for a moment, and suddenly it's all there between us, the years we've known each other. The years I've loved him.

'So that's the story,' I say briskly, taking a bite of my pancakes and instantly regretting it. The maple syrup has not helped. I choke and take another desperate slug of coffee.

'Enough!' Nico snatches the plate away from me. 'I can't take it anymore. I'll admit the pancakes aren't great, if you two stop grimacing. Let's go into town and get something. We can give Lee the guided tour.'

Something like relief flickers through me. Now is clearly not the right time to bring up divorce. It'll have to wait until later.

'I'd love that.'

Chapter Twelve

Lee

'And that's the library,' Phoebe says, gesturing across the square with her arm towards a white building with green trim that looks like something out of *Anne of Green Gables*.

We're sitting on a park bench, eating warm donuts from a paper bag while Phoebe points out local landmarks. So far, between the library, the honky-tonk bar, the coffee shop and the tiny independent bookstore, I'm utterly sold on Roseport. In the light of day the hodgepodge of buildings that lean up against one another are painted in sunny pastels.

Emotion washes over me. It's something like nostalgia, even though I've never been anywhere like this before. But it *feels* like I have. It feels like freshly sharpened pencils, the hushed scratch of a needle coming down on a vinyl record, like heavy, drugging golden light and a Natalie Cole soundtrack.

It's good. It's really good.

There are quite a few people around, and every single person we've passed has called out a greeting to Nico and his daughter, sometimes stopping them to chat while eyeing me with obvious interest. I can't work out if it's nice or creepy. Whatever it is, it's not ideal for someone who finds it difficult to make small talk. Hopefully, my giant sunglasses have hidden all my wincing.

'Is that another dentist's office?' I ask, looking over the top of my sunglasses at a sign that hangs out the front of the building across from us. It's shaped like a giant tooth.

Nico sighs. 'Yes, there are four.'

'Four seems like a lot for a town this size.'

'It's a whole thing.' Nico runs a hand through his dark curls and I'm temporarily distracted from what he's saying by the wiry muscles flexing in his forearms. The sleeves of his shirt are rolled up enough to show them off to their best advantage. He has a new tattoo there, I've noticed, on the inside of his right arm: a small bee drawn in curling black lines. I want to run my fingers over it. 'They were all married to each other and then they split up,' he continues, unaware of my horny mental wanderings. 'Now there are four dentists' offices and it's like the bloody Wars of the Roses but with more root canals.'

'Four dentists were married to each other?' I frown, confused.

'Dr Salt was married to Dr Knox,' Phoebe explains. 'And Dr Parr was married to Dr Felton, but then they got divorced and Dr Knox married Dr Felton instead, and so Dr Salt married Dr Parr, but then Dr Knox and Dr Felton got divorced and then Dr Salt and Dr Parr got divorced, too, and now we have four separate dentists.'

'Goodness,' I murmur, trying to follow this.

'Reality TV producers are missing a trick,' Nico grins, getting to his feet. 'Which dentist you use is a bigger deal here than which football team you support. Feuds broke out, alliances have been forged and broken, friendships ended, it's very *Game of Thrones*. If the Lannisters were obsessed with dental hygiene.'

When we reach the end of Main Street there's another surprise in store: the sea.

I suppose on some level I understood that as we had been driving north up the Maine coast when we left Portland, we *had* to be somewhere near the sea, but I still feel like Roseport has pulled another sneak attack on me.

Lapping turquoise water shifts into navy, melting seamlessly into the horizon and a clear, cerulean sky arcing overhead, making you feel like you're suspended, floating in the middle of all that *blue*. The sun strikes the sea, leaving silver streaks behind. It's dazzling – literally. Spots of light dance, scattered and fragmented like a spinning disco ball.

'Pretty good, right?' Nico asks, clearly enjoying my stunned expression. 'It's quiet now because the season's ended, but you should see this place in the summer, it's crazy . . . nature cruises, fishing trips and lighthouse tours. It's a big tourist spot.'

He gestures towards the harbour in front of us where a handful of large boats are docked. There's a thin strip of pebble beach and a long wooden jetty stretching out into the water. Seagulls wheel over our heads, and in the distance several small islands are covered in trees.

'Wow,' I manage. 'Maybe I can see you living here after all. Even *I* want to take pictures of all this.'

I turn to look at Nico, but he's standing too still, a pinched line appearing between his eyebrows. I can't see his eyes behind the sunglasses he wears, but it's clear something is wrong.

'What did I say?' I ask.

'Nothing.' He shakes his head, and frustration leaps inside of me. More secrets.

Bored with admiring the scenery, Phoebe tugs at Nico's arm.

'Me and Taco think we should go and get ice cream.'

'I didn't know Taco could talk,' Nico says dryly.

'He told me *with his eyes*,' Phoebe insists. 'We have a very special bond. Anyway,' she pulls out a notebook, the same she had in her pocket yesterday, and smiles, 'you owe us.'

Nico eyes the notebook with obvious animosity. 'Fine.'

The old-fashioned ice cream parlour is a short walk away. It's a wide, low building on the corner of Main Street, the front painted a pale blush pink, its windows framed by yellow awnings. The sign over the door is written in powder blue cursive.

SCOOPS!

'Miss Rita makes the best ice cream in the whole world,' Phoebe says reverently.

'And also,' Nico adds cryptically, 'the worst.'

I eye the writing in the window:

Cones ★ *Waffles* ★ *Sundaes* ★ *Splits* ★ *Gossip* ★ *Shakes*

'Gossip?' My brows lift.

'Miss Rita knows all.' Nico opens the door for us, setting a silver bell tinkling over our heads. 'She's the Deuxmoi of Roseport and she's about to have a field day with you,' he carries on, his voice holding a wry warning.

'Phoebe!' a tiny Hispanic woman in her late seventies exclaims from behind the counter. 'Let me guess, the swear jar has filled up again?'

'Yep.' Phoebe bounces forward, Taco hot on her heels.

'Lucky for me your daddy is one of those Brits who's always cursing. You can get away with a lot when it's in one of those *Bridgerton* accents.' The woman bats her false eyelashes at Nico, who laughs.

'I need to clean up my act before my daughter bankrupts me,' he says ruefully, pulling out one of the pink bar stools for me to sit at. 'Miss Rita, let me introduce my friend, Lee Turner-Jones.'

I smile at the woman who is eyeing me like *I'm* the ice cream sundae. Her grin widens. 'Oh, I know who you are,' she says, delighted. 'Bud was in this morning and he said you were pretty as a picture.'

'Bud said that?' Nico asks, taking the stool beside me.

'As good as.' Miss Rita waves a hand in the air. 'You just have to translate the grunts, and I happen to be fluent. I think he was very taken with Ms Ophelia Turner-Jones and now I see why. Is that hair natural or out of a bottle?'

I touch my hair. 'Um, it's got some highlights in it,' I say, casting Nico an uncertain look.

'Maybe I should go blonde?' Miss Rita purses her lips.

I don't know how to reply to that. Should I tell her she'd look pretty as a blonde? Is that a weird thing to say to a stranger? But maybe if I don't agree with her she'll think I'm being rude? In the end I overthink my potential response for too long to say *anything* and remain awkwardly silent.

'Lee isn't just Dad's friend,' Phoebe says, her nose practically pressed to the glass that houses dozens of tubs of ice cream in a full rainbow of colours. 'She's his wife.'

A sound like a broken fax machine comes out of my mouth.

'*Phoebe*,' Nico groans.

Miss Rita lets out a long, booming laugh that seems far too big for her tiny body, before slapping a couple of menus on the counter. 'Oh, don't you worry, I know *all* about it.' She gives me an exaggerated wink.

'News travels fast,' Nico says, and he doesn't seem surprised. He also doesn't sound happy about it.

'You know you're going to need the whole town to pull this thing off,' Rita says.

'What whole thing?' I ask, curiosity outstripping social anxiety.

'What are your specials today, Rita?' Nico cuts in, and my eyes narrow. Something weird is going on here and I don't think I can leave it alone. One way or another I'm going to get the truth out of Nicolas Hart.

'I've got strawberry cheesecake, brown butter pecan and blue cheese and pickle.' Rita says.

'Blue cheese?' I repeat, distracted from my interrogation plans.

'Miss Rita is something of an . . . ice cream maverick,' Nico says, clearly aiming for diplomacy.

The woman in question looks pleased. 'I like to push boundaries,' she says, fluffing her hair. 'Not that people appreciate me around here. I'm a misunderstood genius, not valued in my own time. Anyway, what do you think, you want to try it?' She looks at me hopefully.

I can only blink at her.

'Lee has already taken on my boundary-pushing spinach pancakes this morning,' Nico says smoothly, coming to my rescue. 'Besides, if I know her, she wants brown butter pecan.'

'That's true,' I agree gratefully. 'It sounds like heaven.'

'Okay,' Rita says, though she looks disappointed. 'Phoebe, you want your usual? Cotton candy and chocolate peanut butter?'

'Yes, please,' Phoebe says eagerly, climbing up onto the stool next to Nico. 'With extra sprinkles and fudge sauce.'

'I am the worst dad in the world,' Nico mutters. 'I swear, she's having a plate of broccoli for her dinner.'

'Oh, and a pup cup for Taco,' Phoebe continues. 'He only tried to eat three socks yesterday.'

'That is surely worth celebrating.' Miss Rita grabs a paper cup, which she fills with squirty cream. Taco sticks his entire face into it while his tail wags so hard it almost lifts him off the floor.

'So, Ophelia.' Her gaze is sharp as she puts an elaborate sundae together for Phoebe and I take a seat on one of the high stools. 'That's an unusual name.'

'Um, my parents are both actors,' I say, annoyed with myself for sounding so stiff when she's being friendly. 'They're Shakespeare devotees.'

God, who uses the word *devotees*? *Just relax! Relax!* my internal voice screams in a very un-relaxing sort of way. *Be normal!*

'Max Jones and Caroline Turner,' Miss Rita nods while topping the ridiculous concoction with an insane number of rainbow-coloured sprinkles and even I'm starting to worry about Phoebe's teeth at this point. 'Big Hollywood stars. And that brother of yours . . . we're real fans of his vampire show round here.'

'*Blood/Lust?*' I make an effort to loosen my posture. 'It's great, isn't it?'

'I like it when they fight with their shirts off,' she confides, her eyes going a bit dreamy.

'I mean, I could live without those bits to be honest.'

That big laugh fills the shop again and I feel a strange sense of triumph. I can do this, I can make small talk with strangers.

'Well, I'm his number one fan, a fully signed up member of the official club,' Miss Rita beams. I had been previously unaware there was an official fan club for my brother and I don't know how I'm supposed to feel about it. 'He's a good-looking boy that's for sure, and that fiancée of his . . . well, I don't swing that way – apart from a brief but memorable period in the late Seventies – but if I did—'

'Cynthie is very beautiful,' I cut her off desperately. 'They're really happy together.'

'Do you see much of them?' Rita pushes the sundae across the counter towards Phoebe, who descends on it with about as much dignity as Taco.

'No, not really,' I shrug, immediately feeling self-conscious again. 'They're both pretty busy.'

Nico slides me a look at that, his brows pulled down in a frown, but before he can say anything Miss Rita is already on to the next part of her interrogation.

Thirty minutes and one exceptional scoop of brown butter pecan ice cream later I feel like I've been through the most intense job interview of my life. On the plus side, Rita's seeming obliviousness to how awkward I am, plus Nico's reassuring presence, somehow makes things easier. I answer all her questions; I even start to relax a bit.

The bell rings over the door and Rita breaks off from her deep dive into my teenage years to grin at the man who walks in.

'If it isn't the chief! Get your handsome butt in here and I'll fix you a milkshake.'

'No, thanks, Miss Rita,' he says. 'I was just passing and thought I'd stop in and say hello to our newest visitor.'

He turns to me and holds out his hand.

'Luke Thomas, I'm the chief of police here in Roseport.' He must be in his late thirties, a couple of inches shorter than Nico, but broader in the shoulders. His blond hair is cut short, and his grey eyes are kind as I shake his hand. He's very good-looking.

'Lee Turner-Jones,' I reply. 'Do all of Roseport's visitors get a personal greeting from the police chief?'

He laughs. 'No, ma'am, they don't, but these are unusual circumstances.'

'I take it we're the talk of the town?' Nico asks him.

Luke winces sympathetically. 'Yeah, just wanted to give you a heads up that tonight's town meeting looks like it might be eventful.'

'Oh god.' Nico pales. 'I forgot. I can't believe I forgot.'

'Beers are on me later if you need one,' Luke commiserates.

'Pretty sure I'll be taking you up on that.'

'A few of us usually head to Darlene's after the meeting,' Luke says to me. 'I hope you'll join us.' The smile he gives me is sweet, and I find it's easy to smile back at him even though I don't know what he's talking about.

'That sounds lovely.'

When I turn back to Nico he's watching the two of us and his mouth has thinned. 'We'd better get going,' he says abruptly. 'That bloody meeting tonight.' He glances at his watch. 'Magda will be coming to pick Phoebe up from ours soon.'

'I'll see the both of you later then,' Luke says. 'Nice to meet you, Lee. Miss Rita.' He gives her a little salute as he heads for the door.

'I do love to watch him leave,' she sighs, her eyes on his – admittedly excellent – butt before she wiggles her brows at me.

'Come on,' Nico says, laying some cash down on the counter and turning to Phoebe. 'I need to buy a giant bottle of multi-vitamins on the way home.'

'Why are you so *obsessed* with vitamins?' Phoebe grumbles, sliding to her feet.

'I'm worried you're going to develop scurvy.'

'My ice cream had peanut butter in,' Phoebe says. 'Peanut butter must have loads of vitamins in. Is a peanut a vegetable?'

'A peanut is a legume,' I volunteer. 'They're actually closely related to peas and beans.'

Nico shoots me a dirty look. 'Whose side are you on?' he mutters, but Phoebe is delighted.

'Peas and beans!' she says as the two of them head for the door with Taco dancing alongside. 'They're very good for you. We should have ice cream every day.'

'There's another one the good Lord blessed with a spectacular behind,' Miss Rita smirks. 'And he's a good daddy to that little girl, too.' She pauses. 'It would be a real shame if anyone did anything to hurt them. People around here would not take that well. Not at all.'

It takes me a second to realise I'm being lightly threatened and my mouth drops open. 'I wouldn't . . .' I manage before trailing off.

Rita only continues to fix me with a surprisingly flinty look.

'I've known Nico for most of my life,' I say finally. 'He's . . . very important to me. I'd never do anything to hurt him, or his daughter.'

Whatever she sees in my face has Rita's expression softening.

'I see how it is, honey. You just mind how you go. Those two are going to keep you on your toes.'

I have a feeling she might be right about that.

Chapter Thirteen

Nico

When we get home Magda is waiting on the porch.

'Sorry,' I call, hurrying towards her. 'I can't believe I forgot.' The two of us take it in turns to watch Phoebe on town meeting days. I'm a fan of this arrangement because it means I get out of fifty per cent of them, which is the maximum I'm allowed to miss without getting major grief from my neighbours.

Magda only shrugs, her alligator smile growing wider and wider as her eyes move between Lee and me.

'It's no problem,' she says, bending down to fuss Taco. 'I hear you were giving your guest a tour of the town. Apparently you looked *very* cosy.'

'Who did you hear that from?'

Magda digs into the pocket of her dress and pulls out her phone, which is buzzing even as she holds it up. Notification after notification scrolls past on her screen.

The latest one shows a small preview of a photograph that was clearly taken about ten minutes ago when Lee and I were walking down the street.

This fucking town.

'What did you think of Roseport, Lee?' Magda asks, following Phoebe up the steps to the front door.

'I thought it was charming,' Lee says, and I know she means it. I watched her today, and the way she looked around – delighted and a little wistful – made something ache in my chest.

'That's good,' Magda nods. She darts another look at me. 'So did you two have a chance to talk? Will Lee be staying for a while?'

'Actually—' I begin, ready to shut Magda down as quickly as possible, but I'm surprised when Lee cuts me off.

'That's something that Nico and I need to discuss. In private?'

'That's a great idea,' Magda agrees. 'Why don't you two walk down to the pond? It's so pretty this time of year.'

Lee doesn't blink. 'Excellent.' She turns to me. 'Shall we go?'

'I—' I start, but she's tilting her chin, that stubborn posture that I recognise. 'Sure,' I sigh, resigned to my fate.

'Lead the way,' Lee says, and so I do.

We wander in silence down the footpath that winds through the woodland at the back of the house. The air is full of birdsong, and Lee looks around with obvious appreciation. The afternoon light splinters through the canopy of leaves overhead, touching her hair, and I automatically reach for a camera that isn't there.

Finally, we emerge into the clearing by the pond.

'Wow,' Lee whispers. The banks of the large pond are thick with bullrushes, lined with red and gold trees; the iridescent flash of a blue dragonfly zips across the surface of the water. A single rowing boat is tethered to the wooden boardwalk that crosses the widest part of the pond, looking particularly picturesque.

'I know,' I agree. I point to the trees on the other side of the water. 'That's the woodland that backs onto the inn. It's actually faster to walk there than it is to drive around.'

'It's beautiful,' Lee says, as I lead her out onto the boardwalk and gesture for her to have a seat.

She perches on the edge of the wooden planks next to me, our legs dangling over the water, and for a moment we sit in the quiet.

I wish I could say it's restful. It *should* be restful, but I've spent the whole day feeling like I was going to climb out of my skin. Having Lee here – in my home, in my town – has me on edge, and I have no fucking clue what's going on with me.

It started yesterday, the second she fell into my arms, and it's only been getting worse: the way my heart keeps beating hard when I look at her, the way I find myself wanting to put my hands on her, just to brush a strand of hair away from her face, or to rest my palm on the small of her back.

I don't understand why it feels like she fits here. Why it seemed right to have her sitting at our dining table, or to watch Rita draw her out of her shell over ice cream. She absolutely *shouldn't* belong here.

Take her ridiculous outfit for one thing. She's wearing a simple – and obviously expensive – cream dress with a long, light jacket over it in the same colour and without a single wrinkle in it. She's sitting on the *ground* like it doesn't matter, like she's so perfect and untouchable that the dirt wouldn't *dare*.

She's also forgone her usual deadly stilettos in favour of a pair of brown knee-length boots, still impossibly high heeled and made of some sort of buttery suede. They have gold zips that travel up the inside of her calves, and I've spent the whole fucking day imagining sliding those down. Slowly.

Now, Lee pushes her oversized tortoiseshell sunglasses up onto the top of her head and turns to look at me. Her expression is determined.

'Are you going to tell me what's really going on?'

'What do you mean?'

She keeps her eyes pinned to mine, clearly not buying it.

I sigh, and switch my gaze away from her and back out to the scene in front of us. 'It's not your problem, Lee.'

The moment stretches between us. She's just going to wait me out.

'It's nothing,' I say finally, reluctantly. 'It's this stupid thing with my dad's will. There's been a complication with executing it.'

'Is that *still* going on?' Lee frowns. 'Hasn't it been—'

'Almost eighteen months, yes. Turns out things are convoluted when you're dealing with a six-hundred-year-old estate and an egomaniac who wanted to make his whole family jump through hoops.' The words are bitter and I can't help it. My father was not a good man.

'I'm sorry,' Lee says quietly.

'Apparently my father wasn't going to let a little thing like being dead stop him from trying to fuck around with my life.' I run a hand across my jaw. 'He left me money in his will, a good chunk of it, surprisingly. Only it's bound up in a trust.'

'A trust?' Lee looks puzzled.

'I guess it was important that he make it clear how much he disapproved of my *rootless lifestyle and wild-child antics*,' I say, quoting directly from the letter I received, the one burned into my brain no matter how much I try to forget about it. 'So there are a bunch of stipulations to gain access to the money. A kind of morality clause. I am to be *assessed*,' I bite out, 'by a lawyer, the trustee, and should I be found wanting then the trust will be dissolved and the money absorbed by the estate. I'm sure you can guess which way the *new* duke will be hoping the assessment goes.'

Lee's eyes widen.

'If it was just me,' I continue quickly, 'I wouldn't give a shit about that asshole's money. We've already been through this once when he cut me off because I wouldn't go to university like he had planned. He loved to try and use money to control me and I never let him. But it's not just me anymore.'

'Phoebe,' Lee says with understanding.

I hum in agreement. 'I can't do my job the way I used to.' It's hard not to wince at that, but I force my face to remain as neutral as my tone. No one needs to know how much that admission hurts. 'I have to be here, with her, and photography isn't compatible with that. For now I'm doing some construction work on the inn, but I should be wrapping that up in the next couple of weeks.'

'You—' Lee looks more dazed by this revelation than anything else. 'You've been working on the inn? I didn't know you could even . . .' She makes a gesture with her hands that I think is supposed to symbolise hammering an imaginary nail. It's adorable.

I grin. 'You didn't know I had a contracting licence?'

She shakes her head, eyes round. 'You mean you can . . . build things?' she asks. 'With . . . your hands?'

The slightly breathless way she says it has all the blood running unexpectedly to my groin and I shift in my seat. 'Yeah,' I say. 'That's kind of how it works.'

When she continues to look at me, I keep my tone light, not wanting to let her know I'm affected. 'You forget that I *didn't* go to university. It was a lot of years before photography paid the bills and I took on all sorts of jobs, including working on a lot of building sites. I got trained up in a bunch of different skills – it was a practical choice, meant wherever I was in the world I knew I could always find work.'

'I suppose I didn't really think about it,' she frowns. I'm reminded of this morning when I learned she started university early. I hadn't paid attention back then. Hearing about how lonely she'd been as a kid made me feel like a piece of shit. I know she's always struggled with big crowds, and I remember her tagging along after us sometimes when we were home, but I don't think Jack and I spared her much of a thought.

Now I shrug. 'Why would you? Anyway, you don't require a state-level licence in Maine, just a local one, so that was easy enough. When I got here I needed a steady job and Magda desperately needed work doing on the inn. It was another leap of faith for her, but I do good work, and obviously I'm not charging her anything like she'd have to pay someone else. I owe her a lot.

'I've got a decent amount of cash set aside,' I add quickly, and I don't love how much I want Lee to know I'm a financially responsible adult, but the woman *is* an accountant. 'Mostly because I've never spent money on anything but travelling – I had no house, no furniture, not much more than I could carry in a backpack, so my savings are in a good state, but they won't last for ever. I want to buy the house from Magda, to work to extend it. After everything she's been through Phoebe needs strong roots, stability. I can give her that.'

I tap my fingers against the side of the boardwalk, frustration bubbling in my veins. Lee stays quiet.

'Plus, she's *special*.' My words are heated now. 'She's so bright. Like I-can-hardly-keep-up-with-her bright. My friend Mei is her teacher, and she's mentioned the possibility of Phoebe skipping a grade, just like you did. Phoebe doesn't want to leave her friends, but it's an option.'

Maybe Lee can relate to Phoebe's situation more than I can. Mei says it's about keeping her engaged and stimulated, but Phoebe's pretty set against moving up a grade and I have no idea what the right thing to do is. I don't want her to be unhappy, but I don't want her to be stifled either. It feels like there's no right answer, and I'm the adult, I'm the one who is supposed to know what to do, but every decision I make has such enormous consequences for the rest of Phoebe's life.

The money is part of that, too.

'I want her to know that she has nothing but choices, open doors and a father who supports her. It would be selfish of me to throw a tantrum and turn my back on this money if it can provide a future for my daughter. I can jump through a bunch of stupid hoops . . . for her.'

Lee considers this for a moment. 'So,' she says slowly, 'this is what Magda was talking about. With the trustee investigating you, a quickie divorce from the woman you drunkenly married in Las Vegas is—'

'A disaster,' I finish. 'Ironically, I'm the most stable and responsible I've ever been. Phoebe must have overheard me joking with Magda that the only thing I needed was a pretty, dependable wife to go with the kid and the dog and the house in the suburbs.'

'Of course, nothing screams dependable like a ready-made wife who's an accountant,' she says, and I don't know if I'm imagining the touch of hurt in her voice.

'This is why I didn't want to tell you. It's *my* mess, not yours. Magda means well but she should never have let Phoebe talk her into this. I'll figure something out.'

I have no idea what, but there has to be a way around it.

'When is the trustee coming to assess you?'

'Next Sunday. A week from now.' My jaw tightens at the idea. 'Maybe there's a way to keep this all quiet. Rush through the paperwork.'

Lee shakes her head. 'I don't think so. If this person is any good at their job, they'll have run a background check on you. Our marriage certificate is filed. They're probably *expecting* to meet your wife. It's actually better that you heard it all from me now, rather than having it dropped on you then. At least there's still time to prepare.'

'Bloody hell.' I can't believe that hadn't occurred to me. Of course Lee's right. There's documentation; the wedding might have been a drunken blur but our marriage is *legal*. It's why Lee came all this way in the first place. Obviously my dad's lackey is going to know about it already. If it wasn't such a massive fuck-up it would be funny – I was literally the last person to find out I have a wife.

Lee. My wife.

'What if I stay?' Her voice rings loud in the quiet of our surroundings.

'Stay?'

Lee lifts her chin again, 'That's what everyone's been hinting at, right? What if I stay and pretend to be your wife? It would only be for a little while, wouldn't it? Just until the assessment is over.'

'I don't know how long they plan to be here,' I say slowly, my heart beating a bit faster. 'It could be a few days, it could be longer. I have no idea.'

'But they can't stay indefinitely,' she points out. 'My job is flexible. I can work remotely for a while.'

'What about Gran?' I ask a bit desperately.

Something passes across her face then, something I don't like. 'She doesn't need me. She made that clear.'

'What does that mean?'

Lee doesn't answer; her expression smooths out, impossible to read.

I sigh, realising that Lee has shut the conversation down. I'll get nothing out of her now, but I file it away – a matter for another time. 'You're supposed to be the sensible one here,' I remind her.

Obviously, I've miscalculated. If anything, she looks even more determined now. 'The circumstances are far from typical. Who says this isn't the best plan?'

'A mad ruse in which you and I pretend to be happily married, living in a small town and raising an eight-year-old?' I laugh. 'We should just get you a flight home.'

'Why won't you let me help you?' Lee asks.

'Why would you want to?' I fire back.

She flinches and I hiss out a breath in frustration. 'I only meant that this isn't your problem. I don't see why you need to be dragged into it. I can handle things.'

'I thought I was your friend.' Her voice is small.

'What?'

'I know that you and Jack are best friends. I know I'm just his sister, but I thought . . .' Her hand drops to the boardwalk and she traces an absent circle with her finger. 'Before Vegas. I thought we were friends, too.' She looks up at me then and it feels like someone has taken a baseball bat to my gut.

This morning Lee told Phoebe the story of when we first met, and I realised I hadn't thought about it for a long, long time. That solemn little girl with the big, sad eyes. She didn't even cry that day. Not while her parents were inside the house, screaming obscenities that would make a sailor blush. Not when everyone had forgotten about her and she crept away to hide.

Thinking about it now makes me want to put my fist through a wall.

'Of course we're friends,' I say, hoarsely. 'That's why I don't want you wrapped up in my problems. I care about you. I care about you a lot.'

The words hang in the air between us and I resist the urge to laugh them away, to claw them back or make them smaller.

A delicate pink flush tints her cheeks. 'It's not fair that your awful dad put you in this situation,' Lee says after a moment, getting to her feet. 'It's *insulting*. And what's worse, you won't let me help you when I've told you I can. All that stuff you want for Phoebe? I want that for her, too. If we really are friends then you should know that.' She pulls her sunglasses down, covering her eyes again, but not before I glimpse something in them. Determination.

'You don't need to tell me that Phoebe's special,' Lee continues. 'It's obvious. And,' she adds primly, 'it's fiscally responsible to start preparing for her future now. It sounds to me like Magda has some sort of plan. I want to hear it.'

I stand as well, dusting off my jeans. I'm a mess of indecision. I wasn't lying when I said I didn't want to drag Lee into this mess, but I don't know if I can afford to turn down the help she's offering.

'Fine,' I say finally. 'Let's go and listen to a plan that's been put together by an eight-year-old and a woman who believes that I have a navy blue aura in need of cleansing. What could possibly go wrong?'

I don't know what Magda's been cooking up, but the fact that she's roped Bud and Rita into it doesn't bode well. Lee doesn't know the people in this town like I do.

When we get back to the house, Magda and Phoebe are playing a game of cards at the table.

'She said yes, didn't she?' Magda says, looking between Lee and me. 'I knew she would. The second I saw her, I knew. The vibrations . . . there's no denying it,' she beams.

'Lee hasn't agreed to anything except hearing the pair of you out,' I caution as we take the two remaining seats at the table. 'Against my advice, I might add. *I* think the idea of her pretending to be my wife is insane.'

'It's not pretend, Nico,' Magda says, her voice surprisingly stern. 'Lee *is* your wife. That's the whole point.'

Lee clears her throat delicately. 'Even so, I think there are a few issues we need to discuss.'

'Yeah,' I break in, 'like how do you imagine we'd explain to everyone the fact that I suddenly have a wife, popping up from nowhere?'

'Naturally we considered that issue,' Magda agrees. 'And that's why we already told them. The whole town has agreed to take part in the ruse. We've got a week to get everything prepared. We'll just pretend Lee has been here the entire time.'

'You already discussed this with the whole town . . .' I know my face has lost some colour. 'Christ.'

'Is Christ a curse word?' Phoebe crinkles her brow, already reaching for her notebook.

'You've got to leave me something, Bee,' I plead and my daughter grudgingly chooses to let this one slide.

'When did you even plot this whole thing?' I ask.

'We had an emergency meeting yesterday,' Magda says. 'You weren't invited.'

'Oh, of course. Why consult *me* on the matter?'

'So we'd act as though Nico and I have really been married for a year?' Lee clarifies, ignoring my grumbling.

'That's right,' Magda nods, 'and then any particular absences can be explained by you travelling for work.'

'On your website it says that you do a lot of travelling,' Phoebe says, looking at Lee with interest.

'Not as much as I used to, but yes, I often consult abroad,' Lee agrees.

'And aren't your family all like really famous actors?' Phoebe tilts her head. 'You must be good at pretending.'

'Actually, no,' Lee says. 'I'm not good at it at all. I was always a bit of a disappointment. Still,' she carries on quickly and her voice is too bright, 'it shouldn't be that hard, right? All I have to do is be here looking ... responsible. I'm good at that. I mean, we *are* married. All the paperwork is perfectly legal and correct. We've *been* married for a whole year. We're not lying about the important part. There's no reason to question it, is there?'

'Exactly,' Magda nods, looking pleased with herself. 'And we can discuss all the details tonight at the town meeting. I think it's best on this occasion if we all attend.'

'Including Phoebe?' I ask.

'Of course including me.' Phoebe pushes her glasses up her nose. 'I'm the *mastermind*, Dad.'

'Actually, we're all very excited,' Magda continues blithely. 'It will be a fun community activity. Remember for the Spring Festival when we did the town-wide murder mystery? We have some talented thespians around,' she tells Lee with a wide smile. 'It really brought people together.'

'What I remember is everyone sloping around in trench coats, and Annie forgetting to actually give anybody the murderer card so the game went on for a week, descending into town-wide paranoia, wild accusations and fisticuffs in the town square,' I say grimly.

'But we had so much fun!' Magda trills.

I look over at Lee. She doesn't even have to say anything, I know she's going to agree to this. She'll sign herself up to this foolish, unlikely scheme because she wants to help me and Phoebe. Even though it will complicate her life, even though there's no reason for her to do it.

Three pairs of eyes are trained on me. Four, actually, because even Taco is looking at me expectantly.

'We'll go to the meeting and hear what everyone has to say,' I say grudgingly. Then I meet Lee's gaze. 'But don't say I didn't warn you.'

Chapter Fourteen

Lee

'Wait, wait!' Tara's face is so close to the camera, her tight, dark curls are practically quivering; her voice is breathless with excitement. 'You're going to *stay* and pretend to be Nico's wife for this lawyer person?'

'Well, technically, I *am* his wife,' I say, stretching out on the bed, my voice low so that no one can hear me filling in my best friend.

'Oh my god!' Tara's camera wobbles as she moves around. 'You're doing a marriage of convenience! In a small town! You're practically living in a romance novel right now!'

'Are you making popcorn?' I ask incredulously, even as her microwave dings and I watch her reach inside for the paper bag.

'Listen, I lead a very boring life so I'm choosing to live vicariously through you.' She props her phone up on her kitchen worktop and moves around, emptying the popcorn into a bowl. 'I want to be fully situated so I can appreciate this.'

'I haven't got that long to chat.' I glance over at the door and nerves leap in my stomach. Despite my air of breezy confidence with Nico, I'm far from feeling sure of my own capabilities when it comes to pulling off a proper ruse.

'You know you don't have to do this, right?' Tara pauses and looks up, straight into the camera, clearly trying to read my own expression; there's a flash of concern in her brown eyes. 'You can just come home, no one would blame you.'

'I know. But I want to help. And it's not even really lying, is it? We *are* actually married.'

'That's not what I mean. Don't you think you're a bit . . . emotionally compromised?'

'I care about Nico *and* Phoebe. I want the best for them, that's all.'

'Hmmm.' Tara is giving me serious side eye at this. 'Yeah, I think that we all know that you "care" about Nico.' She does the finger quotes and everything.

'I deeply regret telling you everything about my life,' I sigh.

'You're just upset because you'll never convince me that you don't have proper feelings for Nico.'

'It was a childhood crush,' I insist. 'I've hardly even thought about him for the last year.'

'Sure.' Tara's flat delivery tells me all I need to know about how much she believes that story. 'I just don't want you to get hurt . . . Playing happy families with the guy you've been in love with for decades feels like a real recipe for disaster, babe.' Her brow is crinkled with obvious concern.

'Message received.' I keep my tone light even as her words strike a definite chord. It's not like Nico had exactly been enthusiastic about this plan to keep me around. It's important that I keep a tight lid on any feelings I may have. 'But this really is just a practical thing. It's not Nico's fault his dad was the worst.'

Tara nods slowly. 'Yeah. Absolutely mad that there's an actual trust full of money at stake. And that you're married to a *duke*!' She brightens at this, as if she can't help herself.

'He's not a duke,' I protest. 'His estranged half-brother is a duke.'

Tara pays no attention to this, settling herself on her sofa and digging into the bowl of popcorn. 'In a marriage of convenience with a duke,' she says dreamily between bites. The stacked gold rings on her fingers gleam against the deeper tawny gold of her skin as her hands move. 'And you're the ill-suited peasant who has to save his reputation.'

I choke on a laugh. 'I wouldn't say peasant,' I manage, apologetically. 'There's quite a lot of generational wealth and privilege on my side. Plus I don't do too badly myself.'

Tara waves this away. 'Yeah, but that's like when the duke marries the factory owner's daughter. It's a class thing, isn't it? Worlds apart.'

'We literally grew up next door to each other,' I say dryly.

'Just let me have this!'

'Please stop trying to tropify my life.'

My friend lets out an impatient huff. 'I'll never understand you. We met and bonded over reading romance novels and you're the least romantic person I know.'

'Just because I can appreciate a good romance novel doesn't mean that I believe they're representative of real life. I like them the same way people like reading science fiction or fantasy. It's an *escape* from reality.'

In my experience, the *reality* of getting caught up in an 'epic love story' means excusing a lot of terrible behaviour on both sides. People literally wrote songs about my mum and dad and their passionate romance, but living with them was like being braced in the back seat during a decades-long car crash.

However, this is an argument we've had before, which is probably why Tara simply ignores me.

'So how long are you going to stay out there?' she asks.

'I don't know. I guess that depends on what happens with the trustee.'

'It's not like you to be without a plan,' Tara says after a moment.

I shrug. 'Maybe it's good that it's out of character.' I think about the argument I had with Gran. 'Maybe I need to make some changes. You're always saying I should shake things up.'

'Well, yeah, but I meant get a haircut, a fringe that will look great at the hairdressers but that you're bound to regret as soon as it rains . . . not a husband, a stepdaughter and a dog in another country in a town full of strangers for an unspecified amount of time while some lawyer examines your fake life.'

'Anything sounds bad when you list it all out like that.'

'Hmm,' she murmurs. 'Tell me about this town then, what's it called, Roseport? Sounds cute.'

So I do, I tell her everything, from Bud picking me up and the twilight, Nirvana-fuelled yoga class, to Miss Rita and her ice cream with a side of gossip. By the end Tara is cackling, delighted.

'Oh my god, it sounds amazing!' she says. 'I know you don't want to believe you're in a romance novel, but please tell me there's a gorgeous, aw-shucks police chief and he's going to be caught up in a love triangle with you and Nico?'

'Well, actually . . .'

'No!' Tara exclaims, leaning forward with so much enthusiasm that kernels of popcorn go flying.

'Not the love triangle bit,' I laugh, 'but I did meet the handsome police chief, and he seems very nice. He invited us out for drinks after the town meeting.'

'Lee. Please.' Tara's face is suddenly very close to the camera. 'This is so important. *Please* tell me he was wearing a cowboy hat.'

'I'm afraid not.'

She sighs and sits back. 'I guess you can't have everything.'

'I should probably get ready to go,' I say reluctantly. 'I think they said the meeting was at seven so we'll all be heading off soon. What do you think a town meeting looks like?'

'Chaos from the sound of it,' Tara sounds gleeful, but then she must see the worry on my own face. 'But absolutely nothing you can't handle. You're so clever and so brilliant, and they'll love you.'

'Thanks,' I murmur. 'I hate that I feel so awkward. It seems like it's a really tight community and obviously they all love Nico . . .'

'Oh yeah, *everyone* loves Nico,' Tara grumbles.

'I just meant the fact that they're all so determined to be a part of this plan to help him. That's strange, right? Nice, but strange.'

I can't imagine any of my neighbours enthusiastically hurling themselves into a little light perjury for my benefit. I'm not even sure most of them would be able to pick me out of a police line-up. (Surely correct and normal?)

Tara only shrugs again. 'Things are different in small towns, and they *are* all . . . you know . . . *American*. Who knows how things work over there. They put marshmallows on sweet potatoes – they're capable of anything.'

'Good point,' I agree, getting to my feet. 'Well, thanks for the pep talk. I'll let you know how it goes. Brace yourself, this place seems pretty . . . eccentric.'

'That's because the town itself is a character!' Tara yells, as I end the call.

When I hang up, I notice I have another message from Adrian:

A work trip? Nice. Anywhere glamorous? Xx

I feel another pang of guilt. I know ending the relationship was the right thing to do, and if I'm honest I thought he'd be annoyed, more than happy to disappear from my life, but I guess he's really taking this friendship thing seriously.

I'm in the States, I type, and then hesitate. I can't leave it at that, can I? It sounds so cold and his message was friendly. Don't know about glamorous, but it's very pretty. After a moment's thought I add a couple of kisses . . . that's what he did so it seems polite.

I don't have to dwell on it for long because there's a soft knock on the door, and when I open it Nico is standing there, looking sheepish. In the background I can hear Phoebe and Magda locked in a loud and competitive card game.

'Sorry, can I—' Nico gestures towards me and I pull the door wider, letting him in.

'It's your room,' I remind him.

'You know you really don't have to come tonight.' He lifts a hand and rubs the back of his neck. 'I would understand if you decided you didn't want any part in this.'

He doesn't know he's echoing Tara, but yet again it's a reminder that Nico seems less than thrilled by the prospect of pretending to be married to me. It's hard not to take it at least a little personally.

'It's not such a big deal,' I say with what I hope is an easy shrug. 'Let's go to the meeting and hear what everyone has to say.'

He huffs out a sound that might be a laugh. 'Honestly, I don't know why I'm trying to talk you out of it, you've always been so stubborn.'

'I have not!'

'Yes, you have! You're one of the most stubborn people I've ever met! Remember the thing with the trick or treating when you were seven?'

I blink. 'I have no idea what you are referring to.'

'Oh, please,' Nico scoffs. 'You heard that me and Jack were going trick or treating and your mum and dad said you should leave us boys alone. You snuck out the house anyway and followed us around all night, wearing a bedsheet.'

'That wasn't me.'

'Daisy,' Nico laughs, 'the sheet didn't cover your feet and you wore those shoes you loved with the beads on the laces . . . the ones Gran got you. They literally had your name on them, spelled out in black and white.'

I'd forgotten about those shoelaces. Gran had surprised me with them after I told her some of the girls at school made them for each other and I was feeling left out. They said LEE on one foot and RULES on the other, and there were little pink and purple heart-shaped charms, too. I thought they were extremely cool, but fine, in hindsight, maybe not the best for protecting my super-secret identity.

I feel a wave of love for my grandmother at the memory, followed by the sharp sting of hurt that she hasn't reached out to me since I arrived. I don't think we've ever really had a fight before, and our argument still feels too near the surface for me to be sensible about it.

'Ah,' I manage, returning to the conversation with Nico. 'That could have been a different Lee.'

'But then they wouldn't have ruled,' Nico teases.

'I thought I was so stealthy.'

'I don't know about that. You kept on bashing into things.'

'I couldn't cut proper eyeholes in the sheet!' I protest.

'*Anyway*,' Nico says, 'the point is I know you and I know when there's no point arguing with you.'

'Wow, remind me who's the stubborn one here?'

Nico pinches my chin between his thumb and forefinger and tips my face up so that I'm looking at him. 'Lee,' he growls and, oh no, I like him growling my name quite a lot. I feel a wash of heat rush to my cheeks. 'Stop arguing with me about who is the most stubborn. I'm trying really hard to make a point here, which is that there is absolutely no pressure on you to attend this town meeting. I know being around big groups of people is your worst nightmare. If you're determined to hear the plan then I can go and report back.'

He looks down at me, calm and steady, his hand still on my chin, and the only thing I want to do is touch him, to lift myself up on my toes and press my lips against his, but instead I stare at his face. He's got *such* a great face.

It's the bone structure; so finely drawn that he's beautiful – in that very seriously beautiful way that Italian Renaissance artists strived to capture. It's the sensual mouth, the slightly hooded eyes, the hard line of his jaw that stops him from being too pretty.

The moment stretches out between us. A beat passes, then two as we look and look at each other. The sound of my heartbeat is so loud I'm surprised we're not drawing attention from the next room.

Nico's touch gentles, and his fingers trace a featherlight line up along the side of my jaw. It's a touch that I feel *everywhere*, and I realise I'm holding my breath.

When he reaches the tender hollow under my ear where my pulse thrashes wildly, like some sort of caged animal underneath his fingertips, I exhale, and the breathy sound has Nico's eyes widening. His hand drops, and he takes a step back.

'I don't mind,' I croak.

Nico looks dazed. 'What?' he asks, shaking his head slightly.

I try for a smile to dispel some of the tension. *What just happened?*

'I don't mind going to the meeting. For you and Phoebe I'll even make small talk with strangers.'

I watch my words land, and his body relaxes; a familiar gleam of amusement dances in his eyes. 'Wow,' he says with a smirk. 'You must *really* like my daughter.'

'Something like that,' I mutter. 'Now, tell me, do I need to get changed? What's the dress code for town meetings? Should I wear a suit? Something more dressy? Or is it more of a coastal casual thing?' I worry one of my small pearl earrings. 'I think I have a striped Sézane jumper with me.'

'Hmmm, I don't know. Do you have anything that's somewhere between formal and casual with a touch of elegant whimsy?'

I start mentally riffling through my wardrobe. I wasn't sure how long I was staying for so I packed options but I'm drawing a blank. 'Whimsy? I don't think so, like what?'

'Fake moustache?' Nico suggests. 'Or a small bird that you can perch on your shoulder?'

'You're teasing me.'

'I mean, you're making it pretty easy, Daisy. What the fuck is coastal casual?'

'Right, fine, I'm overthinking it,' I sigh. 'So I'm okay in this?' I gesture to the outfit I've been wearing today.

'As long as you wear the boots, too,' Nico says.

'You like the boots?' I ask, and I would swear that a hot spark briefly leaps in his eyes.

'Yeah, they're nice,' he coughs. 'But it's not for me; my friend Kat has been texting me all afternoon and she'll want to grill you about them.'

'Oh.' I try really hard not to care that Nico has a friend called Kat who has great taste in shoes and access to his phone number. 'How did she—'

'Don't ask,' he sighs. 'Town full of busybodies. But actually I think you'll really like Kat. She's Luke's sister. She's coming out for drinks with us after the meeting, so you'll get a chance to talk.'

'Great,' I say brightly, even though it is *not* actually great and I do not have a good track record for making friends. I try to remember what Tara said . . . I just need to relax and be myself.

I can do that.

'In that case I'm ready to go,' I say, feeling like Joan of Arc or Marie Antoinette as I give him a wide smile. 'Let's go and meet the rest of Roseport.'

Chapter Fifteen

Nico

'You should hold hands,' Phoebe says as we get out of the car.

I swing round to look at her. 'What?'

'You and Lee.' Phoebe nods at Lee who is standing very still. 'You've got to practise being married, haven't you? And married people hold hands.' Her tone implies that this is very obvious, and that – once more – we are deliberately sabotaging her vision. 'They kiss too,' she adds with devastating bluntness. 'Maya's parents kiss *all* the time.'

I think Lee's face has lost what little colour it had, but she sounds calm when she says, 'I wouldn't expect there to be a lot of kissing at town meetings.'

'Yeah,' I say, trying to sound just as relaxed, even though now I am looking at her mouth and the possibility of kissing her flashes through my mind in cinematic detail. 'This is practically a business meeting.'

Phoebe huffs. 'At least hold hands,' she demands.

I look at Lee, who shrugs and holds her hand out. My fingers wrap around hers; her skin is cool and soft.

The meeting takes place at the town hall, a pretty building opposite the church, and – surprise, surprise – today the place is packed to the rafters.

'Yoo-hoo!' Rita calls out and waves when Lee, Magda, Phoebe and I enter the scrum. 'I saved us seats.' She's sitting right in front of the small stage, next to four empty chairs.

'Great,' I grunt as we make our way down the aisle between the rows of folding chairs occupied by the entire population of Roseport. They all watch Lee with avid expressions, more than one pair of eyes travelling to our clasped hands, and I sincerely hope that she's missing all the excited whispering that springs up in her wake. Lee has always been nervous about big social events and I know she must be hating this.

Not that anyone else would guess. She glides down the aisle in her high-heeled boots, and her expression is serene. When someone reaches out and touches her arm, *I'm* the one who starts forward, a weird protective growl in my throat. We left Taco at home with a giant dog chew, but it appears I'll be bringing the watchdog energy myself.

In the end it's only Mrs Kaminski, the apple-cheeked, eighty-seven-year-old retired nursery school teacher, telling Lee that the belt tie on her fancy coat is dragging on the floor. Probably not a threat.

Lee thanks her and drops my hand, straightening her coat before removing it entirely and draping it over her arm. The crowd watch her like she's a matador twirling her cape.

'Thanks, Miss Rita,' I say when we reach her, even though I'd rather not be sitting in the front row.

'No problem,' she winks. 'Gotta have the best seats for the big show!' She rummages around in her pockets before pulling out two sandwich bags full of the candy she uses as ice cream toppers. 'Plus, I brought snacks.'

'Yesss,' Phoebe hisses, bundling past so that she can take the seat immediately beside Rita. 'I'm *starving*.'

'You literally just had dinner,' I say loudly, keen to make it known that I am actually feeding my daughter. She even ate a few mouthfuls of buttered corn, which is at least nutritionally adjacent to a real green vegetable.

Phoebe treats me to a withering look. 'But everyone knows there's a separate kind of hunger for dessert, Dad. It's science.'

With a sigh, I take the seat next to my daughter, and Lee sits in the one beside me, carefully shaking out her coat before folding it over the back of her chair. This, I feel, is incredibly trusting. It's a cream coat, clearly expensive and not the same one as earlier. (Who in the world has one immaculate cream coat, let alone two?) And now she's leaving it vulnerable to anyone with grabby little jam hands. I eye the row behind us, checking for oil-stained mechanics or small, chocolate-covered children but it seems we're safe.

'Are you okay?' Lee whispers, her lips dangerously close to my ear.

'Yep,' I reply quickly. 'Are you?'

'I'm fine,' she says, and her expression gives nothing away. There's not a trace of anxiety on her face and I'm starting to think maybe that's her tell. Lee always looks so unruffled, but the more time I spend with her the more I'm convinced that when that calm mask comes down, it means she's jittering with nerves. I have the overwhelming urge to reach for her hand, to tangle her fingers with mine and reassure her somehow, but I am very aware that I shouldn't.

I don't know what the fuck is going on with me, but I *do* know that I was about five seconds away from kissing her in my bedroom before we left and, honestly, I'm still waiting for the resulting adrenaline kick to die down.

'We'll be getting started in a minute,' Magda says from her place beside Lee where she is waving hello to various people. 'I have to say it's a great turnout . . . we haven't had a meeting this well attended since the last time DeeDee Brady's goose was on the loose.'

'A goose on the loose?' Lee echoes, a quiver in her voice.

'That goose is a fucking menace,' I grumble. 'Any time he gets out he destroys so much property, and squares off with all the dogs. Taco's absolutely terrified of him.'

Lee lets out a strangled 'Mmm.'

'He's a delinquent.' Magda purses her lips. 'I didn't agree with the people calling for the town to build some sort of animal *jail*, but it's hard to know what to do with him. Then of course there's Russell . . .'

'Who's Russell?' Lee asks.

'I believe he's on the docket tonight,' Rita says, leaning across. 'Been bothering that young waitress at the diner again, the old pervert.'

'You have a town pervert?' A line forms between Lee's eyes.

'Certainly we do,' Miss Rita says, as if to be without a pervert would somehow be insulting of our townhood.

'He's a bird, too,' I explain, but clearly not well enough because Lee continues to look baffled. 'Russell the crow,' I carry on, and I am struck by the distressing realisation that this is just my life now. 'He's got this thing about peeking in people's bedroom windows,' I add a little desperately.

'So *you* watch out, Lee,' Rita warns. 'He'll have his beady eye on you, that's for certain.'

'*Goodness*,' Lee murmurs, clearly not knowing how else to respond to this statement. Twenty seconds later she has her phone out of her pocket and she's texting someone, her lips pressed together. When a reply flashes through almost instantly she makes a muffled snorting sound.

'Okay, people!' Art, the head of the town council, yells as he finally takes to the floor, and the crowd quiets. He's a small man in his sixties with a big voice, and he struts along with his chest puffed out. His wife Annie – taller than him and pale with an elbow-length fall of white-blonde hair – drifts along behind. Despite the fact that Art has the look of an officious little twit, and Annie gives the (correct) impression of being extremely vague, they're actually not that bad. Inept, of course, but not bad people.

'Big meeting tonight,' Art booms, rubbing his hands together. 'And we've got a special guest here, all the way from jolly old Blighty!' This last is said in a horrifyingly bad cockney accent. 'Apples and pears!' Art continues, seemingly at random. 'Tea and crumpets!'

He looks expectantly at Lee.

'Um. Hello?' she says. This response is understandable, but if she thinks this is weird she needs to brace herself for what's sure to come.

Art beams at her, and Annie lifts her hand in a gesture that might be a wave, but she seems to forget what she's doing half way through and her arm falls limply back to her side.

Lee darts a worried glance in my direction and I try to look solid and reassuring.

'So,' Art picks up again, 'thanks to last night's emergency meeting, most of us know why we're here, but I'm going to turn the floor over to Magda, to lay out the details.'

'And me,' Phoebe insists, jumping to her feet.

'And Phoebe,' Art agrees. 'Miladies,' he rolls forward into a bow, 'me doth believe the floor is yours.' Looks like the British thing is going to stick, although now he appears to be channelling a medieval squire with awful grammar. Perfect.

Magda and Phoebe shuffle up to the stage, and give a brief overview of the situation we find ourselves in. As this includes my father's draconian will, his position as a member of the British nobility and the scandalising fact that Lee and I got married in Vegas and were too drunk to remember it, I expect an uproar. What I get is the sort of slightly bored silence that means every single person in this room was already well aware of these details. Someone even sucks loudly on an empty drink, the straw making those obnoxious bubbling sounds as they try to hoover up the last drops.

I should have known this gossip would be old news by now – it *has* been almost three whole days since Magda and Phoebe found out.

'So,' Magda concludes, 'we have a week until the trustee will be coming to conduct their inspection. We must integrate Lee fully into the town and make sure, when the trustee arrives, that he or she—'

'Or they,' Annie murmurs.

'Thank you, Annie, or *they*,' Magda corrects herself, 'believes completely that Lee and Nico are in a happy, stable marriage. To do this our entire community must work together, so this meeting today is for us to discuss exactly what that looks like.'

At this a dozen hands shoot up into the air.

'Yes,' Magda says, 'Phil?'

Phil gets to his feet. 'The Roseport Players stand with you,' he says, and his throbbing tones lead me to believe that Art's chivalry is contagious, particularly when the two of them exchange glances and then both pound their fists over their hearts in some sort of weird salute while bowing their heads at Lee.

After darting me another *what-the-fuck?* look, Lee gives a brief nod, which is the sort of vaguely royal gesture that has these idiots beaming with approval.

'Who are the Roseport Players?' Lee whispers out the side of her mouth as Phil continues talking.

'Amateur dramatic theatre group,' I murmur back.

'Their extended performance of *Chicago* last year was surprisingly good,' Miss Rita pipes up, and I wince, thinking about those four hours of my life that I'll never get back.

'We were wondering if we could devise some simple scenes within the group,' Phil is saying, 'small tableaus if you will, for our trustee to stumble across.'

Magda's eyes narrow. 'What sort of thing did you have in mind?'

'A date night at Stefano's?' the woman next to Phil stands up. 'We thought some of the players could go in undercover, and make subtle comments about what a nice couple they are in front of the trustee? Talk about our favourite memories of Lee from the past year.'

'Casually of course,' Phil adds earnestly, which is something. 'But, you know, kinda loudly?' he adds, which seems less promising.

'I like it,' Magda beams. 'This is the kind of thinking we need.'

Buoyed by this success there are several more suggestions. Some – like including Lee in the local craft group – are small and manageable enough. Others – like having a plane fly daily over the town dragging a banner with mine and Lee's faces on it are . . . less so.

'I've been watching YouTube to learn about improvising,' Phoebe says. 'It's important that you go along with whatever someone says to you. You have to say *yes, and . . .*'

Phil and company nod with approval. 'Perhaps a small demonstration?' Phil suggests.

'*Yes, and* we're in space!' Phoebe exclaims, pointing a finger at him.

'*Yes, and* my Quazon laser has malfunctioned!' Phil hurls himself forward, clutching an imaginary gun.

'*Yes, and . . .* Don't worry, commander,' adds Phyllis, the local florist, stepping gamely forward. 'We have a battle-ready space cannon that shoots . . . um . . . green slime.'

'Take that, alien scum!' Mrs Kaminski yells and she looks a lot less sweet and innocent as she bathes in the imaginary blood of her enemy.

'What . . . is happening?' Lee whispers.

I scratch my jaw. 'You just have to let them wear themselves out.'

Although, admittedly, the space opera playing out in front of us is a lot to take. Lee has lost her serene look and is now observing the scene through eyes rounded with shock. She's gripping her phone like it's some sort of life jacket.

'I think that's enough,' I say finally, getting to my feet. I try to put as much authority behind the words as possible. 'While Lee and I both appreciate your . . . *enthusiasm*, it's best to keep things simple. If we do decide to go ahead with this, we just really need everyone to act . . . normal.' I realise the futility of this suggestion at once.

'Lee and I will pretend to be a couple, all we need is for you to act as if you're used to seeing her around. Honestly,' I can hear the desperation in my own voice, 'that's it.' I slump back into my seat.

A chorus of unhappy mutterings greet this. ' . . . no fun,' I hear someone grumble.

'Well, Nico,' Magda says, 'if that's really what you think. Everyone here wants to support you and Phoebe, and Lee as well. After all, she's part of the family now, too.'

There's a murmur of agreement and Lee's posture stiffens. Unthinkingly, I reach out to touch her knee.

Huge mistake. Her dress has ridden up and my palm unexpectedly meets warm skin covered in only a fine layer of silk. It's like holding her hand multiplied by infinity.

I snatch my fingers back, like I've burned myself.

Rita tuts sympathetically beside me. 'You'll have to do a lot more than touch the poor girl's knee if you want to sell this thing, Nicolas,' she whispers in my ear, and then she lets out one of her too loud laughs as I wince.

'So, as long as everyone is happy to agree to our little charade, it seems we're done with the matter for now,' Magda adds. 'Obviously, once we know the details of the trustee's arrival, we'll send out a town-wide alert. Code name Operation Wedded Bliss,' she adds, and everyone perks up again at this bit of subterfuge.

'Not a very subtle code name,' I point out.

'That's what I said,' Phoebe sighs. My daughter's potential for devious machinations is clearly being thwarted by the quality of her co-conspirators.

Magda, however, ignores this. 'So unless there's anything either of you want to add . . .' She looks at me and Lee expectantly.

'Nope,' I say. I stretch my legs out in front of me and cross my arms, glad that this bit is over.

Lee only shakes her head.

'Okay then,' Art says, reclaiming his position. 'With that first matter sorted, let's talk other business. It seems Russell has been up to his old tricks . . .'

Chapter Sixteen

Lee

By the time Phoebe and Magda have headed back to her place, and Nico leads me through the door into Darlene's, I am *extremely* ready for a drink. At this point I could do with being hooked up to an IV that delivers cold gin directly into my veins.

I thought Nico was exaggerating, but if anything he had played down the eccentricities of small-town life. That meeting was a lot of people having very loud feelings everywhere and I'd be feeling overwhelmed even if it hadn't been for the part where they all volunteered to be in on a town-wide lie with me at the centre.

'Come on,' Nico's hand is on the small of my back and I swear I can feel the warmth of his touch through my coat, 'time to return to planet earth.'

'Is there gin there?' I manage.

'I fucking hope so,' he mutters.

We're hit by a wall of heat and sound as we enter the bar, and I instinctively flinch – my body and my brain would quite like a nice dark room to sit down in for a bit – but Nico's hand rubs in small, reassuring circles at the base of my spine.

At least I assume they're meant to be reassuring, and not intensely arousing, which is what they actually are. Even the bizarre scenes at the town meeting weren't enough to distract me from how close the two of us were sitting. Every time his shirtsleeve brushed against my arm, a firework display of endorphins went off inside my brain.

Dragging my attention away from the man beside me, I turn to take in our surroundings.

Quite a few people from the town meeting have drifted over to join the patrons already propping up the long bar that stretches against one wall. At the back of the room there's a small stage with a giant juke box next to it, and a cluster of high-top tables. The walls are covered in music memorabilia, and pictures of handsome cowboys astride gorgeous horses. Across from the bar are a bunch of booths with battered red leather seats. The twang of country music fills the air.

'Nico! Lee!' A woman in one of the booths lifts her hand to wave at us. She's a gorgeous, curvy brunette in a plaid shirt, and she's sitting with Luke and another woman with long, ink-black hair who has her back to us.

'Hey, Kat,' Nico calls back. 'We'll grab some drinks and be right with you.'

We make our way to the bar and join the crowd of people waiting to order. Nico tucks us into the corner with me against the wall, and he puts his body between me and everyone else.

'Thought you could probably use a second before you have to meet more people,' he says, leaning down close to my ear so that I can hear him over the noise. 'We can take a beat.'

I swallow hard, and focus on the buttons of the dark green shirt he's wearing. 'Thanks,' I manage.

Nico lapses into silence and for a whole minute or two – maybe even longer – we stand there, close together but not touching. I concentrate on my breathing as the smell of his aftershave wraps itself around me. All I can see is him, his hard torso like a shield, holding the rest of the world at bay. My nervous system starts to regulate, tension leaves my body. I can feel my muscles relaxing, my shoulders coming down.

That's the thing about being around Nico, it settles something inside me. He makes me feel safe, he always has.

When I finally look up at his face, he's totally relaxed, idly scanning the room, one arm resting against the bar. I get a funny feeling in my stomach when I realise he would stand here quietly, comfortably like this with me for as long as I wanted.

I take another deep inhale and breathe out slowly, then I reach out and touch his arm.

'Thanks,' I say again. 'You were right. I did need that.'

He smiles down at me. 'Don't worry about it. You know we can skip out on drinks?'

I shake my head. 'I want to meet your friends. Plus, I've got to start . . . what did Magda say? . . . fully integrating myself into town life.' I try not to feel too nervous about that. Integrating isn't exactly my strong suit.

'It definitely sounded like they were trying to get you to join their cult,' Nico muses.

'Right!' I exclaim, glad it wasn't just me. 'Tell me the truth, have you been indoctrinated? Blink twice if you need me to save you.'

'As far as I know I am not in a cult, but maybe I'm in so deep I can't even see it.'

I nod wisely. 'They've been boiling you like one of those frogs.'

Nico frowns. 'What frogs?'

'It's a metaphor. Apparently, if you put a frog in boiling water it will jump straight out, but if you put it in tepid water and slowly heat it up then the frog will stay and boil to death.'

Nico's eyes widen. 'Okay, Daisy, first of all . . . dark.' He runs a hand over his face. 'And second of all, yep, I'm a boiled frog, that's exactly what's happened. Half of that stuff in there didn't even sound weird to me anymore.'

I laugh. 'At least it seems like one of those nice cults. You know, the ones that are more about tending a communal vegetable patch than . . .'

'Establishing a hierarchy of sister-wives?'

'I mean . . . they have kind of married you off,' I point out. 'But you should probably stick to just the one wife.'

Our eyes meet and his are lit with amusement, whisky gold light that I want to sink into.

'I'm really a one-wife-at-a-time sort of guy.'

'That's good to hear.'

'So . . . that meeting didn't scare you off?' Nico asks me, his face suddenly serious. 'We're really doing it? You and me. Married.'

'For a little while anyway,' I agree lightly, trying desperately not to show that this is the culmination of every birthday candle wish I made between the ages of eleven and fourteen. Okay, sixteen. *Fine*, maybe eighteen.

'I still don't know if it's the right thing to do, but the situation is pretty desperate,' he says, which doesn't feel like the greatest compliment. He fixes me with a steady look. 'I don't know what I'd have done if you hadn't come along. Probably bollocksed this up as badly as I manage to do with everything else. I promise I won't let you down, and if you ever need to walk away then I get it.'

'We'll be fine,' I insist, wishing I could smooth the worried expression from his face.

'*You'll* be fine,' he says. 'Whatever happens. I promise you that. Now, shall we get that drink?' Nico turns to lean over the bar and catch the bartender's attention.

'That would be great.' I look around. 'It feels like we're in Nashville. What's a bar like this doing in a small town in the middle of Maine, anyway?'

'You're about to find out.'

'What do you . . . *Dolly*!' I gasp, and I hear Nico's laugh ring in my ears as if it's coming from far away.

I blink, but the scene doesn't alter. Dolly Parton is standing in front of me about to take my drink order.

'Not quite,' she says in a honey-thick Southern drawl. She holds her hand out over the bar and I take it. 'Darlene,' she grins. 'Welcome to my place.'

'I'm so sorry,' I stammer. 'You look . . .' I trail off.

Darlene laughs. 'I know. It's uncanny, right? I got it my whole life so eventually I decided I'd just lean in.' She gestures to her big, blonde hair and rhinestone-studded outfit. 'No one better to model yourself on than Ms Parton.'

'Oh, I agree,' I say, still feeling vaguely starstruck. 'I'm a *huge* fan.'

'Then we're going to get along just fine,' Darlene nods. 'Now, what can I get the two of you to drink? Nico, you want your usual?'

'Yes, please, Darlene.'

'And for you, Lee? Wait, let me guess. It's a particular skill I have.' She runs her eyes over me, her lips pursed in a glossy, pink pout. 'Gin martini,' she says slowly, like a clairvoyant communicating with spirits in the afterlife. 'Very cold. But . . . not olives . . . with a twist?'

'Heaven,' I agree, and she nods again in satisfaction.

'Randall!' Darlene yells over her shoulder. 'You pour Nico a beer while I mix up a mean martini for Miss Lee, here.' She sends me a wink and then sashays off to start making my drink.

'Oh my god,' I whisper and I realise I'm clutching Nico's arm. 'You could have warned me. I love Dolly Parton!'

'I know.' Nico is clearly pleased with himself. 'You had that photo of her on your wall for years. I couldn't resist.'

'I know she's not Dolly,' I say, watching Darlene out of the corner of my eye, 'but is it weird that I'm still fan-girling?'

'I think Darlene's used to it. Sometimes tourists refuse to believe it isn't her, they think Dolly Parton is living some secret double life, pulling pints in a bar in Maine.'

'But what if . . .' I say, wide-eyed, and Nico laughs again.

A rail-thin Black man with a dazzling smile props a pint of beer on the bar in front of Nico. 'Lee, this is Randall, Darlene's husband,' Nico introduces us. 'Randall, this is Lee.'

'Your wife!' Randall shakes my hand with great enthusiasm.

'Er, yes,' Nico takes a deep sip from his drink. 'Better get used to that, I suppose.'

Randall nods. 'Nice to meet you, Lee.'

'You too,' I manage.

'Hey,' Nico looks down at me. 'You okay?'

I nod tightly.

'I'm right here with you,' Nico says. 'And if you want to leave, you say the word and we'll go.'

'What word?'

He tilts his head, looking at me with a smile. 'Coastal casual.'

Against the odds, my own mouth curves up. 'Fine, coastal casual it is,' and getting a tight grip on the stem of my martini glass, I make my way over to Nico's friends.

Chapter Seventeen

Nico

'Hi, Lee.' Luke shoots to his feet as we approach the table. 'Good to see you again.'

I narrow my eyes. He seems a bit too eager for my liking, but his warm welcome has Lee's shoulders coming down.

'You haven't met my sister Kat or our friend Mei yet, right?' he continues, making the introductions. Lee smiles shyly at the other two women, but Kat bundles her straight into a hug.

I wince and Mei rolls her eyes underneath the blunt cut of her dark fringe.

'Kat, *release*,' Mei says firmly, like she's talking to Taco when he's chewing up one of my shoes.

'Sorry!' Kat pulls away from Lee, who looks a little flustered. 'I forget not everyone is a hugger.' She beams at Lee. 'I'm Kat and I'm obsessed with you already. I need to know where you got those boots, and this coat!' She strokes Lee's sleeve reverently. 'I'm *dying* over this coat.'

'Kat,' Luke sighs.

'Okay, yes.' Kat pulls back again with a rueful look in her eyes. 'I'm doing it again. In my defence I have had two of Darlene's strawberry margaritas and I'm tipsy.'

She's still smiling as she eyes Lee expectantly.

'Um, I think the boots are old Ralph Lauren,' Lee says finally.

'Dang!' Kat exclaims. 'I knew it was too much to hope for that you'd say you got them from Target.'

'What's Target?' Lee asks, shooting me a worried look.

Kat gasps. 'Oh, you poor, sweet child. You don't know what you're missing out on. Don't worry, I'll take you.'

'Thanks,' Lee manages, but a small smile tugs at her lips. Maybe Kat's steamroller approach is actually going to pay off. It would be nice for Lee to have friends if she's stuck here for the next few weeks.

Mei leans over and holds her hand out for Lee to shake. 'I'm Mei,' she says, 'I'm tonight's designated driver so I'm nursing one beer and unfortunately not tipsy at all.'

'Not that Mei talks as much as Kat even when she's hammered,' Luke puts in, earning himself a shove from his sister.

We all take our seats and Kat holds up her glass. 'Okay, a toast to the newlyweds!'

'Do they count as newlyweds if they've been married for a year?' Mei muses.

'I think if you found out you were married less than a week ago, you should definitely qualify for newlywed status, right?' Lee says, her posture still stiff. 'We shouldn't have to miss out on our honeymoon period just because we got so drunk we didn't *know* we were married. That sort of thing could happen to anyone.'

'That's right,' I agree as the others laugh and again I watch something like relief flicker across Lee's face. 'In fact, I think we should still be able to register for gifts at this point. There's a crêpe pan I've been eyeing up.'

'Please god, no more pancakes,' Lee groans before smiling at me. It's a real smile, one that shows off her dimples, and it feels like a wave of sunlight falling across the table.

'You said you liked them,' I protest, trying not to look flustered.

'I said they had a *unique flavour*,' Lee corrects me. 'And you knew exactly what that meant.'

'A very polite way of saying they tasted like sewage?' I ask.

'Exactly.'

When I laugh and look away from her it's to find the other three members of our group watching us with avid interest.

'All this British banter,' Kat swoons, and Lee blushes. I think for a moment she'd forgotten it wasn't just the two of us. I know I had.

'Please don't try and do the accent,' I grimace. 'I haven't recovered from Art's Victorian chimney sweep moment.'

Luke grunts in agreement.

'Congrats on surviving your first town meeting, Lee,' Mei says. 'Was it everything you imagined it would be?'

'There were a lot more bird-related issues than I'd anticipated,' Lee says diplomatically.

'Fucking Russell,' Kat murmurs into her cocktail glass. 'Talk about ruining the mood when I finally got Tyler back to my place last week.'

'Can we not get started on your sex life?' Luke groans.

'I'm not going to have any sex life if Russell has anything to say about it,' Kat grumbles darkly into her drink. 'I swear that bird *knows* when anyone's about to get lucky.'

'Frankly, I think if he stopped you from sleeping with Tyler, Russell's doing a community service,' Mei says, and she and Luke tap beer bottles in their own toast.

'That guy is the worst,' Mei tells Lee in an exaggerated whisper.

'Listen, not all of us can accidentally marry a hot single dad in Vegas,' Kat says and takes another sip of her drink. 'It's slim pickings out here.'

'Actually,' Lee pipes up, 'my friend was saying that we're basically a marriage of convenience trope.'

'Yes!' Kat hoots.

'What do you mean a trope?' I ask.

'Like a romance novel,' Kat puts in, as if that clears anything up.

'He's also . . .' Lee leans in towards Kat, 'my brother's best friend.' She half whispers the words like an admission of guilt.

'Nooooooo!' Kat yells, clearly delighted. I have no idea what the fuck is going on, but as Lee seems to be relaxing and enjoying herself and she and Kat are bonding, I have no problem with it.

'So you two go way back, then?' Luke asks.

'Yep.' Lee sips her drink. 'I've known Nico since I was five.'

'Okay,' Mei rubs her hands together, an evil glint in her eye, 'so you have *all* the good embarrassing stories.'

'Please tell us that Mr Smooth here had an awkward adolescence,' Luke says and settles back in his seat.

'Oh yes,' she replies. 'Let's begin with the saga of Tansy Bennet and Nico's ill-advised foray into amateur BMXing.'

'Let's not.' I choke on a laugh. I can't believe she even remembers that. Fortunately, I'm saved from that particular story by the arrival of Randall with a giant plate of loaded nachos. As we all dig in, the others pepper Lee for more details and she seems to relax more with every answer.

'Shall I get us another round?' she asks, a little shyly, a few minutes later.

'Yes!' Kat exclaims, twirling her finger in the air. 'Let's keep this party going.'

When Lee disappears into the crowd, Kat reaches across the table and grabs my hand.

'I'm sorry, but I have a massive crush on your wife.'

I choke on the last of my beer.

'Join the club,' Mei says. 'She's gorgeous . . . and that *accent*! She's so hot.'

'*So* hot!' Kat echoes.

I look at Luke, who smiles and shrugs. 'You've got to admit that she's a very attractive woman.' My face must do something that I'm not in control of then because his smile widens and he holds his hands up in a gesture of surrender. 'Objectively speaking, man. I'm obviously not going to hit on her when she's married.'

'Good,' I say, and the word comes out a lot more snarly than I'd anticipated. 'Let's keep it that way. Lee's off limits,' I gesture to them with my empty bottle, 'to all of you.'

'Oh my god!' Kat hisses, leaning in again, her eyes darting over her shoulder to make sure the coast is clear. 'Nico. Do *you* have a massive crush on your wife?'

If I had any beer left, I'd be choking again. I actually wish everyone would stop referring to Lee as my wife all the fucking time.

'Lee?' I laugh. 'Of course not. We grew up together, I care about her a lot. She's . . . like a little sister to me.'

'If you really felt that way, you wouldn't be going all growly caveman about Luke,' Mei says. 'He's a genuinely good guy and a catch.'

'Thanks, Mei.' Luke lifts his drink in a small salute.

'If I wasn't exclusively attracted to women, I'd have locked him down years ago,' Mei continues breezily.

'The point is,' I say stubbornly, 'Lee is doing me a huge favour. It's a complicated situation and I'm not going to make it any worse. And neither are you,' I say firmly, shooting all three of them a pointed look. Luke flashes me a boy scout salute, but Mei and Kat only smirk.

'Sorry, it took a minute,' Lee reappears, carrying a tray full of drinks.

'Hey, Randall,' Kat catches the man by the arm as he speeds by, 'will you take a photo of all of us to commemorate Lee's first night?' She brandishes her phone at him.

We pose for the photo and when Randall hands her phone back, Kat coos over the picture, leaning over to show it to Lee.

'Such a good one of all of us, even if the lighting is terrible,' Kat says.

'Yes, we need Nico to take one on his proper camera.' Lee sends me a quick smile, and my heart sinks.

'Oh!' Kat exclaims. 'Nico, do you have a fancy camera or something?'

A line appears between Lee's brows. 'What do you mean?' she asks. 'Nico's an amazing photographer.' When everyone looks blank, she carries on uncertainly, 'It's his job.'

'I thought you were a contractor?' Mei says slowly.

'I *am* a contractor,' I agree, and there's a hard knot of anxiety making its presence felt in my chest. 'I used to take photos but I don't anymore. It's not a big deal.' I take a swig from my fresh beer bottle.

There's an awkward silence, and Lee is looking at me like I just sprouted a load of tentacles and declared I'd arrived from a different solar system.

I quickly turn the conversation to other things, and the rest of the night is relaxed and mercifully uneventful.

By the time we leave it's late, and we make the short drive home in silence. Lee looks out the window, clearly lost in thought. I remind myself that, however overwhelmed I'm feeling, she's been through a lot more today.

'You must be exhausted,' I say, as I open the front door. Taco leaps up to greet us, running straight past me as if I don't exist to dance around Lee's feet. He lets out several excited yips, then rolls over while Lee crouches down to rub his belly.

'I am also here,' I say dryly, but they both ignore me.

'I'm not feeling too bad at the moment,' Lee says, her attention on my dog. 'My body has no clue what time it is, and I guess it'll all hit me soon. I'll sleep well tonight.' She straightens up and gives me a smile. Taco parks himself next to her feet, gazing worshipfully up at her.

I clear my throat. 'Hopefully, I will too. I usually hate it when she's gone, but at least I can crash in Phoebe's room tonight.' I'm definitely looking forward to sleeping in a real bed; I'm not twenty anymore and the sofa did a number on my back.

I walk towards the kitchen. 'Do you want a drink?' I call over my shoulder.

'Um, just a glass of water, please.' Lee comes to perch on one of the stools at the breakfast counter and Taco retires to his bed where he can curl up and still keep an eye on her. 'Does Phoebe stay with Magda often?'

'One or two nights a week.' I pull a glass down from the cupboard. 'It's good for them to have the time together, but with the inn being renovated, Magda's moved out to one of the other cottages and there's not as much space as she's used to.' I fill the glass from the tap and place it in front of Lee. 'We've all been trying to work out the right balance. She had a whole life with Magda and Tom before I came along so it's sort of like shared custody.'

Lee wraps her hands around her water glass. 'It's complicated,' she says quietly, 'trying to do what's best for her.'

I lean against the other side of the counter. 'Yeah. I hate it when she's away,' I admit. 'I've missed too much time with her already . . . I feel so guilty whenever we're apart. And then sometimes I think I hold on too tight because of that. I'm struggling with making decisions for her. Like this thing with her skipping a grade . . . I don't know what to do. Magda thinks she should, but I'm not so sure. What if I choose wrong and fuck up her life?'

If I sound freaked out, it's because I am. 'What do you think?' I ask.

'Oh, I'm not sure it's any of my business . . .'

'You've been there,' I point out. 'I'd like to hear your opinion.'

Lee exhales. 'Honestly? I don't think my experience would necessarily be the same as hers, or that all of Phoebe's future happiness will ever boil down to a single decision. If Phoebe wants to stay where she is and that's your instinct too, then trust it. You can always revisit it later if it becomes an issue. You don't need to have it all figured out right now.'

She's so calm and steady, and the relief that I get from having someone I know and trust to talk about this stuff with is out of all proportion.

'Nico,' Lee says tentatively after a moment.

'Hmm?'

'Where's your camera?'

The change of topic throws me for a second. I gesture towards the bedroom, trying to keep my words easy. 'It's in storage somewhere. I don't have much need for it at the moment.'

'I know you said you couldn't work like you had been ...' Lee says carefully, 'but I didn't realise you weren't taking pictures *at all*.'

I shrug, helpless. 'I have to be here for Phoebe.'

I don't know how to explain it to her, but maybe Lee understands anyway. Her gaze softens, and she bites her lip as if physically stopping herself from saying something. My eyes are on her mouth. I want to run my thumb along her bottom lip. I want to tug it free from her teeth and claim it with my own.

I want it with an intensity that leaves me shaken.

There's something crackling in the air, an atmosphere that fills the room, like the minutes before a storm hits. I don't know when I started feeling so out of control around her, when being around Lee turned into some sort of extreme sport. It feels thrilling, it feels ... dangerous.

As if she's thinking the same thing, Lee takes a step back.

'You know, I am actually pretty tired,' she says. 'I think I'm going to head to bed.'

'Of course,' I cough. 'Let me know if you need anything. I'll be ...' I gesture towards Phoebe's room. Then I turn and grab my own glass from the cupboard, keeping my hands busy so that they don't reach for her.

'Okay, goodnight,' I hear her say.

''Night,' I reply, but I don't look around. I don't watch her disappear into my bedroom, getting ready to climb into my bed.

Because there's only so much a guy can take.

Chapter Eighteen

Lee

I wake up to the low murmur of Phoebe and Nico starting their day, and I drag myself out of bed and get dressed, sending Gran my daily text requesting proof of life. She sends back a photograph of today's paper and a ticket for this evening's performance of *Magic Mike Live*. It's Monday, and my first official day as a fake resident of Roseport.

When I leave my room it's just gone 8 a.m., and I find a set of keys sitting on the kitchen counter along with a short note.

Had an early start and didn't want to disturb you. I'm walking to the inn – left the keys to the truck so you won't be stranded here.
N x

Nico must have taken Taco with him as well because the house is eerily quiet. I drift around the kitchen, pouring myself a glass of orange juice and drinking it while looking out of the window. The silence is soothing and I sit down to do some work, but despite the fact that I did an intense amount of socialising yesterday, it's only a couple of hours before I start feeling restless.

It's another beautiful day, and even though I know all those people at the meeting last night are out there, the urge to venture outside is overwhelming. Kat told me she owns a coffee shop in town and invited me to stop in any time. Coffee doesn't sound too scary.

I grab my laptop and slip it into my bag before heading out. I don't drive much, and Nico's car is the size of a small tank, but thankfully the wide American roads are a lot more forgiving than London streets. Still, it takes me several minutes of driving around before I find a parking space enormous enough that I feel comfortable pulling into it.

'Morning, Lee,' someone calls as I clamber down from the truck.

I start. 'Oh, yes, good morning,' I say to the man passing me with his small, fussy-looking dog. I have no idea who he is, but it doesn't seem to matter as he carries on his way.

I turn in the direction of the café, and get about three steps down the street, before a woman pushing a toddler in a stroller stops to say hello. 'Good morning, Lee!'

'Morning,' I reply faintly, and I swear the toddler waves a tiny fist in greeting.

On the remaining walk to the café – which can't be more than fifty metres from the car – *seven* more people say good morning to me. This is more social interaction than I typically have with people over a forty-eight-hour period.

When I push open the door to Bean & Gone, the handful of customers inside all turn and greet me in the sort of cheerful chorus you'd hear in one of those arty horror movies about a Stepford community that wants to offer up the newcomer to devil worship.

I mutter my weak hellos, and make my way to the counter where Kat stands, her hair scrunched up in a messy bun, a cloth thrown over her shoulder.

'Morning, Lee!' she deliberately echoes the creepy singsong voices.

'Who are all these people?' I whisper.

'Is that a genuine question?' Kat asks. 'Because you are going to have to get to know everyone. I was thinking that you could use some flashcards.'

I brighten at this. 'Actually flashcards would be great.' If there's one thing I am good at, it's studying.

'I was joking,' Kat laughs, but when my face falls she quickly adds, 'but I'll get Mei on it – that's the kind of crafty shit she gets a real kick out of. It's the teacher in her.'

'I'll take all the help I can get,' I say nervously. 'I'm going to be terrible at this.'

She looks surprised. 'No, you're not.'

'Oh yeah,' I nod, 'I am. I'm such a textbook anxious introvert. I have a very limited social battery, it can get drained pretty quick.'

Kat hums thoughtfully. 'Yeah, we are a lot in this town. I'm used to everyone being in my business and having an opinion but I can see how it could be difficult. Actually, it may surprise you to hear this, but I myself *thrive* on the attention.' She tosses her hair and fixes me with a wide grin, making me laugh.

'I'm the total opposite,' I admit. 'I don't love being *perceived*. If I could exist as a sort of nebulous energy cloud in public, that would be great.' I sigh happily at the thought.

'If I promise to try and perceive you as a nebulous energy cloud in great boots, will that help?'

'Maybe,' I smile. 'Thanks.'

'What are friends for? Anyway, I'm glad you took me up on the invitation to visit my place. What can I get you?'

I look over the giant chalkboard on the wall behind her. 'A maple-oat latte, please, the biggest size you have,' I say before turning to linger over the glass case of pastries. 'These look amazing.'

'Try the pecan muffins,' Kat advises. 'I buy them in fresh from this baker in the next town over. They'll change your life.'

'Sold.'

Kat gets to work making my coffee, chatting the whole time. I can't believe how easy it is to be around her. In between the slightly overwhelming town meeting and the weirdly charged conversation I had with Nico, last night was surprisingly fun. Nico's friends are great, and I actually managed to relax and enjoy myself with them.

I can't remember the last time I felt so comfortable with new people.

'This place is lovely,' I say, looking around in appreciation. 'The perfect spot to get some work done.' And it is: it's light and airy and full of dark shining wood and splashy green plants. Kat grinds some coffee beans and the rich smell fills the air.

'Thanks,' Kat nods as she moves easily around the giant silver coffee machine. 'It's been a lot of effort, but I love how it turned out.'

She hands me my coffee, and I reach for my purse with my other hand, but she stops me with a wave. 'Nope, first one's on the house.'

'Oh!' I stop, tucking a strand of hair behind my ear. 'That's so nice.'

The bell over the door rings.

'Hello, Kat. Good morning, Lee,' the dapper-looking man approaching us calls out as the door closes behind him.

'Hi, Gerald. You want the usual?'

He nods in agreement.

'Hi, Gerald,' I repeat after Kat, trying to commit his face and name to memory.

We make conversation for a couple of minutes while Kat makes his coffee, and I feel unnecessarily proud of myself for asking him *two* questions instead of just nodding politely. Look at me! I'm doing it! I'm integrating!

By the time Gerald heads back out the door (with a coffee for his husband Carl) a queue has formed, and just as I realise that I'm being trapped in a sinking quagmire of small talk, Kat interrupts.

'Lee has a ton of work to do, so stop yapping at her and concentrate. Who wanted the maple scone?'

As the hungry crowd turn their attention to Kat, she winks at me and mouths the words *nebulous energy cloud*. Gratefully, I take my coffee and muffin and head for a table in the back where I pull out my laptop.

For the last couple of weeks I've been working on a complicated money laundering case that involves investigating several years of accounts across multiple businesses and I lose myself for a while in the soothing familiarity of the work, sipping my delicious coffee, devouring the sweet and spicy cake and hoovering up all the crumbs as I try to untangle the puzzle in front of me. They look innocent enough, but my gut says there are secrets hiding inside all these numbers, and I'm going to ferret them out.

'Lee,' a voice breaks through my concentration and I blink, lifting my eyes from my computer screen, like I'm coming out of a deep sleep.

Kat is standing over me, her hands on her hips. 'I said your name, like four times.'

'Sorry,' I wince. 'I get a bit involved in my work.'

'I can see that,' she says, eyeing my computer screen. 'It looks like you're trying to crack the Matrix.'

'Something like that,' I agree, and when I catch sight of the clock in the corner of the screen I realise I've been sitting here for over two hours.

'Nico called in his lunch order and I wondered if you wanted to take it over for him?' she asks. 'He's working up at the inn, and you have his truck, right? I think Luke was going to pick it up for him later but as you're here . . .'

'Oh,' I say, glancing back down at my computer. 'Sure. I'll get something, too, if that's okay.'

I order a sandwich, as well as a bag of muffins to take home with me, aware that I've been taking up a table all morning without paying for anything, not that Kat seems at all bothered. She wraps everything up, her fingers moving deftly as she talks a hundred miles an hour the whole time.

'Anyway, me and Mei want to take you out for a girls' night,' Kat says as I tap my card against the card machine. 'So let me know what evening suits you.'

I smother a laugh. 'I literally have no plans,' I say. 'Also, like I said, I don't exactly have a thriving social life, so I think it should probably be what suits you.'

'Sweetie,' Kat gives me a pitying look, 'you didn't think you were getting away that easily, did you? Every social club in town has pencilled you in as their guest of honour. Plus it looks like you and Nico have a couple of date nights planned, right?'

'What are you talking about?'

'You do know you and Nico have a public calendar?' Kat asks. 'He and Magda set it up.' She swipes at her phone and shows me a calendar absolutely teeming with appointments.

'What the . . .' I stare at it in mounting horror. What is displayed before me is literally the stuff of an introvert's worst nightmares. *This* is my Stephen King novel.

'Take it up with your husband,' Kat shrugs, handing me a weighty paper bag and a cardboard tray with two to-go cups in it.

'Oh, don't worry, I intend to,' I agree as I head for the door. I can't believe Nico would set this up without talking to me about it.

'And text me about girls' night, okay?' Kat calls after me as I leave.

By the time I bump off the road and down the drive towards the inn I'm wound up pretty tight, my fingers drumming an anxious tattoo against the steering wheel.

I pull to a stop and open the door, already forming my imaginary arguments. I *won't* freak out, I tell myself, but I will, *calmly*, lay out the facts.

Unfortunately, literally every coherent thought leaves my head when I round the truck only to be greeted by the sight of Nico in battered, low-slung jeans, a worn, white T-shirt that clings lovingly to the long lines of his torso, and an actual *toolbelt* coming towards me.

I'm not sure if he's *really* walking in slow motion and being soundtracked by Ginuwine or if my brain is doing that, but *Oh. My. God.*

As he swaggers closer I have to lean back against the bumper, my knees dissolving from under me. This feels indecent, filthy. Someone should do something! This is pornography! Happening right in our streets!

'Lee,' his mouth kicks up, and he's pulling off a pair of work gloves, tucking them into the back pocket of his jeans. Why is that the sexiest thing to ever happen? 'You didn't need to bring my lunch. Luke said he'd pick it up.'

You know the sound that the dial up internet used to make when it connected? The horrible disjointed whirring and beeping then the long, shrill scream? That is what is happening in my brain right now.

'No car,' I gasp finally, the words absolutely airless.

Nico frowns. 'What?'

'You don't have a car,' I swallow, my eyes flickering all over him, unable to settle on any one detail. His arms, muscled and tanned against the white T-shirt, his biceps definitely more . . . substantial than the last time I saw him, the tattoos, the heavy work boots, the unshaven jaw, the gleam of the tiny gold hoop in his ear, almost hidden behind the fall of his dark curls. He's all dusty and dishevelled and . . .

'. . . get there all right?' he asks and I realise he's been talking this whole time.

'Yep,' I squeak. 'Yes. Sure. Fine.'

'Are you okay?' he asks, suddenly concerned. 'You look a bit flushed.' He steps right up to me and lays his hand over my forehead, the other cradling my cheek. Big, callused man hands.

I whimper and clutch the giant paper bag full of food to my chest, holding it like a barrier between us.

'I'm fine,' I say, staggering away from him. 'A bit warm from the . . . truck. I think I had the heating up too high. I don't have the controls figured out yet.'

'Oh,' he pries the bag gently out of my death grip, hefting it lightly on one arm, 'I can take a look at that before you head home.'

'No need,' I say, feeling a bit steadier. As long as I don't look directly at him everything is fine. I find myself fascinated by a patch of gravel to his left. 'I'm going to walk back. You said it's faster, right? And I figured you might need the truck for your . . .' My eyes dip to his belt of their own accord and I feel lightheaded again. '*Tools.*'

'Yeah, we need to sort you out with your own transport while you're here,' Nico says. 'Luke said his mum's old car is just sitting in their garage. He's going to check with her to see if you can use it, but he doesn't think it will be a problem.'

'Oh,' I push my hair back away from my face, trying really hard to focus on the conversation, 'that's so nice of him.'

'It's not *his* car,' Nico says, his voice suddenly gruff.

'I know, but it's nice of him to think of it,' I say. 'I really like him.'

'You really like him?'

I nod frantically. 'Yup.'

'What exactly do you like about him?' Nico's eyes are fixed on me, and I think he must be realising how flustered I am.

'Oh, you know,' I say, barely able to remember what we're talking about. *Luke! Right, Luke.* 'He seems like a good guy. He made me feel really welcome last night.'

Nico's posture softens. 'Of course he did. All my friends loved you.'

'Really?' I ask hopefully. I'd want his friends to like me anyway, because they're important to Nico, but I realise now that I want them to like me for *me*, too. Last night was a bit like that first morning with Nico and Phoebe ... a glimpse at the sort of life I always wanted but never felt I could have.

'Yes,' he huffs out a laugh. 'They've formed a Lee Turner-Jones fan club. Mei told me they're only using me to get access to you from now on.'

I can't hold back a laugh at this. 'Kat did invite me out to girls' night,' I confide, trying to sound cool about it but failing miserably.

'That's great,' Nico says with another smile. 'So,' he turns and gestures behind him to the inn, 'do you want the tour? Are you going to stay and keep me company over lunch?'

'Yes, please. All of it.'

He leads the way towards the door. 'Do you need me to wear a hard hat or something?' I ask.

When he turns back to look at me there's amusement in his face. 'As much as I'd like to see you rocking a hard hat, the structural work is long finished. That's why the rest of the crew are done ... the whole project is wrapping up. It's all cosmetic now, so you're fine, just watch where you step – especially in those heels.'

'I think I'd look great in a hard hat,' I say, following him through into the entrance hall that I saw briefly the other night, which is acting as a bit of a storage space – boxes, tools and tins of paint are stacked against the walls. Nico puts the bag of food down next to a rolled-up rug.

'If anyone could pull it off, it's you,' he says, and it's not even a real compliment, but try telling that to my face because I can feel the broad, delighted smile stretching across it. So much for playing it cool.

'Come on,' he gestures towards the staircase, 'let me show you what I've been up to.'

Chapter Nineteen

Nico

'Okay, I know I said this about the *last* room but this one really is my favourite,' Lee says, standing in the middle of the small suite and turning in a circle.

'You're just saying that because it's called the library room.' I watch her as she runs her fingers over the floor-to-ceiling shelves that I built into three of the walls.

'Maybe,' she agrees. 'I love the dark blue, so dramatic, and it makes it feel all decadent and cosy. And the bed will fit in that alcove there?' She points to a space cut into the shelving for the headboard.

'That's right.'

'So you'll be able to sleep surrounded by all the books!'

'And read them by the fire.' I walk over to the fireplace that I'm in the process of cleaning up. 'Magda has ordered some hand-painted tiles from a local artist. They've got illustrations and book quotes on them. And there are two wingback armchairs that will be arranged just here.'

Lee makes a sound that goes straight to my groin, but fortunately her attention is on the door through to the bathroom and she wanders off to explore while I try to get myself under control.

'Oh, this bathtub!' she calls back to me. 'You'd never get me out of here.'

That image is not particularly helpful in my current situation.

When she reappears, she's flushed with excitement. 'I love it so much. This place is a dream.'

'It's definitely getting there,' I agree. 'Magda should be able to start putting the furniture back in in the next couple of weeks.'

Lee drops suddenly to her knees in front of me and I swear to god all the blood leaves my head.

'Hardwood?' she asks and I let out a strangled laugh.

'What?' I wonder if the universe is actually fucking with me as she runs her hands reverently over the floor.

'Is this the original hardwood?'

I clear my throat. 'Yeah. It was a nice surprise to find it hidden under the old flooring.'

'Sorry, I know I'm being weird. I have such a weakness for home renovation TV shows,' she says and gets back to her feet. I still don't understand how she moves so gracefully in those death traps she calls shoes. 'And you're living inside one. I can't believe you did all this. I can't believe you fixed all these things and built all these things and made everything so gorgeous.'

'I didn't do it by myself.' I scratch the back of my neck, feeling suddenly bashful. 'And Magda and Tom were pretty solid on the upkeep. The place has good bones.'

'Still,' Lee moves back to the longest wall and the bookshelves that Magda asked me to paint a deep, navy blue, 'it feels strange that you're capable of something like this, and I had no idea.'

'I think it's good that we still have stuff to learn about each other,' I say, realising that I mean it. I don't know as much about adult Lee as I thought I did. We've never spent this much time together – particularly without the buffer of her family around – and it's addictive. When I saw her drive up with my lunch this afternoon the feeling of pleasure I experienced took me by surprise, although maybe it shouldn't have been a shock . . . I find myself thinking about her fairly constantly at the moment.

Lee looks struck by this, too. 'You're right,' she says. 'It's nice, being friends. As adults, I mean.'

Friends. Right. I could be overthinking it, but it seems like maybe she's re-establishing some boundaries after last night when I definitely wasn't thinking purely friendly thoughts about her. It *must* have been obvious.

'I like us being friends, too,' I say, and it's not exactly a lie, I'm just starting to understand it's not the whole truth.

'You know what this room needs?' Lee says, turning away from me and changing the subject.

'What?'

'A ladder.'

'A ladder?' I frown. 'What for?'

'For the shelves, of course!' She spins back to face me. 'They go so high and all the way around the room . . . it's basically a crime not to have a ladder on wheels.'

'I had no idea you felt so strongly about this.'

'Please, Nico, any young bookworm who grew up watching *Beauty and the Beast* knows that the way to a woman's heart is through a magnificent . . . library.'

She grins at me, and yet again my body responds like I'm an overeager teenager. I hook my fingers in my tool belt and make what I hope is a subtle adjustment, but as her gaze instantly flies to my hands I don't think I got away with it.

Her eyes snap back up to meet mine and there's colour in her cheeks, the same slightly hectic flush she was wearing when she arrived.

'I—' she says.

'Do—' I start at the same time. We both fall silent.

'Sorry, what were you going to say?' Lee asks.

'I was going to ask if you wanted to eat lunch,' I say quickly, worried that I've made her uncomfortable.

'Great!' she replies. 'I was going to say the same thing. I'm starving.'

'Let's take it outside. It's a nice day, and you have your coat, right?'

'In the car.'

This is good, I think as we grab the bag of food from downstairs and head outside. After she picks up her coat, I take her through the gardens to one of the benches that Magda has dotted around. Being outside is good. More air, more space between us. Less chance that I'll do something stupid like tell my best friend's sister how much I like the sight of her on her knees in front of me.

'So you did head over to Bean & Gone this morning?' I ask, digging into the turkey sandwich Kat sent over.

'Yeah,' Lee nods, chewing on her own sandwich. 'It's so nice. Although I can't believe how many people stopped me to . . .' Her eyes suddenly widen. 'Oh my god!' she exclaims.

'What?' I ask, bewildered.

'I can't believe I forgot.' She shakes her head. 'I got distracted, and I forgot what I came here to talk to you about.'

'Okay,' I say, still no clearer. 'What did you need to talk to me about?'

'The calendar, Nico!' she bursts out, as if that is supposed to mean anything to me.

'The calendar?'

She takes a deep breath, all animation leaving her face. Shutting down. 'I know I agreed to the plan, but I'd really appreciate it if you'd talk stuff like that over with me. I get that this town has its own . . . personality, but it makes me feel uncomfortable to have that much on my plate. Maybe that's pathetic, but—'

I hold up my hand to stop her nervous ramble mid-flow. Something has really upset her. 'Lee, I have no fucking clue what you're talking about. Who's made you feel uncomfortable?' I try not to worry that I immediately want to rip that person's arm off and beat them with it. That's probably a perfectly normal response.

'You did!' she exclaims.

'I . . .' I trail off, horrified. I was right, she did notice that I was behaving weirdly last night and it's freaked her out. I'm the worst. I'm a monster. I might as well go and live in the woods with Russell.

'With the calendar,' Lee adds miserably.

Wait, what?

'What calendar?'

In response, Lee pulls her phone from her pocket and flicks through until she finds what she's looking for, then she hands it to me.

On the screen is a calendar with dozens of events scheduled in it. When I look closer I see that they say things like 'Lee and Nico: Doubles tennis tournament'; 'Lee: Crafty Crew circle'; 'Lee and Nico: Date night!' 'L&N: Attend post-game bonfire.'

'What is this?' I say slowly.

'You don't know?' Lee sits back and looks at me. '*You don't know,*' she says again, and this time there's relief in the words. 'Kat told me you helped set it up.'

'Kat did this?'

Lee shakes her head. 'She said it was you and Magda.'

I close my eyes, take a deep breath as the truth settles. '*Phoebe,*' I sigh.

'Phoebe?'

'Well, I didn't have anything to do with it, and there's absolutely zero chance Magda knows how to set up a shared calendar like this on her own. This particular scheme has my daughter written all over it.' I run my eyes over the calendar again and can't help but notice there's a daily appointment to take Phoebe and Taco with us on an 'ice cream date'.

'I'll take care of it,' I say shortly.

Lee gnaws on her lip. 'But won't people be upset with us for cancelling things now they've booked us in?'

'Fuck that.' I give in to my instinct and throw an arm around her shoulder, pulling her into my side. 'They can't check you in and out like a library book. That's not how this works. You look through that monstrosity and see if there's anything you *want* to do. The rest of it goes.'

Lee relaxes into my hold, her body softening against mine. I try not to notice how well she fits there.

I'm still holding Lee's phone (and Lee) when a text alert comes through. Adrian, I notice the name before I make myself look away and hand it back to her.

'I'll go over the schedule at home,' Lee says, pulling back and slipping the phone into her pocket while I concentrate on not blurting out *who is Adrian?* 'I'm sure there are a few things on there that will be okay.'

'It's up to you.' I nudge her arm. 'I'm happy to tell them all where they can shove it.'

Lee's eyes are warm. 'As you have to live here after I'm gone, let's attempt some diplomacy first.'

'Whatever,' I grumble.

After we finish eating, and I watch Lee disappear through the woods towards my house, I head for Magda's.

'Nico!' Magda says when she opens the door. 'What a nice surprise!'

'We need to talk,' I say, and she steps back to let me in.

Magda's cottage had originally been a temporary arrangement – she and Tom had their own generous living quarters in the inn – but as the work progressed and she'd settled in, she decided she wanted to stay here. A new start for her, she said, and I could understand that.

The layout of the house is the same as mine, but Magda hasn't wasted any time putting her own personality all over it. There are dream catchers in all the windows, candles and cushions and blankets everywhere. She painted the whole place a sunny, happy yellow and copper pans hang from the ceiling over her kitchen. The second bedroom is Magda's crafting space, but it also has a daybed for Phoebe when she stays. It's a nice set up.

'Is something wrong?' Magda asks now, gesturing to her oversized sofa, too big for the space, but incredibly comfortable. 'Can I get you a calming herbal tea? You're looking very . . . ominous.' She makes a gesture around me that I know her well enough to recognise as a reference to my aura.

'I need to talk to you about this calendar business.'

'Oh,' Magda's face clears, 'smart, huh? Phoebe showed me how to do it.'

I concentrate on breathing slowly, through my nose. 'I need you to take it down right now.'

Magda's brow crinkles. 'What do you mean?'

'I mean that for *anyone* outside of this nosy, interfering town it would be too much, but for Lee it's torture. I'm not kidding, you need to tell everyone to back *way* off.'

As Magda drops down on the sofa, I realise I'm still standing, but I cross my arms across my chest, thinking about Lee's blank expression, the anxiety that I felt coming off her.

'I had no idea . . .' Magda trails off. 'I'd never do anything to upset Lee. She seemed so happy with the plans at the town meeting, I just assumed—'

'Well, those assumptions stop here,' I say sternly. 'Lee isn't a shiny new toy for you all to play with. She's *my wife*.' The words spill out before I can think about them, surprising me. I hesitate. '. . . while she's here, taking part in this charade, anyway,' I add quickly. 'Lee might come off confident, but she's shy and she finds social stuff overwhelming sometimes. I'm not having anyone upset her or make her uncomfortable, is that understood?'

I expect Magda to be hurt or angry. I've never spoken to her like this before, but instead she's beaming up at me.

'What is that look for?' I ask suspiciously.

Immediately the grin drops and she looks chastened. 'Nothing, you're totally right, Nico. I'm so sorry, I got carried away. I'll take the calendar down, and I'll apologise to Lee myself.'

'Okay,' I say, still wary.

'So now you've got that off your chest, will you sit down and have a cup of tea?' She glances at her wrist. 'We've got time before I need to pick Phoebe up.'

Grudgingly, I sit down. 'Fine, but none of that herbal muck. I want a cup of real tea.'

'Coming right up,' Magda nods, and as she makes me a cup of tea with the proper teabags she keeps in just for me, I feel myself soften. I know Magda only had the best of intentions, but seeing Lee upset had me seeing red. It's *possible* I overreacted, racing over here.

'So you and Lee already had a chance to catch up today?' Magda asks, placing a perfectly brewed cup of tea in front of me.

'She came by the inn and I gave her the tour.'

Magda's face lights up. 'What did she think?'

'She loved it,' I admit. 'Apparently she's into house renovation projects. She wanted to know if you have a Pinterest board.'

'Ooh,' Magda claps her hands together, 'fun! I can't wait to pick her brains. It's obvious she has fabulous taste. You only need to look at her style. Then again, I suppose her mother . . .'

'Yeah,' I agree. Say what you will about Caroline Turner – and I could say plenty – the woman knows how to dress. 'And her grandmother's the same – in looks at least.'

'That's the one you're close with?'

I grin. 'Yes. She kind of ruled the roost when we were kids. Jack and Lee's parents were very checked out, and once Ma came back to the States I spent most of my school holidays with them rather than flying back and forth, some weekends too, so Gran took me on as well.'

'You and Jack were a package deal, I take it?'

'We were pretty inseparable,' I agree, and I feel a pang of guilt that Lee and I haven't spoken about Jack. 'We were already best mates when we went off to boarding school together. Stayed there until we turned eighteen, so he's more like my brother than my actual half-brothers. His family is my family.'

'Including Lee?' Magda looks at me over the top of her own teacup, and I shift in my chair.

'Including Lee,' I repeat, and I know it's true, I just don't exactly understand how to fit all the pieces neatly together anymore.

'So which was her favourite room?' Magda asks, changing the subject.

'The library room. She's a big reader . . . said we need to put a ladder in.'

Instead of looking confused, Magda nods. '*Beauty and the Beast.*' She tips her head. 'Maybe you should build one.'

'Maybe I will.' I sip my drink, as if I'm considering it. As if I hadn't decided to build one the second Lee looked at me with that smile and asked for it.

I am so utterly fucked.

Chapter Twenty

Lee

Nico doesn't get home until after six, with Phoebe and Taco in tow. I've been sitting at the kitchen table, trying to concentrate on work, but it's difficult to focus. Especially when my mind keeps helpfully serving up images of Nico-the-handyman and remembering the way he held me and told me in a growly voice that he'd take care of everything.

I swear to god I felt the feminism leaving my body.

See also: waiting around at home like a lost soul, hoping he'll come through the door.

The thing is, it's so quiet here. Usually I love quiet, I *thrive* in quiet. Noise and chaos stress me out, but the house feels wrong without the three of them in it, and the relief that I experience when they finally do get home is absolutely disproportionate to the situation.

'Hi!' I jump to my feet.

Taco is already on me, dancing around on his hind legs, and letting out excited yips. I'm beginning to understand the previously elusive draw of dog-ownership . . . it feels incredible to be greeted as if I'm back from war every time he sees me.

'Who's a good boy?' I say as I fuss him. 'Who's such a good, handsome boy?'

Taco's tongue lolls out of his mouth and I'm convinced that he grins at me, his tail wagging.

I look up and over at Nico. He's in the process of gathering up the trail of items Phoebe sheds as she comes inside. Phoebe reaches down to pat Taco's head on her way to the kitchen where she turns some music on the speaker and opens the fridge, declaring that she's starving.

'Didn't your grandmother *just* feed you?' Nico asks wearily to a soundtrack of Disney songs.

'I brought some pastries back from Bean & Gone,' I say tentatively, glancing at Nico to make sure it's okay, but he's busy hanging up Phoebe's coat.

Phoebe's eyes widen behind her glasses. 'Did you get cinnamon buns?'

I shake my head, feeling like a failure. 'I got some of the pecan muffin things, though.'

'Oh,' Phoebe shrugs. 'Those are almost as good.'

'I think what my daughter means to say is "Thank you, Lee, for that thoughtful gesture",' Nico grumbles.

Phoebe turns a wide smile on me as she rummages through the paper bag and extracts a muffin. 'Thank you, Lee,' she says and then she surprises me by rushing over and briefly squeezing me round the waist. My hands barely have time to flutter to her shoulders before she's gone.

'I'm gonna go play on my Switch,' she says, heading for her bedroom door.

'I'd say I don't know where she's putting all this food, but I think she grew another inch this week,' Nico sighs, rubbing his shoulder in a weary gesture as he reaches down to untie his boots.

'She hugged me,' I say, slightly dazed. I mean, sure it lasted approximately 0.3 seconds, but *still*.

Nico chuckles. 'Her black cat energy is constantly fighting the fact she's been raised by a family of huggers.' He must see something in my face then because he adds, 'But you should be honoured. She doesn't hug just anyone, you know. It took me much longer to wear her down.'

I *do* feel honoured, even though I know it's silly.

'Do you want a muffin?' I ask as I switch on the kettle. 'I got one for you, too. And a cup of tea?'

Nico collapses into the armchair with a groan. 'Don't threaten me with a good time.'

I smile as I pull out the mugs and teabags.

'Did the rest of your day go okay?' I ask when we're both settled with our drinks and pastries.

'Yeah, I managed to get that tiling finished in the kitchen so that's another big job crossed off.'

I sip my tea. 'You're all back late,' I say. 'I thought Phoebe finished school at 3.30?'

'Shit, sorry.' Nico glances up. 'I'm not used to sharing plans with someone, I should have said. She does finish then, but Magda picks her up and keeps her until I finish for the day, which is usually around five-ish, then we go and pick up Taco from the dog-sitter.' He picks up his tea, blows on the surface. 'My schedule can change depending on what work I have on, but Magda's flexible. Sometimes I pick up Phoebe from school myself, sometimes I work late . . . but this is pretty standard for us.'

I put my cup down and pick at my muffin. 'You know, while I'm here, maybe I could keep Taco for the day?'

Nico looks surprised. 'Really?'

I shrug. 'It's no big deal. He's a good dog.'

Nico lets out a loud laugh at that, and I look pointedly at the ball of fur currently curled up tightly beside me on the sofa, his chin on my knee.

'I'm trying really hard not to take this personally,' Nico frowns, 'because I think you must have some sort of secret dog whispering ability.'

'Pretty sure your dog is a little baby angel,' I coo, rubbing Taco's ears while he lets out a happy grumble that presumably signals his agreement.

Nico shakes his head. 'Sure, we can try it and if it doesn't suit you, he can go back to Suzy.'

'Okay,' I agree. 'I think he'll be good company. And Luke texted me about his mum's car – apparently I can pick it up tomorrow.'

'Luke texted you?' Nico asks, his face suddenly blank. 'I didn't know he had your number.'

'I think Kat gave it to him,' I say hesitantly. Maybe Nico isn't keen on me muscling in on his friends. 'Is that a problem?'

'No, sorry, of course not, I just . . . he didn't mention it when we spoke earlier.' He pauses as if having some sort of internal struggle. 'Luke's a good guy,' he says eventually.

'I got that impression,' I agree, still confused by Nico's tone.

When he only stares moodily into his mug of tea, I take a breath. 'I wanted to say thanks for today. It did get me thinking,' I start nervously, 'about this plan of ours. I know that the whole shared calendar thing was a bit overzealous, but maybe you and I should discuss what we want this thing to actually look like?'

'And by "this thing" you mean . . .'

'I . . .' I flush. 'I suppose what our pretend marriage should look like. The stuff that Magda and Phoebe and everyone else put on the calendar,' I press on bravely, 'the me and you stuff. We probably do need to talk about that, right? I mean, the trustee is going to be watching us so we have to . . . look married.'

I know Nico and I are *technically* married so I keep telling myself it's not really lying, that I don't have to do anything in particular to convince this trustee. But of course, that isn't the whole truth.

There's the small detail I haven't really acknowledged yet: we're going to have to pretend to be in love.

The irony is that I've spent most of my life pretending I *don't* have feelings for him. There's something seriously messed up about the fact that acting madly in love with Nico Hart will be the most honest I've been for years.

Nico straightens. 'To look married,' he repeats my words slowly.

'Exactly. It's not going to be enough for me to be living with you, or for people in the town to be comfortable seeing me around. It's you and me, we're going to have to ... act like a real couple.'

Nico's expression is blank. 'Okay,' he says eventually. 'Let's talk about that. I don't want there to be anything that makes you feel awkward.'

'Right,' I nod. 'Same.'

There's a long silence.

'I actually did make some notes,' I say, reaching for my notebook on the coffee table in front of us. 'Laying out some general rules and guidelines.'

'Of course you did.' Nico's voice holds a note of fondness.

I hide my face behind the pages, reading the list I made earlier while feeling increasingly hysterical over the whole thing. 'So we probably *should* go on some dates in public. Once the trustee is here at least.'

Nico's head dips into a nod of agreement. 'Right, and we should agree on our history—'

'I don't think we need to complicate things there,' I jump in. 'We stay as close to the truth as possible. We met as kids, and we knew each other for a long time before anything ... romantic happened.' I break off, feeling light headed, but force myself to push through. 'It was a whirlwind and we got married in Vegas, then we moved here when you found out about Phoebe, although I'm still travelling back and forth for work.'

'Seems like you've thought this through.' Nico sits back and gives me a long, measuring look. 'I agree that all of that sounds reasonable.'

'As long as you don't know us,' I force a laugh. 'I'm not really the type to inspire whirlwind romances and spontaneous weddings, but luckily the trustee doesn't know that. You'll just have to pretend you've had feelings for me for longer than you let on.'

'That should be fine,' Nico says neutrally. 'And I suppose you'll have to do the same.'

I almost burst out laughing, but I manage to control my facial expression just in time. 'I'll do my best.'

I look back at my notebook. 'I'm going to attend a couple of town events,' I say, and then I hold up my hand when Nico looks like he's going to protest. 'I don't mind doing a few things, and I know it really will help if it looks like I fit in here. It'll make things much more convincing.'

Nico exhales. 'Lee,' he says softly. 'I don't know where you got this idea that you need to try so hard. You fit in here just as you are.'

'Oh!' I don't know what to say to that, and I tuck my hair behind my ear in a quick, nervous gesture. 'Well, I . . . still . . .'

Nico waves his hand. 'Never mind. If you're happy to hang out with a few more people and it's your choice, then sure, I think that's a good idea. Just know that it *is* your choice, okay?'

'Okay,' I murmur, my eyes glued to my notebook.

'So what's next on the list?' he asks.

I feel my already pink cheeks flush harder. I told myself I would be cool about this.

'The next thing on the list is physical intimacy,' I say, sounding like a robot trying to learn the ways of humans.

I'm pretty sure Nico pales.

'Physical intimacy?' he repeats.

I nod. 'Phoebe brought this up the very first night but we didn't talk about it. Because if we're going to be seen in public – or even here in the house, assuming there will be home visits – and we're supposed to be a happy couple, we're probably going to have to . . . touch each other.'

'Right,' Nico says distantly. 'Touching. Yup. That makes sense.'

'So we should talk about what that looks like,' I press on, outwardly calm while everything inside me riots.

Nico hums in agreement again and shifts in his seat. 'Well, I don't have any problem with you . . . touching me.'

Gah.

I nod thoughtfully, like this is a business negotiation. 'Great. I don't have a problem either.'

I actually have a huge problem, but as it's about how much I *want* him to touch me it's not relevant to this conversation.

'Although, I think we're probably going to have to be really clear about what that looks like,' Nico says carefully. 'I'd never want to cross a line that would make you uncomfortable. How exactly would you like me to touch you?'

That high-pitched noise fills my head again. How would I like him to touch me? *Everywhere and as much as possible* does not seem like the appropriate answer.

'Obviously we can hold hands,' I say instead. 'You can, um, put your arm around me.' *What else do couples do?* I wonder desperately while my brain helpfully supplies a long list of X-rated answers. 'I could sit on your lap, we could . . . hug?'

'I can do all of that,' Nico agrees, and I notice he's clutching his mug quite tightly. God, this is so awkward.

I retreat to the safety of my notebook and tap the page. 'And there's kissing, of course.' I can't believe how calm I sound. All these years of hiding my feelings have been training me for this one, single moment. This is my emotionally repressed Olympics.

I look up and Nico's eyes have dipped to my mouth. A muscle in his jaw tics. 'You think we should kiss?'

'According to Phoebe married people kiss *all the time*,' I joke weakly. 'We're friends, so we don't need to make this a big deal, just a couple of quick, friendly kisses here and there.'

He is really looking at me now, serious eye contact, an unreadable expression on his face. 'I think I need a bit more guidance.' I swear his voice has dropped even deeper than usual. There's a gravelly quality to it that has my thighs clenching. 'Maybe you could . . . show me.'

'Show you how you could kiss me?' I almost stumble over the words.

He doesn't say anything, only nods.

'Okay, sure,' I say, trying to act casual while a thousand hysterical swear words run rapidly through my head. This is like my dream and my nightmare combined. I'm going to kiss Nico Hart. I'm going to kiss *my husband*, who must under no circumstances realise that this is anything more to me than pretend.

'I can do that,' I say. 'That's . . . practical.'

'By all means.' Something like amusement flickers in Nico's face. 'Let's be practical.'

I get awkwardly to my feet, but he stays seated.

'How do you want to . . .' I gesture towards him, and he treats me to another long look.

His hand reaches out for mine, and he tugs me closer.

'You want me to sit on your lap?'

His expression remains enigmatic. 'It was one of the things you mentioned.'

'Right, yes.' I hover for a second and then slowly lower myself onto his right thigh. I sit, rigidly, concentrating on how to breathe. In and out.

'You okay?' Nico asks.

'Uh huh,' I nod.

'Can I . . .' He pulls me gently into his chest, smoothing my hair back and away from my face, before his palm traces a slow line down my spine.

I know I should be embarrassed about how easily I melt into him, but I can't help it.

'So this is good then?' Nico asks, and I can feel his voice rumble in his chest.

'Yes,' I affirm, the word a little too close to a sigh.

'What comes next?'

I can tell by the way he's asking that he's giving me the opportunity to step back, but I'm so wrapped up in him – literally – that I can't bring myself to do it.

'Well, you could kiss me on the cheek,' I suggest, trying to sound confident.

I move, tipping my face up towards him. 'Like this.' I brush my lips against his cheekbone, and his arm tightens for a second, his fingers flexing against my hip.

'Like that,' he murmurs. 'Got it.'

'Or . . .' I turn slightly, and my hands coast up until I'm cradling his face, the rasp of his stubble against my fingers like the sweeping friction of a match being struck, sending ripples of heat travelling through my body. When he looks down at me, his eyes are hooded.

'If we're trying to be really convincing, you might have to kiss me,' I whisper. 'Like you mean it.'

Before I can overthink it I press my mouth to his. It's the lightest touch, barely there, but my body goes wild. I can *taste* him. My heart is pounding. My lips press firmer and part, only a little, just enough to exhale, enough for a gentle scrape of my teeth against his bottom lip. I squirm closer to him, sliding against his thigh.

That is when I realise that he's sitting underneath me, absolutely unmoving, his hands at his sides so that he isn't touching me.

I pull back.

His face is completely blank. There's zero sign that he's anything like as affected as I am.

Shit.

Shit, shit, shit.

'So something friendly like that,' I say, trying not to worry about how breathless I sound. I unfold myself casually from his lap and get to my feet, dusting off my trousers without meeting his eye. 'Like I said. No big deal.'

'Right,' Nico says, and he doesn't sound happy. 'No big deal.'

On a series of muttered excuses I grab my notebook, escape to my room and turn to press my back to the door, my eyes closed.

I think I just made a total fool of myself.

Again.

Chapter Twenty-One

Nico

What the hell just happened?

I stare at the closed door that Lee disappeared behind and try to catch up with the events of the last ten minutes.

One moment I was drinking tea, and the next the girl I've known for most of my life was kissing me and it felt like the whole universe turned upside down. If doctors had been doing one of those scans on my brain at the time, they'd have watched it light up like a slot machine paying out.

It was barely anything. But her lips were so soft, and her hair smelled like honey, and then she made that noise – that breathy little exhalation – and she'd shifted against my leg and I was so relieved she couldn't feel how absolutely rock hard I was. It had taken every ounce of control I possessed not to pull her across to straddle my lap, to hold her right where I needed her and to kiss her like I wanted to: slowly, deliberately until she begged me for more.

Instead, I'd had to hold myself like a statue, every muscle in my body tensed so that I didn't react, so that I didn't cross every line we'd literally *just* established.

She'd had a notebook of *rules*. We were in the middle of a

discussion about boundaries for fuck's sake, and what did I do? Drag her into my lap and practically dare her to kiss me.

Because I wanted to. Because I wanted to so intensely that I ignored the tiny voice of reason telling me it was a bad idea. And now, here I am, *immediately* faced with the consequences of my own actions. Because I think maybe . . . *maybe* for a second she wanted to kiss me too. My head sinks into my hands and I exhale a shaky breath.

I have no idea how to handle this.

After a few minutes of staring into space, I realise I'm not equipped to deal with this mess on my own, and I drop Luke a quick text. Then I go and check on Phoebe, who is absorbed in catching Pokémon.

'Hey, Bee. I think I need to go and see Luke about Lee's car,' I say, leaning casually in her doorway. 'If Lee's okay with it, are you happy to stay here with her by yourself?'

'Sure,' Phoebe nods, not even lifting her eyes from the screen.

Easy part done, I steel myself and knock on Lee's door. When she calls for me to come in, I find her sitting in the middle of the bed, her phone in her hand.

'Sorry to interrupt—'

'No, you're good, I was just texting with someone,' she replies, lifting her phone like it's evidence.

I swallow down the urge to ask her if that someone is called Adrian and who he is to her. 'I just heard from Luke and I thought I'd go and pick up the car we talked about. Would you mind keeping an eye on Phoebe for a bit?'

'Oh!' Lee's eyes widen comically. 'Yes, of course. Are there any instructions? I should write them down.'

It's enough to loosen some of the tension I feel, and I actually manage to squeeze out a laugh. 'She's very low maintenance,' I promise. 'Practically a cactus. Magda fed her and helped her with her homework, so Phoebe'll probably want to chill in her room – she likes time to decompress.'

Lee nods in understanding.

'If I'm not back by eight, if you could coax her back to the real world long enough to put on her pyjamas and brush her teeth that would be great, but otherwise I can't think of anything. Just make sure the house doesn't burn down.'

'Does she have any allergies?'

'She's allergic to penicillin, but as long as you're not whipping up antibiotic smoothies I think you'll be fine.'

Lee nods, exhales. 'Okay, got it.' I watch as she carefully writes 'no penicillin' in her black Moleskine notebook and underlines it twice, followed by '8 p.m., get ready for bed. Check oven and all potential fire hazards.'

Her expression is so earnest that I swallow my laughter this time. 'Thanks,' I say, 'I appreciate it.'

She waves a hand. 'No, no, you're doing me a favour sorting out the car.'

'Text me if you need anything,' I call on my way out, and then I head for my truck and over to Luke's place faster than I ever have.

When I arrive he's sitting on the porch with a cold beer in his hand.

'I take it you need this,' he says, handing it to me, and pulling another out of the cooler beside him.

I sink into the wooden Adirondack chair beside him. 'You have no idea.'

We sit for a while in silence, and this is what I like about Luke. He's a patient guy, he'll let you work through stuff at your own pace, he's a good friend.

'It's Lee,' I say finally.

'No shit,' Luke smirks into his beer.

What a dickhead.

'We kissed,' I blurt. 'Or . . . she kissed me.'

'And that's . . . bad?'

I huff out a breath. 'It's complicated. We were talking about being fake married. Or real married but with fake feelings, or maybe real feelings but a fake relationship. I have no idea. But she wasn't *really* kissing me.'

'She was kissing the *idea* of you,' Luke says wisely.

'What?' I ask, startled.

'I don't know, man,' he shrugs. 'I'm trying to follow what you're saying but you're a mess. I took a shot.'

'Okay, let's turn down the radio-call-in therapist persona.'

'You know I can't resist a good *Sleepless in Seattle* moment,' he says easily, 'so why don't you tell me what happened in plain English?'

'It wasn't like she chose to kiss me, it was practice.' Even as I say the words I know they sound insane.

Luke lifts his eyebrows, but stays quiet as I tell him what happened.

'Hmm,' he says at the end.

'*Hmm?* That's it?'

'Honestly, I don't know what you want me to say. Obviously you're into Lee.'

I freeze with the bottle half way to my lips. 'I don't think I said that.'

'First of all – I've seen the two of you together. You look at her like she's a double chocolate chip cookie. And secondly, you said that you shared an incredibly PG-13 moment and it freaked you out so much that you're here drinking beer on my porch instead of talking to her about it.'

'I know,' I start desperately, 'but . . . it's Lee.'

'I don't know what that means. I thought we already went over this part. You know I'm not about objectifying women, and I mean this very respectfully . . . but Lee is *crazy* hot.'

'Oi!' I growl.

His smirk is back. 'And there's that. You're in so deep, my friend, and you don't even know how you got there.'

I take a moment to absorb this. 'I don't understand how this happened. I've known her most of my life. Why do I feel like this all of a sudden?'

'You're telling me in all those years there's never been *any* attraction? You've never even thought about it?' He sounds sceptical.

I run a hand over my face. 'I don't know ... maybe there have been times, *glimpses*,' I admit. 'But she's so much younger than me, almost seven years. I never really ...'

I trail off, remembering the first time it happened. I was back from travelling somewhere and I'd arranged to meet Jack for drinks but I went to drop in on Gran beforehand while he had some awful dinner with his parents. I hadn't seen Lee for months. She must have been around eighteen and she opened the door in an oversized university sweatshirt, leggings and fluffy socks. Her gold hair was loose, falling down her back, and when she saw me her face lit up.

It was like being hit by a truck. She was so beautiful it knocked the air out of me for a second. But I was almost twenty-five, and she was Jack's sister and I told myself it was a weird moment, a blip. I moved past it. If there were times where I found myself thinking about her over the years, I pushed it aside and put a little more distance between us.

'I get that when you were kids, seven years felt like a lot, but I don't think the age difference really means anything now,' Luke points out. 'You're telling me there's been nothing in the last decade?'

I take a deep pull on my beer. 'Fine. Maybe when we ran into each other last year I was ... attracted to her.'

Because I had been. Because that morning when I woke up with her in my arms had rewired something in my brain. Which is probably why I'd freaked out. And *maybe* I'd thought about her quite a bit since, but that didn't necessarily mean anything. We're friends, after all. I'm *allowed* to think about her.

'She's an attractive woman,' Luke says.

'Yes, thanks, you've already made your thoughts on that very clear,' I say sourly. 'But none of this explains why I suddenly can't get her out of my mind, why I think about her all the time. Why I'm so desperate to undo the zips on her stupid fucking boots!'

'Ah,' Luke murmurs, but I'm on a roll now.

'It's not even just that I want to get her into bed. Although, I *definitely* want to get her into bed. It's all this weird shit. Her laugh. Her dimples. The way she always smells like honey. I'm obsessed with her wrists! They're so fucking pretty. I want to wrap my fingers around them and take her pulse.' I rave, feeling totally unhinged. 'What the fuck is that?! You know the stories about how the Victorians were so prudish that they had to cover the legs on tables in case they made men have dirty thoughts about women's ankles? You'd hear that, and laugh and say, "wow, who *were* these perverts?" Well, I get it now. It's me! I am the Victorian pervert!'

Luke is staring at me, his mouth slightly open. He closes it with a click. 'I'll admit that's not ideal.'

'No, Luke, it's *not* ideal. The question is, what am I going to do about it?'

He thinks about this for a moment. 'Have you considered sleeping with her?'

'Are you listening? All I do is consider sleeping with her!'

'I think you're overcomplicating this. Why not see if she's interested? For what it's worth I'm pretty sure she is.'

'Do you think?'

'Look, I know I'm just a lowly small town police chief and not a big city detective or anything, but I'd say that anyone who agrees to pretend to be your wife for an unspecified amount of time in a batshit crazy town on the other side of the world from her home, who then sits in your lap and kisses you right on the mouth is sending out some fairly clear signals.'

'Yeah. But then she's also always calling us friends, and *she's* the one who said we needed to have rules in the first place.'

'Sure,' Luke nods. 'But, again, I'm going to make the potentially outlandish suggestion that you just . . . ask her.'

'I get it,' I sigh, because of course I do, 'but I honestly don't think it's that simple. *Maybe* she has some feelings for me, too.' I try to suppress the instinctive leap of pleasure I feel at the possibility. 'But she's hard to read, so I could be wrong. Maybe she's being careful for a reason – there are a lot of other factors to consider before we open that whole can of worms.'

'Such as?'

'Such as we're in this situation because she's doing me an absurd, there's-no-way-to-ever-pay-it-back level favour and she's staying in my house in a town where she knows no one and has no real support and it feels like the dynamics are messy, like I'd be taking advantage of the situation if I made a move.' I grimace as that thought really lands.

'Such as, she's my friend. Her brother is my *best* friend of almost thirty years. Whatever roots or family I have, they're tangled with hers. And you know I love Phoebe more than anything, and if I had the choice, I'd choose being her dad every single time, but it doesn't change the fact that my life as I knew it basically imploded a year ago and I'm still sorting out the pieces. I'm a mess, I have no idea what I'm doing – not just as a dad, but in pretty much every area of my life. I'm so far from ready for a serious relationship, and if that's not what I'm offering her then what am I even thinking? Lee doesn't do flings, and that's all I've ever done. If I hurt her I'd lose everything, but I'd deserve it because I'd never expect anyone else to forgive me . . . I'd never forgive myself.'

My chest is squeezed tight by the time I finish, and I pick at the label on my beer with my thumb, staring out into the darkness.

'Yeah . . .' Luke exhales a long breath. 'Okay, that is kind of complicated.'

His hand comes down on my shoulder in a comforting thump.

'Thanks,' I manage a laugh.

'If you want my advice . . .' Luke says, after a moment.

'I genuinely do,' I agree. 'At this point I'm desperate.'

He tips back the last of his beer. 'You and Lee . . . I can see it. I think your feelings for her are stronger than you're letting on, maybe than you're admitting to yourself, and if there's a chance you could have something real then you shouldn't throw it away. That shit is hard to find, trust me.'

'So you think I should tell her how I feel?'

'No. I think you should *work out* how you feel and be really fucking sure. Because if you don't think you can offer her the relationship she wants then you're right – you're just going to hurt her. And I think you'll hurt yourself, too.'

'Shit,' I sigh. 'I think that's actually good advice.'

And I hate it.

'I need to keep things as they are,' I say slowly. 'Protect the friendship. Not complicate the situation any more than it is already.'

'I'd say that's a good starting point.'

'I need to keep my hands to myself.' I close my eyes.

'Unless you're fake kissing her in front of your dead dad's lawyer?'

I groan. 'Fuck. This is going to be hard.'

'That's what she said?' Luke nudges me with his elbow, and I understand this is a gesture of manly affection, which I truly appreciate.

'Thanks for your help,' I say, putting the empty beer bottle down by my feet. 'But now I need another favour . . . I told Lee I was coming to pick up your mum's car so I can't exactly go home without it.'

Luke gets to his feet and slaps me on the back again.

'Give me a ride over to my mom's then. I'll drive it to your place and then you can drop me back here.'

'I appreciate it, man.'

'Hey, what are friends for if not arranging transportation for their friend's fake wife who their friend definitely has real feelings for?'

Chapter Twenty-Two

Lee

The next three days pass quietly. I spend the mornings in Bean & Gone, catching up on some work but often getting distracted talking to Kat, and sampling items from her extensive coffee menu. (She makes me an iced blueberry latte that is so good, I swear I hear angels singing.)

Yesterday afternoon I attended a meeting of the craft club with Magda, which was actually really nice, even if my crocheting skills are going to need work. When I came home exhausted from a day of socialising, Nico took one look at me and knew exactly what I needed – an evening spent crashed out on the sofa watching home improvement shows together in comfortable silence.

By some unspoken agreement, Nico and I haven't talked about the kiss, and I think it's for the best. We've been having lunch together every day, with Taco acting as chaperone, and he's made enough comments about how *great* it is to have a *friend* from home around that the message has been received. Loud and clear. I've made a concerted effort to keep all the lustful/objectifying thoughts to a minimum, and that's been mostly going fine. Mostly.

(There was a rough moment yesterday where he took his jumper off, peeling his T-shirt up with it, and I caught a glimpse of his taut stomach and a set of ridiculously defined abdominal muscles, but I put that image firmly out of my mind and it hasn't haunted me *at all*.)

The thing is, I genuinely enjoy being with Nico. I always have. Over the past couple of days, I've found myself opening up – about my job and the travel involved, Tara and the book group – and he's shared with me about the first weeks settling into town, getting to know Phoebe and the work he's done on the inn.

Getting to know him is my new favourite hobby. I thought I already had him all figured out, but this version of us – open, honest, learning about the lives we've built – feels different. Nico has a way of making even the smallest detail about me feel important.

'What do you *mean* you've never changed a tyre?' he asked on Tuesday, his tone outraged.

'I have breakdown cover!'

'Princess, this is an important life skill and a safety issue. Come on, I'm going to show you how to do it *right now*.'

What followed had been the sort of competent, muscle-flexing scene that I was trying very hard to avoid, but by the end of it I'd successfully changed a tyre (in high heels) and I had to admit that was very satisfying.

Today, it's too overcast to sit out in the garden, and Nico has spread a blanket over the floor in the inn's dining room so that we can have an indoor picnic. I have absolutely no thoughts about that or how adorable it is. None.

'So, did you manage to get that report sent off this morning?' Nico asks.

'Mmm,' I nod, digging my fork into the enormous salad that Kat made, while Taco lies next to me, looking hopeful. 'Which is good because there are a couple of jobs I've been asked to consult on that I really need to take. I might have to put in a few late nights,' I add apologetically.

'Oh, that's a shame,' Nico takes a sip of his coffee, 'because I was going to ask you if you were up for dinner tonight?'

'Like . . . a date?' I ask tentatively. We haven't talked any more about the whole fake-dating-as-a-married-couple thing, as it had been rather overshadowed by the kissing debacle.

'No!' he says quickly. *Too quickly*, some might say. 'Not a date. I was thinking we could invite people over to our place for something to eat.'

Our place. I try not to shiver.

'Tonight?'

'Yeah, just Kat, Mei and Luke. We could order Chinese, open a bottle of wine once we've packed Phoebe off to bed. What do you think?'

'I think that sounds really nice,' I say, surprised to find I mean it.

Nico hesitates. 'I got an email this morning from my dad's lawyer,' he says after a moment. 'The trustee – his name is Charles Saunders – is flying out the day after tomorrow as planned. Apparently his intention is to stay for two weeks, which he feels will be enough time to *build an accurate report*.' This last bit is said with a tinge of bitterness.

'Oh!' I blink. 'Right, well, at least that's some solid information. And two weeks, that's not so bad, right?'

'At least it means you can make your own plans,' Nico says, looking down at the floor. 'I know it's all been really up in the air. You must have been feeling so out of control.'

That's a complicated statement. It's true, but not in the way he means . . . being around Nico makes me feel out of control. Being stuck in Roseport for an indeterminate length of time has felt . . . well, it's felt lovely, actually. I realise with a sinking heart that this trip now has an expiry date.

'On the fifth of November you get your life back,' Nico says, and it seems like he is also struggling with exactly how to handle this.

'If you want to check out flights home then obviously I'll buy your ticket.' He attempts a smile that doesn't quite meet his eyes. 'Can't have my daughter showing me up in the chivalry department. It's the least I can do.'

'Sure,' I murmur. 'I'll look into it. That's . . . good news then.'

An awkward silence falls, and when I look over, Nico is glaring down at his untouched lunch. I expect finally hearing from the lawyer has put him in a bad mood. The whole process is going to be one long, awful reminder of his relationship with his father.

'You can let Gran know when you'll be back,' he says finally. 'I know you've been worrying about her.'

That's true. I even texted Jack and asked if he'd check in with her more while I'm away, because presumably she'll share more information with the grandchild she's actually speaking to. He assumed I was on a business trip and I didn't correct him.

Now, I make a noncommittal sound in my throat, and Nico's gaze sharpens.

'You keep doing that whenever I bring her up. Are you going to tell me what's going on with you two?'

I hesitate, but actually the fight between Gran and me has been slowly eating away at me, and Nico is one of the only people in the world who really understands our relationship.

'We had an argument,' I admit. 'Right before I came here, and we haven't exactly spoken since.'

A worried frown crosses his face. 'Was it about our situation?'

'No, I didn't tell her about it. I wasn't sure you'd want her to know. She thinks I'm in the States for work.'

'I don't mind if you talk to her about this,' he says gently. 'I know the two of you don't keep things from each other.'

'I have no idea how I'd tell her right now. We've never gone this long without talking before.'

'What happened?'

'Honestly, I don't really know. We were talking about . . .' I trail off then, realising I'm going to struggle to tell this story without mentioning Adrian, and for some reason that feels weird. I tell myself not to worry about it – Nico hardly cares about my love life.

'. . . the man I was seeing. In London. Gran didn't approve,' I finish, the words coming fast.

Nico's posture stiffens. He opens his mouth then closes it. 'Why didn't she approve? Did he . . . do something?'

'No!' I exclaim. 'He's a very nice man,' I add, and Nico's shoulders, which had just started to come down, seem to tense again. 'Gran didn't approve because she thought he was boring.'

This shocks a choked laugh out of Nico. 'I don't know why I'm surprised,' he says. 'That sounds exactly like her.'

'I know, and then I got a bit . . . annoyed, I suppose, because I couldn't understand her problem with me seeing someone who's kind and respectful and even-tempered.'

Nico only makes a humming sound that could be agreement or encouragement to continue with the story, and I can't see his expression because he looks down at his coffee.

'Anyway, I told her that I didn't want to be anything like—'

'Your parents,' Nico finishes, already nodding. 'That makes sense. Growing up with the two of them must have been traumatising as fuck.' There's no judgement in his tone, and unlike Gran he doesn't try and reassure me, only listens. Maybe that's why I find myself opening up.

'Exactly. I don't know if she realises how bad it was. I mean, I suppose she must have done because eventually she took me to live with her, but we didn't ever talk about it.'

Nico frowns. 'How old were you when you properly moved in with her?'

I tilt my head, considering. 'Sixteen? It was after Mum and Dad had split up the last time, before they reconciled again six months later. They'd had a huge row, absolutely *trashed* the house – it looked like a hurricane had been through. The neighbours called the police but Dad managed to smooth that all out before he left. Gran found me the next morning trying to clean everything up, and Mum refused to get out of bed. Gran took one look at all the broken furniture, the empty bottles, the smashed-up china and told me to pack my bags.'

Nico looks stunned. 'I didn't know any of this.'

I shrug. 'Why would you? Jack was at uni, you were travelling.'

'Did Jack know?' Nico's voice is gruff.

'I don't think he realised I'd properly moved out at that point,' I say. 'And I didn't want to tell him. You know how hard Mum and Dad were on him, wanting him to be part of their grand acting dynasty. It was awful the way they treated him, and he didn't need me piling on with my problems. I could tell he was struggling, but I couldn't do anything. It was horrible. Mum and Dad were . . . addicted to their own drama, I suppose, and I didn't know how to cope with being around it.'

'You were just a kid.'

'I suppose. I didn't feel like one at the time. Anyway, because I'd skipped a year at school everyone knew I'd be applying to universities soon enough. At first they all thought I'd go away to study, but I wasn't ready for that. I liked living with Gran, I felt safe . . . steady for the first time. And there are great universities in London.' I manage a small smile. 'Mum and Dad were pretty pissed off that I turned down Cambridge. Choosing my own university was the first thing I ever did for myself, and Gran went to battle for me. She told them both to back off . . . only in much less polite language.'

Nico manages a smile. 'I can imagine.'

'When I finished uni and moved out of Gran's place I really missed her,' I confess. 'So later, when she started needing a bit more help, it made sense for us to buy a place together.'

'And this argument you had was about . . . the man you've been seeing?' Nico asks carefully.

'It started that way,' I sigh, 'but it led to her making some less than welcome remarks about my behaviour and general demeanour. And I think she's frustrated because she feels like I'm hovering over her. Which . . .' I exhale. 'I probably am. But I don't think she gets how scary it was for us last year when she . . .'

'Yeah,' Nico agrees, and I know that, like me, he's remembering Gran, small and frail and suddenly *old* in that hospital bed, hooked up to a bunch of machines.

'Maybe there were things that we'd both been bottling up.' I shrug helplessly. 'When you – or rather Phoebe – sent me that plane ticket it seemed like an opportunity to escape. Like the space would be good for both of us.'

'Hopefully it will,' Nico says, but there's still a pinched groove between his brows.

'So,' I say eventually, trying to make the words sound light, 'tonight's our last night of freedom then. We can spend all day tomorrow getting ready for this Charles Saunders. I'm organising your whole house. He's going to be deeply impressed.'

Nico groans, but his expression lightens. 'You're about to colour code my spice rack, aren't you?'

'Obviously not!' I huff. 'What sort of a system is that? I'll alphabetise it.'

He laughs (even though I'm not joking) and we go back to our lunch.

Later, while he's nagging Phoebe to get ready for bed, I call through to him from the kitchen, 'Nico, where are your table linens?'

There's a short, heavy silence, and then the sound of Phoebe and Nico dissolving into laughter.

Phoebe appears first, her freshly washed face all pink and glowing, her pyjamas covered in pictures of donuts and slices of pizza. '*Table linens*,' she says in what I assume is supposed to be an impression of my accent. She sounds like Lady Bracknell.

'I forget, Phoebe,' Nico comes up behind her, with Taco trotting alongside, 'where *did* we put the table linens? Was it in the larder with the decanters and the finest porcelain?'

My hands are on my hips. 'You're telling me you don't even have napkins? How am I supposed to create a charming tablescape in these conditions?'

'*Tablescape*,' Nico's lips quirk.

'No, wait, we *do* have napkins,' Phoebe says, and she starts rummaging around in the kitchen drawers before emerging with a triumphant yelp. In her hand she clutches a crumpled packet of paper napkins printed with tiny unicorns. 'They're from my birthday party last year,' she explains.

Nico chokes on a laugh, but I shoot him a glare. 'Perfect, thank you, Phoebe. Now, let me show you how to fold them into the shape of a rose.'

'A rose?' Phoebe wrinkles her nose. 'Really?'

'Yes, really. And Nico, you can get the nice wine glasses down. I know you have those – I saw them in a box at the back of the cupboard.'

Phoebe settles down beside me at the table and I show her how to fold the napkins.

'How did you learn how to do this?' Phoebe asks, her brow creased in concentration.

'My gran taught me.' I run my fingers over the purple unicorns. 'She's good at making things special.'

'My napkin doesn't look right,' she grumbles, and I lean over, smoothing out some of her corners.

'Looks great to me.' I twist the paper flower this way and that for her to admire.

'What else does your gran do to make things special?' Phoebe is interested.

'Um, she always makes me the best birthday cakes. Even now that I'm a grown up.' I pull out my phone and flip through my photographs until I get to this year's offering, which was shaped like a high-heeled shoe. 'When I was your age she'd sometimes take me out of school for the afternoon and we'd put on our best dresses and lots of her jewellery and go for tea at the Ritz.'

'What's the Ritz?' Phoebe asks, intrigued.

'It's a fancy hotel in London.'

'So she taught you how to do this stuff?' Phoebe gestures at the napkins, at the pitcher that I filled with slender branches of autumn foliage from the garden, the white tea light candles that I unearthed in the back of a cupboard and dropped inside empty jam jars. It looks pretty. Festive.

'She taught me how to do just about everything,' I admit.

'Remember that time she built you a den in your bedroom?' Nico smiles. 'It was epic.'

'What kind of den?' Phoebe asks.

'She made it out of all these vintage tablecloths, stitched together like a circus tent,' I say. 'It had fairy lights in and silver stars hanging from the roof. I loved it.'

'I think *I* need a den like that,' Phoebe muses.

'With your dad's skills you should go full tree house.'

Nico runs a hand over his face as Phoebe visibly brightens.

'That's a *great* plan,' she says admiringly.

There's a knock at the door and as Phoebe runs to answer it, Nico turns to me. 'You think you're so clever.'

'Hey, you're the handy one!' I laugh. 'You can singlehandedly build an entire inn, I think you can stretch to a teeny little tree house. You live in the woods!'

'I already told you, I didn't build it singlehandedly.' He reaches up and tugs teasingly on my hair. 'I'm going to teach you how to use a hammer properly, then *you* can build Phoebe a tree house. I can already tell you she'll be a nightmare client.'

'I *would* be unstoppable if I could wield a hammer,' I agree, as Kat and Mei spill inside from the cold in a flurry of chatter, and Taco jumps all over them, delighted.

'We brought wine!' Kat holds out a bottle in each hand.

'Ohhh, look at the table!' Mei exclaims. 'This is so pretty!'

'Are those just branches from outside?' Kat touches the paper-thin amber leaves. 'It looks like a Pottery Barn commercial.'

'I think that's a compliment on your tablescape,' Nico murmurs in my ear.

'I helped fold the napkins,' Phoebe says proudly, while Mei and Kat make appreciative noises. 'Lee's good at making things special, right, Dad? Like her gran.'

'That's right, Bee,' Nico agrees.

'No Luke?' I ask, changing the subject.

Kat lifts her shoulder. 'Mrs Platt called him out to talk about her neighbours' fence again. She's convinced it's a good two inches over the boundary line and she wants them arrested. Poor Luke, he's going to be there a while.'

I try to picture Mrs Platt and come up with a deceptively sweet-faced old lady.

'We'll save him some food,' Kat says and hunts around for a cork-screw. 'But let's order now. I'm borderline hangry.'

'I can stay up for a bit, can't I?' Phoebe turns big eyes on her dad.

'Only until the food arrives,' he says firmly and when her expression becomes hopeful he lifts a finger. 'But you're not having any! It's too late and you've already eaten.'

'I'll save some and hide it in the fridge,' I whisper, and Phoebe gives me another one of those lightning-fast hugs that make me feel invincible.

Nico pulls out his phone and tries to place his order at the Chinese place while Kat yells, 'Make sure you get extra dumplings!' and Phoebe shares her own strong opinions about the correct number of dumplings per person.

Before I can weigh in, my phone buzzes in my pocket.

'It's Tara,' I murmur, surprised, and I glance at Nico who has just finished his own phone call. 'Isn't it after midnight back home?'

'Get it,' Nico says, but I've already answered.

'Tara? What's wrong? Are you okay?'

'I think I did something ridiculous,' my best friend's breathless voice reaches me. 'It seemed like a great idea at the time, but you're going to think I'm insane.'

I dart Nico a quick look and shrug, no idea what's going on. 'Never,' I say firmly. 'I will never think that. Whatever it is, we can fix it. Did you murder someone? Because I will fly back right now with a shovel.'

Tara laughs. 'If I did, I don't think it would be wise for us to discuss it over the phone.'

I laugh as well, some of the tension leaving me. 'No. I suppose not. So, what's going on?'

'Okay, this is the mad bit.' Tara sounds nervous. 'Please don't freak out, but . . . *the call is coming from inside the house*.'

'What do you—'

There's a knock at the door.

Chapter Twenty-Three

Lee

'Woah, the delivery driver's fast tonight,' Kat says, but I beat her there, swinging the door open, holding my breath.

Because she's there. Standing right on the doorstep with her phone held up to her ear, and an anxious smile on her face.

My best friend.

She's here.

'Okay, maybe the call is coming from right *outside* the house,' she says, 'but that didn't sound as dramatic.'

I don't even hang up the phone, I just charge towards her, and then we're in each other's arms and we're both laughing and squealing and talking all over each other.

It takes me a second to register that we've never done this before, that as well as we know each other we've never physically been in the same room. Part of me had always been scared that I'd manage to make it awkward when we did eventually meet, but it looks like I didn't need to worry.

'Oh my god! You're real! I can smell you! You smell so good!' Tara sniffles. 'Sorry, I sound insane. I'm so happy to see you.'

'I'm so happy to see *you*!' I exclaim. 'I can't believe this. What are you doing here?'

'I was worried about you,' she admits, taking a step back. 'I knew you had so much going on and you were basically here by yourself without, you know, anyone who was *Team Lee*, and I had all this holiday I needed to use up, so I thought I'd surprise you. It was only when I got here that I realised it was such a strange thing to do, that we've never even met in person and—'

I cut her off, squeeze her arm. 'No, no. You were right. It's the best surprise. I can't believe you did this for me.' I find myself blinking back tears.

Tara's smile widens, and it's so strange seeing her standing in front of me. I knew she was pretty, of course I did, but in real life she's stunning. Shorter than me in my heels, and all rounded curves. She's wearing a leopard-print coat over the top of a pair of high-waisted jeans and a white T-shirt. Her dark curls are loose, her skin glows, her eyes are dark and sparkling with mischief.

'Well, it wasn't totally selfless,' she says. 'You had me intrigued about Roseport and I wanted to see it for myself. This place is amazing.'

'Right?' I agree, delighted to have someone to share it with, and then I realise we're still standing outside. 'Come in, come in!' I tug her arm, pulling her inside where the others are all standing around trying not to look nosy.

'Guys, this is my friend, Tara.'

Nico steps forward first, and Tara's eyes widen before she darts a look in my direction. I shrug. *Yup.* I accidentally married the most handsome man in the world.

'Tara,' he says warmly. 'Lee's told me so much about you, although she refuses to let me join your book group.'

'Are you a big romance reader?' Tara asks, taking the hand he offers.

'Well, no, but I'm always happy to try new things.' He looks at me then and I feel flustered.

'*I* am a big romance reader,' Kat says, inserting herself into the conversation. 'And I don't know about this book club.'

'Oh, Kat can definitely join,' I say.

'Did you just get into town?' Mei asks Tara.

She nods. 'Yeah, I dumped my bag at the Airbnb and got a cab over. I didn't even need an address, just told the driver I was looking for Nico and Lee and he drove me straight here. It was only when we were on our way that I realised this was either a really cute surprise, or the sort of thing a psychopath would do.'

'Or a serial killer,' Phoebe puts in, considering my friend. 'Although that's statistically unlikely as only sixteen per cent of serial killers have been women.'

'Well, of the ones they caught,' Tara points out, and Phoebe looks much struck by this.

'I don't think you're a psychopath or a serial killer,' I grab her hand. 'I'm *so* happy you're here. It's the best surprise.'

'Let me get you a drink,' Nico says. 'Wine?'

'I'm interrupting,' Tara says, looking around, and everyone protests at the same time.

'You'll stay for dinner?' Nico asks. 'We ordered an insane amount of Chinese food.'

'Chinese food and wine?' Tara laughs. 'Sounds like heaven.'

'Did you say you're staying at an Airbnb?' I ask.

'Yeah, there's one above the bar in town.' Tara accepts a glass of wine from Nico with a smile. 'There aren't a lot of places to stay around here with the inn shut but it's nice . . . except I am sharing a room with quite a lot of wigs.'

'Darlene's wig room,' Mei explains. 'She has a pretty extensive collection.'

We're interrupted at that moment by more banging at the door, but it's still not the food. Instead, a harassed-looking Luke stands on the step.

'Hey, Lee,' he greets me, 'sorry I'm late.'

'You're not late, dinner hasn't even turned up yet.' I gesture him inside. 'This is my friend Tara from home, she just arrived.' I turn to Tara but she's staring at Luke with wide eyes.

'Hello,' she whispers.

The harassed look melts off Luke's face, and his own eyes are doing something funny; his pupils are ginormous.

'Hi,' he says, and he leans over me like I'm not there to take her hand. He doesn't exactly shake it, but holds it for a moment in his own while staring at her.

I clear my throat and he jumps back, pink spreading across his cheekbones.

'I—' he starts. 'Sorry. I—'

Fortunately for him, the delivery guy *does* make an appearance then, and there's a brief flurry of activity as Nico pays him, Kat and Mei spirit the boxes over to the kitchen and Phoebe heads off to her room, complaining the whole way, with Taco sneaking in behind her to sleep on her bed.

Amid this chaos, Tara stands completely still beside me and I wonder if she realises that she's dreamily humming 'Cowboy Take Me Away' under her breath. Probably not.

We all help ourselves to the food on the counter, piling up our plates before taking our seats around the dining table. Luke practically sprains something throwing himself into the one beside Tara.

Kat is openly laughing at him, but he doesn't seem to notice.

'So, Tara, how long are you in town for?' Luke asks.

'Just a week,' she says. 'Lee made this place sound so interesting, and I thought maybe the big plan would benefit from having someone from Lee's side of things here to help out.' She bats her lashes, and – for some reason – starts talking in the breathy accent of a Southern belle. 'Y'all, Lee and Nico sure are the cutest couple I've ever seen.'

'You know you don't need to do an accent, right,' I ask, 'if you're supposed to be my friend from home?'

Tara pouts. 'Another tragic instance where I cannot put my drama degree to use.'

I close my eyes. 'This town is going to love you.'

'How do you feel about improv?' Mei asks.

'Extremely positive,' Tara beams. 'So, the guy is turning up when exactly?'

'The day after tomorrow,' I say uneasily. Despite his visit being the whole reason I'm here, I've been trying not to think about it.

'That reminds me,' Mei says. 'I have a gift for you. Ta da!'

From her copious tote bag she extracts a large envelope. Inside are a stack of laminated cards with photographs on them.

'My flashcards!' I squeal.

'I used the school laminator and everything.' Mei looks proud.

'Ugh, I *love* a laminator,' Tara puts in, only providing further evidence of our soulmate connection.

'My students helped me with the info,' Mei gestures to the cards, and I realise that underneath the photographs are short biographies that include facts like ages and spouses' names and other, more specific insights such as: *Obsessed with an old movie called* Clueless; *Has a mean dog*; *Smells kinda soupy*.

'They're such little jerks,' Mei says fondly.

'Please don't tell me they really think *Clueless* is an old movie?' Kat asks, forlorn.

'We're ancient,' Luke sighs into his glass.

'Hey, speak for yourself. I'm eighteen months younger than you.' Kat digs her elbow into his side.

We pore over the cards for a while, talking and laughing as I try to commit as much as possible to memory. We polish off most of the food, and I slip a plate of leftovers into the fridge for Phoebe, while Nico shakes his head. Kat opens another bottle of wine.

Then Nico opens another.

This is how I end up with a card attached to my forehead with a piece of washi tape from Mei's bag, and a slight slur to my words, asking, 'Am I older than sixty-five?'

Luke, who has a picture of Annie stuck to his own head, squints at me and snorts out a laugh. 'I guess so. The kids have written "one hundred and ninety", but that can't be right.'

'The oldest person to ever live was one hundred and twenty-two when she died,' Tara nods wisely, listing a little to one side. 'So something fishy is going on.'

'A clue!' I exclaim. 'I must be someone very old.'

Nico grins at me, his arm thrown across the back of my chair. 'Calm down, Poirot.'

'You're just upset because you're still miles off,' I say, though in fairness, he does have a picture of Button, Art and Annie's Yorkshire terrier, taped to his head so it's not really any wonder he's confused.

'Wait, wait,' I say, banging my hand on the table. 'Am I mean?'

'Mean as a rattlesnake,' Kat agrees.

'I'm Mrs Platt!' I hoot, ripping the card from my head and everyone cheers and does the same.

'Lee wins,' Mei declares. 'We're such good tutors.'

She offers up her hand for a high-five and I accept happily. I don't get enough high-fives in my day-to-day life, I decide.

Luke points at the Mrs Platt card, his expression haunted.

'That woman's going to be the death of me. Her granddaughter got her a smartphone and now she WhatsApps me surveillance reports on her neighbour's cat's "suspicious behaviour".'

'Poor baby,' Tara croons, and she reaches out to pat his hand, while Luke stares down at her fingers, dumbstruck.

'I think my friend likes your friend,' Nico whispers, his lips brushing against my ear and sending delicious shivers through me.

'It must be bad, he usually has way more game than this.'

I smile. 'I think you're right.'

'Always, Daisy.' His voice is a low rumble that does things to my insides. 'I'm always right.'

Chapter Twenty-Four

Nico

It's after midnight by the time everyone leaves and Lee and I are clearing up the takeout containers and empty wine bottles.

'That was fun,' she says, sounding surprised.

'It was. It's nice that Tara came out here to surprise you.' I watch as her smile widens, as she shakes her head like she can't believe someone would show up for her like that.

For the last few days I have kept my word and done nothing except be an excellent friend to her. Instead of avoiding her, I've insisted on us spending time together so that she'll know precisely how *fine* I am with everything.

The reality is that I haven't been able to stop thinking about that kiss, which despite its innocence has taken over the top spot as one of the most erotic moments of my life. At night while I toss and turn uncomfortably on the awful sofa, and Lee sleeps on the other side of the wall, I think about her face and her voice and her soft, laughing mouth until I fall asleep and dream about her.

I want to ask her more about this man she was seeing in London. Was it this Adrian guy who's still texting her? Is it over or are they still seeing each other? Does she want him the way that I want her?

I'm a mess. But Lee doesn't need to know that. I told Luke I wasn't going to make the situation more complicated and I meant it. Still, maybe there's a casual way I can ask her about her love life. Friends do that, right?

'Do you—' I start, but our quiet conversation is interrupted by a heart-stopping scream.

'Shit!' I exclaim, already running for Phoebe's room.

I open the door, turning on the light as Phoebe struggles up, her eyes wide, her face wet. Taco whines at her side, trying to lick the tears from her cheeks.

'It's just a bad dream, Bee,' I say quietly, moving to the side of her bed to hug her. She nestles against me, and I can feel her heart hammering, her small shoulders shaking. 'Just a dream, it's okay. You're okay.'

'It was too dark,' she murmurs, her face pressed to my chest. 'I couldn't get out and there was a monster. He was coming to get me.'

I hold her tighter, Taco curls up against her side. 'Nothing's coming to get you. I'm here and everything's okay.' I feel her relax into my arms. 'Do you want to play the game?'

She sniffles. 'What letter shall we do?'

'How about D?' I ask. It's a technique I read about, for kids who have nightmares – getting her back in the room by naming five things beginning with a certain letter.

'Um, dog,' she says, 'Dad, drawers, door.' She looks around, more of the tension leaving her. 'Daisy,' she finishes.

I look up and see that Lee is standing in the doorway watching us anxiously. Catching my gaze, her eyes widen and she mouths an apology before slipping away.

I turn my attention back to Phoebe. 'Good job. Now, why don't you lie down and we'll read for a bit?'

'You won't leave?' she asks, snuggling back against her pillow. 'Not until I'm asleep?'

'I won't leave. I promise.'

It doesn't take long. It surprised me, at first, how quickly she'd fall back to sleep after a nightmare, but I stay for an extra couple of minutes to make sure she's fully out before I pull the door shut behind me.

Lee is sitting at the clean dining table, staring at a glass of water. When she sees me she jumps up.

'Is Phoebe okay?' she asks, gripping the back of her chair.

I nod. 'Nightmare. It's been a while since she had one. I was sort of hoping we'd left them behind.'

'She has them a lot?'

I nod again, my jaw tight. 'Used to. They started after Tom died. Apparently it's common for kids dealing with grief, but they're hard on her.'

'Hard on you, too.' Lee tilts her head, her expression sympathetic.

I exhale a shaky laugh. 'I don't know how to protect her from her own brain. If you know how to beat up monsters in people's dreams then I'm all ears. Mostly I feel useless.'

'I used to have nightmares,' Lee says carefully, not meeting my eye. 'When I was a kid. I wish my dad had come running.'

I'm struck by the same hot flare of anger that I experience whenever Lee talks about her parents. I hate thinking of her being so alone.

'It doesn't feel like enough,' I say, and I'm not just talking about Phoebe. I wish I could do more for Lee. I wish I could go back in time and stop anything or anyone from hurting her.

Lee, however, is frowning. 'You keep saying that, that it's not enough, that you don't do enough, but I've been here, living with both of you and I don't know how you could do *more*.' She reaches out and squeezes my arm. 'It's obvious to everyone that you're a good dad, you're being too hard on yourself.'

I shake my head. 'That's the thing . . . it's not enough to be a *good* dad. Phoebe didn't even know her mother and then eighteen months ago she lost Tom, the only father figure she'd ever had. It's too much. If I'd known that she existed I'd have been here but I wasn't, and I can never make that right for her. She's a child, and all she knows is that I *wasn't there*.' There's a pain in my chest like a knife, and I can see an echo of it in Lee's eyes.

'I swore to myself I'd never, *never* abandon my kid like my dad with me. I missed so much stuff, Lee,' I say, the words soft like a secret, the kind I can't say out loud to anyone else because I know Magda carries so much guilt over this too, because I know that she was doing the best she could but that it hurts anyway. 'Her first smile, her first steps, her first word. I think about those moments and how there's no getting them back, and it kills me.'

'Of course it does. That's grief.' Lee comes to slip her arms around my waist. She presses her body to mine, rests her cheek against my chest, holding me tight. For someone who isn't much of a hugger, she's excellent at it. I band my own arm around her back, pulling her close like I want to, deciding not to question the comfort I get from her touch.

'I'm so sorry,' she murmurs. 'You deserved to have all those things. It's okay to be sad about it.'

We stand locked in each other's arms as the clock on the kitchen wall ticks gently, as the seconds stretch out. I know I should let go, but I don't want to.

'Do you like working at the inn?' she asks.

'What?' I pull back, thrown by the question.

'You've done an amazing job there, it looks beautiful, but do you enjoy it?'

'Sure. It's hard work but it's satisfying. I like feeling useful.'

'Yeah,' she points her finger at me, 'that. You know, when I used to ask you about your job you would light up. You couldn't wait to tell me about what you'd been doing, what you'd seen. You didn't go anywhere without your camera. Not since you were *fourteen*, Nico!'

'What do you want me to say?' My chest feels tight.

'I want you to tell me why you've stopped taking photographs.'

'You know why. I have to be here. I can't drop everything and disappear for weeks to take photos on the other side of the world.'

'But is that really the only option?'

'Why are we talking about this? I don't . . .' I trail off, try to organise my thoughts. 'I don't know how to do it,' I say finally.

'To do what?'

'I don't know how to do the job I love without it being all that I am. Before, I took the assignments I liked, I went where the whim took me, in search of something . . . beautiful or moving or wild. I've never had any other ties or responsibilities before, and so my work *was* my life. But now my life is . . . something else.'

And that's the problem. I don't really understand what the something else is, but how do I explain that to Lee? How can you have a clear picture of the future when you've spent a year with your head down just putting one foot in front of the other? The only thing I know for sure is that I need to be here for Phoebe. Photography has always been such an all-consuming presence in my life that it never left room for much else, but my daughter deserves one hundred per cent of me and I have no idea how to keep a hold on any part of my old life without bringing my new one crashing down.

'I get that,' Lee says slowly. 'I understand why you want to be the *perfect* parent, but surely it doesn't mean pretending such an important part of your life doesn't exist?'

'It feels easier to pretend that it doesn't exist than to try and live with only a piece of it.'

Lee's expression softens. 'Nico,' she breathes, and I'm temporarily distracted from whatever she's about to say by that – the shape of my name on her lips. Her eyes are so pretty, I notice, such a deep blue, fringed with long, dark lashes. Am I drunk? I only had a few glasses of wine but suddenly I *feel* drunk. 'I know that you have this idea of yourself . . . that your dad made you feel . . .' she hesitates, as if sorting through the words. 'I need you to know that you're not some . . . reckless wastrel.'

'Wow, Daisy!' I can't help but smile at that. 'Don't think anyone has used *wastrel* in a sentence for quite a few decades.'

She squeezes my arms as if she wants to give me a shake. 'Shut up and listen! You have this deep-held belief that you're unreliable or careless, because that's what *he* told you over and over again, but it's not true. You said it yourself: you could travel where you wanted *because* you weren't beholden to anyone.'

'*Beholden*,' I murmur, but she ignores me, all lit up with something and, whatever it is, my heart is beating harder.

'But as soon as you found out about Phoebe, you were here. No questions asked. You changed your entire life for her. That's not what a careless person does. You don't need to change who you *are*. You don't need to give up the thing you love like some sort of penance.'

Fuck. There's a real tender part of my soul that she's reaching right into here. I'm startled by an intimacy between us that I've never really acknowledged before, that Lee *knows* me this way, that she understands what's bothering me without any need to explain myself. I guess this is what almost thirty years in each other's lives looks like.

'Being a parent is the ultimate responsibility,' I say, and my voice is rough. 'And I've never done responsibility before. My dad loved to remind me of that at any opportunity. Even from beyond the fucking grave with this whole inheritance nightmare. I can't be the person I was a year ago. I don't know how to trust myself with that, to trust myself with Phoebe. She's precious and I'm so scared I'm going to fuck it up.'

Lee smiles. 'I think that's standard for any parent. But if it helps, I know you won't fuck it up.'

'You do?'

'If Jack or Gran were in trouble, they'd call you, Nico. Your mum, too. You're not irresponsible. You've always taken care of people, it's a huge part of who you are. Who sat in the grass making daisy chains with me? Who was right there in the hospital with Gran last year? *You.*'

She's looking at me with this earnest expression and I swear my chest is aching.

'And you?' I ask, suddenly needing to know the answer. 'If you were in trouble. Would you call me?'

Her lashes lower so I can't see the look in her eyes. She lets go of my arms and takes a step back, the movement careful.

'You've always been my safe place, Nico,' she says softly. 'So . . . yes, even though I probably shouldn't. I'd call you.'

'I'm glad about that,' I murmur, and I give in to the urge to brush the loose wave of golden hair away from her face, to tuck it tenderly behind her ear. 'I'd want you to.'

There's a beat of silence while we look at each other, and something sweet and vulnerable dances in her eyes, then Lee looks away. 'Anyway, I think that's enough excitement for one night,' she says. I can almost see her reeling all her emotions back in until her smooth mask is in place. 'I'm going to head to bed.'

'Sure.' I try to keep my voice even. 'Sleep well.'

She makes it to her bedroom door before she turns back. 'Nico . . .' she pauses, fixes me with those blue eyes, her expression serious. 'I really do think there's a way you can be Phoebe's dad, and still be *you*. Just think about it. Please.'

Chapter Twenty-Five

Nico

The next morning I wake up sprawled uncomfortably on the too-small sofa with a drumline playing in my head and Taco licking my face.

'Okay, okay,' I mumble, getting to my feet so that I can put some food down and let him outside. Despite the fact I only had a few glasses of wine last night, I'm still feeling a certain tenderness in body and spirit. Getting older sucks.

The corner of my laptop sticks out from under the sofa where I shoved it before I eventually fell asleep last night and I eye it warily for a moment.

Last night after my conversation with Lee I opened up the pictures from our night in Vegas, and as the screen comes to life now they pop up in front of me.

They're some of the last photos that I properly took the time to edit, and seeing them now is strange. First of all, there are some great shots in there, and I remember how buzzed I was about them at the time. Frankie Martelli and his friends have the most incredible faces, their personalities sing through every image, and the way I've worked on the pictures really makes the most of the moody setting, emphasising a curl of cigar smoke through the diffused light here, a vibrant pop of deep red there.

I click through the photographs until I get to the one I'm looking for.

It's of Lee.

She's sitting at the poker table, an enormous stack of chips in front of her. Her fingers are pressed over a fan of cards, still face down. No one knows yet that it's a winning hand.

Her face is turned towards one of the other players, and she's grinning at something they said, her eyes half shut, the dimples in her cheeks on display. Her hair is falling out of the long, mermaid-y braid she had it in; the top two buttons of her white silk shirt are unbuttoned, revealing the hollow at the base of her throat.

There's something about this picture, something magic. It's Lee. She's luminous. Strands of gold thread through her hair, her skin is all pearls and moondust. She's not just sitting *in* the light. She *is* the light.

I draw in a shuddering breath. *Look at her.* Is it any wonder I married this woman? I probably dragged her down the aisle. She never stood a chance.

There was this moment last night where she had one of those stupid flashcards taped to her head, and she was laughing at some story Tara told, and the light from the candles I'd teased her about flickered over her face. I heard the camera shutter go off in my head. I wanted that picture so badly, my hands shook. I wanted to catch her in that instant and keep her for ever.

I have no idea what I'm supposed to do with all these feelings.

Suddenly, the bedroom door opens and Lee tiptoes out. She's wearing bright pink cotton pyjamas, covered in photographs of cats. Her hair hasn't been brushed, and she startles at the sight of me.

I slam the laptop shut, looking guilty as hell.

'Sorry,' her eyes widen, 'I thought you'd still be asleep. I was going to creep past for a glass of water.' She winces. 'Maybe some ibuprofen.'

I dread to think what she imagines I was doing . . . Still it might be better than the reality, which is mooning over a photograph of her face.

'Yeah, it's no Vegas hangover,' I manage, getting to my feet, 'but half a bottle of wine is a pretty heavy night for me these days.'

'Me too,' Lee agrees. After a second's hesitation, she crosses to the kitchen and pours two glasses of water from the jug in the fridge, before extracting matching his and hers doses of painkillers from the First Aid box.

I'm about to call Taco back inside, but clearly he's heard his beloved's voice because he comes barrelling past me like a bullet. I open my mouth but instead of jumping all over Lee as I expect him to, he sits and gently leans against her leg.

'He knows I'm feeling delicate this morning, don't you, my sweet boy?' Lee asks, scratching him behind his ears while he whimpers in delight.

'Before you got here it used to take me fifteen solid minutes of swearing and threats to get him back inside.'

Phoebe's door opens then and she comes in, wearing her black cat hoodie. 'Oh, good, you're both up,' she says and climbs up onto one of the kitchen stools, last night's bad dream forgotten. I guess I should be happy that they don't seem to linger in her mind, but each one takes a week or two off my life.

I grab my glass of water and swallow my pills before turning to her. 'Let me guess. You're starving and you want something disgustingly unhealthy for breakfast.'

Sensing weakness, she blinks at me. 'There's half a tub of Miss Rita's peanut butter ice cream left in the freezer.' Her eyes widen further. 'And peanuts are *legumes*, Dad.'

'I told you that was going to come back and bite me,' I mutter to Lee, but I extract the tub of ice cream and a spoon and hand them to my daughter.

'Hey, I like your pyjamas.' Phoebe waves her spoon in Lee's direction.

Lee glances down and grimaces, clearly registering her outfit for the first time. I bite back a smile. She looks so cute.

'This is the first time I've seen you look . . .' Phoebe purses her lips. 'Un-fancy.'

'Oh,' Lee looks flustered, running a hand over her hair to smooth it.

'Phoebe,' I chide.

'What?' Phoebe asks around a mouthful of ice cream. 'I like it. Lee fits in with us.' She gestures to the two of us – me in my pyjamas, her in hers with the cat hoodie over the top.

Lee's cheeks are pink. 'I like silly pyjamas,' she says, like it's a confession. I suppose the bright pink PJs are not exactly what I'd imagine Lee to wear in bed. Not that I've spent a lot of time imagining what else she might wear as she slept in my bed . . . lace . . . or silk . . . or nothing at all.

'Coffee?' I bark, hustling over to the machine.

'How come you like silly pyjamas?' Phoebe asks, and this is great . . . let's all remain focused on Lee's sleepwear.

Lee swipes a mug from the cupboard and hands it to me, her attention still on Phoebe. 'I think,' she starts tentatively, 'that my clothes are a bit like my armour. I love them, but they also make me feel . . . more confident? More in control. When I'm just hanging out around the house I don't need that so much. I can just be . . . silly.'

I'm suddenly struck by a memory from Vegas of those pyjamas covered in the little tropical fruits and my heart feels bruised, tender like a peach.

'Yeah,' Phoebe nods thoughtfully. 'Like how I always feel *so powerful* when I wear my soccer uniform. But we like you when you're silly. You don't need to wear your armour with us, right, Dad?'

When my daughter looks at me with her sweet, serious face I feel as if I've been punched in the solar plexus by my love for her. Lee's stunned expression leads me to believe she might be experiencing something similar. Underneath her snarky attitude, my girl has the biggest heart.

'That's right, little Bee,' I agree, my voice a bit hoarse.

'Cool,' Phoebe nods, like she hasn't just totally decimated the emotional wellbeing of two adults, and turns her attention back to her ice cream. I busy myself making coffee while Lee casually runs a finger under her lashes.

'Cool,' Lee echoes softly. 'So, I was thinking maybe we should go and get hot chocolate at Bean & Gone this week,' she says to Phoebe, and the words are hesitant like she's not sure her invitation will be welcome. 'I could pick you up from school one day. There might be cinnamon buns, too.'

Phoebe perks up at this and agrees enthusiastically, and I don't even think it's about the buns.

While the two of them chat, I start making some toast. Ice cream isn't going to cut it for me and Lee – not that it looks like there's any going spare – when we have a busy day with plans to take Tara out sightseeing, as well as getting everything ready for the trustee's arrival tomorrow.

'Shall we watch cartoons now?' Phoebe asks, but before I can answer, we're interrupted by a sharp knock at the door.

'Who can that be?' I mutter.

There's a man standing on the front porch. He's probably in his sixties, he's wearing an immaculate three piece suit, and his thinning brown hair is swept back from his long face. He blinks at me from behind a pair of round, wire-rimmed glasses.

'Nicolas Hart?' he asks in a plummy English accent.

My stomach sinks. 'Yes,' I agree reluctantly.

The man reaches into his pocket and pulls out a business card. 'Charles Saunders,' he says, confirming my worst fears. 'Of Saunders, Saunders and Sneed. You've been expecting me?'

'Not until tomorrow.' I look down at the card in my hand, which is thick and embossed and clearly the business card of someone not to be messed with. It also looks like the trustee is a *partner* in a prestigious law firm. I'm sure he's delighted to be spending two weeks in small-town America, observing me like a high school science experiment.

Charles frowns. 'I apologise. My assistant must have forwarded incorrect details. I will look into the matter.'

My brain is working slowly, but after a long, awkward moment I realise he's waiting to be invited in. I glance over my shoulder, to where Phoebe and Lee are still chatting in the kitchen.

'Er, come in,' I say finally. 'I'm afraid you've caught us having breakfast.'

When I turn back into the house, Lee glances up and I catch her eye. '*Honey*,' I say brightly. 'It looks like we had the date wrong. Charles Saunders, my father's lawyer, is here.'

The coffee cup slips from Lee's fingers, shattering on the kitchen floor. Taco is barking like mad, charging around in circles, while Lee tries to stop him stepping on any of the broken splinters.

'Oh!' Lee exclaims. 'Oh, no, I . . .'

I head towards her, grabbing a roll of kitchen towel as I go. I put a hand on her arm. 'Don't move,' I say as calmly as I can manage, mopping up the small amount of coffee she had left in her cup. 'You have bare feet.'

'Sorry,' she says. 'I'm so sorry, I . . .'

I grab a dustpan and brush from under the sink and sweep up the mess, while Lee stands in her pink pyjamas looking deeply traumatised.

'Hey,' my daughter – utterly unruffled – spins on her stool to face the lawyer, who is standing neatly inside the front door. She lifts her ice cream spoon in a little salute. 'I'm Phoebe. Do you want some ice cream?'

'Phoebe!' I straighten, moving to dump the bits of broken cup into the bin. I turn to the lawyer and let out a loud, and extremely fake, laugh. 'She's not having ice cream for breakfast! I mean . . .' I flounder, 'she is, but—'

'It's peanut butter flavour, and peanuts are legumes,' my daughter adds helpfully. 'Like peas and beans.'

'I see,' Charles says in the kind of mild, even tone that leads me to believe he is judging me very hard.

Now that it's safe for her to move, Lee starts forward, a frozen expression on her face.

'Mr Saunders. I'm Lee Turner-Jones,' she says, holding out her hand, and she sounds calm at least. Steady and reassuring. 'I'm sorry for the . . . unfortunate greeting. I'm afraid we weren't expecting you.'

'So Mr Hart explained.' Charles takes her hand and shakes it. 'I apologise for the inconvenience. I will be looking into the miscommunication, I assure you.'

'No, no,' Lee shakes her head. 'Welcome to . . . our home?'

It's not ideal that it sounds like a question.

It's also not ideal when she suddenly blurts, 'I snore!'

For the first time, Charles's face displays some emotion. 'I beg your pardon?' he asks, clearly startled.

I can't say I blame him, I have no idea what's going on. Lee is wringing her hands and I follow her gaze to the sofa, which has my pillow and bed sheets still spread out on it.

I close my eyes.

When I open them, Lee is nodding frantically. 'Yes, yes, I snore terribly. It's awful. So loud.'

'Yes, *and*,' Phoebe leaps in, eager to show off her improv skills, 'it's real bad. Like, woah, is that an earthquake? No, it's Lee snoring.'

'Right,' Lee blinks. 'That's right. And poor Nico. My *husband*, Nico,' Lee gestures at me as if Charles might not know who she's talking about. 'He sometimes has to come out here on the sofa, just to get some sleep. I wouldn't want you thinking . . . or getting the wrong impression about . . . we're *very happy*.' She takes a step towards me, and slips her arm around my waist, leaning against me so that I can literally feel her vibrating with anxiety. 'And obviously we sleep together. We *love* to sleep together . . . sorry, I don't mean that we love to *sleep together*, not that there's anything wrong in that area, oh no, we have a very active . . . but that's not . . . that is, I just mean we love sleeping, *actually sleeping*. In the same bed.'

All three of us are staring at her now, and there's a long moment of silence.

'I see,' Charles says neutrally. I fear this is going to be a response I hear often from him, and I'm worried about how much he *does* actually see.

'Want to have a look at my room?' Phoebe pipes up.

'Certainly.' Charles inclines his head and follows her. Phoebe turns to glance back over her shoulder, shooting Lee and me a look that very clearly says *get it together!!!*

Once they're out of sight, Lee steps away from me and slumps, her hand reaching out to hold the back of the sofa.

'Oh my god, I'm going to be sick,' she whispers.

'I can't imagine why,' I manage. 'That went great.'

'I think I blacked out for a second there.' She closes her eyes. 'Did I—'

'Start rambling about our very active sex life?' A hysterical laugh is making its way up from my chest. 'I had some trouble following, but I'm pretty sure you did.'

'Oh my god,' she moans again. 'I can't believe that happened.' She looks down at herself. 'I can't believe I'm wearing pink cat pyjamas. I had such a good outfit planned for this meeting. I was going to wear a jacket with shoulder pads, Nico. Shoulder pads!'

'I—' I don't know how to respond to this, but it seems my response is not needed.

'Not like, Eighties *Working Girl* shoulder pads or anything,' she continues, her eyes slightly wild. 'But an extremely tasteful, tailored suit in understated neutrals. And Louboutins. Very high ones, immaculately polished. I was *not* going to be barefoot, wearing novelty pyjamas with unbrushed hair.'

I take a step forward, and put a hand on each of her un-padded shoulders.

'Daisy?' I say.

'Yes?' She blinks helplessly up at me.

'Take a breath.' I pull her gently against me, and her arms wind around my waist. Her cheek rests on my chest.

'Okay,' she murmurs, her eyes fluttering closed as she exhales. 'Okay. I can fix this.'

'*We* can fix this,' I agree.

'You know if *we're* going to fix this you're actually going to have to say something,' she grumbles. 'Not just stand there looking shell-shocked.'

'I think you were talking enough for the both of us,' I laugh, and she pokes me hard in the chest, but there's the ghost of a smile on her lips.

'. . . and that's why Pluto is included even though it is only a dwarf planet,' Phoebe is loudly explaining to Charles as her bedroom door opens.

Charles holds a small notebook and makes an annotation in it with a shiny gold pen. Presumably giving me negative marks on my astronomy knowledge.

I'm about to offer him a cup of coffee, when there's another knock at the door.

'Wow.' I force a smile. 'We *are* popular this morning. I wonder who that is.'

When I open the door it is to find an extraordinarily glamorous woman, swathed in a fur coat and matching fur headband, peering at me from behind enormous sunglasses, a wide, gleaming white smile on her face.

'Darling!' she exclaims, throwing her arms out wide.

Chapter Twenty-Six

Lee

'Ma?' Nico gasps and I freeze.

I absolutely must be dreaming. This has to be a nightmare. There's no possible way that Nico's mother is here on his doorstep, while the terrifyingly unimpressed-looking lawyer sent by Nico's dead father to evaluate his life hovers nearby. And certainly not while I am wearing my pink cat pyjamas. That is too absurd to be real.

I pinch myself, but the results are disappointing.

'What . . . what are you doing here?' Nico asks, blocking the doorway so that Claudia can't get in.

'Darling, Magda told me all about this lawyer your absolute bastard of a father was sending . . .' I hear her say with devastating clarity. Her clipped, American-English hybrid of an accent carries beautifully.

Nico lets out a strangled cough. 'Yes,' he interrupts hastily. 'Mr Saunders. He actually arrived a few minutes ago.'

There's a heavy silence. While I can only see Nico's back, I'm certain that there is a very intense soundless exchange happening between the two of them. Finally, Nico steps back, a frozen smile on his face. 'Why don't you come in?'

Claudia glides into the house, her tall frame draped in furs, and she pulls off her sunglasses, her gorgeous green eyes sweeping the room until they land on me. 'Lee!' she exclaims, her arms thrown out as she approaches me. 'My beautiful daughter-in-law! How are you, darling? You look . . .' There's a hitch in her stride as she actually registers what I look like, but it's barely noticeable . . . 'So charmingly cosy,' she finishes, bundling me into a Chanel No. 5 scented hug.

'Hello, Claudia,' I say robotically. 'What a nice surprise.' I haven't seen her for almost two decades, but honestly, if anything, she looks younger than the last time. Her skin is absolutely poreless; the perfect bone structure that put her face on the cover of every major fashion magazine still looks sharp enough to be dangerous. Her hair is a long, straight dark curtain underneath the unnecessary fur hat. It's not really that cold outside, but she looks like she's stepped out of a glamorous '70s après-ski photo shoot.

Claudia turns the focus of her attention on Charles. 'Of course, *you* must be Mr Saunders, hello, *I* am Claudia Hart.' She delivers the line in a way that makes it clear that she knows that he knows who she is, but she's graciously not going to make a big deal of it . . . which somehow makes a very big deal of it.

Even Charles Saunders' professional game face can't stand up to this, and there's a light flush on his cheeks, his hand goes to touch the knot of his tie.

'Ms Hart. I'm a great admirer. How lovely to meet you.'

'Oh, Charlie!' Claudia tinkles. '*Can* I call you Charlie?'

'Well, I—' Charles begins, but Claudia ruthlessly cuts him off.

'Charlie, I'm *so* sorry to come crashing in unannounced when you're just beginning your work here, but I can never *bear* to be away from my precious family for too long.'

'Hi, Granny,' Phoebe pipes up, her smile angelic.

Claudia swings around and her eyes narrow. 'Now, Phoebe,' she says sweetly, but there's steel at the back of her words. 'I believe we discussed this before. You're to call me Claudia.'

'Oh, right,' Phoebe says with zero contrition. 'I forgot.'

'I'm sure you did,' Claudia murmurs, but she leans down to give Phoebe a careful hug. 'I have brought you some fabulous Murano glassware in my luggage,' she tells her granddaughter.

Phoebe darts a look at her dad, who runs a weary hand over his face. 'Thanks,' she says finally.

There's an urgent knock at the door, and I let out a desperate choke of laughter. *What now?*

Before anyone can answer it, the door swings open and Magda comes flying in. 'Nico!' she yells. 'Bud's been to the airport and . . .' She comes to a screeching halt in the middle of the room, taking in the scene in front of her. 'Ah,' she clears her throat. 'I see everyone else beat me to it.'

'Magda!' Claudia recovers almost instantly, delivering airy kisses to both of Magda's cheeks. 'How *gorgeous* to see you, I was just telling *Charles* the *lawyer* here that I can never stand to be away from my family for too long, particularly my *beloved* daughter-in-law, Ophelia.'

I don't think anyone can claim to be surprised that Claudia never followed the model to actress pipeline.

'Right,' Magda nods with way too much enthusiasm. 'That's exactly right. And very normal.'

There's another beat and Charles steps forward.

'Charles Saunders,' he says, introducing himself to Magda. 'Of Saunders, Saunders and Sneed.'

'Which Saunders are you?' Phoebe asks. 'The first or the second?'

'The first.' Charles dips his head.

'Yeah, but I bet you'd still say that even if you were the second,' Phoebe muses. 'That's what I'd do.'

Charles pauses. 'The second Saunders is my son, so I think it's safe to say that I come first.'

'Ah,' Phoebe says wisely, 'a nepo-baby.' Then when we all look surprised, she shrugs. 'Hey, I see stuff on TikTok.'

'Hahaha!' Nico breaks in. 'No you don't! As if my eight-year-old daughter would be allowed access to TikTok!' He fixes her with a hard stare. 'That would be ridiculous, because *my* daughter and I have had *several* conversations about the dangers of social media and she knows that using my phone to go on TikTok would result in an immediate grounding.'

'That's right,' Phoebe agrees instantly. 'Sorry, did I say TikTok? I meant Wikipedia, which I sometimes use for educational purposes.' The angelic expression is back.

God, she's good.

'Well,' Magda says heartily, 'it looks as if I'm interrupting, but I wanted to come and pick up Phoebe for our usual . . .'

'Pancake breakfast,' Phoebe supplies helpfully. 'I'll go and grab my stuff.' And with that she dashes out of the room.

'Perhaps Mr Saunders would like to join us?' Magda offers him a friendly smile. 'It looks like Nico and Lee have had quite the morning, and I'm sure they'll want to catch up with Claudia.'

'Well, I—' Charles begins again, but once more Claudia steamrolls him.

'What a *wonderful* idea, Magda. You and Phoebe really must show Charles the delights of this *charming* town. Charlie, I do hope that you'll be able to make time for dinner with me while you're here? After all, no one knows Nico better than his mother!' She's fixed him with a hypnotising, unblinking stare and it must be working, because Charles only nods, his throat bobbing as he allows Magda to guide him towards the door.

'That would be my pleasure,' he murmurs. 'Mr Hart, now that I've introduced myself, my secretary will be in touch to set up a more formal appointment.'

'Can't wait,' Nico deadpans.

Phoebe barrels out of her bedroom, dressed and carrying her backpack. 'Okay, let's go. Come on, Taco!'

She grabs his lead and clips it onto Taco's collar, dragging him along with her. I manage a weak goodbye as the three of them head out, and Magda shoots me a reassuring thumbs up as she passes, already chattering to Charles about the town's many excellent qualities.

When the door closes behind them, I crumble to the floor, my head in my hands.

'This is a dream,' I say firmly. 'This is a bad dream. We cannot possibly be this awful at this. He's only been here for half an hour.'

'Maybe it wasn't as bad as we thought.' Nico is slumped over the kitchen counter looking haggard.

'I don't know what you're worrying about,' Claudia says breezily, pulling off her hat and fluffing her perfect hair. 'I thought it went great.'

'Ma, I say this with love,' Nico pulls himself up, 'but what the fuck are you doing here?'

Claudia pouts. 'Where else would I be in my son's time of need? I came to help, of course.'

'Right.' Nico pinches the bridge of his nose. 'And how exactly do you plan to do that?'

'Well, for a start I'm going to seduce Charles Saunders for you.'

A groan comes from somewhere deep in Nico's chest. I pull myself to my feet and go to stand beside him, rubbing soothing circles on his back as he drapes himself over the counter again.

'Yes,' Claudia muses, coming to take Phoebe's recently occupied seat at the breakfast bar across from us. 'And it might not be that bad. He was very sweet, wasn't he? And distinguished-looking. I do like a man in glasses.'

Nico's mouth is set in a straight line. 'I think it's probably best if you leave the man alone.'

Claudia waves a perfectly manicured hand in a casual gesture of dismissal. 'Darling, you keep your attention on your own role and I'll handle mine.' She looks between the two of us. 'I must say this informal set up for your first meeting was quite the *choice* . . . I guess it does scream domesticity.'

'We thought he was arriving tomorrow,' I jump in. 'I was going to wear a suit. It had shoulder pads,' I add desperately.

Unlike Nico, Claudia appears to understand the significance of this because her face crumples in sympathy (or at least as much as someone very clearly pumped full of Botox *can* crumple).

'Terrible,' she murmurs. 'Still,' her voice perks up, 'you really *did* look like a normal family.'

'I suppose,' I agree, still trying to process the last thirty minutes. 'But it wasn't the most auspicious start. I don't think I made a great first impression.'

'You?' Nico shakes his head. 'What about me? Hungover and feeding my daughter ice cream for breakfast. That just screams responsible parent, doesn't it?'

'Now listen,' Claudia says suddenly all business, 'you two are going to have to get your shit together. You can't let a little blip like this get in your way. Not when the stakes are so high. I swear to god, if that rat-bastard ex-husband of mine was still alive I'd murder him myself for putting you through this.'

She leans over the counter and presses a hand to Nico's cheek.

'My sweet boy,' she coos. 'So smart and so very, very good. You didn't get any of that from your sperm donor.'

'You were married for three years,' Nico protests weakly. 'I don't think we should refer to Dad as my sperm donor.'

Claudia sniffs. 'He might as well have been. You know, he *tricked* me into that marriage, showering me with gifts and affection and taking me to *fabulous* parties, then the second he had that ring on my finger he thought I was going to turn into some little housewife. Can you imagine?' She turns to me, wide-eyed. 'Me?'

'Um, no,' I say, because I can't. Also she's not wrong. Nico's father was a horrible man, a bully, a philanderer, a really nasty piece of work. According to Gran, Claudia was wise to get out when she did. I only met him a couple of times in passing, but the man had strong Disney villain vibes.

'Marriage,' Claudia pouts. 'It's not all it's cracked up to be.'

'Says the woman who's been married five times,' Nico snorts.

She smiles. 'What can I say? I'm a *romantic.* Of course that's how your father got me in the first place, the cad. So attractive, but so withholding,' she sighs. 'Still, I have to admit he was *marvellous* in bed . . .'

Nico is groaning again.

'And I did enjoy my time being a duchess,' she continues blithely. 'In hindsight I should have kept hold of the title for longer instead of remarrying, but *c'est la vie.*'

'How long are you here for, Claudia?' I ask, trying to turn the conversation in a better direction.

'As long as you need me, my doves!' Claudia beams. 'I've cleared my schedule. It will give me a chance to spend time with Phoebe as well. Do you know, I do believe she has inherited some of my moxie.'

'Oh yeah, she's full of moxie,' Nico agrees, resigned.

'And Lee, it really is *so* good to see you again.' Claudia reaches across to take both my hands in hers and give me a good once over. I would sell my soul for a hairbrush. 'You've grown into such a *gorgeous* woman. I always knew you would. Beauty *and* brains, everything a mother could ask for in a daughter-in-law. You're an absolute doll.'

She gives me one of her enchanting smiles, and I find my own mouth pulling up in response. This is the thing about Claudia – she's a tornado in designer couture, but she's also completely irresistible. When I was small I idolised her. Although I had my own impossibly glamorous parents, Claudia somehow transcended even their standards. And she wasn't only beautiful – she was so much fun, always up for an adventure, or pulling me aside, away from the boys to play with her perfumes and have 'girl talk'.

When she moved out of the house next door to us and went back to the States I'd been devastated.

'It's good to see you, too,' I say, suddenly a bit shy. 'Are you staying in town?'

'As it happens there isn't any accommodation available in Roseport, so I'm staying in a *darling* little hotel in the next town over. Your local driver – Bud, is it? – has offered to chauffeur me around as needed, and I did some light snooping when I checked in.' Her smile widens, showing off her sparkling white teeth. 'It seems your Mr Saunders is staying down the hall from me. *Très* convenient.'

'Ma, please, just . . . keep a lid on the seduction plans for now, yeah?'

Claudia blinks at Nico. 'Of course I could *try*,' she says doubtfully, 'but I'm afraid the wheels are already in motion.'

'You met him for about ninety seconds,' Nico huffs.

His mother's shrug is languid. 'I don't know what to tell you. It's my gift . . . and my curse. Besides, if I'd been in his confidence this morning, he never would have been able to spring this surprise visit on you. Think how useful it will be to have a mole on the inside!'

'Right.' Nico only nods because I think it's clear to both of us that there's little point in arguing further, and Claudia is already picturing herself as a femme fatale in a trench coat.

Claudia's phone dings and she pulls it from her pocket. 'Ah, Bud awaits! I'll leave the two of you to your morning, but we'll catch up for dinner later, won't we? My treat.'

'We already have plans today, Ma,' Nico says gently. 'I'm sorry, but I had no idea you'd be here. Tomorrow?'

Claudia looks supremely unbothered. 'Whatever suits you. You know I never have any problem entertaining myself.'

'Precisely what I'm worried about,' Nico mutters under his breath.

'And before I forget.' Claudia pulls something else from her pocket with a flourish, placing it on the kitchen counter. 'I brought you these.'

Nico eyes the small black box with suspicion. 'What is it?'

'Your grandparents' wedding rings,' Claudia sings, already heading for the door. 'They're nothing special, you know, but I assumed you wouldn't have thought about it. Unlike Phoebe, you, my treasure, inherited *none* of my devious wiles. Speak soon!' She wiggles her fingers at us as she slips outside. 'Bud! You darling man!' I hear her cry, before the door swings shut behind her.

Nico and I look at each other and then down at the box. It feels like Claudia just tossed a grenade at us and then left.

'This is a very strange morning,' I say finally, trying to break some of the tension.

'Even by Roseport's standards,' Nico agrees, but he's still looking at the box. 'We shouldn't have done this, any of it. I should never have agreed.'

My heart sinks. 'I'm sorry,' I say miserably. 'I know I'm not a very good actress.'

His eyes fly to mine. 'No!' He steps towards me. '*I'm* sorry. I can't believe I roped you into this insanity. And now,' he gestures to the small and innocent-looking jewellery box as if it's a live tarantula, '*this*. I hadn't even thought—'

'It's just a costume, Nico,' I say, even though I get why he's freaking out. Pretending to be married is one thing, but wearing actual wedding rings feels like a whole other level, one that I foolishly hadn't considered. I thought if I ever wore a ring it would be put there by someone who loved me. It feels like cheating us out of something, this particular moment of pretence, but it can't be helped.

'It was a good idea,' I carry on firmly, trying to convince both of us. 'It would have been conspicuous to anyone looking for holes in our story. As it is, we can get away with it because I had obviously just got up so I wouldn't necessarily have my ring on yet.'

He doesn't say anything, only nods tensely and picks up the box, as if it might explode. He opens it and looks inside, the expression on his face unreadable, then he turns it to face me.

I gasp before I can stop myself. Inside are three rings: a man's gold band; and a woman's set – another gold band and a diamond engagement ring. By Claudia's standards I suppose they're nothing special, but I think they're lovely. The engagement ring has a small round central diamond, surrounded by eight smaller diamonds. It looks like a snowflake, or a tiny flower.

It looks like a daisy.

There's a lump in my throat that I'm trying hard to ignore.

'You don't have to wear one,' I manage to choke out. 'Some men don't.'

I feel his gaze on my face. 'I would,' he says, his voice deep with a rough edge to it. 'I'd wear one.'

I swallow. 'Okay, then,' I say as calmly as I can manage. 'We'll wear them. If they even fit.'

I take the two women's rings from the box before he can do anything – I absolutely couldn't handle having Nico put a ring on my finger – and slip them on.

And of course they fit. As if they were made for me.

Nico has put his own wedding band on, and he spins it around his finger. 'It's a bit loose,' he says. 'But that's fine.'

I look at the gold band on his ring finger and feel a spike of something weird and primal at the sight of it. I like seeing it there. I like it a lot. When I tear my gaze away, he's watching me.

'So I think there's something else we need to talk about,' I clear my throat. 'After this morning it's pretty clear . . . you need to move back into your bedroom.'

There's a long pause. 'And where will you sleep?' Nico asks slowly.

Wow. Okay.

'I'll sleep in there, too.' I wish I didn't sound so defensive. 'We're both adults, it's not a big deal. We even shared a bed before, once.'

Bringing up Vegas right now is probably not a great idea, and Nico's scowl only confirms that.

I swallow. 'Look, when I got here we had no idea I'd be staying for three weeks. I should have said something anyway, even before Charles arrived unannounced. You can't keep sleeping on that tiny sofa. I'm surprised you haven't seriously damaged your back.'

'I'm fine,' Nico grinds out.

Okay, so he *really* doesn't want to do this. That doesn't feel great. 'Is it—' I hesitate. 'Have I done something to make you feel uncomfortable?' I manage to push the question past my lips. I think about the awkward kissing moment, and I want to die.

His expression softens. 'No, you haven't.' He twists the ring on his finger again, an absent gesture. 'You're right,' he says at last. 'We can be adults about this. We can share a bed.'

He sounds like he's trying to convince himself rather than me.

'Great,' I say.

'Great,' he echoes grimly.

Somewhere inside my brain an alarm is blaring, but it's too late to back out now.

Chapter Twenty-Seven

Nico

'I want to try the sun-dried tomato one again,' Tara says, leaning over the table to dig her spoon into the luminous orange ice cream. 'I still don't understand what the black bits are?'

'I think it's olive tapenade,' Lee muses.

Luke makes a horrified noise low in his throat.

'It's honestly not as bad as it sounds,' Lee insists. 'It's sort of . . .'

'European,' Tara nods pensively. 'Like a gazpacho.'

'I don't care. It's an abomination,' Luke mutters.

'Shhh!' Tara swats his arm. 'Miss Rita will hear you.'

Luke looks chastened for a moment, but when Tara doesn't move her hand from his arm right away, his expression melts into something smug.

I'm glad one of us has their love life under control, seeing as I just found out I'm spending the next two weeks sharing a bed with the woman I'm in very serious lust with but definitely shouldn't touch.

Fantastic.

'I brought you a new one to try.' Rita hustles over with another single-serve tub of ice cream. 'This is a little something I've been playing around with. It's a bit unusual, but I think I'm close to cracking it.'

As the ice cream in question is a vivid yellow with veins of green sauce running through it I dread to think what this means.

'Thanks, Miss Rita,' Tara sings, beaming at the mad scientist. Rita leaves with a cheery wink, humming to herself as she goes. Obviously, she's delighted to find someone who is willing to try her wild experiments, and our table in the front of the parlour is covered in small tubs of half-eaten ice cream.

'What do you think?' Tara pokes the new flavour in front of her with her plastic spoon. 'Banana?'

'That is extremely optimistic,' I say.

'She said unusual,' Lee wrinkles her nose. 'It could be some sort of cheese?'

'Isn't there a type of chard that's yellow?' Tara ponders. 'That might explain the green bits.'

'Okay, I definitely draw the line at chard,' Luke grumbles. 'Ice cream should come in one of three flavours: vanilla, strawberry or chocolate.'

'Boooooooooo!' Tara pokes him in the side. 'Where is your sense of adventure? For that I think you have to be the one to try it.'

She scoops a spoonful of the yellow mixture and holds it up. She's grinning at him, an obvious dare.

When Luke takes the spoon into his mouth and licks it clean, Tara's breath catches, her eyes glued to his lips. I think she's humming something under her breath.

'Well?' Lee asks, her amusement clear.

Luke grimaces. 'I don't know. Is there such a thing as fish ice cream?'

'Oh god,' I wince.

Luke takes a long sip of his vanilla milkshake, while looking a bit pale, and Tara tells him how brave and manly he is.

We've spent the afternoon giving Tara her tour of Roseport, and when Luke *happened* to bump into us, he tagged along too. Phoebe opted for a playdate with Maya instead, and Maya's mum offered to drop her back later, so it's been just the four of us ducking in and out of shops, enjoying the crisp autumn weather, while Tara and Lee ooh and ahh over every single building, lamppost and picket fence in Roseport.

It's been good, actually, a welcome distraction from not only the catastrophic events of earlier, but also the absurd and overwhelming crush I have on my wife, the one that increasingly threatens my sanity.

Seeing that ring on her finger this morning almost had me on my knees, offering her a lot of things I have no business offering her.

But come on, when I opened that box and found a daisy made of diamonds nestled against the velvet I knew the universe was fucking with me. If I *had* ever actually proposed to Lee then it's the ring I would have chosen. It looks so right on her finger it makes me want to howl. Honestly, everything about this woman has me feeling feral. I'm slightly concerned about what the next full moon will bring. It's possible she's *awoken* something in me.

'Alert! Alert!' Rita comes barrelling back towards us, her phone clutched in her hand. 'The Operation Wedded Bliss group chat is hopping! Your lawyer guy's wandering around downtown and Ern's keeping him busy at the hardware store but he's going to pass by here any minute, so you two need to start looking way more married.'

'What does that even mean?' I ask. 'We're sitting right next to each other.' It's bad enough that whenever we're in public together Phoebe is constantly making sure Lee and I are holding hands, I don't need Rita micromanaging me as well.

Rita rolls her eyes at me. 'Good lord, Nico, it's no wonder you can't get a date.'

'Hey!' I protest. 'Just because I *haven't* been dating doesn't mean I *couldn't* if I wanted to.'

Tara and Luke are already pushing away from the table.

'It'll look more convincing if it's just the two of you,' Tara says innocently. 'Me and Luke are going to go and check out . . . the bookstore again.'

'Yup,' Luke nods eagerly. 'Don't worry, you guys. I'll make sure Tara gets home safely.'

'Such a gentleman,' Tara murmurs. 'We're still on for dinner?' she asks Lee. 'You're not sick of me yet?'

'Stop by around six.'

'Nico! Get your arm around your wife RIGHT NOW!' Rita snaps as our best friends melt into the distance, their hands almost touching. 'I can't believe you young people today, do you need me to tell you how to do *everything*?'

'I think we've got it from here,' I grit out.

With another huff Rita leaves. Ern's hardware store is a few shops down from Scoops, and we're sitting at one of the small pastel pink tables in the long window facing onto the street. If he's coming this way then Rita's right that Charles is going to get a great view of us.

'You ready?' I ask Lee, being very careful about our communication here. We haven't talked about the physical contact issue since the kiss.

She turns towards me, a look of determination in her eyes.

'We did a rubbish job this morning,' she says. 'So let's make this count. Get your hands on me!'

She blurts the last words and then winces, but that is all the encouragement I need. It's for the *ruse*, I tell myself. I'm *supposed* to look like I want to lift her up onto this table and do unspeakable things to her.

I push my chair back and reach for Lee's, grabbing the edge of her seat and dragging the whole thing across the floor so that she sits with her legs at an angle, caged between mine.

She lets out a little squeak of surprise and her hand drops to my thigh, the diamond ring on her wedding finger catching the light.

The wolf that apparently now lives inside me approves of this situation greatly.

I drape my arm around the back of her chair, and toy with the ends of her hair. She has it down today, a silky fall of honey-coloured waves.

'How's this?' I ask in a low voice, leaning in so that my face is closer to hers.

'Mmm,' she murmurs, and when she turns towards me, I can see every shade of blue in her eyes, the slightly darker ring around her iris. So pretty.

She leans further into me, her hand grazing higher up my thigh.

A low sound hums in my chest. 'Daisy,' I rasp, and our noses brush. I'm half a breath away from taking her mouth with mine, and I know there are reasons I shouldn't, but right now I can't for the life of me think what they are.

'Yes, Nico,' she whispers, and I don't know if it's a question or permission. Her eyes round as she looks past me through the window. 'He's coming,' she breathes.

She said I could kiss her, I remember that very clearly. *Kiss me like you mean it.* Oh, I can do that. I can *definitely* do that.

I cup her cheek, closing the tiny distance between us. The first touch of her mouth is soft, tentative, but I'm no passive participant this time, and I want *more*. I want *everything*. I cradle the back of her head, bury my hand in her hair, and trace the seam of her lips with my tongue. With a small, surprised gasp, her mouth opens and I sink into her. She's soft and lush and she tastes like strawberry ice cream. Dimly, I hear the bell ring over the door. Her fingers curl into my thigh, and I rumble appreciatively against the sweet, sensitive corner of her mouth.

'Ahem.' A sound interrupts us, and Lee jerks back, away from me, blinking like she's waking up from a dream.

Standing about two feet away is Charles Saunders, his face

impassive as he looks down at us. As we put on that entire show for his benefit I shouldn't be feeling so annoyed by his interruption, but I am and my whole body crackles with frustration. It wasn't enough. It wasn't close to enough. A drop of water in an ocean of need and longing.

Then Charles frowns and steps back. 'Good grief!' he exclaims.

I follow his gaze to the window, and there, leering at us through the glass, is an enormous black crow. His beady eyes move from Lee to me and back.

'Oh my god,' Lee whispers. 'It's really him . . .' She looks rumpled and flushed, like she's just had all the sense kissed out of her.

I rap my knuckles against the glass until the bird grudgingly flaps away.

'He's a pervert,' Lee tells Charles, still sounding dazed. 'The crow. Russell.'

There's a pause.

'I see,' Charles says. He clears his throat again. 'Anyway . . . I was just passing, and I saw you in here. I wanted to apologise once more for the mix up this morning.'

I glance over at Lee and she's summoned up a smile. I have no idea what she's thinking. I had all but forgotten this man's existence, but maybe she really did only kiss me so that he could see? That was the plan, right? Maybe she's not as completely turned around by it as I am?

This is exactly why this whole mess is so complicated.

'Really it's no problem,' Lee says smoothly. 'I'm only sorry we weren't at our best.'

Charles gives a thin smile. 'I'm not here for your best, Ms Turner-Jones. Just as an impartial third party observer. It would be helpful if you continued to live as you usually do.'

'Is this the sort of work *you* usually do?' I ask, leaning back in my chair and crossing my arms. I know I sound belligerent, but I can't help it.

'No.' Charles fixes his steady gaze on me. 'However, your father was one of our most valued clients, and he made the request personally before his death. These are exceptional circumstances, and as we continue to act in the interests of the estate, your brother—'

'Half-brother,' I correct him, because I can probably count on one hand the number of times I've spoken to Ward – or his younger brother Rupert – since my parents' divorce.

'Your *half-brother*,' Charles tilts his head in acknowledgement, 'the new duke, considers it a priority and is *keen* to resolve this matter as soon as possible.' He gives me a significant look from under his brows.

'As are we,' Lee says, placing a warning hand on my knee before I can say what I think about the new duke and his priorities. The man who employs Charles Saunders has every reason to want me to fail. It hardly seems like a fair deal.

'Please,' she continues, 'do let us know if there's anything we can do to be of assistance while you're here. I've compiled all the documents relating to our marriage and the housing agreement with Magda, as well as the paperwork from Phoebe's school, should you require copies of those.'

She has? I feel steadier, just listening to her talk, and there might even be a glimmer of approval in Charles's eyes. My super-organised wife. Now that she's had time to prepare, she's playing the part beautifully – even without the shoulder pads.

'Thank you,' Charles manages to say, before Rita comes bustling over.

'Lee, Nico!' she exclaims, several decibels too loud. 'My very favourite married couple! Who do we have here?'

She turns and wags her finger at Charles.

'You must be new, everyone around here knows better than to interrupt these two when they're canoodling. Still like a pair of newlyweds, one year in! I ALWAYS say that their love for each other is like something OUT OF A ROMANCE NOVEL.' She's yelling directly into his face by the end of this tirade.

I can feel my eye twitching as Lee jumps in to make the introductions.

'How are you liking our town, in which both Lee and Nico are pillars of the community?' Rita asks casually.

'It's charming,' Charles declares. 'And the people have been making me feel very welcome. Magda and Phoebe took me for breakfast at Bean & Gone, and the owner was extremely friendly. She seemed quite keen to talk about Nico's volunteer work.'

'My . . .' I trail off.

'With the ORPHANS,' Rita jumps in.

A frown puckers Charles's brow. 'I understood it was something to do with rehoming animals?'

Rita's eyes widen and she sneaks a look at the phone clasped in her hand. 'Oh,' she mutters, 'I thought we'd agreed . . .' Her head snaps up and her smile broadens. 'The PUPPIES. Of course. But so many of them are orphans, aren't they, Nico?'

'I—' I look at Lee in desperation.

'Taco, who you met this morning, is one of the dogs that Nico took a special interest in,' she jumps in and I nod. This isn't even a lie. I am very interested in Taco. I love that little shit, and I guess as a stray it's possible he is an orphan . . . well, was. *I'm* his father now.

'Yes, he's a very interesting . . . dog,' Charles says doubtfully. 'My ex-wife had one a bit like him, a sweet, simple creature.'

I bristle at this. Taco is not simple. If anything, he's *too clever* for typical training methods. They're not challenging him enough. I'm ninety per cent certain that if I really tried I could teach him how to read.

Fortunately, while I've been internally raging over this slight towards my dog, the conversation has moved on. '. . . Ern showed me a significant number of different hammers despite my explaining that I had very little experience with DIY.' Charles sounds bemused now. 'Honestly, I had no idea there were so many, but he was certainly very passionate and knowledgeable on the subject. He must have spoken about them for a solid fifteen minutes.'

I wonder how many times Ern said *yes, and.*

'That's Ern!' Rita manages. 'He's always been very . . . passionate . . . about . . . hammers.' The woman is undoubtedly about to start giggling, so it's lucky that Charles says his goodbyes, reiterating that we'll hear from his assistant in the coming days.

'In the meantime, I wouldn't worry,' he says. 'I'll be keeping a low profile. Just a fly on the wall. You'll *hardly know I'm here*.' Again he gives me another significant look.

'Great,' I agree, even though that actually sounds very creepy.

Still, whether we want them or not we seem to have a town-wide network of not-at-all covert spies who will know where the lawyer is at all times. This fact is underlined by Rita recording a voice note the moment Charles leaves the ice cream parlour.

'The crumpet has left the nest,' she hisses into her phone. 'Repeat, the crumpet is on the move!'

There is zero chance we're pulling this off.

I look at Lee, my pretend wife, who I *really* kissed only a few minutes ago. My best friend's sister, and the woman who is driving me out of my mind. The woman I'll be sharing a bed with tonight.

Yup. We're doomed.

Chapter Twenty-Eight

Lee

The next morning I wake up in a state of bliss. Which is to say, I wake up in Nico's arms.

Last night, after a long and very fun dinner with Phoebe and Tara (and yes, Luke, who arrived holding her hand and looking at her like she was made of diamonds), the pair of us had been extremely polite and formal about our sleeping arrangements.

After we'd both used the bathroom – where we changed into our pyjamas – I politely offered him his choice of side of the bed, he politely demurred to me, and this went on for a while before we slipped quietly under the sheets, both clinging to our separate edges of the mattress, a wide gulf of bed linen between us.

Then Nico turned out the light and I lay there for ages obsessing over the fact that he was in bed with me, and I could hear him breathing, when only a few hours earlier he had kissed me. Actually kissed me. Not that either of us had mentioned it.

We'd certainly showed Charles, though. And that was the whole point.

Right?

Eventually, I *must* have fallen asleep because I wake up, and even though the room is in gloomy darkness, it feels like a morning kind of gloom. I'm not lying at the edge of the bed anymore, I'm right in the middle of it, and I'm wound around Nico like an invasive plant species.

My head is tucked under his jaw, my cheek resting on his chest, one arm flung over his torso as he lies on his back. One of my legs is thrown over his, so I'm basically straddling his thigh. His hand, large and warm, cups my backside.

I don't move. I hardly dare to breathe. I have no idea if Nico is still asleep or not. When his chest continues to rise and fall in a steady rhythm, I relax a bit, let myself enjoy this, the feeling of being held by him. Unfortunately, the hand he has on my ass is extremely distracting, and when I move, he makes a sleepy sound, pulling me even closer. The pressure of his thigh between my legs increases and I swallow a gasp.

Nico's fingers flex, digging into my flesh, and he mutters again. He rolls over, taking me with him, and now his front is plastered to my back, his heavy arm pinning me to the mattress as he spoons me. At this point it becomes *very* apparent that I am not the only one at the mercy of their hormones, because the long, hard length of him is pressed against me, so close to where I want him, that this time, when his hips move, rocking against me, I do make a sound – a sort of pained whimper.

There's a brief, charged silence, and his breath catches. *Is he awake?*

He makes the same movement again, the same lazy thrust, and I keep my eyes tightly closed. I'm pretty sure he's awake, but right now both of us have plausible deniability, and I have no intention of putting a stop to things. Instead, I grind lightly against him, and he's the one who makes a noise, a slow hiss of air between his teeth.

When his arm shifts, his hand coming to rest, flat against my abdomen, I wonder just how far we can take this, lying here in the quiet and the dark. He nuzzles at my neck and I stretch, lean back, giving him better access. His lips trail a gentle line along my nape, his teeth scraping against the tender skin there. His hand slips down, lower, lower, his index finger dips beneath the waistband of my pyjamas . . .

A sudden banging on the door has us springing apart.

'It's six a.m.!' Phoebe yells. 'Rise and shine!'

'Waaa,' I make an inelegant noise, levering myself up into a seated position just as the alarm on my phone starts blaring. I smash around on the nightstand until it turns off.

Beside me, Nico sits up, looking as shell-shocked as I feel.

'Good morning,' he says, his voice a low rasp in his throat.

'*Early* morning.' My response is bright. Too bright? 'Remind me who thought it would be a good idea to be up at six a.m. on a Sunday?'

'That would be you,' Nico says, scrubbing a hand over his face. 'You're the one who wanted to go up to the overlook and catch the sunrise.'

'Only because you and Phoebe said it was so beautiful,' I protest.

Nico only grunts. 'Why don't you use the bathroom first?' He shifts his weight, pulling at the sheets, and *of course* my eyes drop instantly to his crotch.

'Yup!' I agree, leaping out of bed while my cheeks flame. I grab the pile of clothes I'd already laid out for this morning. 'I'll be quick, don't worry.'

'No rush,' I hear him murmur dryly as I close the door to the bathroom.

I stand with my forehead pressed against it for a moment. Did that really just happen?

By the time I emerge, dressed in black wool trousers and a thick, cream jumper, Nico seems to have got his *situation* under control because he's out of bed and rooting around in the closet.

'Magda has some walking boots out by the front door,' he says over his shoulder. 'With a pair of thick socks, they should work.

There's a bit of a climb up to the lookout. It's not far, but it'll be tricky in your stilettos.'

'Thanks,' I manage, slipping out the room as fast as humanly possible.

'*There* you are,' Phoebe grumbles, while Taco dances excitedly around her feet. 'This was *your* idea, remember.'

'I know, I know,' I agree, flustered. 'But you only just beat the alarm on my phone so . . .'

Phoebe digs out Magda's boots from the pile by the door, and I pull them on. They're a tiny bit big, but they'll do.

'Okay.' Nico comes blasting out the bedroom, dressed in the sort of thick grey woollen jumper that has me writing fisherman fantasies in my head featuring storms outside the window of a small stone cottage and a fire crackling in the hearth as we slowly remove our – oh no! – soaking wet clothes.

His dark curls are dishevelled, the stubble along his jaw could almost be called a beard at this point and a green canvas backpack is thrown over one shoulder. He stalks through to the kitchen, setting a flask under the coffee machine and pressing buttons, before grabbing cereal bars and bottled water and throwing them into his bag. This level of efficiency is really doing it for me.

He screws the lid on the flask. 'Let's get going, we don't want to miss it.'

We pile into the truck and a fifteen-minute drive later we're winding up the steep side of one of the hills that flanks the town. At the top of the road, there's a small car park, and we're the only ones there.

Phoebe and Taco lead the way, already familiar with this route, and Nico and I linger behind. The gloom is lifting, and the world is draped in an unpromising grey as we follow the dusty footpath, carved between lumbering rocks and scrubby undergrowth. So far Nico and I have not said one single word to each other, and I'm busy trying to convince myself that it's because we've fallen into a companionable silence, rather than because we're both feeling awkward about what happened in his bed.

I concentrate on putting one foot in front of the other as the path grows steeper, and when I stumble over an exposed root, Nico's hand is instantly there, in the small of my back, steadying me. The brief moment of contact has me sucking in a sharp breath, and he pulls away at once.

After a couple of minutes, we round a corner, and the world drops away almost underneath our feet, the view suddenly opening up, a wide and dazzling panorama.

'Oh!' I exclaim, unable to come up with anything more eloquent.

'Just wait,' Nico murmurs, his face turned towards the scene below: the rolling blanket of trees gilded with gold and amber, tumbling down towards the sea, Roseport laid out like a toy town in the middle of it all. He squints out at the horizon where the first, sleepy light of the day gathers, smouldering like embers in a grate.

'I saved you a seat,' Phoebe calls, patting the space beside her on the simple stone bench where she sits, Taco at her feet.

I drop down beside her, burrowing further into my coat as the wind whips around us.

'Chocolate milk for you,' Nico says, holding out a carton to Phoebe, who happily accepts.

'And coffee for you.' He pulls out the flask and pours me a cup, strong and dark in an enamel mug. I cradle it in my hands enjoying the warmth, trying to take in every detail of the scene in front of me. Minute by minute, the light is intensifying, streaks of pink and orange paint the sky, and it's so beautiful it doesn't look real.

Nico still hasn't sat down, and he roots around in his rucksack a moment before he pulls out what is undeniably a camera case.

I freeze, whipping my gaze forward again, determined not to make a big deal of this.

Aside from a blink-and-you'd-miss-it moment of hesitation, there's nothing about Nico to justify my concern. He handles the camera easily, moving quietly around, the only sound the rapid click of the shutter.

As the minutes pass, and the light pours over us like water, Nico's posture relaxes more and more. He climbs up onto a rock at the edge of the drop, his step sure and steady as he pauses to adjust some of the settings on his camera.

'Are you going to take one of us?' Phoebe calls after a few minutes, seemingly unaware of or unbothered by the significance of this moment.

'I am.' Nico jumps down, while Phoebe gets to her feet, encouraging Taco to pose in front of the view. The two of them look so cute together, and I see Nico smile from behind his lens.

I lean forward, my elbow on my knee, my chin resting in my hand as I look at them, the three of them together. I watch while Nico calls out instructions, and Taco jumps up to lick Phoebe's face, while she giggles, and the whole world unfurls glowing and beautiful below them, and I feel for a moment like my heart is going to burst.

That's the instant that Nico captures with his camera, the instant before I draw back, embarrassed that he's turned the focus on me.

'Come and stand with us, Lee,' Phoebe demands. 'I bet *you* can get Taco to sit properly.'

'Can you take a selfie with that fancy camera of yours?' I ask Nico.

'Let's find out,' he grins, and he pulls me in tight while I sling an arm over Phoebe's thin shoulders, manoeuvring her in front of us, a triangle of smiling faces. 'Say flax seed,' Nico sings.

The sound of the shutter merges with our groans.

'Was it worth getting up early for?' Nico asks, his arms still around my waist.

I look up at him. The wind is ruffling his hair, his smile is wide, I can feel his giddy pleasure in this moment. Something important just happened.

'Yes. It was worth it,' I say.

Chapter Twenty-Nine

Lee

'Did you say "wow it's beautiful", while looking at the view, and then he said "yes it is" but when you turned around he was actually looking at you?' Tara asks, her eyes wide.

'What? No.'

My best friend groans. 'Such a wasted opportunity.'

'I have to agree.' Kat leans across the table to grab a nacho. 'It feels like the scene really called for it.'

'Again,' I sip at the pink, frothy drink that Mei returned from the bar with a couple of minutes ago, 'I'd love it if you stopped trying to turn my life into a romance novel.'

'Babe,' Tara sounds exasperated. 'We're not *trying*, this is happening.'

'If it was actually happening then wouldn't Nico have made some sort of move by now?' I blurt out.

The three women look at me with sympathy. When Tara texted me this morning saying that we needed to have my long-promised girls' night at Darlene's, I'd been relieved. My situation with Nico is so complicated, and for the first time, I have friends who I can actually talk to about this stuff. At first I was worried about Kat and Mei's obvious loyalty to Nico, but Mei had held my hand and looked me dead in the eye.

'This,' she said, gesturing around the bar, 'is a safe space. Tonight is girls' night. The four of us are entering into a sacred covenant. You can tell us anything and we will be completely on your side. Anything at all. Please. We're actually dying for all the juicy details.'

'*Dying*,' Kat chimed in.

So I gave in and spilled the whole story.

We're sitting at one of the high tables next to the juke box, and tonight is a highlight in Roseport's social calendar – the monthly 'Dollyoke' night, when Darlene and her patrons get up to perform stirring renditions from Dolly's extensive catalogue. In honour of this special occasion, Kat took me to Target (which I loved) and the four of us are decked out in denim and matching pink cowboy hats. I even found a pair of shiny gold cowboy boots that Kat insisted I must have. They are definitely made of plastic and they pinch my toes, but I love them.

When I looked in the mirror before I left I barely recognised myself, but what I couldn't miss was my wide smile, the excitement in my eyes.

'So what about the last few days?' Mei asks now. 'After the whole sunrise hike?'

I shrug. 'Nothing. Every morning Nico's been gone before I wake up.' This is presumably so that we don't have a repeat of Sunday, but as I've withheld the details on that particular incident, I keep that part to myself. 'Sometimes I get a text saying that Charles is in a specific place and the two of us will rush over so that we "happen" to bump into him.'

'Oh yeah, I heard about the run-in at the grocery store,' Kat says, and I'm fairly sure she's trying not to laugh.

'It wouldn't have been so bad if Rita and her pals hadn't put together that little decoy shopping basket and shoved it into my arms just as he arrived.' I take another deep slug of my drink, wincing at the memory.

'Wait, why would they do that?' Tara asks, understandably puzzled.

Kat leans forward, unable to hide her smirk. 'I think the idea was to have Charles see what was in there, right?'

'Oh god,' Mei whispers. 'What *was* in there?'

'I don't want to talk about it.' I drop my head to rest on the tabletop.

'You have to tell us now!' Tara shakes my arm until I sit back up.

'A giant box of extra-large condoms, a bag of kale, a copy of the *Financial Times* and an energy drink,' I list, ticking each one off on my fingers and remembering the wild look in Nico's eyes as we'd watched the items sail along the conveyor belt in front of Charles's startled face.

All three of them burst out laughing.

'It certainly tells a story,' Mei grins.

I groan again, and Tara pulls me in for a reassuring sideways hug.

'But aside from the town's schemes, we haven't been alone together for days,' I carry on mournfully. 'If Phoebe isn't there, then his mum is around, or Magda, or Charles. I can't tell if he's avoiding me or not.'

'It sounds to me,' Tara says, 'like Nico might be waiting for *you* to make a move.'

'What do you mean?' I ask, exasperated. 'I kissed him! I kissed him right on the mouth! Twice!'

'Okayyy.' Mei tilts her head. 'But have you considered that men are . . .' she casts around for the right words. 'Useless?' she settles on finally. 'Devoid of emotional intelligence? Uneducated in the language of subtlety?'

'I think what Mei is trying to say is that Nico might have thought the whole kissing thing really *was* just part of the act,' Kat says more diplomatically.

'How much more obvious can I be!' I exclaim. 'It's humiliating at this point.'

'Again,' Mei gestures widely with her drink in her hand, 'Men. Simple. Have you actually said, "Nico, I want to get in your pants?"'

'Not *out loud*,' I say, horrified by the very idea. 'But there have been signs. Clear signs. He must not be interested.'

All three of them start laughing again.

'Girl,' Kat shakes her head, 'Nico is so into you that he might as well be walking around wearing a T-shirt with your face on it.'

I try to suppress the flutter of excitement I feel. 'But he's supposed to be acting like that, remember? He's *supposed* to be my husband.'

'The Roseport Players made him audition for Shakespeare in the Park this past summer,' Mei grimaces. 'Trust me, the man isn't that good an actor.'

'Did they really?' I ask, temporarily diverted.

'Mei has a video on her phone,' Kat grins evilly. 'It's painful to watch. Let's just say Nico doesn't have the skill to pull off the role of "Lee's husband" the way he has been.'

'Luke thinks he's a mess over you,' Tara puts in, slurping her cocktail – which is apparently called a pink squirrel – through her straw.

'Nico mentioned something to Luke?'

'Definitely,' Tara nods. 'I haven't been able to get the whole story . . . apparently the men have their own sacred covenant, but from what he's let slip it's obvious Nico's all tied in knots. I think if you want anything to happen then you're going to have to take charge of the situation.'

'Tell him how you feel,' Kat begs.

'Then grab him and stick your tongue down his throat,' Tara advises.

'And he'll probably get the message,' Mei weighs in, before narrowing her eyes. 'Although I wouldn't count on it.'

I take another long sip of my pink squirrel. I have no idea what's in it; it tastes like a dessert, sweet and innocent. I know it's not too strong because we all agreed that getting drunk on a school night was unwise. Darlene suggested these were the perfect solution, just enough for a happy buzz, and I trust her bartending judgement. Plus, they feel festive.

'Maybe,' I say finally. 'But that's enough about me and Nico for a minute. Can we talk about Tara and Luke?'

'Yesssss!' Mei slams her hand down on the table.

'I'm conflicted about this one but in the spirit of girls' night, I'll allow it,' Kat points a finger at Tara, 'but no grisly details.'

'I want all the grisly details,' Mei and I say at the same time.

Tara smiles a wide, Cheshire cat grin. 'Ladies, let me tell you, that man has the best hands . . .'

'Gahhhhhh!' Kat covers her face. 'Immediately too much, Tara. *Immediately*.'

My friend giggles, and she looks so happy that I might even temporarily be able to put my own romantic worries out of my mind.

'I knew it was all about to kick off the second you saw each other,' I say smugly.

'Was it that obvious?' Tara asks.

'Well, you do start humming "Cowboy Take Me Away" every time you see him,' I say.

Tara's mouth drops open. 'I thought that was happening in my head.'

'I get it.' Mei scoops up another nacho. 'It's easy to imagine Luke as a sexy sheriff. If you're into that sort of thing.'

'Gross,' Kat grumbles, but Tara is nodding eagerly.

'Right?' she says. 'I'm trying to convince him that he needs a Stetson.' She flicks a glance at me. 'He actually asked if I'd consider changing my flight home, maybe stay a bit longer. What do you think?'

'Are you kidding?' I exclaim. 'Of course you should stay, and not even because the sexy sheriff asked you to. *I* want you here, I just didn't know it was an option.'

'We're all just fine with *sexy sheriff* now, are we?' Kat huffs.

'Sorry,' I say. 'We'll wait until you're in the bathroom to talk about your hot brother like the respectful friends we are.'

'That's all I ask,' Kat replies.

'So you're going to stay a bit longer?' Mei asks Tara, who nods. 'Then I think we should definitely celebrate with another round of pink squirrels.'

'I'll help you.' Kat jumps up from her seat. 'I think I saw Tyler over by the bar earlier, and I want him to get a good look at me in this miniskirt.'

'God, that guy is the worst,' Mei mutters as the two of them disappear into the crowd. Clearly, Dollyoke is quite the event, because the place is packed tonight and we only have such a prime spot because Darlene put a hot pink 'Reserved' sign on the table for us.

'I'm so glad you're going to stay.' I give Tara's hand a squeeze. 'When do you think you'll head back?'

'I'm not sure,' she says and bites her lip. 'You know I can do most of my job remotely and my boss can't function without me, so he'll be fine. Another couple of weeks, maybe. After that . . .' She blows out a long breath. 'I know it's insane, I know I only met him a few days ago, but this thing with Luke . . . I don't want to jinx it, but I figure there's no harm in sticking around, to see if there's anything there.'

I experience a pang of jealousy at her words, at the way she feels free to explore her feelings for Luke.

'What about you?' Tara says. 'How long will you stay?'

'The trustee is due to leave on the fourth of November,' I say, fiddling with the edge of a beer mat.

'That's not what I asked.' Tara's voice is soft.

I shrug. 'That's the answer, though. I've booked my flight. I can't stay in Roseport, I have to get home.'

'To your grandmother?'

I nod. 'She's not the only reason, but she's the main one.'

'Are you two talking yet?' Tara asks, her voice laced with sympathy. She may not have been in my life as long as Nico, but she knows me well enough to understand how important my relationship with Gran is.

'We've been texting. I keep thinking I should call her,' I say. 'But somehow the longer it goes without us talking, the harder it is. This silly argument seems to have taken on a life of its own. And she doesn't know I'm here, doesn't know about Nico. I'm not even sure what I'd tell her.' I summon up a weak smile. 'It's less than ten days until this whole situation is all sorted and I'm back home. I suppose we can talk about it then.'

'If you only have ten days left here, don't you think you should make them count?' Tara asks.

'What do you mean?'

She gives me a long look. 'You know exactly what I mean.'

Fortunately for me, my phone pings and I turn it over. 'It's another text from Adrian,' I tell Tara with a frown. 'I swear he texts me more now than he did before we broke up.'

'Are you sure he got the message?' She sips her drink.

'Definitely,' I nod. 'He was really nice about it.' But . . . was he *too* nice about it? I honestly don't think he was that attached to the relationship, but have I got it wrong?

My concerns are interrupted when Kat and Mei return, both carrying a cocktail in each hand.

'That asshole,' Kat fumes, hopping up onto her seat. 'I swear to god, this is the last time I even look in his direction.'

'Tyler's here with a date,' Mei murmurs.

'What a bastard,' Tara leaps in immediately.

'I hate him,' I growl. 'I knew he was the worst.'

'Me too,' Tara agrees. 'I've always said that.'

'You haven't even met him.' Kat manages a small smile.

'As if we need to actually *meet* him,' Tara huffs. 'Gross.'

There's a screech of feedback then as Darlene takes to the stage. 'Good evenin', friends,' she says into the microphone. She's resplendent in a tightly fitted white jumpsuit covered in rhinestones, her hair teased high. The whole room starts cheering.

'Welcome to Dollyoke,' Darlene continues when we simmer down. 'Make sure you have your name down with Randall if you want to sing . . . it looks like we've got a pretty full ticket tonight.'

'Don't worry,' Kat leans across the table, 'I already put us down for multiple songs.'

'Excellent,' Tara approves while I clutch my pink squirrel.

'What? To sing them?'

'No, to represent them through the medium of interpretive dance.' Kat rolls her eyes at me. 'Of course to sing them.'

'Absolutely not.'

She turns her big eyes on me. 'Lee, I need this tonight. The only thing that's going to get me through is Dolly and my girls.'

'Oh no,' I whisper as the truth sinks in. '*We're* your girls.'

How has this occurred? What happened to successfully lone-wolfing my way through life? This is what comes of making friends . . . one day everything is fine and normal and the next you're doing Dolly Parton karaoke in a pink cowboy hat.

'I'd advise you to start sucking down that pink squirrel,' Mei says kindly. 'It'll go a lot easier.'

'Don't worry,' Kat says brightly. 'I didn't put you down for a solo performance, I'm not a *monster*.'

'Right,' I manage. 'That's fine then.'

At that moment, Darlene launches into a pitch-perfect rendition of 'Jolene', and I get so caught up that when it's time to perform '9 to 5' I actually let my friends drag me up with them. Sure, I stand at the back, far away from the microphone, mostly laughing as Kat and Tara ham it up for the crowd, but I still do it. And I only hate ninety-five per cent of it. There is a tiny five per cent sliver of me that can admit to having fun, which is completely mind-blowing.

The crowd cheers. People shout out words of encouragement – they call my name, and I recognise so many faces and it feels . . . nice? There's a warm glow in my chest and I'm not sure I can blame whatever Darlene's putting in these pink drinks.

Other people get up to sing. Tara belts out an excellent version of 'Harper Valley PTA', one of the most underappreciated Dolly numbers. Kat sings 'Here You Come Again', and somehow makes the whole thing sound like a threat directed pointedly at Tyler. Mei and I hoot and holler and dance in our seats.

When Darlene winds up the show with a storming performance of 'Dumb Blonde' the audience goes wild, but I'm distracted thinking about Nico again.

Perhaps Tara was right. If I only have a few days left with my husband . . . maybe it's time to start making them count.

Chapter Thirty

Nico

I'm not sure what I did in a past life to deserve this, but as I sit through this interminable dinner, forced to watch my mother flirt with the lawyer who has been sent to destroy my life, I'm guessing it was pretty bad. Like Vlad the Impaler bad.

'Oh, Charlie,' Claudia giggles, her hand lingering against his arm. 'That is *so* fascinating.'

As Charles had been talking about the importance of good estate planning, I think *fascinating* is a stretch, but he only looks at my mother with a small, dazed smile on his face.

I have to hand it to her, the seduction plan is working a treat. I just don't know if it's going to help or if – more likely – she's going to shatter his heart into a million pieces, leaving me worse off than ever.

The restaurant at the hotel where Ma and Charles are staying is all hushed piano music and crisp white table linens. After working late, I thought I was having a quiet mother-and-son dinner with Claudia, but she had other ideas, and now I'm on edge, trying to second guess what's going on behind Charles Saunders' professional mask.

'I interviewed Magda today,' Charles says, as he cuts his chicken, working neatly around his plate in a clockwise direction. 'She's very fond of you.'

I clear my throat. 'I feel the same way about her. She's done an incredible job raising Phoebe.'

'I can see that,' Charles concedes, and I feel some of the tension loosen its grip on my chest. 'And you and Ophelia seem to have taken to parenting very well.' He dabs at his mouth with his napkin. 'The two of you were already married when you found out about Phoebe, is that right?'

The tension is back, time to try not to trip over myself in this web of lies. 'That's right,' I say, attempting to sound casual. 'About a month.'

'Mmm.' Charles takes a mouthful of wine. 'And the wedding in Las Vegas, that was . . . a spontaneous decision?'

'Goodness no,' Claudia jumps in, leaning over to top up Charles's glass and offer him a look down her dress at the same time.

God, I could do with a whisky.

'Nico and Lee are a love story for the ages, Charlie! Written in the stars and decades in the making. You should have seen the way Lee followed Nico around when they were children. We called her his little shadow.' Her eyes have gone misty.

'The sweetest girl you've ever seen, but so shy. Like one of those nervous rescue animals that Nico works with,' she says airily, and I wince because this keeps coming up – the whole town has made me out to be Dr Dolittle, and yesterday someone thrust a small (and extremely vicious) kitten into my arms just as Charles rounded a corner.

I suppose I should be glad it wasn't the Gerbers' teacup pig as originally planned. That little bastard has surprisingly sharp teeth and a real shitty attitude.

'Lee knew straight away that my boy was special,' she continues. 'The *most* gentle soul. She felt safe with him, and I don't think she felt safe very often in those days. Then again, it went both ways … Nico was at his best when Lee was around. They balance each other out, always have.'

I'm surprised by this insight, and I think about Lee standing in my kitchen, telling me I was her safe place while also allowing me to open up about something I'd been carrying alone. It *does* go both ways.

'I'm just glad that Nico finally woke up and realised what he was missing.' My mother treats me to a long look over her wine glass. 'Only a real fool would let a woman like Lee get away.'

'Yes,' I say, mechanically. 'A real fool.'

'Good job you married her then,' Charles arcs a brow, 'otherwise I'd have to write that in my report.'

It's another hour before I can prise myself away, and despite the fact that my mum has been pouring drinks into the man all night, I still can't tell what Charles thinks about me.

He's spent the last few days fading into the background, popping up just often enough to keep my blood pressure elevated. As well as interviewing Magda more formally (as both my employer and Phoebe's other guardian), he's spoken to Mei about Phoebe and her education.

He dropped by the inn to see me at work and I gave him a tour while he made nondescript humming sounds and wrote things in his notebook. He set up an interview with Lee and me for Saturday, which marks the halfway point of his two-week visit. It already feels like he's been here for ever. I'm definitely not made for a life of deception.

It doesn't help that outside of our encounters with Charles I've been trying to keep a bit of distance from Lee. Every morning without fail I've woken up pressed against her, wanting nothing more than to pick up where we left off on Sunday, and every morning I've forced myself out of bed and into a cold shower instead.

I had a plan, dammit, and it was one that didn't end with Lee being hurt or confused so I'm sticking to it . . . even if my resolve is hanging on by a thread. At least tonight, with Phoebe at Magda's, I can stay in her room and give myself a break from having to try and sleep next to the woman of my increasingly lustful dreams. I'm totally exhausted and running exclusively on caffeine at this point.

As I turn off the highway I realise there's no point in going home. Lee's gone out with the girls tonight and I offered to pick her up. It's almost closing time at Darlene's so I head towards town instead, and I've only just pulled into the car park when my phone rings.

'Hello?'

'Nico!' Lee exclaims happily. 'You answered!'

'Of course I did.' I can't suppress a chuckle at how pleased she sounds. 'I'm outside waiting for you.'

'You're here?' She breaks off to talk to someone else. 'I'm coming out now, two minutes. Don't leave!'

'I'm not leaving. Does anyone else need a ride?'

'No, most people went when the Dollyoke finished. Kat and Mei already left, and Tara's staying here.' She lowers her voice to a whisper that somehow still manages to be very loud. 'Luke's coming over so they can have sex. Apparently Luke is *great* at sex.'

'I'll be sure to let him know,' I say dryly.

I get out the truck and stand, leaning against the door, my arms folded across my chest as I wait for Lee to appear. When she does, it takes me a second to recognise her.

I didn't see Lee before she went out, and part of me is glad about that because I don't know how I would have sat calmly through dinner with this particular image in my brain.

Her legs are totally bare apart from the briefest excuse for a denim miniskirt and a pair of gold cowboy boots. They've been paired with a matching denim waistcoat, snug fitting with a dangerously low neckline and a row of buttons marching down the front. Her hair is down, a sexy tumble of snaky waves, and there's glitter dusted on her cheeks. Instead of a coat she holds a pink cowboy hat in her hand.

I feel like I'm having an aneurysm.

'Hey, pretty girl,' I call before I can stop myself. 'Where's your coat?'

She spots me and her face lights up. She rushes over to me, grabbing my arm.

'Nico!' she whispers, and her eyes are sparkling. 'I did a crime! A very small crime!'

I'm already undoing my coat and slinging it round her, trying not to touch her bare skin, but it's hard . . . there's a lot of it.

I swallow. 'What do you mean a crime?'

She glances furtively around the car park, which is empty apart from the two of us. 'We mayonnaised Tyler's truck!' she blurts. 'He was out with some other girl even though he's been sniffing around Kat again, and so we wrote on his truck with one of Darlene's mayonnaise dispensers. Tara wrote "wanker", but I made her change it to "banker" because that would be too much of a clue that the British girls were behind it! And everyone hates bankers!'

She looks so pleased with herself.

'Excellent work, my little mastermind,' I laugh, trying unsuccessfully to thread her arm through one of my sleeves.

She nods, biting her lower lip which is a deep rosy pink. 'I did leave some money under his windscreen wiper,' she confesses in a low voice. 'So he could pay to have it cleaned off. But don't tell the others.'

'Your secret's safe with me. Now, about your coat . . .'

'I don't have one,' she says. 'Kat said it would ruin the look. She was quite insistent that I wouldn't feel the cold later.' She glances around in surprise. 'And she was right.'

Her eyes flicker to mine. 'You called me pretty girl,' she says. 'You think I look pretty?'

She steps back, and my coat falls from her shoulders while she holds her arms out. I swallow again, and bend down to pick up my coat. This is a mistake as I'm treated to an up-close look at those legs, and I find I want to sink my teeth into her thigh.

'You look very pretty,' I say mechanically, and she doesn't seem appeased.

'It's because of the clothes,' she says, suddenly forlorn. 'Because I don't look like me.'

'No, Daisy.' I can't stand the look on her face. 'It's not the clothes. You always look pretty.'

She lifts her eyes and focuses on me with a startling intensity. 'Nico,' she says, her voice suddenly serious. 'I'm going to kiss you now. Not for pretend or practice.' Her gaze drops to my mouth. 'But because I want to.'

She starts towards me, and I'm frozen, my brain trying to catch up with what she just said.

I manage to hold up a hand, and she stops, right in front of me. 'Lee,' I croak.

'Don't you want to?'

'Of course I want to,' I grind out. 'But—'

I don't get any further because she drops her hat, reaches up and fists the front of my shirt, dragging my mouth down to hers.

And the entire world detonates.

There's absolutely nothing tentative about this kiss. It's open mouths and the stroke of her tongue against mine, the drag of her canine against my bottom lip, a husky whimper into my mouth as she presses herself against me.

My coat falls to the ground again as I lift one hand to cradle her head, my fingers spearing through her tangle of gold hair, pulling her closer. I spin us around, pressing her into the side of the truck, and she makes a sound of raw approval as I rock against her, my mouth devouring hers. Her legs come up around my hips, and I'm holding her up now, pinned between my body and the truck, my fingers digging into the backs of her thighs, the feel of her bare skin under my hands almost undoing me.

I kiss a delirious trail down the side of her neck. 'Honey,' I murmur, and my voice sounds like it's coming from far away, 'you always smell like honey.' I press my tongue to the hollow at the base of her throat and she moans, writhing against me.

'Nico,' she murmurs.

She pulls on my hair, dragging my mouth back to hers and I have no problem with that. This kiss is a demand, she knows what she wants and I'm happy to give it to her, to give her anything, everything.

It's only when her hand dips between us, towards my belt, that I come briefly back to my senses. I pull away too fast, and Lee stumbles. I reach out to steady her, my fingers wrapped around her arm and her back against the truck as she blinks up at me.

Both our chests are heaving. Her mouth is swollen, her eyes enormous. The top button of her waistcoat is undone and I have no memory of doing that. There's a glimpse of black lace on display and a low, wild sound rumbles through my head. At least I hope it's in my head.

We're parked in the middle of town, right outside Darlene's where anyone could walk by, and she's been drinking.

Fuck.

My gaze drops to Lee's legs, and the impression of my belt buckle is pressed into the tender skin on the inside of her thigh. Something about that is so obscene and such a turn on that my brain fogs again. I want to run my fingers over those pink lines, to soothe them away with my tongue.

'I'm sorry,' I force out. 'I shouldn't have let things get so out of hand.'

'I'm not sorry,' Lee says quietly. 'I want to be out of hand with you.'

I step forward, tucking a strand of hair behind her ear, letting my fingers trace a slow, deliberate line along the side of her throat.

'Tomorrow,' I say in a low voice. 'When you're not full of alcohol, you and I need to have a talk about this.'

'About my neck?' she murmurs, dazed.

I feel my mouth kick up. 'About every fucking inch of you, Daisy.' I scoop up my coat and her silly pink hat. 'Now, get in the car.'

Chapter Thirty-One

Lee

By the time Nico opens the front door I'm still jittering with adrenaline. I can hardly believe I've managed to make it inside on my own two feet, because my legs feel like they're made of rubber.

I knew that kissing Nico properly would be good. I didn't know that kissing Nico properly would be the sort of earth-shattering experience from which there was no coming back. I can still feel it, little aftershocks of need and pleasure rippling through my body.

There is no possible way he could kiss me like that if he wasn't interested. There was no one for us to perform for, no reason to pretend, no excuses between us – that was just Nico and me, and he wants this as much as I do. The thought has me giddy, I'm high on the sudden rush of complete confidence, a totally alien emotion.

'I need to grab a few things,' he says now. 'I'll sleep in Phoebe's room tonight.'

I spin to look at him in disbelief.

'What?' I manage. I want to kiss him so badly that I don't realise I'm actually walking towards him to do it until he puts out a hand to ward me off.

'Hold up, let's get you some water.'

My mouth drops open. 'I don't want water,' I say slowly. 'I want sex. With you.' Maybe Mei is right and he really needs me to spell this out for him? 'I want to have sex with you,' I enunciate clearly. 'Right now.'

He lifts a hand to his eyes. 'Fucking hell,' I hear him mutter as he turns and goes to get me a glass of water. When he returns I haven't moved.

His jaw is tense as he holds out the glass to me. 'Drink this.'

I frown. 'I don't understand what's going on. It seemed like you wanted to . . .'

His eyes are dark, his mouth set in a firm line. 'I told you already, we'll talk about this tomorrow.'

'I want to talk about it now.' I ease closer and he takes a step back like he's scared of me.

'Lee,' he says firmly. 'You've been drinking. I'm not touching you tonight.'

'But . . .' I frown, sorting through this. 'I consent. I consent wholeheartedly. I am a fully consenting, very enthusiastic participant in this arrangement.' I gesture between the two of us with my hand. And it's true! I might have a little bit of a buzz, enough to give me some Dutch courage, but I'm not drunk . . . it's a school night! I stopped drinking well over an hour ago.

I know my own mind and what I want. And what I want is Nico and his hands all over me. 'I'm not drunk. It's very nice of you to be concerned, but I'm really not!'

I wonder if I should stand on one leg or recite the alphabet backwards or something?

'Not. Touching. You,' he says again.

The confidence falls away and cold doubt crawls over me. Did I read it wrong after all? I'm offering myself up on a platter here and he's turning me down.

'I can't believe this,' I murmur, finally accepting the water from him and holding it in front of me.

'If it makes you feel better, neither can I,' Nico says, and he sounds grumpy.

My phone buzzes and I pull it out of the pocket of my microscopic miniskirt.

'Who is it?' Nico asks.

'It's Adrian again,' I sigh, reading the message.

I'm in New York for work. Maybe we could meet up for the weekend somewhere? I'd love to take you for dinner. Xx

My heart sinks. Oh god, that definitely doesn't feel like a *friendly* message, does it? Is he hoping we'll get back together?

When I glance up from my phone, Nico is looking at me through narrowed eyes. 'Who *is* Adrian?' he asks and it probably makes me a bad person but I can't help the thrill that runs through me when I detect a hint of jealousy in his voice.

'He's a man I was seeing, in London,' I say casually, slipping the phone back into my pocket.

'*Was* seeing,' Nico repeats carefully.

'Well, I wouldn't be here doing my best to get you into bed if I was with someone, would I?' I snap, and something like amusement lights Nico's eyes.

'No, I suppose not.' He takes a step towards me. 'But he's still texting you?'

I frown down at my phone. 'Yes, a bit. I should probably put a stop to it but I don't want to be rude. What would I even say?'

Our gazes tangle for a long moment, then Nico steps even closer, towering over me, invading my space. My face is tipped back to look at him, and it feels like I'm exposing my throat to a predator. I swear

I see a flash of hunger in his eyes as he lowers his head, as his mouth traces the line of my neck so lightly that I'm not sure if he's actually touching me, or if the featherlike sensation is his breath skating over my skin. Finally, his lips are next to my ear.

'Tell him you're married,' Nico says in a voice like velvet rubbed against the grain. 'And that your husband doesn't share.'

Oh.

I catch my breath, ready to swoon into his arms, ready to be ravished like some sort of historical romance heroine. I give in. Tara was right. I can't even be mad about it.

Only instead of ravishing me, Nico wraps his fingers around the glass in my hand and drags it up until I'm holding it to my lips. 'Now drink the fucking water, Daisy.'

I blink at him, my mouth hanging open. When he continues to frown at me, I sip from the glass, then I turn and head for the bedroom, shutting myself into the bathroom with a sulky click of the door.

'You'll be glad about this in the morning,' Nico says from the other side. 'You'll know I was right.'

'Not likely,' I mumble, yanking off my cowgirl outfit and slipping into the pyjamas I also bought at Target today. I curse myself for not taking the opportunity to buy sexy nightwear, but in my defence I didn't know Nico was going to force me to seduce him, and I have a weakness for cosy pyjamas. These ones are a soft cotton pair of shorts and a T-shirt, covered in tiny pumpkins.

In the bedroom, I can hear Nico moving around collecting his belongings and I brush my teeth with more vigour than usual. If I thought I was sexually frustrated before, it's nothing compared to whatever this is. I'm currently too annoyed to feel embarrassed, but I know that it's going to hit me later.

'Have you seen my headphones?' Nico calls, and then he mutters something about needing a soothing meditation.

'My AirPods are in the side of my carry-on,' I call back. Maybe he wants me, just not enough to actually do anything about it, not enough to cross the line from friendship into whatever this is. I shouldn't really be mad at him for that, but I am.

I'm so deep in thought that it takes approximately twenty seconds for me to realise what I've done, but it's twenty seconds too long. By the time I come skidding out of the bathroom, Nico has my bag out on the bed and is staring down at something in his hand, a thoughtful look in his eye.

'It's . . .' I start.

'Lee, it's been a while, but trust me, I know what this is.' He lifts the small air pulse vibrator so I can see it.

I swallow. As a sexually active woman who travels a lot, I have zero shame about the handy sex toy I carry in my luggage. For me it's as routine as packing my toothbrush. However, I was *not* prepared for the sight of it in Nico's hand. I was *not* prepared for the heat in his gaze when he turns to me. That look is back, the wolfish gleam in his eyes, and my body approves of it wholeheartedly, even as my emotions are pinballing all over the place.

He considers the toy for a moment, rubbing his thumb over the buttons. 'Have you been using this?' he asks, his tone conversational.

'What?'

'I was just wondering. Have you been using this here? In my bed? In my shower?'

'Maybe,' I manage.

He tilts his head, running his eyes over me. It's a look that I feel everywhere, and I squeeze my thighs together.

'And what did you think about?' He takes a step towards me. 'When you used your toy to get yourself off . . . did you think about me?'

I hesitate.

'Tell me,' he says. It's a demand, but there's the bite of something desperate underneath.

My tongue darts out to lick my suddenly dry lips. 'Y-yes,' I whisper.

He looks pleased by this confession. 'Good,' he murmurs, taking another step forward. I don't even realise I've moved as well, until my back hits the wall.

'So when I leave you here alone tonight,' he says, still in that mild tone, his hand coming up to rest on the wall by my face as he leans in. I turn my head, watching the flex of the muscles in his forearm, close enough for me to sink my teeth into. 'Are you going to use it then?'

My eyes slash back to his.

'Yes,' I admit, my fingers curling into the palms of my hands so that I don't reach for him.

He looks at me, something frantic thrashing in his stormy gaze.

'Still not going to touch me?' I whisper, the words a taunt and a challenge.

His jaw tics. 'No.'

But he wants to. It's in every taut line of him. He wants to touch me very badly. Whatever the reason is that he's stopping himself . . . it's not because he doesn't *want* me.

The realisation settles. I smile up at him. 'So you don't mind if I . . . take care of matters myself?'

Slowly, I reach out and take the vibrator from his hand. There's a gentle hum as I turn it on.

He inhales sharply. His expression is one of surprise. 'Now?' he asks.

'Now,' I agree.

The moment stretches between us. A dare thrown down.

I more than half expect him to leave, but he leans even closer, his body a welcome cage around mine. 'And will you be picturing my mouth on you, my fingers inside you when you come?'

Oh my god.

'Yes,' the word is little more than a breath of shared air.

There's another pause, a feeling like being suspended at the top of a rollercoaster, the instant before the freefall.

'Show me,' he says, somehow making the rough words a demand, a plea and a question all at the same time. His posture eases back, giving me a chance to escape.

But that's the last thing I want.

This time my smile is victorious. My fingers are shaking as I slip my hand into my shorts, and press the toy where I'm already wet and ready.

My eyes fly to his and Nico watches, his face impassive.

'Turn it up.' His voice is low.

There's a click as I press a button and I gasp as the intensity of the air pressure increases.

'Hold it there,' he says. 'Right there.' I hold the vibrator firmly against my clit where it pulses over and over. 'Press it again.'

The pressure grows, a beat hammering between my legs as he tells me when to ease off the intensity before turning it back up. As he has me do it again and again.

Click, click, click.

'*Nico*,' I moan, the sensation almost unbearable.

'Such a good girl,' he murmurs, and I jolt, the words like a shock of electricity hitting my nervous system. He lets out a rumble of approval, his gaze trailing over my face. '*Look* at you.'

My legs are trembling. His arm brackets me, but he's not touching me anywhere, and I don't know why it's *so* good, but it is. The way he's watching me unspool, come undone right in front of him, while he's totally in control, only the edge of something hot and hungry in his eyes.

I can feel my climax building, can already tell it's going to shatter me, and he hasn't even laid a finger on me.

I have to hold myself up and I'm not sure I'll be able to do it for much longer. Air saws in and out of my lungs, a bead of sweat runs down my spine.

I try to tell him how good it feels but I can't form full thoughts let alone words. Every nerve in my body is alive and spitting sparks. I'm lightning in a bottle. I'm coming apart at the seams.

'Let me see, baby,' Nico whispers, his mouth close enough to the shell of my ear that I can *feel* his voice like a caress. 'Let me see how pretty you look when you come.'

The orgasm hits me hard and fast, my hips bucking as my eyes flutter shut. Behind my eyelids there's an explosion of scattered light. 'Oh god,' I moan as my body riots.

When I open my eyes, he's still there, looking back at me. His pupils have eaten up his irises, his chest is rising and falling almost as heavily as my own. Slowly, he peels himself back from the wall.

He looks at me for a long moment, and nods like a decision has been made.

'Okay,' he says.

Then he turns and leaves the room.

Chapter Thirty-Two

Nico

There's no use pretending anymore, and in a way it's a relief. What happened last night can't be waved away as a misunderstanding or played off as part of our charade. It's pretty damn clear that what exists between Lee and me is a lot more than friendship. Tonight, when I get home from work we're going to have to talk about it, and I'm experiencing a confusing mix of anxiety and anticipation over that.

Last night I pinned Lee to a wall and watched her climax and it was without question the hottest fucking thing I've ever witnessed. Seeing those blue eyes flutter closed, the pink that spilled across her cheeks, the way that perfect rosy mouth of hers opened as the orgasm hit her. Every detail of it is imprinted on my memory, and will be for ever.

It was a moment that there was no coming back from, and when I realised that, instead of panic all I felt was . . . satisfaction. The kind of overwhelming, primal satisfaction I've never experienced before, swiftly followed by something else: need.

The way I need her is like a disaster. Something violent, painful, thundering through my body like a hurricane, obliterating me and testing the very fragile hold I have on my own control to its limits.

In that moment I wanted to touch her so badly that I had to leave the room before I did something we'd both regret. Unfortunately, that noble gesture meant that I spent a long uncomfortable night alone, followed – if I'm honest – by a long, uncomfortable morning at work.

As I wasn't sleeping anyway, I came in ridiculously early. I'm so close to finishing up this renovation at the inn that there isn't even anything for me to smash up. What I wouldn't give for a good demolition job right now.

Instead, I've been carefully reassembling the desk in reception at the base of the stairs. A hundred years old, this desk has greeted guests upon arrival through the front door, since the inn first opened. I couldn't leave it in situ when we were hauling all the building materials in and out and using this space as a holding area, so I took it apart and it's been in storage for months. Putting it back together in its rightful place was supposed to be a milestone, a sign that the renovation was almost at an end. It was supposed to give me a sense of satisfaction.

The irony is not lost on me. The last thing I feel right now is satisfied.

I'm almost done, on the floor, screwing one of the doors to the desk's cupboards into place when it hits me: the scent of honey and smoke that's haunted me for almost two weeks now, that lingers in my house, on my clothes, chasing me around town reminding me of her presence twenty-four, fucking seven.

When I look up, Lee is already inside the front door.

'Hi,' she says, tucking a strand of hair that has come loose from her braid behind her ear in a nervous gesture. She smiles.

I lever myself up from the floor.

'Hi.' My voice is little more than a growl.

'I know you said in your note that we'd talk later, but I couldn't wait.' She takes a step forward. 'There are some things I need to say.'

Thankfully the desk is between us so she can't see that the sound of her voice already has me hard. I am so *gone* for this woman it's humiliating.

'Are you okay?' I ask carefully.

She nods, takes a deep breath. 'I'm feeling confused about last night,' she blurts. 'I thought you were rejecting me . . . and then you . . .' She flushes. 'So I thought maybe . . . but then you left.'

My stomach swoops as I parse these half sentences and understand exactly what she's saying. *Shit.*

'I wasn't,' I say quickly. 'Rejecting you, I mean. Not at all.' I rub the back of my neck. 'Fuck. I've made a mess of this.'

I was trying to do the right thing and all I did was make her feel bad about herself.

'Maybe.' She tilts her head, considering me. Something is going on with her, her cheeks are still flushed. Her eyes keep dipping to my chest and my arms. 'Why don't you explain it to me?'

'You'd been drinking,' I say, a desperate edge to my words. 'I didn't want you to do anything you'd regret. I didn't want anything else to happen until we'd talked about it, about what it would mean. There are a lot of things to consider before you and I . . . before we take any steps that change what we have.'

She thinks about this for a moment, and her expression softens. 'I knew what I was doing last night. You didn't take advantage of the situation. I wanted it. I wanted more. I still do.' She lifts her chin as if daring me to disagree.

I can't pretend I'm not relieved. A tiny part of me worried that we'd taken things too far, whatever I convinced myself of in the moment. Still, the rest of her words hit me like a sledgehammer.

'More?' I manage eloquently.

She takes another step forward, and there's a light in her eye I've never seen before. It looks like I'm not the only one confronting my baser nature this morning.

'We should . . . talk,' I say.

'Yes,' Lee agrees distantly, her eyes sliding over my torso again. 'That's why I came here. To talk. Only now . . .'

'Now, what?'

'Now I really want you to kiss me.'

The confession hangs in the air between us. She's blushing and I don't think she's as calm and confident as she sounds. I think she probably spent all morning psyching herself up for this. I think last night she really did believe I was turning her down, and she made herself drive over here and talk to me anyway.

I need to handle this the right way, but as there is no blood left in my head it seems unlikely that I'm going to be able to work through the subtle nuances of our current situation. All I want to do is touch her.

I watch her as she rounds the desk, her fingers trailing over the surface.

'This is beautiful work,' she says, and her voice is breathy. Static electricity buzzes across my skin. There's nothing I can do but stand here, my heart pounding, as she comes closer.

'I think it's very impressive . . . what you can do with your hands.' Her pupils are enormous, she looks high but I'm sure I do, too. I'm absolutely off my face on lust.

She reaches out and runs a finger down my forearm, until she finds my hand. She strokes over my palm. 'Such good hands,' she says.

'Yeah?' I take a step towards her, meeting her where she is, seeing the relief light her eyes at my movement, feeling it as if it were my own. 'Where would you like them?'

'All over me.' The answer is instant, no hesitation. She wants me to hear how certain she is. She tips her head back to look up at my face, her gaze steady.

'I'm sure that can be arranged.' Hooking my finger into the belt of that ridiculous cream coat she's wearing, I tug her flush against my body. Then I wrap one hand around the side of her throat and pull her mouth to mine.

I don't just kiss her. I devour her. I let some of that savage need out from the place I've been holding it back, let her feel what she does to me. I bite down on that full lower lip, until she moans. There's nothing gentle about it, we don't ease in, we kiss like we're fucking, like we're picking up exactly where we left off last night.

When I tug at the knot, the belt of her coat falls apart and I push it off her shoulders to the floor. Underneath it she wears one of those silky buttoned-up shirts that drive me crazy, tucked into a pair of dark, high-waisted trousers. It's like the outfit she was wearing that night in Vegas.

I stop for a moment, taking her in. My gaze drops to her feet. Deadly-looking black stilettos. 'You're wearing your armour,' I murmur.

'I thought I might need it.' Her teeth sink into her bottom lip.

I run my thumb across her mouth, gently tugging her lip free. 'You don't.'

Then I kiss her again, my fingers going to the button at the base of her throat, popping it open. Her pulse skips under my thumb. I dip my head, already desperate for that extra inch of skin.

'Fuck, Daisy,' I groan. 'Why do you always smell so good?'

'It's my perfume,' she manages, sounding dazed. 'It's honey and tobacco.'

I hum in appreciation as I undo another two buttons, biting down on the tender curve between her neck and her shoulder.

She's unbuttoning my shirt too, her movements quick and neat. When her fingers hit the bare skin on my chest we both exhale in relief. I want her touch everywhere. I need her hands on me the same way I need oxygen.

I pull the bottom of her shirt out of her trousers and make quick work of her remaining buttons, running my knuckles down the narrow strip of skin I've revealed, over the pale pink lace between her breasts. I watch her nipples pebble through the thin fabric of her open shirt.

'I thought you might not like this as much as the cowgirl outfit,' she admits, and when I look up, there's uncertainty in her eyes.

'Do you know how wild you drive me in your fancy clothes?' I say against her lips. 'Do you know how obsessed I am with the idea of messing you up, tidy girl?'

Breathless, she shakes her head.

'Why don't I show you?' I flick open the button at the top of her trousers, ease down the zip. She mirrors my movements and when her fingers graze my cock through my boxers I hiss out a curse.

I kiss her again, pushing her shirt from her shoulders, and down her arms, but the tight cuffs catch around her wrists. Taking advantage of this situation, I twist the fabric behind her, tugging her arms with it so they're pinned, her hands in the small of her back, and her body arched towards me.

The bra she's wearing is one of those low cut balcony ones, a barely there scrap of silk and lace that has my mouth watering. I lean forward, pressing kisses to her soft flesh, running my tongue over that silk, sucking gently on her nipple through her bra while she moans, restrained by the shirt that I fist tight behind her.

'Oh god, Nico,' she pants. 'That's . . .' She loses her train of thought as I tease her with my teeth.

My attention dips lower.

'Well, well, Daisy,' I murmur. 'Aren't you full of surprises. Shoes off.'

She steps out of her heels without comment, suddenly several inches shorter. I release my grip on her arms, dropping down to my knees in front of her, my hands on her waist. I rub my mouth along her stomach, up under the curve of her breast where black ink swirls across her ribcage.

'I like this,' I say, tracing my tongue over her tattoo. *Mine*, my blood sings.

Lee shivers. She's managed to free herself from her shirt, and her fingers curl into my hair, tugging lightly, the sensation in my scalp on the very edge of pain. I look up.

'Take your shirt off,' she demands. Those cool blue eyes are hot now. I laugh, but shrug off my open shirt. I'm immediately rewarded by the feeling of her hands running over my shoulder, my biceps. It's like my skin is thirsty for her. Everywhere she touches me is a relief and a torment all at once.

More, the voice inside my head snarls. *More.*

I tug on her trousers and they fall to the floor with a whispered sound like a sigh. She steps out of the pool of fabric, and I stay there, on my knees, looking up at her, clad in nothing but her underwear.

'Fuck,' I manage.

She smiles, her dimples popping out. 'I'd be delighted,' she says, like we're at a tea party.

Lust and affection and a million other emotions crash through me, and I surge to my feet, scooping her up and spinning her around, depositing her on the edge of the desk with a muffled squeak.

'You want to know what you do to me?' I growl, tugging off my boots and shucking off my socks and jeans with an almost inhuman speed, until I'm standing in front of her in my underwear. There's no hiding how affected I am, and her eyes widen gratifyingly as she looks her fill.

'I want to take you to bed,' I say, watching her, all glowing skin and pink silk, and swollen lips as she gazes back at me. 'I've thought about it a million times. A million ways. You make me so desperate, the first time I fuck you isn't going to be anything like I planned. It's not going to be slow and careful. It's going to be right here on this desk. Now.'

She shivers again, and I step between her thighs, kissing her before she can say anything. I unclasp her bra and it falls away. My hand closes over her breast and she makes the sort of sound I could get addicted to hearing.

She reaches for me with greedy fingers, freeing me from my boxers, and when her hand wraps around my cock I groan, my forehead dropping to hers. I look down to where she touches me. The diamond on her finger catches the light, and I could come from that image alone: her getting me off while wearing my ring.

I run my fingers along the seam of her underwear and push the damp fabric aside, teasing, sliding a finger slowly inside her. 'I want to watch you come again.' I add another finger, and her muscles clench around me. 'I want to watch that pretty pink blush spread everywhere.'

'I want you inside me this time,' she gasps.

That sounds like an absolutely fucking great idea, but I've just realised there's a problem. 'No condom,' I sigh, pumping my fingers again. 'Sorry, baby. We'll have to do this another way.'

'In my pocket,' she snaps, and she grabs hold of my wrist, stilling my hand, her eyes wild as she looks at me. 'There's a condom in my coat pocket.'

I let out a surprised laugh, but she only looks at me. I step back, fumbling around for her coat.

She doesn't have a condom in her pocket.

She has seven.

'Jesus, Daisy,' I shake my head. 'What exactly did you have planned?'

'I don't know *exactly*,' she says, wiggling her skimpy underwear down over her hips. 'But this is better.'

After that things move fast. After that it's a blur of desperate touches and needy groans. Her nails on my back, my mouth on her honey-scented skin, her teeth on my neck, her hands braced on the desk and a sigh on her lips as I finally, finally sink inside her.

And my heart *stops*.

It actually stops beating for a moment, before it picks up again, twice as fast. I should probably be worried, but what a way to die: buried inside my wife.

My hips move, slow at first, testing, stretching, as we learn each other, as our bodies find their fit, and then faster as we discover our rhythm. Lee is incoherent, murmuring words that I don't think are even English. She feels incredible around me, and her muscles contract, a ripple of thought-obliterating sensation. She's close, I can tell she's close. Thank fuck, because I'm already seeing stars.

'Lee,' I start, 'I—'

She lifts a hand and presses it over my mouth. Her eyes are closed, a frown pinches her brows.

'Shhh,' she says. 'I'm concentrating.'

I smile under her palm and that feeling is back again, a pressure in my chest that matches the relentless one building everywhere else.

I slip my hand under her ass, changing the angle a fraction, hitting her a bit deeper and we both make a choked sound of pleasure. My thumb finds her clit and her eyes fly open. She still has her hand over my mouth. 'Yes,' she says very definitely. '*Yes*.'

And then I watch as Lee Turner-Jones climaxes for the second time. Only now I fall over the edge with her.

And I have a feeling nothing is ever going to be the same.

Chapter Thirty-Three

Lee

'Oh my god!' Tara squeals. 'You slept together!'

'Shhh!' I glance around the thankfully quiet coffee shop. In my short time here I've learned that gossip spreads like wildfire in Roseport and I'll admit this is particularly juicy gossip. If I'm not careful, Rita will be passing the news out with her ice cream sundaes and people will be high-fiving me in the street.

'Sorry,' Tara whispers, eyeing me over the top of her latte. 'But also not sorry. *Finally!*'

I manage a smile. Honestly, it's been three hours and I haven't even started to recover my equilibrium. My body feels achy and used in the best possible way, my heart rate has yet to return to normal. The shower that I had before driving over to meet Tara hasn't washed the smell of Nico off me, and I swear I can still *taste* him. Someone once told me that you can get hooked on heroin the first time you use it. Well, I get it now. All I can think about is having sex with Nico. My body still hums with the force of what we did, but I want it again. And again. And again.

I don't know how to sit in a coffee shop and hold a conversation. I don't know how to be around people. I don't know how I'm just supposed to function like a normal human being anymore.

'Was it amazing?' Tara asks.

'It was . . . He . . . We . . .' I trail off, unable to find the words and gazing hopelessly at her.

'Woah,' Tara says reverently, and I nod.

'Yeah. Woah.'

'Okay, tell me everything.' She settles in and I give her a brief recap of events, the tasteful highlights, only occasionally losing my train of thought.

'Holy shit,' Tara hisses. 'Right on the desk? That's so fucking hot.'

'I know,' I nod, taking a long sip of the chamomile tea I ordered in the hope it would calm me down.

'So you just, like, pounced on him? I'm so proud!'

'I went there to talk to him,' I say. 'I really did. But when I got there . . .'

'What?'

'He was on the floor, *fixing things*.'

'Oh no.' Her eyes widen.

'And he was . . . he was wearing . . . *a plaid shirt*.' I sound desperate.

Tara puts her cup down with a clink. 'With the sleeves rolled up?'

I nod. It had been a disaster. It was like walking into some sort of soft porn film made specifically for the female gaze.

She reaches across for my hand and squeezes it. 'Babe, there was simply nothing else you could do in the circumstances. You're only lucky he wasn't wearing the tool belt as well or you'd probably be knocked up by now.'

'Tara!' I exclaim and she giggles.

'Although maybe not, seeing as you're apparently the queen of prophylactics. Tell me again how you went over there to "*talk*" with a pocket full of condoms.'

'Obviously I was planning to seduce him if the opportunity *presented* itself,' I huff. 'Last night you told me I needed to be clear and direct. I was being *responsible*.'

'Sounds like there wasn't much seduction required.' Tara's grin widens.

I feel a matching smile slip over my own face. 'Not really.'

'Okay, you're starting to lose the scary eyes. Welcome back to planet earth.' She holds up her mug in a small toast. 'So I take it you two didn't actually get around to having the talk?'

'No, we only just managed to get our clothes back on before Magda turned up.'

I flush at the memory. Thank god she hadn't been ten minutes earlier when I'd been transcending the boundaries of the observable universe and having an orgasm so intense I think I sprained muscles I didn't know I had.

Magda didn't seem to catch on to what she'd walked in on, but she *did* keep talking about the *incredible energy* in the room, and fussed at length over the sex-desk, which is apparently some sort of priceless antique.

I shot Nico an appalled glance at this, but he only looked smug. I suppose it was a very sturdy piece of craftsmanship.

'Magda dropped by to ask him to take her to pick up some furniture in his truck, but he did say he's going to take me out tonight so we can discuss . . . things.'

'Like a date?'

I shrug. 'He didn't use the word *date*. He said *dinner*.' What he actually said, once Magda finally left the room, was *dinner somewhere public where we won't be tempted to rip each other's clothes off*.

'Sounds like a date to me.'

'What are you two whispering about?' Kat drifts over to clear the table beside us while there's a lull at the counter. We're currently her only customers and she looks grateful for the break.

'Lee and Nico have a date tonight!' Tara sings. 'Guess who finally acted on our advice!'

Kat swings her attention towards me. 'No!' she says.

'Yes,' I nod.

The bell rings over the door.

'Sorry, Clyde!' Kat trills. 'We're closed.'

'It's four o'clock,' Clyde grumbles, looking at his watch.

'Fine, let me grab you your bran muffin, but we're closing for the next hour.' Kat hustles to the counter, popping a muffin in a paper bag and thrusting it at him. 'This is a girl talk emergency.'

'You don't need to close the café for me,' I say.

The look she gives me is scornful as she shoos Clyde out the door and slaps the 'Closed' sign in the window. She drops into the seat across from me, her phone already in her hand. 'I'm texting Mei right now, but I can't wait until she gets here. Tell me *everything.*'

That evening I stand in front of Nico's bed, wrapped in a towel, deliberating over what to wear for this date-that-maybe-isn't-a-date. At this point I have tried on and discarded every single item I have access to.

The tone that I need to set is very specific. I need to look casual! Unfazed by the extremely intense sex we had this morning! Ready to talk about what it means to be having sex when we are actually married and involved in an elaborate legal deception!

I know what I *should* wear – jeans. Jeans would say all of these things. Only I don't own any and I don't think a denim miniskirt is going to be the right call. I make a mental note to ask Kat to take me back to Target.

Tragically, staring at the clothes is not making a new and perfect outfit magically appear. I've already worn pretty much everything here in differing combinations. (I am a master at packing the capsule wardrobe, but even my ingenuity has been stretched by an unexpected three-week trip.) I wish Gran was here. She'd throw together the perfect thing in five seconds flat, and I'd feel confident and *right*.

I experience a wave of sadness because we've barely spoken – only exchanged a few texts here and there, which isn't like us at all. I know that physically she's fine, but not what's happening in her life. And for the first time ever she *really* hasn't got a clue what's going on in mine.

She'd probably get a kick out of it, actually.

I pick up my phone to text her, just to check in again and make sure she's taking all her medication, that she's feeling good. What I get back is a blurry photograph of her pill organiser next to a half-empty bottle of champagne. Still, at least today's compartment looks to be empty.

I try not to fret over the fact I'm not there to keep an eye on her, that she's still sending me snarky photos instead of an actual message.

Please don't forget about your appointment with the GP on Wednesday, I text. That one gets no response at all, but I can tell she's seen it. I suppose that will have to do.

With a sigh I turn back to my clothes, eventually settling on a soft, oversized cream jumper paired with buttery tan-coloured suede trousers.

I add some simple gold jewellery and understated makeup, pull my hair back into a loose braid, spritz myself with perfume, and it's only taken around ninety minutes to make myself look like a human woman who hasn't tried too hard. God, this is exhausting.

Unsure how to proceed at this point, I sink onto the edge of the bed and stare at the door. Through it, I can hear the low murmur of Nico and Phoebe's voices, the soft hum of occasional laughter, like it's just a regular evening.

I twist the small gold hoop in my ear and take a steady breath. So why am I sitting in here alone? What am I waiting for? Nico to knock on the door with a corsage?

It's not even necessarily a real date, Lee, and it's certainly not the bloody prom.

I take a deep breath and open the door.

Chapter Thirty-Four

Nico

'I don't know why you get pizza but I had to eat *carrots*,' Phoebe is whining. 'You know how much I love pizza. It's cruel of you to go without me.' She gives me a look that would do a winsome Victorian orphan proud.

'First of all, may I remind you that it was your bright idea for Lee and I to have date nights where it's just the two of us,' I say, even though we've already had this conversation three times. Parenthood, I'm learning, has much to do with repetition. 'You said *many times* that it was crucial to your "master plan". Second of all, you have already emotionally blackmailed me into a family ice cream date on Sunday, so I'd quit while you're ahead if I were you.'

Phoebe pouts, but goes back to the book she's reading while I help myself to a bottle of beer from the fridge. It's after six, and I'm not driving tonight so I deserve it.

It's *not* because I'm jittery and nervous about waiting to take Lee out and I'm not feeling weird about lying to my daughter about this not being a real date. At least . . . I think it's a real date. We didn't exactly get a chance to discuss things properly with Magda tripping all over the place banging on about 'intense vibrations' while I tried not to look like a man who had just had the best sex of his life on her reception desk.

I don't know who I'm trying to kid. Of course I need a beer. This would be complicated enough without every cell in my body obsessing over the fact that Lee and I are sharing a bed tonight and this time everything is different.

As if she could hear me thinking about her, the door to Lee's room opens and she steps out.

'Cool pants,' Phoebe offers from her spot on the sofa.

'Oh!' Lee runs her hands self-consciously over the soft leather that clings to her thighs and I realise I'm staring at her with my mouth open. 'Do you think? I wasn't sure about the dress code . . .'

My daughter wrinkles her nose. 'I don't think Stefano's *has* a dress code.'

'No,' Lee laughs, but it's a high, anxious sound. 'I guess not.'

She hovers awkwardly in the doorway for a moment, and I know I should say something, but I'm still recovering from the sight of her in those tight, tight trousers. She smiles at me, fusses with her earring.

Click. The camera in my head goes off. The real thing is right there on the kitchen counter. I've been using it more and more the last few days, taking pictures of the work around the inn. It feels good, it feels like a relief.

'What are you reading?' Lee asks Phoebe.

'It's part of a series about these three magic sisters who find a mermaid.' Phoebe scoots up on the sofa. 'Do you want to see?'

Lee's expression lightens. 'I'd love that.'

The two of them sit side by side, their heads close together as Phoebe talks Lee through the complexities of the fantasy world she's been inhabiting. Taco drapes himself over Lee's feet, pinning her in place.

This time I do reach over and grab my camera. I silently snap a couple of pictures without them noticing.

'Do you want a drink?' I blurt out, my voice too loud.

Lee tips her head back to look at me. 'I'd love a glass of white wine, thanks,' she says before she goes straight back to peppering Phoebe with questions.

I grab the bottle of fancy stuff she bought out of the fridge. When I lean over the back of the sofa with her glass, Lee reaches to take it, and her fingers brush against mine.

'Thanks,' she says with a smile, and I let myself touch my hand quickly to her cheek. It feels sweet, habitual, this sort of touch. Touching her because I can. I like it.

The moment is interrupted by the sound of my phone ringing and when I pull it from my pocket my eyes widen.

'Oh, shit,' I murmur. 'It's Jack.'

Lee gets abruptly to her feet, much to Taco's disgust, and Phoebe darts a look between the two of us.

'Does he know . . .' She points to Lee and then to me.

'I don't think so?' I glance at Lee, who has her arms wrapped around her middle. She doesn't say anything, just shakes her head.

'Cool!' Phoebe sits back with a smirk. 'This is going to be fun.'

'Should I tell him?' I ask as the phone continues to ring, and I feel my panic rising. 'About the wedding,' I clarify, because what happened today is a whole other story.

Lee chews her bottom lip. 'Not yet,' she says. 'It'll only make things more complicated.'

'Right,' I agree. I'm not exactly prepared to have that conversation either. Still, I definitely *should* tell Jack. About the marriage, anyway. The sleeping with his sister part is something that probably needs a bit more build up.

I position myself so that the camera won't show Lee when I pick up the call. The screen blinks, and then, there he is, my best friend of almost thirty years.

'Where the fuck have you been?' he greets me.

'Hey, watch your mouth,' I manage to smile. 'There are children present.'

Phoebe slips in beside me, beaming innocently up at the camera, and I throw my arm around her. 'Hi, Uncle Jack!'

I glance across at Lee who is standing frozen in place, and something in her expression makes my chest hurt.

'Sorry, Pheebs,' Jack says, contrite.

'Don't worry, Dad can put a dollar into the ice cream fund for you,' my daughter sings.

'Nice,' Jack chuckles. 'I'll make sure to drop a few more swear words before we hang up, okay? So don't settle for less than ten bucks.'

'You've got it,' Phoebe agrees. 'Hey, I'm reading that book Aunt Cyn gave me.'

Lee shifts on her feet and makes a sign that she's going to head back to her room. I give an infinitesimal nod, and she disappears, closing the door behind her.

When I tune back in to Jack and Phoebe's conversation, I watch my friend, his dark hair shorter than the last time I saw him, laughing with my daughter, and it's easy to see how happy he is. Ever since he and Cynthie managed to get their shit together he's been like a new person.

I'm happy for him, of course I am, but for the first time I feel a real pang of envy. Don't get me wrong, I've always thought what they had looked pretty great, and since meeting Phoebe it's definitely occurred to me that having a partner – a real, all-in partner – would make life easier, but I'd pretty much resigned myself to single life. The idea of dating someone wasn't even on my radar, but here I am ... about to take a beautiful, brilliant woman out to dinner. And she's Jack's sister.

'I'm gonna go and read in my room,' Phoebe says after a couple of minutes and I nod.

'Why don't you get in your PJs, little Bee? Your grandmother will be here soon.'

'I don't know how you managed to make such a cool kid,' Jack says once Phoebe's gone. 'I miss you guys. We need to get something in the diary.'

'Definitely,' I agree. 'Are you in New York any time soon?'

'You know, you could actually invite us to this town we've heard so much about,' Jack laughs. 'And what was that about Magda coming over tonight?'

'It's not Magda, it's my mum, she's here for an unexpected visit and she offered to babysit,' I say with a wince.

'Hang on,' Jack perks up. 'Don't tell me you're actually going out, you hermit?'

'Yeah,' I rub the back of my neck, 'it's a dinner thing.'

'Fuck me!' Jack exclaims with delight. 'You've gone all shifty! You've got a date, haven't you? Cyn!' he shouts over his shoulder. 'Cynthie! It's finally happening, Nico has a date!'

There's a muffled response from another room that has Jack chuckling. 'She wants details,' he explains.

'There are no details,' I say firmly. 'It's not a date . . . it's just a . . .'

'A what?'

I shrug helplessly. 'A . . . casual evening.'

Jack's famously blue eyes narrow. 'Wait, I know this look. This is the panicked look. You *like* this woman.'

'I—' The words are stuck in my throat. This is my nightmare. 'She's . . .' I trail off.

'Woah.' Jack leans back. 'No words. This is big. I honestly don't remember the last time this happened. We were probably about fifteen. So, tell me all about her. Cynthie will murder me if I don't get all the gossip.'

His eyes flicker to the top of the screen and he laughs again. 'She just texted me a message with those exact words. She's trapped in a chair while Patty does her hair right now or she'd be in here interrogating you herself and you'd stand no chance.'

'There isn't any gossip,' I say firmly. 'I am going out for dinner with a *friend*. She's . . . great.'

'Great?' Jack looks unimpressed. 'What do you mean *great*?'

'I mean she's funny and clever and so fucking gorgeous I can't see straight, okay?' I snap. 'But we're . . . it's . . . complicated.'

Jack looks stunned by this outburst, as well he might because I was definitely not planning to say any of it, but there's only so much a man can stand. This whole situation is having a catastrophic effect on my blood pressure and I'm a father now, I need to think about these things.

Eventually, Jack lets out a low whistle. 'Okay, it sounds like you have a lot going on,' his tone has softened, 'and look, I'm not claiming to be an expert on love—'

I snort. 'I should fucking hope not. Do you even remember how you and Cynthie met?'

'*But*,' Jack pushes on regardless, 'if you care about this woman that much then you should really tell her. Trust me on this . . . you don't want to waste time, life's way too short, man.'

I wonder how he'd feel if he knew he was giving me this advice about his sister. I honestly don't have any idea how he'd react, but I do know that not telling him feels wrong.

'Maybe you could bring her as your date to our wedding,' Jack says casually. 'It's only a couple of months away now.'

I settle for making a vague humming sound of agreement and change the subject to ask about Gran.

'Yeah, she's good,' Jack nods. 'Apparently her cholesterol numbers aren't great but they're getting better, and the cardiologist gave her the all clear, although I usually have to squeeze that sort of info out of Lee.'

Because Lee's the one taking care of her, I feel the sudden urge to say, but I bite my tongue.

'I'm pretty sure something's off between her and Gran. I think they might have had a bit of a falling out,' Jack muses.

'About what?'

'No idea,' he shrugs, 'I don't think it was anything serious. You know those two are thick as thieves. Apparently Lee's away on business at the moment so Gran's living her best bachelorette lifestyle, which I really did *not* need to hear the details on, but which she was happy to share anyway.'

Something compels me to ask, 'Where *is* Lee at the moment?'

'Good question.' His brow wrinkles. 'She texted me a few days ago asking me to check in on Gran but she didn't mention where she was. Thinking about it, she hasn't been travelling for work as much as she used to.'

'Since Gran's heart attack,' I can't keep the sharpness out of my voice. 'She probably feels like someone has to be there.'

Jack grimaces. 'Fuck. You're right. I can't believe I didn't put that together. Do you really think she's worried? I mean, obviously straight afterwards, but it's been a year . . . Gran's doing so well . . . right? There's no reason Lee can't be away. She never said anything to me about it.'

I shrug, not ready to ease his guilt on this one. I think it's time he started paying more attention where Lee's concerned. It's obvious she feels like she's alone in looking after her grandmother, but Jack loves both of them – she should be able to lean on him a lot more. The two of them definitely need to communicate better.

'You and Lee aren't in touch much?' I ask, even though I already know the answer.

Jack frowns, troubled. 'Not as much as we should be. Cynthie's pretty good about messaging her and stuff, but we haven't caught up in person for a while.'

'It must be hard on her,' I say. 'Being on her own.'

Jack looks startled at this. 'Lee? I don't think so, you know what she's like, it's tricky to get stuff out of her, but she's always been so self-sufficient.'

Thankfully, before I can say anything to *that*, he shakes his head. 'But you're right that I should make more of an effort. Hey, maybe all of us can get together some time. I bet her and Phoebe would hit it off. You guys should do a trip to the UK, introduce your daughter to her roots.'

'Maybe,' I say. 'In the summer break.'

'Summer break!' Jack shakes his head again. 'So weird that you're dealing with school holidays now.' His smile grows. 'You know I'm really happy for you, right? I know how hard it's been, but what you've built with Phoebe . . . I'm so fucking proud of you. You're an amazing dad, and she's the best.'

'She really is,' I say, and now I feel even worse.

'Okay, I'll stop being a soppy bastard and let you get ready for your *casual evening*.'

'Dick,' I scoff, but there's no heat in it and we say goodbye, promising to catch up soon.

While I stare at the blank screen I try to organise my feelings. Jack might not have known who he was giving me advice about but that doesn't mean he was wrong. Part of me – a part of me that keeps getting louder and louder – knows that there could be something real, something scarily real and serious between Lee and me, but apart from the fact we slept together I have to ask myself what else has changed?

The answer is nothing. I'm still an unemployed single father who has no clue what he's doing with his life, and she has responsibilities of her own and a life on the other side of the world. Is there even the slimmest chance this won't end in disaster?

Chapter Thirty-Five

Lee

'So I'm guessing a pizza joint is not a typical Lee Turner-Jones date night,' Nico says as we look at each other from our vinyl seats across the small table.

I try not to react to him calling this a date.

'What's a typical Lee Turner-Jones date night?' I ask, sipping at my water.

He narrows his eyes, considering. 'Hmmm. Maybe drinks at a wine bar, one of those fancy tasting menus at a slick London restaurant. Finishing off with a glass of expensive brandy somewhere with moody lighting.'

As this is exactly what Adrian and I did the last time we went out I only shrug hopelessly.

'But do you know what?' There's a glint in Nico's eye, his lips curl into that devastating half smile. 'I know you pretty well, Lee Turner-Jones. I think you'll enjoy this more.'

I feel the answering smile pull at my mouth even as I try to fight it. 'I think you're probably right.'

I glance around the pizzeria, which is a bright, cheerful space. The table is covered in a red gingham cloth, and there's an electric tea light flickering in a glass holder next to our bread basket.

Buzzy bossa nova comes over the speakers, and the place hums with conversation as other customers dig into pizzas the size of carriage wheels. There are several families sharing a meal together.

'I like this place,' I say. 'I never got to go to this kind of restaurant as a kid.' It's almost impossible to imagine my parents anywhere without actual silverware. Gran wasn't exactly a fast food enthusiast either.

'Phoebe had her birthday party here.' Nico looks haunted. 'Eleven eight-year-olds. It was like being in a war zone. I still have nightmares. I should warn you we'll both be dead to her if we don't take some leftovers home.'

'She already made me promise I would,' I say.

Nico barks out a laugh. 'And me. Did she do the big eyes on you?'

'From behind the glasses?' I touch a hand to my heart, shaking my head. 'It *kills* me. I'd give her both of my kidneys if she asked me while making that face. Even though I know she'd only sell them on the black market. I haven't spent a ton of time with kids, but I love hanging out with her.'

'She's very into you, too,' Nico says and leans back in his seat.

'Do you think so?' I ask, impossibly pleased.

'*CIAO!*' a voice belts from beside me, making me jump. 'My favourite married couple!'

'Hi, Stefano,' I greet the older man with the salt and pepper moustache whose real name I know perfectly well is Steve, mentally thanking Mei's flashcards. 'Is Rosie in tonight, too?'

Stefano beams. 'She isn't, but when I saw the reservation I let her know you two were coming and she said to tell you she hopes she'll see you at craft club on Tuesday. You were a big hit!'

We make small talk for another couple of minutes and then Nico orders a pizza with an irresponsible number of toppings and a bottle of house red, and Stefano disappears back to the kitchen. A short time later we're digging into the biggest pizza I've ever seen.

'Oh, this is so good,' I moan. 'Maybe Stefano *is* actually Italian?'

'Stefano is about as Italian as a plate of chicken nuggets,' Nico snorts. 'And are you actually going to eat your pizza with a knife and fork? Come on, tidy girl, live a little.'

He holds his slice of pizza out across the table.

'Sorry for having excellent table manners,' I scoff, but I lean over and take a bite.

'Even the way you bite into things is neat.' He shakes his head. 'I can see your perfect little teeth marks.' Under the table his leg presses against mine and I smile.

By the time I push my plate back and away from me, stuffed, my fingers are sticky. I wipe them on a napkin and then extract a bottle of hand sanitiser from my handbag.

When I look up, Nico is grinning at me. 'Ate a fully loaded pizza with your fingers while wearing a cream top and didn't spill a thing. A miracle.'

'Thank you, Nicolas,' I say primly, taking a sip of my red wine – which is actually very decent – 'I can, and have, eaten my meals for many years now without throwing food down my front.'

'Okay, princess,' he says, and then he crooks a finger, gesturing for me to lean over the table towards him. When I do he picks up a napkin and presses it to my cheek, softly swiping over the corner of my mouth. His finger brushes against my lip, and it feels like a tiny electric shock travels all the way down to my toes.

'You have a little sauce,' he murmurs, 'just here.'

When he pulls back, I ease myself away, falling into my seat with an audible thump.

'So,' I say after we spend a full thirty seconds staring greedily at each other. 'We should probably talk.'

'Mm hmm,' Nico rumbles. 'We should definitely talk.' He reaches across the table, tangling his fingers with mine. 'Do you know,' he says mildly, 'that it feels impossible not to be touching you all the time?'

I clear my throat. 'I might know something about that, yes,' I watch as his fingers toy with my own, as he gently twists the diamond ring that I'm still not used to wearing.

'It's been difficult for a long time,' his eyes are still on our hands, 'the not touching you part.'

I choke back a laugh at this. 'Try going twenty-seven years.'

His fingers tighten briefly. When he looks at me, his eyes are wide. 'Daisy . . .' The way he says my name is full of too many things – wonder and tenderness and compassion and worry.

I pull my hand back, embarrassed. 'I shouldn't have said anything,' I mutter.

'I'm glad you did,' he says gently. 'But do you really mean—'

'That I've had a giant crush on you since I was a kid?' I ask ruefully. 'Oh, yeah. Sorry. Have I freaked you out?'

'No! I just had no idea. I'm trying to wrap my head around it.' He exhales a long breath. 'That's a lot to live up to.'

He sounds so nervous that I smile. 'Are you worried that I've idealised you,' I ask, 'that I think you're perfect?'

He lifts a hand to the back of his neck, embarrassed. 'Um . . . maybe?'

'I *know* you're not perfect.'

'You don't have to sound so sure about that. What's wrong with me?'

'You want a list?'

His mouth quirks. 'I *dare* you to come up with a list. I'm delightful.'

'You're cocky. That's on the list.'

'I don't see that as a flaw.' He puts a little extra bass into his voice and I laugh.

'You're stubborn.'

'So are you!'

'We're not doing *my* list.' I wave this comment away with my hand. 'You'd never hurt someone on purpose but you can be careless with people's feelings, you're slow to forgive people, and you get *so* grumpy when you're hungry that I think you should consult a doctor about it. You're messy. You don't own an iron. You are an awful cook. You have terrible taste in books—'

'What do you know about my taste in books?' he cuts in.

'You have a stack by the bed. They're all about Spitfires and the Second World War.' I look at him. 'Why are you smiling?'

'Because you're about to feel *so* bad,' he smirks. 'Phoebe was doing a project for school and I wanted to be able to answer her questions so I was reading up on stuff on the sly.'

'No!' I bang my hand on the table. 'You were being an adorable single dad? You're not a military history bore?'

'Sorry.' He leans back in his seat, crosses his arms across his chest. 'I guess I'm closer to perfect than you thought.'

'Damn it,' I grumble. I really needed that one.

'In fact,' he's looking at me with obvious enjoyment now, 'I like to read *all sorts* of things. I even asked Tara for some good romance recommendations.'

'You did not!'

He pulls his phone out his pocket and clicks through until he gets to the notes app which contains a list of a dozen of my favourite titles. 'I already asked Mrs Penny to place the top three on hold for me at the library.'

I sink my head into my hands. 'Fine, I give up. You're perfect, too good to be true.'

He laughs, a light, happy sound. 'No, I'm not, and everything else you said was totally right. I don't know why hearing a list of my flaws felt so good, but here we are. I'm reassured. I'm a monster and you like me anyway.'

'Yeah,' I smile. 'I suppose I do.'

'I like you, too.' He says it softly. 'You know how much I care about you. That's partly why *this* is so complicated.' He gestures between us. 'We're so tangled up together, us, your family . . .'

'I know,' I agree.

'Plus . . .' He hesitates. 'You know my situation, you know what my life looks like right now. I'm not sure I'm in a place to be a good partner to someone. I'm barely keeping my head above water as it is.'

Maybe because you need a partner, I think, but I don't say it . . . it's not like I can offer to be here with him, sharing the load.

'And we live approximately 3,085 miles apart,' I add instead, trying to ignore the dull ache in my chest.

'You Googled it too,' he sighs.

We both fall silent.

'So,' he says after a moment. 'You know what that all means.' He's trying to make this as easy on me as possible.

I sit with it for a while, knowing that we need to be realistic. There's no future for the two of us.

And yet.

'I don't want to be practical,' I say finally.

He frowns. 'What?'

'Look, I understand what you're saying . . . or working your way up to saying. I know that the practical choice is for us to draw a line under what happened today, to try and go back to the way things were.'

'That is definitely the practical choice,' he agrees slowly.

'And I'm saying I don't want that.' I think about the argument Gran and I had, about the way I've been closing myself off so much – not just over the last year, but for much longer. How I've made my world as safe as possible by keeping tight control on every element of my life. I haven't truly risked anything. Not for a long time . . . maybe not ever.

This thing with Nico is a huge gamble. It will almost certainly end with my heart smashed into a million pieces, and yet right now, in this moment, while I look at him across the table, I don't care. I know I'd take all the promised pain if it meant another week of us together. I know I'd accept it in exchange for another hour.

'I think we should take the next week. Like a gift,' I say, my voice steady. I feel strangely calm about the decision. 'We both know that it can't last. We're going in with our eyes wide open. We won't leave things on bad terms. We won't hurt each other.'

He hesitates. 'I'm not sure that's true. I think you could hurt me, Lee. I think you have enough of me already to do that. And I don't ever want to be the one to make you unhappy. We wouldn't mean to, but that doesn't mean we wouldn't hurt each other. Another week isn't going to make that any less of a problem.'

I press my lips together. Nod. 'You're right. It would be naive to say we'll come out of it unscathed. But . . . I think it's worth it. I understand if you don't feel that way, trust me.' I force a smile. 'I'm not usually one to gamble on my feelings like this.'

It's his turn to be quiet, long enough for my heart to start beating hard, for disappointment to well in my throat.

'You forget I've played poker with you,' he says finally. 'I think you know exactly when to gamble.'

'Is that a yes?' I'm holding my breath now.

He rubs a hand over his mouth and nods again. 'Of course it is. You can add "not doing the noble thing" to my list of flaws. I know I shouldn't, I know it's selfish, but I'm keeping you. For as long as I can. All of you.'

I exhale slowly. 'Want to go and get a proper drink?'

Chapter Thirty-Six

Nico

I honestly don't know how we ended up here, but I am line dancing. More accurately, I am stumbling around, bashing into people while *Lee* line dances.

After dinner, we walked over to Darlene's hand in hand, as if it was the most normal thing in the world. When we arrived at the bar the high-top tables had been moved, leaving a large empty space.

'Oh god,' I winced. 'Dancing.'

'Line dancing?' Her face lit up.

'I'm not doing it,' I said firmly. Lee took years of ballet classes and she genuinely loves to dance but I, on the other hand, have two left feet.

'Oh,' she pasted on a smile, so careful not even to *glance* at the dance floor again, 'of course. Let's just grab a drink.'

And *that* is how I ended up line dancing: because when her eyes were sad and resigned all I cared about was making her happy. Because I couldn't be another person who didn't put her needs first. If she wanted to dance then fuck it, we'd dance all night.

And I should be hating every second, but I'm not. Because Lee *loves* it. While the music plays and Randall calls out indecipherable phrases like 'right jazzbox', I flail about like an idiot, and Lee moves effortlessly into formation with the twenty other people who also speak this secret language.

'How are you doing this?' I hiss when I knock into her side for the fourth time.

She laughs, her eyes sparkling. 'It's easy once you lock into it . . . it's just patterns. Follow me.'

She places a hand on my arm and starts counting, pushing and tugging at me to change direction. I'm still terrible, but at least now I'm facing the same direction as everyone else.

'You're doing really well,' Lee encourages me, when I manage to hit several correct steps in a row. 'You're so good.' Her sweet encouragement, the words that she keeps murmuring in a low, excited voice are unfortunately leading to impure thoughts on my part. As is the jumper that keeps sliding on and off her shoulder, revealing a tantalising glimpse of her bra strap, the tiny freckle by her collarbone.

I almost head in the wrong direction again, but she hooks her hand around my arm, spinning me towards her, and her giggle is the loveliest thing I've ever heard.

It doesn't really matter what Lee and I discussed, I know there's only one way this thing ends . . . with me picking up the pieces of my obliterated heart as she flies away. I've never been close to feeling this vulnerable before. I've never cared enough about anyone to get hurt, but with Lee we're starting something with a lifetime of history behind it. I'm already in so deep, I feel wild – reckless, exhilarated, ecstatic. Scared.

The song finally finishes, and the group breaks, ready to go and grab more drinks, but a few dancers stay behind. When the juke box hums and clicks, sliding in the next record, and the opening bars to 'To Know Him is to Love Him' fill the air, there's a murmur of appreciation and a handful of couples start to dance.

'This is a bit more my speed,' I say. I hold out my hand and Lee slips into my arms without hesitation, like she belongs there.

One of my hands rests on the small of her back, holding her close. The other is tangled with hers, and I pull it against my chest, over my erratically beating heart.

'Thank you for dancing with me,' she says softly, as we sway gently around the dance floor.

'Any time.' I lift my arm, sending her out into a spin and then twirling her back into my arms. She crashes against my chest, laughing.

By some unspoken agreement we carry on dancing, even when the song ends and another begins.

'So, how did it go, talking to Jack tonight?' she asks after a moment.

'I felt like a dick keeping this a secret from him,' I admit.

'I was surprised to hear Phoebe talking about Uncle Jack and Aunt Cyn,' Lee says. 'Have you guys spent a lot of time together?'

She keeps the words light, but I catch the faint trace of yearning in them, and I know what's going on: she feels left out. I introduced Jack and Cynthie to Phoebe, and Lee didn't even know she existed.

That didn't seem like a strange idea before, but now it does. Now I feel awful about it, actually.

'We've met up a few times, and they talk on FaceTime,' I say carefully. 'Last time Jack and Cynthie were in New York, Phoebe and I stayed with them for a few days, and we've hung out in Boston a couple of times, when our schedules lined up. But they've never come here.'

Lee's eyes widen. 'They haven't been to Roseport? Why?'

I allow myself a laugh at that. 'Think about it: can you imagine how this town would react to Jack Turner-Jones showing up? There's literally a chapter of the *Blood/Lust* fan club based here. Rita is the president. Sometimes she wears a T-shirt with a picture of his face on just to mess with me.'

Lee laughs and I feel her relax in my arms.

'And that would be *nothing* compared to Cynthie showing up. I genuinely think they'd throw a parade with floats and everything.' Sure, my best friend is a celebrity, but his wife-to-be is an Oscar-winning, mega A-lister, and I am utterly certain that this whole town would lose their collective minds.

'They'd make her the mayor,' Lee grins. 'They'd force her to join the Roseport Players. They'd have a Cynthie Taylor look-a-like competition and get her to be the judge.'

'Now it just sounds like you're pitching ideas.'

'They'd create a shared calendar so unhinged that Cynthie wouldn't have time to brush her teeth.'

'Exactly.' We reach the edge of the dance floor, and I use the opportunity of turning to draw her a little closer. The smell of honey invades my senses. 'But also . . . I don't think I was ready to have them here. Not yet.'

'Why not?'

I take a moment to think about it. 'Because I felt like I was still working it all out, I suppose. How to . . . *be*. Here.'

'And you didn't actually invite me, either,' she frowns. 'I just turned up.'

'Maybe,' I shrug, 'but I'm so fucking glad you're here.'

'You are?'

She looks so hopeful that I throw any remaining shred of common sense I possess to the wind. 'I am. I love having you here, I love sharing this place with you.'

'You're lucky, you know? It's so . . . bright and alive here.' She glances around the bar with a touch of wistfulness in her expression.

'It is.' I can't take my eyes off her. 'And you're helping me to appreciate that. I think I was afraid if Jack came here, he'd know something was off. That seeing him here would be like pulling out my camera, that it would hurt, make me want my old life back . . . and I feel like a shit dad for even *thinking* that.'

Lee gives a low murmur of protest, but I shake my head.

'This was never part of my plan.' A rough laugh escapes me. 'Not that I really had one. But *this*,' I remove my hand briefly from her back to gesture around us, 'this isn't even close to where I thought I'd end up. I suppose I was worried that I'd feel trapped, that bringing any part of my old life here would only make me want what I couldn't have.'

My hand goes back to her waist and I look down at her.

'I haven't stayed in one place, had a home, a *real* home in a long time. I didn't think I needed that . . . or wanted it, but I was wrong. I've been running around for years just trying to find somewhere I could breathe. It wasn't until you arrived that I finally realised I don't feel trapped at all, that everything I didn't even know I wanted . . . it's right here.'

Her cheek is on my chest as I hold her tight against me, and as 'I Will Always Love You' plays on the juke box, my words hang in the air.

Because maybe everything I want *is* right here in Roseport, now, in this moment. But it won't be. Not for much longer.

Lee and I don't speak. We let the song wash over us, we keep on dancing.

If one week is all I have then I'm making every second count.

Chapter Thirty-Seven

Lee

It's a pretty perfect date night, and to cap it all off, we're home by eleven. I could say that's because we're being responsible: we've got our meeting with Charles tomorrow, and we need to relieve Claudia from her babysitting duties. I'd love to pretend that's why we rush home from the bar, why we sit next to each other in the back of Bud's cab, our hands resting on the seat between us, close but not quite touching while the air between us trembles.

But we're not being responsible. We're being horny little monsters.

'Darlings! I do hope you had fun,' Claudia twinkles from the sofa where she's flicking through a fashion magazine. 'Although I thought you'd be hours yet.'

'Did it all go okay?' Nico asks, studiously ignoring this.

Claudia waves her hand. 'Of course! We had a *wonderful* time.'

Nico gives her a grateful smile. 'I'll quickly look in . . .' He gestures towards Phoebe's door.

Claudia and I watch him go. 'He's such a great dad,' she says, her eyes soft.

'He really is.'

'I always knew he would be.' Claudia looks suddenly sad. 'Nothing like his own father. He loves that little girl so much.'

'She loves him, too.'

The wistful expression disappears, and Claudia smiles. 'She does. But then, how could she help it? My son is a very loveable man . . .' The look she gives me is arch.

Thankfully, we're interrupted by Nico coming back into the room.

'Did she wake up?' Claudia asks.

'For a second,' Nico grins. 'But she's back out like a light. Taco's all snuggled up with her. I take it from the state of her walls you two had a good night . . . Who exactly is Patty Felton and how did she earn a spot on the grudge list?'

Claudia's alligator grin widens. 'A *ghastly* woman who has outbid me at the last three auctions I've attended. She follows me around and then jumps in with all that gauche crypto money her husband makes or downloads or however it works.' Claudia sniffs. 'I guess you can't buy good taste so she's always trying to steal mine. Anyway, Phoebe and I had a great time discussing vendettas and plans for vengeance.'

Nico groans. 'I don't think I want to know.'

'No, no.' Claudia is airy. 'Phoebe had some excellent ideas. She definitely takes after me. Apparently Magda is very *love and light* about things, which I find so admirable, but ultimately very unsatisfying, don't you think? Anyway, my sweet ones, I'm sure you're *dying* to get to bed.' This last line is delivered with all the subtlety of a brass marching band, and she winks as she throws a giant cashmere pashmina around herself. 'And Bud is still outside waiting for me. Such an intelligent man, we do have the most *insightful* conversations. Goodnight!'

She shuts the door behind her, and the house falls silent.

In the quiet, the throb of my own heartbeat rings in my ears; my skin suddenly feels too tight. All the tension that tangled between us in the back of the cab comes rushing back in an instant.

When I glance at Nico he's running his eyes over me like he has a list of wicked things he wants to do and a pretty good idea of where he's going to start.

I don't say anything, can't say anything. I only turn and head for the bedroom. Nico follows in silence, his steps unhurried. I shiver, but don't let myself turn around, totally aware of his presence.

I stop by the foot of the bed, my gaze unfocused on the sheets and my heart hammering. I realise I'm nervous. The anticipation that has been building all night . . . it feels brand new. It feels like the first time. There's the sharp click of a lock turning.

When I turn to face him, Nico's eyes are dark. 'It's lucky that this place was part of the inn,' his voice is low, 'or I'd have had to fit a lock myself. Now I have you where I want you. No interruptions.'

He takes another step towards me, nudges me backwards so that my legs hit the edge of the bed.

'Oh?' I look up at him. 'And what exactly do you have planned?'

His smile unfurls slowly. 'I have some thoughts.'

Lowering to his knees in front of me, he runs one warm hand down my leg, rumbling his approval at the feeling of the soft suede under his fingertips.

'But if you want me to touch you then you're going to have to be quiet.' Slowly, he traces the seam of the fabric along the inside of my calf. 'Do you think you can do that?'

'Yes,' I whisper, wetting my lips. Phoebe's room might be on the opposite side of the house, but I know we have to keep the noise down.

'These shoes,' he says almost absently. 'I still remember when I first saw you in Vegas, sitting at the bar, flirting with the bartender in your fuck-me heels. I wanted to punch that guy in the face.'

'If it helps,' I manage, 'I was very bad at flirting.'

Amusement flickers across his face. 'Sit on the edge of the bed,' he demands, and when I do, he eases my right shoe off, pressing his thumb into the arch of my foot in a way that has my eyes fluttering shut. 'I don't know how you walk in these things.'

'Practice,' I smile as he repeats the action, his big, warm hand wrapping around my other foot. He stands up, towering over me.

'I've thought a lot about this,' Nico murmurs. 'About fucking my wife in our bed.'

My breath catches. *His wife.* He says the words as if he likes the feel of them in his mouth. I let myself fall a bit further into the fantasy. Nico's wife. For the next week that's what I am. I'm not going to let worries about the future ruin this, I decide, and I feel fiercely protective of this moment, like some sort of feral Zen master. I'm living in the now, and the now is *spectacular.*

Nico leans over me, grips the hem of my jumper and pulls it up over my head. Cradling my face between his hands he finally kisses me, easing us back on the bed. He tastes like whisky, his mouth a hot, slow tease. I try not to black out as his tongue slides against mine, and the sandpaper scruff on his jaw scrapes against my skin. He traces my cheekbone with his fingers. My teeth close around his earlobe, the metallic touch of his earring cold on my tongue, and he shivers.

The room is full of quiet sighs and whispered encouragement. His fingers are deft as they undo my bra, as he turns his attention to my breasts, nipping and sucking and teasing me all while he unbuttons my trousers. He kisses his way down my body as he slides them off, and my fingers thread through his dark curls while he places open-mouthed kisses across my thighs, one big hand pressing lightly on my stomach in a silent command to keep still.

I make a choked, desperate noise and he lifts his head. 'What did I say, baby? I need you to be quiet, or I'll have to stop.'

'I'll be quiet,' I promise, feverish. 'I'll be so quiet. Please don't stop.'

He hooks his fingers into the sides of my underwear and drags them slowly down my legs, and then his mouth is where I want it, where I *need* it to be, and I squirm and press my hand to my lips to keep from crying out as he fucks me with his fingers, with his tongue – leisurely, languidly, *relentlessly* – until my vision hazes over and I come apart. I press my hand harder over my mouth, swallowing a scream as the heat uncurls inside me, starting in my toes and travelling up, up, up until I'm nothing but stardust, a supernova exploding across the sky.

When I come back to earth, Nico is lying beside me, wearing a self-satisfied smirk. He's also fully dressed and I don't have a stitch on. This would usually make me feel self-conscious but I think he blew up that part of my brain.

'No fair,' I grumble. 'Why do you have all your clothes on?'

'We can remedy that situation any time you like.'

'Great.' I press my hand to my heart, which feels like it's trying to escape out of my chest. 'Just give me two to three business days to catch my breath.'

'We're in no hurry,' he says, and as if to prove the point he leans over and gives me a lingering kiss. His fingers trail down my side, and stop at my tattoo – he traces the letters with his fingertips, a barely there touch that has me thinking maybe I don't need that long to recover after all.

'Tell me about this,' he whispers. 'It's from *Pride and Prejudice*, right?'

I lift my brows in surprise and he laughs. 'I Googled it,' he admits. '*Everything nourishes what is strong already*,' he reads the elegant, looping script that trails over my ribcage.

'I got it last year,' I say as he continues to touch me. 'Tara and I both agreed to get bookish tattoos and it felt . . . daring, actually. Unexpected. Like a secret.'

'Mmm . . .' He leans down and kisses the ink. 'Knowing that underneath those tidy clothes it's silk underwear and secret tattoos . . .

That's going to make my life more difficult. I have enough trouble focusing around you as it is.'

I laugh, and he grins and kisses my neck.

'So what does it mean?' he asks.

'Elizabeth Bennet says it.' I close my eyes, relaxing into the feeling of his fingers stroking my skin. I want to purr like a cat. 'She's being funny, talking about someone writing bad poetry for her sister Jane, and how there's no quicker way to kill off romance, and then Mr Darcy says something about how he thought poetry was the food of love. She tells him it probably is if people are really, properly in love with each other, that "everything nourishes what is strong already".'

'I like that,' Nico murmurs.

'I do too,' I agree sleepily. 'People think love is all poetry and tempests, but I never wanted it to be like that. I think there's something romantic about saying that a love story doesn't sprout because of a few pretty words, but that when you're *in* love, really in love, then art – then *everything* – can be *for* you.'

'Like when you hear a love song, and you finally feel like you really understand it,' Nico muses.

'Exactly. You don't fall in love *because* of the song, the song says something about how you feel already and in that moment you feel it even more. It feeds it. Something strong that only gets stronger.'

He's quiet for a moment, and I feel hazy, drugged, slipping into that place between waking and dreaming as he strokes my side, as he feathers kisses across my shoulder. He manoeuvres the bed sheets, dragging them over my sensitive skin. I prise my eyes open to see him unbuttoning his shirt.

'What are you doing?' I ask.

'Shhh, go back to sleep,' he says.

'I'm not asleep,' and I feel cross about this comment, until his shirt hits the floor and I get to drink in all those beautiful muscles, all that delicious gold skin. He shucks off his jeans and slips into bed beside me, wearing only his boxers. He reaches out and pulls me against him, his fingers sliding over my stomach, as he brushes a kiss against my neck.

'You were definitely asleep,' he murmurs against my hair. 'You were making cute little noises.'

I wrinkle my nose. 'I certainly was not. And anyway,' I press against him, 'I seem to remember something about you wanting to fuck your wife in this bed.'

Nico lets out a pained hiss, and I can feel him hard and ready against me.

'But only if you can be *very* quiet,' I whisper, turning in his embrace and winding my arms around his neck, kissing him and rubbing my extremely naked body against his.

'Fuck,' he bites out. 'I want you so much.'

'Who's stopping you?' I ask, as my fingers drift down, pushing into his underwear, curling around his erection. He pumps into my hand with a needy growl, and I smile against his mouth. 'Shhh,' I murmur.

'You think you're so funny,' he mutters, something dangerous sparking in his eyes. 'Let's see who's laughing when I'm inside you and you're the one trying not to scream my name.'

'Promises, promises . . .' My words are swallowed up by his kiss, and then his hands are everywhere. There's no part of me that's left untended. It's chaotic in the best way. He keeps getting distracted by something new: Did I know how soft my skin is in this precise spot behind my ear? Did I know the freckles on my back are shaped like the Eridanus constellation? Did I know – as he licks across my pulse – that my wrists have been a real problem for him? I'm so pretty everywhere, he tells me, I'm delicious, he claims, as he tastes and samples and takes. I smell like honey and I feel like I was made for him.

When he finally rolls on a condom and slides into me I'm a mess; shuddering, pressing my face into his neck, trying desperately not to make a noise.

He stretches over me, opening the nightstand, a smirk on his lips, and moments later he reaches between us, sliding the vibrator over my clit while he's inside me. The movement of his hips presses the toy harder against my over-sensitised flesh, the flicker of the air pressure pulses in a relentless rhythm and I'm so full of him, stretched to the limit, right on the edge of pain.

My control is a fraying ribbon, a thousand broken threads. He grinds into me, and the pressure on my clit is devastating. It takes about five insane seconds before I'm coming harder than I ever have in my life. I bite down on his shoulder, completely unravelling as I feel him fall over the edge with me.

'God, that was incredible,' he murmurs when we finally return to earth, when the aftershocks of my orgasm are tingling through my heavy limbs.

'Think how amazing we'll be with some practice,' I agree.

He lifts an eyebrow. 'We need practice?'

'It does make perfect,' I say primly.

He smiles, a wolf smile, leaning in to kiss me again. 'Then by all means. Let's get started.'

Chapter Thirty-Eight

Nico

The next morning I wake up in bed alone. I stretch against the sheets, my hand resting in the space where Lee was curled up, sleeping against me. The pillow smells like honey and my entire body is aching. We crashed out after round three last night, and there's a deep, heavy satisfaction in my limbs. I want her again, I want her now, and it's a hunger that scares me.

I drag myself up, jump in the shower and pull on my clothes. When I open the bedroom door, Lee and Phoebe are in the kitchen and the smell of bacon fills the air. No wonder Taco is sitting hopefully at Lee's feet. There's music on the speaker, a Disney soundtrack that Phoebe has been playing relentlessly lately.

'Hey, Dad,' Phoebe says, waving a spatula in my direction. 'We're making pancakes. Chocolate chip pancakes. And bacon.'

My stomach rumbles. Lee looks at me over her shoulder and smiles. She's wearing those pink cat pyjamas again. Her feet are bare. I want her more than I've ever wanted anything in my life.

'I thought you didn't know how to make pancakes?' I say, pouring myself a cup of coffee from the pot that Lee has made and grabbing a seat at the table. *Look at me, I'm so civilised.* I feel like a wild creature pretending to be a normal human man.

'I don't, but I found a recipe online,' she replies, frowning as she ladles batter into the pan.

'And there's nothing gross in them at all,' Phoebe is gleeful. 'They're just regular pancakes, and they're delicious.'

'Phoebe had to try the first one,' Lee explains. 'Just to be safe. And because it was wonky.'

Phoebe nods solemnly. 'I took one for the team.'

'Okay,' Lee says to her now, 'I see bubbles, let's flip.'

She moves aside and holds the pan so that Phoebe can get in and carefully flip the pancake over, her tongue held between her teeth as she concentrates. Obviously the two of them have a system.

I want this every morning for the rest of my life.

It's quite the realisation, and I sit frozen in my seat, letting that sink in, as the two of them laugh and talk. Did my entire world just get turned upside down over a chocolate chip pancake?

'. . . and then we did line dancing,' I finally tune back in to hear Lee say.

'*Dad* danced?' Phoebe groans. 'Did other people see? That is so embarrassing.'

'He did pretty well, actually.' Lee slides a plate of pancakes and crispy bacon in front of me.

'I was terrible,' I say, trying to pull myself together. 'But not all of us are former ballerinas.'

'You used to do ballet?' Phoebe asks Lee, interested.

Lee tips another pancake onto a plate for Phoebe and nods. 'From when I was four until . . .' she tilts her head, thinking, 'about fourteen I guess.'

'Why did you stop?' Phoebe asks, bringing her plate to the table and sitting next to me.

'My parents wanted me to go professional,' Lee replies, leaning back against the counter. Her feet are crossed in front of her, and her toenails are painted a delicate shell pink. 'But I really hated performing. I got terrible stage fright. I wanted dancing to be fun but they didn't understand that, and it led to too many disagreements so in the end I quit.'

I digest that fact for a moment, another dark mark against Lee's parents.

'Why? Are you interested in doing ballet?' Lee asks.

I snort out a laugh at that, but *instantly* realise my mistake. There's a little flash of something hurt and vulnerable in Phoebe's eyes and I put it there.

'Sorry, sorry,' I rush to say. 'I didn't think ballet would be your thing but if it is then I'm all for it.'

I glance at Lee, panicked. I hate this, the times where I fuck something up, where I think, with an awful clarity, *wow, here is a moment my daughter will be bringing up in therapy someday.*

Lee only blinks, her face calm as she brings her own plate with her to the table and takes the seat on my other side. She leans towards Phoebe and lowers her voice. 'How can someone so pretty be so silly?' she sighs, before turning to me, resting her chin in her hand. 'Nico Hart, don't you know women contain multitudes? Your daughter can be a badass grudge-holding astronomer *and* rock a tutu.'

Phoebe bursts into giggles, her expression instantly lightening. 'Yeah, Dad,' she echoes, her voice a verbal eye roll.

I know I'll always be fighting a losing battle when it comes to these two. Why do I love it so much? 'You're absolutely right, I apologise.'

Lee gives a regal nod, which Phoebe copies.

'Anyway, I think the dance studio in town offers beginner ballet classes,' Lee says, sipping her coffee. She looks at me over the top of her cup. 'Doesn't Lacey teach them?'

'I have no idea,' I say, wondering how she knows about this, but Phoebe nods.

'Yeah, some of the kids from school go. It's on Mondays.'

'So why don't I take you on Monday?' Lee asks, sending me a questioning look. 'We can see if you like it.'

I nod eagerly. 'Absolutely.'

'Really?' Phoebe looks so happy my heart squeezes.

Thank you, I mouth to Lee over Phoebe's head when she's not looking. Lee just smiles, gives a little shrug.

'But before that we need to talk about Halloween,' Phoebe says around a mouthful of pancakes. 'It's on Wednesday and we haven't even discussed costumes.'

'That's right.' I stifle a groan. No one mentions how many costume ideas you have to come up with as a parent. Every week at school seems to bring some new, themed event that I find out about at the last minute, leaving me scrabbling to make something impressive out of bin bags and parcel tape.

'This year we can do a family costume!' Phoebe declares.

'A family costume?' Lee repeats the words.

Phoebe slurps her juice. 'Oh yeah, Charles will *love* it.'

It's a bucket of cold water. My eyes meet Lee's as the two of us remember what we're all actually doing here. The lines between pretend and real shifted a long, long time ago, but Phoebe doesn't know that, and I can't tell her about it. Why confuse her when Lee is leaving in a week?

As far as my daughter is concerned, we're *pretending* we're one happy family, and if that thought hurts me it's absolutely nothing to what I know Lee is feeling in this moment. Because she's the one who has to leave all this behind, and I have a horrible feeling she wants to keep it just as much as I do.

Under the table I put my hand on her leg. She gives me the sort of blank, calm look that I know means she's going through some serious emotional turmoil.

'What about the Three Musketeers?' Phoebe muses. 'Taco can be Dogtanian.'

'Maybe,' I say distantly.

'Sounds good,' Lee says neutrally.

Phoebe picks up her plate and licks the maple syrup off it, and I don't even have the heart to stop her.

'Shall we watch a movie before your meeting?' she asks.

'Sure,' I agree, and as Phoebe keeps up a stream of cheerful chatter, Lee and I descend into silence.

'Why am I so nervous?' Lee asks me later, as she moves around, straightening cushions and smoothing the curtains so they fall just so. Magda has collected Phoebe and Taco so it's just the two of us in the house, getting ready for our interrogation.

'I don't know.' I walk over and take her hand in mine, holding her still. 'I let you rearrange the spice rack and everything.'

'You'll be glad about that when he tells us he's doing a surprise inspection,' Lee mutters, but she squeezes my fingers. 'He'll say, *wow, this is truly the spice rack of a responsible adult*, and you'll say, *thank you, Lee.*'

'Thank you, Lee,' I say, and I drop a fleeting kiss on her mouth.

We haven't spoken about the awkward moment at the breakfast table this morning. What is there to say about it that we didn't discuss last night? I thought about bringing it up, but what if it pushes her further away? Lee and I agreed on the parameters of this relationship, and I can't immediately start asking for more, knowing she might not be able to give it.

'Besides,' I say now, keeping my tone light. 'Nothing can be as bad as the first time he came over. We've got this. It's not our first rodeo.'

'I hate it when people say that,' Lee grumbles. 'Would you consider someone who had done *two* rodeos to be an expert? That doesn't seem like enough rodeos.'

'How many rodeos would be sufficient?'

'I don't know!' she huffs, exasperated. 'Maybe if someone said "this isn't my seventeenth rodeo" I'd think, huh, this person probably knows a thing or two about rodeoing.' She pauses, frowns. 'Wait, is rodeoing a word?'

'How did we end up here?'

'I have no idea!' She has a wild look in her eye. 'It's your fault! You're the one who started going on about rodeos.'

'You're absolutely right,' I agree. 'But it's all going to be fine. You're wearing your shoulder pads and everything.'

She deflates, leaning against me, and I press my cheek to the top of her head. 'That's true,' she says. 'We can handle this.'

'We're a good team,' I agree.

We're still standing wrapped around each other like that when there's a knock at the door.

'Show time,' Lee says, pulling her shoulders back.

It is 3 p.m. exactly. Charles Saunders waits neatly on the doorstep. Lee invites him inside, all calm politeness, while I fix everyone a cup of tea.

'Thank goodness,' Charles says gratefully. 'I haven't had a proper cup all week.'

It's incredibly civilised.

We arrange ourselves around the table and Charles pulls an embossed, leather portfolio from his briefcase, unscrews the cap on his gold fountain pen and begins going through his questions.

'Most of this is standard,' he says, looking at us over the top of his glasses. 'Obviously the terms of a clause such as this one are very broad. It's a trifle unorthodox and leaves a certain amount of latitude to the trustee.'

He puts a lot of emphasis on those last words. Essentially, everything rests on his assessment. No pressure there then. The first questions he asks are easy enough: some family background, a little more about Lee's personal history, education and work.

Lee is serene and businesslike throughout. I try not to get distracted by how hot and competent she is.

'Now about your intelligence work,' Charles says to her, sliding his fingers over the notes in front of him. 'Could you elucidate on some of these contracts? I noticed in the records you provided that several of them are rather sizeable.'

He hands her a piece of paper and she scans it while I try not to look thrown. What intelligence work?

Lee leans forward and runs her eyes over the document. 'Certainly,' she says. 'Do you mind if I consult my notes?'

'Not at all.'

Lee bends down and opens up the slim briefcase next to her chair. When did she put that there? She pulls out a leather portfolio that matches Charles's and his eyes light with approval. Oh god, there are two of them now.

Lee uncaps her own pen and starts annotating the sheet of paper Charles gave her. Her focus is absolute, the only sound is the clock ticking above the stove. Finally, she slides it back to him. 'I've marked out the various agencies and provided you with contact details in case you need to confirm anything,' she says. 'Obviously I can't go into detail, a lot of my work is sensitive . . .' she trails off delicately, and Charles nods in understanding. I'm glad one of us has a clue what's going on.

'For my purposes, I suppose the key question is whether or not you enter into any field work.' Charles tilts his head. 'This would obviously have repercussions in terms of the safety and security of Mr Hart and his daughter.'

Field work? What the fuck?

Lee doesn't look thrown at all, just shakes her head. 'The work I do is purely as an analyst and on a freelance basis. I am under no specific obligation to any of the security services, and certainly pose no threat to anyone's safety.'

'Excellent. Charles makes a note while I gawp at Lee.

She lifts her brows at me and I snap my mouth shut. Fine, so I unknowingly married the James Bond of accountants; now isn't the time to freak out about that.

'And I can see that your financial records are extremely thorough,' Charles says and again there's a definite note of approval. I had no idea that Lee had even had to provide her financial information; god, that's so intrusive. I shift in my seat, but Lee places a reassuring hand on my leg.

'I *am* an accountant,' she says dryly, and Charles gives a short laugh.

'There was no prenuptial agreement before your wedding took place, is that correct?' Charles looks back down at his papers.

'Why would we need a prenup?' I manage to sound more polite than I'm feeling.

'You're poised to inherit a substantial sum of money, Mr Hart,' Charles chides gently. 'We would certainly have advised—'

'As you can see,' Lee jumps in, 'I am financially independent. I make a very comfortable living. Should Nico and I ever divorce . . .'

My stomach twists. Divorce. Of course we're going to have to get divorced. Why does the thought make me want to Hulk out and rip the room apart?

'I would not expect there to be any kind of settlement,' Lee finishes calmly.

'And would you be willing to sign something to that effect?' Charles asks. 'A postnuptial agreement? My office would be happy to draw one up.'

'Certainly,' Lee says at the same time as I growl, 'Over my dead body.'

Lee turns to me, her eyes wide, as she clearly tries to communicate *what are you doing?*

I know that one way or another we're going to have to dissolve this marriage and that Lee isn't going to ask me for a penny anyway, but everything inside me is rioting at the thought of her signing something like that. I don't care how illogical it is, it's not happening.

'No prenup or postnup or whatever you're calling it. No,' I say, the words unyielding.

Charles only lifts his brows and continues. 'Very well.' He clears his throat. 'In that case, we should turn to you, Mr Hart. I understand that you have been working in construction, but that your current project is shortly to be completed?'

'That's correct,' I say, my throat suddenly dry.

'And may I ask you what your plans are? Will you be continuing in this line of work?'

'I've considered it,' I manage. 'Maine doesn't require a state-level contracting licence, so I could take local jobs and still be available to . . .' I almost say Phoebe, but shift at the last moment, 'my family. But, it would take time to build a client base, particularly in such a small area. And although I've made some good contacts in the last eleven months, it would be difficult to sustain a small business of my own right now. One option is to join a local crew. I have several potential leads on that in the short term.'

Charles nods. 'I understand that prior to your move to Roseport you were working as a photojournalist?'

'That's right,' I say tightly.

'Is that an area of work you may return to?'

'That work is not compatible with the needs of my family,' I say mechanically.

'I see.' Charles hums and makes another note. The scratch of his pen against the paper feels judgemental. I can only imagine what he must think of me. No plan, no way of providing for my family, apparently depending on my *financially independent* wife and the big payout I have coming from my dead dad. What a winner.

'You don't have a private pension set up, is that correct?' he asks.

'I do, but I haven't contributed to it for a while.' I swallow. 'I'll see if I can find the details for you.'

'I see,' he says again and I can't even look at Lee. 'And what provisions have you made thus far for Phoebe's future? Is there a college fund?'

'Not as yet.' I swallow. 'I do have some savings but obviously that's a priority for me.'

My own failures as a father are thrown into stark relief. Guilt claws at me. I'm letting my daughter down. I'm a terrible dad.

'We're still working out our best options for the future,' Lee cuts in here, and her voice is all steel. 'Nico's primary concern – and mine – is Phoebe's wellbeing. For the last year he has demonstrated nothing but level-headed and practical responsibility. He is taking this moment to explore his options and make the best decision for everyone involved. That isn't something to be rushed simply because his father has sent someone to rake his life over the coals in an act of petty control.'

It's my turn to stare at her.

'I didn't—' Charles begins, but Lee interrupts, her eyes flashing. She's on a roll now.

'Nico is one of the best people I know,' she continues hotly. 'No, scratch that. He's *the best person.* I have been lucky enough to have him in my life for twenty-seven years and he's a kind, generous, caring, intelligent man. Just because he refused to follow the path his father wanted him to, he's had to spend his whole life being made to feel like some sort of ungrateful, irresponsible waste of time.

'He's been belittled and snubbed by that side of his family while making his own way in the world – without a penny from his father by the way – and climbed to the top of a wildly demanding and impossibly competitive field through hard work and talent alone. Now you want to make him feel as if he's letting that little girl down, when he'd give up his whole life for her happiness? Well, not today, not on my watch.'

She's standing now, and Charles and I exchange a look of bewilderment.

'This entire process is insulting and Nico is handling it with more grace than you or I ever would. The *idea* that he should have to prove he's some sort of saint before he inherits what's rightfully his, from a man who – let's be honest – was one of the most morally bankrupt individuals I've ever met, and I'll remind you that I occasionally investigate terrorist organisations for a living . . .'

Wait, what?

'. . . is an irresponsible and disgusting misuse of the legal system and you ought to be *ashamed* of yourself.'

Her cheeks are pink, her chest is heaving. There's a moment of ringing silence. Charles closes his portfolio and slides it into his briefcase.

'Thank you. I think I have all I need for now,' he says levelly. 'I'll show myself out.'

He pushes his chair back and Lee and I both watch as he leaves, closing the front door behind him with a click.

I exhale.

'Well, Daisy. That was some second rodeo.'

'Oh my god,' she whispers. 'I did it again.'

'Yup.'

'Why are you *smiling*? This is a disaster. I basically just told the trustee to go fuck himself.' Her fingers are in her hair, her expression is panicked.

'Yup.'

She waves a hand at my face. 'Stop it. Why are you looking at me like that?'

I walk over and reach for her waist, and then I bend down, and unceremoniously haul her up over my shoulder. She beats at my back with her fists. 'Nicolas Hart!' she yelps. 'What are you *doing*? Put me down, *right now*.'

I kick the door to the bedroom open with my foot and toss her on the bed, where she bounces. She pushes her hair out of her face and looks up at me, furious.

'What on earth has got into you? Have you lost your mind?'

I stare down at her, and start unbuttoning my shirt. My hands go to my belt. Her mouth drops open, her pupils blow out like drops of ink in water.

'Yup. Now get naked.'

There's a tapping sound against the window.

'Fuck off, Russell!' Lee and I both shout at the same time.

And then I show my wife just how out of my mind she makes me.

Twice.

Chapter Thirty-Nine

Lee

It has been over twenty-four hours since I went nuclear on the man who's deciding his entire fate, and Nico's being surprisingly relaxed about it. Admittedly, the multiple orgasms probably had a calming effect, but even after we dragged ourselves out of bed and Magda returned with Phoebe, he remained unnaturally cheerful.

I cannot believe I blew up like that. I never lose my temper. Prior to yesterday afternoon I didn't even know I *had* a temper to lose. I still feel a bit sick and shaky whenever I think about it. As the poster child for avoiding conflict, this marks a significant shift in my sense of self.

I also can't believe I jeopardised the future of two people I care about so much. There has to be a way to fix it. Perhaps if I find Charles and apologise . . .

'What is this movie, again?' Phoebe asks, carrying an enormous bowl of popcorn to the coffee table in front of the sofa.

'It's called *Bringing Up Baby*. It's Lee's favourite.' Nico is in the kitchen, pouring multiple bags of American candy into different bowls.

Today Nico took one look at me and declared it a 'stay-inside-and-talk-to-no-one' day before popping out to get ice cream and snacks for us. As a result, there's a genuinely deadly amount of sugar in this house and Phoebe is delighted. No wonder the town manages to sustain the business of four separate dentists.

We've already watched a film, three episodes of a show where a couple are renovating a French chateau, and spent an hour lounging around reading our books. It's the strangest turn of events, but spending time with Phoebe and Nico is as restorative and soothing to me as spending time alone. I haven't had that with anyone but Gran before.

'I've never heard of it,' Phoebe muses, dragging a pile of blankets out from her bedroom. 'Did you say it's black and white?' She sounds suspicious.

'I really think you'll love it,' I promise, hoping that I'm right. 'I was about your age the first time I watched it.'

'With your gran?' Phoebe asks. Unfortunately, Phoebe is very interested in my grandmother, this mystical figure of fun, and so she brings her up quite often.

'That's right,' I agree, because of course it is. All my best memories are with Gran.

'Well, I guess if Gran likes it then I'll try,' Phoebe sighs heroically.

'Oh good.' My dry tone is lost on her and Nico shoots me a sympathetic look.

He grabs the final bowls of sweets and brings them over, the table practically groaning under their weight, and the three of us arrange ourselves on the sofa – me at one end, Nico at the other, Phoebe in the middle, and Taco pours himself into a tiny gap between Phoebe and me. Phoebe arranges the blankets over us and, once she's satisfied, Nico hits play.

I glance over at the two of them. They're both glued to the film, wearing matching expressions of enjoyment, and I vow that I'll make everything right before I leave. It's the least I can do.

The film plays and I get drawn into the familiar story of

Katharine Hepburn and Cary Grant hunting for their tame leopard while being ridiculously funny and extremely gorgeous. Every time Phoebe giggles, little starbursts go off in my chest. She leans against me, a small, warm weight. Six more days. Not only six more days with Nico, but six more days of this, of all of us together.

'That was excellent,' Phoebe says, when the credits roll. 'Even if it was in black and white. I can't wait to show Maya, she's going to love it.'

'You can watch it with her next week,' Nico says. 'You're spending the day at hers on Sunday, don't forget.'

Sunday is when my flight home is booked, and Nico's gaze meets mine. For the first time since Charles left, anxiety tightens around his eyes. Perhaps it's finally sinking in how little time we have to fix everything.

I can do it, I tell myself. I can make everything better. All I need to do is track down Charles and apologise for my outburst. I wonder if it's too soon to send his assistant a third email. I barely included any exclamation marks in the last one.

'Maybe *I* should have a pet leopard,' Phoebe wonders. 'He could be friends with Taco.'

'Trust me, leopards don't make good pets outside Hollywood,' Nico says, stretching and getting to his feet to clear away the empty bowls. (Phoebe demolished everything in sight with the horrifying, if impressive, efficiency of a swarm of locusts.)

'And your dad would know,' I say, an idea occurring to me. Maybe there's something else I can help to fix before I go. 'You took photos of them in the wild, right?' I turn to look at Nico over my shoulder. 'Where was that?'

'Yeah,' he says shortly. 'Botswana.'

'You *did*?' Phoebe asks. 'He never talks about that stuff,' she tells me.

I grab my phone and pull up the pictures with a few taps on the

National Geographic website. In one of them a leopard stares directly into the lens, as it prowls through the scrub towards the camera. I turn the screen to Phoebe and she huddles over it.

'Woah!' Her voice holds an awed note. 'You took these, Dad? You got this close to them?'

'Not as close as the picture makes it look.' Nico comes to stand behind the sofa, looking at the image over my shoulder. His voice is stiff, but Phoebe doesn't seem to notice. 'I was on top of a jeep about fifty feet back.'

'That is so cool.' Phoebe is still looking through the photos.

'My favourite was the whales in New Zealand,' I say, taking the phone back and clicking through to the pictures that I have saved. There's one that Nico took of an enormous southern right whale, suspended in the endless blue water; next to it a diver swims, like a tiny doll.

Phoebe's eyes widen. 'You went in the water with them?'

'Your dad does all sorts of cool stuff,' I say. 'One time he rappelled down a glacier in Iceland. There's probably not a mountain range he hasn't climbed all over. And he swam with sharks in Australia.' I shudder. 'I have to admit I don't love those photographs.'

'Show me!' Phoebe demands. She reaches over the back of the sofa and grabs Nico's arm. 'Dad! Show me the sharks!'

Nico sends an unreadable look my way, and I can only hope I haven't massively overstepped. Either way, he's defenceless in the face of Phoebe's enthusiasm.

'I'll grab my laptop,' he says finally. 'Hang on.'

While Nico and Phoebe huddle over his computer and he clicks through, showing her different images, telling her about his travels, I try to melt into the background. I pull up some work on my own computer and sit at the kitchen table with a glass of wine, letting their chatter wash over me as I work, losing myself in the numbers. I have plenty to catch up on.

At some point, Nico presses a hand to the back of my neck before he throws together a vegetable stir fry and I watch Phoebe eat it with a feeling of relief. Nico's no longer the only one worried about getting vegetables into this child. Yesterday I ordered a giant tub of children's vitamin gummies online that apparently taste like Skittles.

'If you could take pictures of one animal, which would it be?' Phoebe asks, slurping noodles into her mouth.

'Snow leopards,' Nico says instantly. 'But it's basically impossible. They're extremely endangered. No one sees them in person, they're like ghosts, but they've caught them on camera traps so we know they're there.'

'Where did they see them?'

'A couple of places. Kyrgyzstan would probably be best.'

'Kyrgyzstan,' Phoebe rolls the word around in her mouth. 'Have you been there?'

'Once.' Nico digs a fork into his own bowl of noodles. 'I did a story about the rangers working up in the Tian Shan mountains.' He pulls up a folder full of photos, of impossible snowy conditions and staggering peaks; of people, wrapped up in winter gear, crossing streams on horseback. It's all so beautiful it punches the air right out of your chest.

'Maybe one day you could take me,' Phoebe says, her eyes still glued to the screen. 'I would love to have adventures like this.'

Nico's gaze meets mine over the top of her head. 'Sure, one day, Bee.'

'I should have a camera. You could show me how to take pictures, couldn't you?'

Nico darts me a look. His throat bobs. 'Yeah. I could show you.'

'And you've done lots of travelling, too, right, Lee?' Phoebe turns to me.

'I have, but accountants don't have as many adventures as photojournalists.'

Nico snorts. 'Right,' he says, and I remember how stunned he looked by Charles's comments yesterday. I often get this reaction when people find out about my work, but honestly, I don't know why they're all so surprised. I'm a forensic accountant. *I* never said my job was boring.

When I pointed this out to Nico last night he scoffed, 'Okay, Ethan Hunt. Just let me know next time you're bringing a terrorist organisation to its knees so I can put the kettle on.'

'Mostly I work in different offices,' I say now.

'And where would *you* go?' Phoebe asks. 'If you could go anywhere?'

I think about it. 'I've never seen the Northern Lights. I'd love to go somewhere snowy and quiet and see them. Norway or Iceland maybe.'

'I've never been anywhere but here,' Phoebe says. 'Well, and Boston. And New York once.'

'You've got lots of time,' I point out.

'I guess.' Phoebe pushes her glasses up her nose. 'Still,' she sounds wistful, 'it would be nice.'

'Maybe we should sort out your passport,' Nico muses. 'Uncle Jack suggested we could all take a trip to England next summer.'

Phoebe's entire face lights up. 'England! Really? We could see Lee and Gran!'

There's a fist around my heart and it's squeezing tighter and tighter.

'All right, Phoebe,' Nico cuts in. 'I think that's enough excitement for one day. Why don't you get ready for bed?'

'Okay,' Phoebe agrees. 'But I want Lee to come with me tonight. We can read my book together. She wants to know what happens to the mermaid, don't you, Lee?' She turns to me, her eyes enormous behind her glasses.

Nico slides a glance at me.

'Of course,' I reply.

Getting Phoebe ready for bed is quite the ordeal. She's not a *baby*, I have to understand. She doesn't *need* someone to put her to bed, she doesn't want to be read *to*, but she does like reading *with* someone. Especially if that someone commits to doing silly voices. She'll even graciously concede to a small amount of snuggling, only for my benefit of course, and as we read we lie back against all her many, many stuffed toys, my arm around her shoulders.

She smells like clean laundry and strawberry toothpaste. Taco curls up in his position at the foot of the bed, heaving the occasional happy sigh.

We read until Phoebe starts to drift off, and I extract myself as gracefully as possible from the mountain of stuffies, ready to turn off the light.

'Hey, Lee,' Phoebe murmurs sleepily.

'Yes?'

'Do you think it's funny that my dad calls me Bee and he calls you Daisy? We're like a set.'

I freeze, my finger on the switch on her bedside lamp. 'Yes,' I croak, 'I suppose we are.'

She snuggles down into her pillow, the window between awake and asleep snapping shut in an instant. She looks so small and defenceless all of a sudden. I can see the baby in her, the younger version of who she is now. Her lashes fan against her round cheeks. There are freckles on the bridge of her nose.

My heart does something catastrophic inside my chest. The bottom drops out of my world.

When I glance up I find Nico leaning in the doorway, looking at us. His arms are crossed over his chest, his jaw is granite hard, his expression flat.

My heart is pounding, as we stare at each other. I feel like I've been caught out, doing something wrong.

Nico peels himself away from the door and hooks his thumb over his shoulder gesturing towards the living room. 'I think you and I need to have a talk,' he says, his voice low.

I swallow, and nod.

Then I turn off the light and follow him.

Chapter Forty

Nico

'I'm sorry,' Lee blurts, pretty much the moment the door shuts behind her.

Seeing as I've just realised I'm going to have to bare my soul to her and I'm in a state of extreme anxiety, it takes a moment for these words to land.

'Sorry?' I frown. 'About what?'

'About what Phoebe just said. About getting . . . too attached to her. I know I shouldn't let it happen.' She's literally wringing her hands now. 'I know it will make everything harder. I didn't mean for it to all get so tangled up like this, for *me* to get so tangled up in your life.' Her breath is coming fast. 'I know it's bad. I know it's all going to hurt. I don't want to hurt her. God, Nico,' she looks at me and her eyes are glazed with tears, 'I didn't even realise I *could* hurt her before this. We should have talked about this ages ago. You're angry and you're right to be. I can't believe . . .' She's so panicked, I reach out and wrap my fingers around her arms.

'Stop,' I say. 'Breathe.'

I actually have some idea about what she's experiencing. When I first met Phoebe it didn't take long for me to understand that if

I wanted to be in her life that meant holding her vulnerable little soul in my hands. Everything I say, every decision I make has consequences for her. It's incredibly overwhelming and Lee is actually handling it better than I did. My epiphany was accompanied by a whole bottle of Jack Daniels.

'But . . . Nico . . .' she looks at me, wild, 'I *love* her.' She presses a hand to her mouth. 'Oh god, I love her. I love her so much.'

My entire universe comes into alignment in a single moment.

'How has this happened?' Lee mutters, clearly not experiencing the same sense of cosmic euphoria. 'I'm not someone who has girls' nights and family dinners, and . . . craft clubs! I'm learning to crochet, Nico! Mrs Penny told me she ordered in a special book about it for me. It's at the library *right now*!'

Okay, now she is losing me a bit.

'This isn't me!' she carries on. 'I'm careful. I'm distant. I don't have all these *people* that matter. I never even met my best friend in person, before this week! Oh god, Gran was right . . . I'm *cold*.'

'What?'

'It's what we argued about, she said I was cold, and I didn't agree with her. I thought she didn't understand me, but she's right. I keep myself apart, I just ran away from her, I shut down—'

'Enough,' I can't stand watching her tear herself apart anymore. 'Lee,' I say, my voice gentling, 'come and sit down.'

I tug her over to the sofa and she sits, her back poker straight while she continues to look traumatised. I crouch down in front of her and take her hands in mine. Her fingers are freezing.

'Listen. Listen to me. You are *not* cold—' I choke off an anxious laugh as I press her hands between mine. 'I mean, physically you are right now, your poor fingers are like ice, but Daisy . . . you're sunshine.'

She's looking at me now. 'You think so? You really . . . believe that?'

I sigh. 'Lee, of course I do. I *know* it. Do you think there's anything cold about what there is between us?'

'I—' She looks thrown by this. 'No, I suppose not.'

I arch a brow at her. 'You suppose not?'

'Well, we've been friends for a long time,' she says hopelessly.

'That's true,' I agree. 'We've been good friends, and never in the last twenty-seven years would I have described you as a cold person. And it's not just me . . . Magda, Phoebe, my mum, they all love you. Kat and Mei and Luke, they think you're amazing. And Tara? She's obsessed with you. She told me about all the times you were there for her. She told me that if I hurt you, she'd spare my life for Phoebe's sake but I'd have to say goodbye to any further plans to procreate.' I shudder, and some of the tension leaves Lee's face; there's a trace of amusement in her eyes and I'm glad someone finds the threat of castration funny.

'But that's not even what I'm talking about.' I push my hands through my hair, frustrated that I can't find the right words 'The feelings *I* have for you – they're not *polite* feelings, okay? They're not lukewarm or friendly. They're wild, Lee. I've been called that my whole life: wild. The things I've done, the way I lived, always chasing some big adventure, the next adrenaline rush, but *nothing* has ever made me feel the way I do about you. You make me feel more alive than I ever have. This thing between us, it's all consuming, it's burning me up inside. I am not a rational human being anymore. You've broken me, in the best possible way. Do you understand? You're not cold, you're *dazzling*.'

She's looking at me now, her eyes wide. I push to my feet, and run a hand over my face, nerves hopping inside me.

'I'm not angry with you. Seeing you with Phoebe only confirmed what I already knew, that I was going to have to talk to you about this, that I was going to have to tell you that I'm not okay with the plan we literally *just* made. That I can't cope with the idea of only having you for six more days. Cards on the table: I'm in love with you.'

Lee continues to stare at me, her face blank.

'I think I need to sit down,' she says eventually.

'You are sitting down.'

'I—' She looks around. 'Right. I'm sorry, I just . . . I'm honestly not sure if this is real. You're in love with me?'

'Pretty fucking desperately, actually.'

'I see. This is . . .' she trails off, frowning.

'You don't seem thrilled about this development,' I manage.

'Thrilled? Nico, there's a Fourth of July firework display going off in my brain right now.'

'Really?'

She nods, and a smile finally breaks over her face. Pure sunshine. My heart starts beating again.

'I mean, I've had a long time to get used to the idea of *me* being in love with *you*,' she says. 'You need to give me a minute to catch up here.'

'Fuck that.' I grab her hand and haul her up into my arms.

The instant her lips touch mine is like holding a match to an incredibly short fuse. I kiss her with everything I have, with all the feelings I want to share with her, and she kisses me back like it's *necessary*, like she needs this as much as I do in order to simply keep surviving. It's not a kiss, it's a claiming, it's a riot, it's our whole lives.

'*Cold*,' I murmur, amused, against her mouth, when we finally pause for air.

I feel her lips curl into a smile against mine. 'Fine. You've made your point,' she says.

'I can make it again,' I trace the curve of her neck with my lips. 'I can make it better.'

She laughs, but catches my face between her hands, looking straight into my eyes. 'We need a plan here.'

'You're right,' I sigh, resting my forehead briefly against hers. 'Okay, if we're actually going to talk I need you to sit over there.' I gesture to the far side of the sofa and after a careful adjustment to my jeans I sit in the armchair as far away from her as possible.

She purses her lips in obvious amusement. Crosses one leg over the other.

'So,' her tone is businesslike, 'cards on the table, isn't that what you said? You're in love with me. I'm in love with you. What are we going to do about it?'

There's a long silence. The amusement slowly leaves her face. I watch as she chews on her bottom lip.

'The idea of being in a relationship doesn't scare me,' I say into the quiet. 'Not with you anyway. My life is a mess, it's far from perfect, but I don't want to wait . . . I want us. In this. Together. All in.'

'Your life doesn't look like a mess to me. It looks busy and joyful and chaotic, but in the best way.'

'And can you cope with that, tidy girl?'

'I *want* that,' she says. 'I want it very much.'

I smile.

'But,' she starts, and my smile slips. 'I can't leave London. We might be fighting right now, but it doesn't change anything . . . I can't leave Gran.' Her expression is earnest as she looks at me. 'She's one of the most important people in my life. She's been there for me through so much, and she's the only parent I have. I love her. She's also eighty-three years old. I might not like to think about that, *she* might not like to think about that, but it's the reality of the situation. Her health isn't going to suddenly start getting better. Difficult times are coming. I'm not going to leave her on her own on the other side of the world.'

'I get it,' I say softly.

'I don't think I could forgive myself if I wasn't there for her,'

Lee pushes on. 'Even being away this long . . . I keep worrying I'm going to get a message saying something has happened. It would kill me . . .'

'I know,' I say again. 'Lee, I *know*. I love her, too. I understand what you're saying, you don't need to explain it to me.'

She nods, relief in her eyes.

'But,' it's my turn to speak, 'I can't leave Roseport. I can't uproot Phoebe when what she needs is stability and structure. I can't take her away from Magda. My life is here, and I can't change that.'

Lee smiles again, but it's a sad sort of smile. 'I understand,' she says, and she really does. She doesn't need me to explain.

'But—' I say, and Lee cuts me off.

'No more buts. *Please*.'

'*However*,' I correct myself. 'I'm not giving up on this. I get that it won't be easy. I get that we'll have to do long distance, but I think we can make it work. I will take as much of you as you can give me, and I will give you as much as I possibly can.'

'What about Phoebe?' Lee asks tentatively. 'Don't you think it will be difficult and confusing for her? Me coming and going?'

'Honestly?' I huff out a breath. 'I don't know. But I do know that she's better off with a parent who's in a loving, stable, healthy relationship than one who's walking around feeling broken in half. I know her life will be better with you in it. She's never had a conventional upbringing, and she understands that families look all different ways. For the rest of it I think it's about good communication, checking in with her.'

Lee nods. 'As long as we both agree that she comes first. If it ever feels like it's not right for her, we reassess.'

I think I fall a little bit more in love with her at that moment.

'Deal,' I say, getting to my feet and holding out my hand.

The smile she gives me then is shy. 'Deal,' and she slips her hand into mine.

'I think we can seal this some better way than with a handshake,' I say.

'Oh?' She tilts her head. 'What did you have in mind?'

I pull her towards me. 'I have a few ideas.'

Chapter Forty-One

Lee

The next day, before I take her to her first ballet class, Nico and I sit Phoebe down to talk to her about the change in our plans.

'Bee,' Nico begins, following our decision for him to take the lead, 'Lee and I want to talk to you about something.'

''Sup?' Phoebe asks, slurping at the carton of chocolate milk I've handed her.

'Over the past couple of weeks, Lee and I have been spending a lot of time together,' Nico continues mechanically, delivering the short speech the two of us sweated bullets over. 'And we've realised we have feelings for each other that go beyond friendship. We want to be a real couple. We love each other.'

Phoebe's eyes move from her dad to me and back again. 'Duh.'

Of all the potential responses I forced Nico to workshop with me, *duh* had not made the list.

'What do you mean . . . *duh*?' Nico asks.

I am watching her very closely for any signs of emotional distress, but there's nothing. She just gives a one-shouldered shrug that looks like a gesture Nico would make.

'Like it's a surprise?' Phoebe continues, observing us with genuine perplexity. 'You've been in love for ages.'

'We have?' Nico says, dazed, and I don't even mind how unromantic this answer is because I am feeling equally thrown.

'Yeah. *Everyone* knows.'

'Everyone?' I repeat.

Phoebe considers for a moment. 'Nana says your auras are blended together, but even if you can't see your auras it's so obvious.' Phoebe takes another thoughtful sip on her drink. 'Plus, I totally *Parent Trap*ped you.'

Again, none of this is going to plan. I eye the notebook in front of me where I had jotted down some potential concerns and talking points. 'I don't think I've heard "*Parent Trap*" used as a verb before,' I say cautiously. 'What does it mean?'

'You know,' Phoebe waves her hand airily in the air. 'I made you come here, and then I made you both go on dates and hold hands and stuff. Didn't you notice that I kept playing "Kiss the Girl" from *The Little Mermaid* on the kitchen speaker?'

'I just thought you were really into *The Little Mermaid*,' I admit.

Phoebe shakes her head. 'Sebastian says it's all about creating the mood.'

'Who's Sebastian?' I ask, lost.

'He's the lobster from the film.' Nico sounds distant, and I bet – like me – he's rethinking every interaction we've had with Phoebe over the last couple of weeks.

'Sebastian is actually a crab,' Phoebe corrects him.

'Okay, putting aside the fact that you schemed to bring us together using a talking crab as your mentor for a moment . . .' Nico rubs a hand over his face. 'You're saying you feel okay about it? I know it's another big change and you've had plenty of those lately.'

Phoebe traces a little circle on the table in front of her with her finger. 'I think it's cool. Does that mean Lee is going to stay?'

She looks so hopeful and all the air squeezes in my chest. Nico and I exchange a glance.

'I can't stay, Phoebe. I have to go back to London because of Gran and my job.'

Her face falls, and even though I told myself I'd been braced for tears or shouting, seeing her look unhappy is an absolute killer. Oh god, is this what it's like being Nico? No wonder he's so terrified of hurting her. I feel like a monster.

'But I'm going to call all the time and come and visit as much as possible,' I press on, my mouth dry. 'I hope you'll come to London, too, in the holidays and stay with me.'

'With you and Gran?' Phoebe looks up.

I swallow. 'Yes. At our house.'

'Will she bake me cookies? Will she make a den for me? Will we have tea at the Ritz?' Her words fall over themselves, and I should be happy that she's excited, but this line of questions presses on another tender part of my heart.

'I'm sure she'll be happy to do all of those things,' Nico breaks in, and under the table his hand is on my knee, his leg pressed against mine. *We're in this together.*

'The most important thing,' he continues, 'is that you know we're here for you. If you have any questions. If you're worried. If you need to talk about anything, you can talk to us.'

Phoebe's lashes flicker as she glances at me. 'We can talk?' she asks. 'Even when you're not here?'

The lump in my throat is back, but I force a bright smile. 'I'm going to insist on it,' I reply. 'I want to hear all your news, and you know your dad can't be relied upon to keep me up to date on town gossip.'

She cracks a small smile. 'Yeah. That's true. Okay.' She shakes off the entire conversation as only an eight-year-old can. 'Can we go to ballet now?'

*

'So that went well, right?' I ask Nico later as I finish cleaning my face in the bathroom. 'She seemed fine? She definitely had a good time at ballet so I guess she wasn't totally traumatised.'

I come back through the door and find he's stretched out on the bed, in his jeans and the fisherman-fantasy jumper, one hand behind his head on the pillow. He looks tired, and I know he's working hard to get the final touches in place at the inn – he'd gone back when I took Phoebe to ballet and stayed until late.

'It went well,' he agrees, looking up as I stand beside him. 'I mean apart from the part where my daughter revealed she's playing 3D chess with my love life. Not sure what the correct parental response is to that.'

I try not to smile. 'At least she's using her powers for good.'

He reaches out, his hand brushing under the hem of my pyjama top, stroking along my hip. It's an affectionate touch, a touching-me-just-because-he-can touch, and it still makes my whole body go haywire.

'Uh oh,' he laughs. 'Horny eyes.'

'I do not have horny eyes!'

I definitely do, but it is impolite of him to comment on them.

Taking my hand, he tumbles me down into his lap and presses a line of soft kisses along my neck. 'You have the prettiest eyes I've ever seen,' he murmurs against my skin. 'I want to take photographs of your eyelashes.'

I shiver into his touch. 'Of my eyelashes?'

He draws back for a moment, and now I know what he meant by horny eyes. 'Of all of you.'

'Okay,' I manage eloquently.

We're interrupted by the shrill ring of my phone and I squirm on Nico's lap to reach for it on my side of the bed. He lets out a pained hiss.

'Sorry, sorry,' I mutter. 'I have to check.'

It might be Gran, I don't say, but he knows what I mean.

I look at the phone screen. 'Oh.'

'Oh?' Nico lifts a brow, tugs my wrist so that he can see. 'Adrian,' he reads the name.

'I don't know why he's calling,' I say, flustered. 'I'll just . . .' I go to decline the call, but Nico stills the movement.

'Answer it,' he says mildly.

'What?'

He gives me his wolf smile. The one I know means trouble, but he only shrugs. 'Answer it.'

'Okay,' I reply slowly, but when I try to stand up he holds my hip, my back pressed firmly to his chest.

'Answer it, Lee.' This time the words have that edge of command to them that makes everything inside me feel heavy and liquid.

Rattled, I press the accept button. 'Hello,' I say into the phone.

'Lee!' Adrian's voice is in my ear, as Nico brushes the hair gently back from the side of my neck, pressing his lips there. 'I wasn't sure if I'd manage to get hold of you. I'm in New York for work, and I was hoping we could meet up.'

The words take a long time to reach me, because Nico's other hand is trailing over my thigh, his fingers tracing lazy figure-eights across my bare skin, and my nerves snap and spit like a freshly lit sparkler.

'I – I'm not in New York,' I manage. 'I'm in Maine.'

'Maine?' Adrian echoes, and Nico feathers kisses down the side of my throat. I finally gather my senses enough to try and bat him away, but he only laughs softly.

'What are you doing in Maine?' Adrian asks.

'Tell him what you're doing, Daisy.' Nico's hand skates up higher, his fingers play under the hem of my pyjama shorts.

I try to move from his lap, but his other hand holds me firmly in place and all I succeed in doing is grinding against his erection.

Both of us freeze for a second, and when he returns to his unhurried exploration of my neck, tasting my skin with his tongue, I have to bite back a whimper.

'Lee?' Adrian says, and I scramble for coherent thought.

'I'm visiting friends,' I temporise, and Nico lets out a rumble of disapproval. His teeth scrape across my collarbone and I almost jump.

'Oh,' Adrian huffs out a sigh. 'That's disappointing, but we can grab dinner when you're back.'

'I'm not sure that's a good idea,' I reply.

'Why not?'

With a Herculean effort I organise my thoughts. 'Because we broke up?'

Adrian laughs. 'Oh, that. I thought you'd have realised that was a mistake by now.'

Nico has finally gone still underneath me.

The pompous certainty in Adrian's voice makes me frown. 'No,' I try to sound apologetic, 'I don't think it was a mistake.'

'Why not?' He seems genuinely mystified. 'There isn't any *reason* for us to break up. We're very good together.'

'I'm sorry, Adrian.' I close my eyes, because I'm so rubbish at this. 'I don't think we're right for each other. I should have said something sooner. The last thing I wanted to do was hurt you or lead you on.'

'You're saying you don't want to get back together?' He sounds put out. 'Look, I'm willing to overlook this whole … *incident*. Clearly, you've been under some pressure at work and you're not thinking clearly.'

I'm trying very hard to hold onto my empathy for him, but it's a struggle. His persistence is all the more confusing because our relationship was so … tepid.

Shit. Gran was right. Maybe not about everything, but she was definitely right about this.

As if echoing my thoughts, Nico huffs a laugh. '*This* guy?' he says, and he nuzzles the skin behind my ear. 'Put him out of his misery, baby. Tell him.'

'I—' I start, and Nico's hand slips up, under my T-shirt, his thumb brushing over my nipple. 'I'm married!' I blurt.

'You're what?' Adrian asks, shocked.

'And?' Nico hums. Unthinking, I rock in his lap, and he draws in a sharp breath, but drops the hand under my T-shirt back to my hip, holding me still. He nips my earlobe. 'Not yet,' he reprimands me softly, and his voice is top-shelf whisky, caressing my senses. 'You know how to get what you want.'

'And . . .' I take a breath, 'my husband doesn't share.'

Nico takes the phone from my hand and hangs it up before throwing it across the bed.

'I can't believe you did that,' I say as I slump back against his chest. The words are airless. I know I should be annoyed, but my brain is so confused, at cross-purposes with my body, which is lit up with pleasure.

Particularly when Nico pushes my pyjamas roughly aside and slides a finger inside me. I gasp, a shocked sound mingling disbelief and desire. He makes a noise of approval, deep in his chest at finding me so ready for him.

'No pretending anymore, Daisy.' His voice is low, as I ride his hand, and I can feel him hard and ready underneath me. 'We're in this for real. You and me. Only you and me.'

My head lolls back against his shoulder, and I'm sure there are things I should be saying, things about domineering, bossy men not being in charge of me, but I'll have to do that later, I'm not convinced there are two working brain cells in my head right now.

I'm too focused on the touch of his hand, his mouth on the tender skin underneath my jaw, the warm, golden feeling in my abdomen, and the tendrils of slow heat spreading through my limbs.

'Say it, Lee.' His thumb flickers over my clit as I grind in his lap, and I whine with need. 'Only you and me.'

'Only you and me,' I whisper, and then I come apart.

Chapter Forty-Two

Lee

'So this is a Roseport Halloween?' I say two nights later, observing the scene in front of me.

'Is it everything you hoped it would be?' Nico asks.

'It's . . . a lot.'

'Yeah, well,' Nico sighs. 'Roseport doesn't really do subtle.' He looks around, appreciating it as well. He wasn't here last Halloween, and it feels good that we're doing something for the first time here together.

'This really is excellent hot chocolate,' I say, sipping from the steaming cup cradled in my hands. It's cool out tonight, and Phoebe wouldn't let me wear a coat because it would cover my costume.

'I told you Kat makes the best hot chocolate every Halloween. I like the crunchy orange sprinkles on top of the whipped cream.' Phoebe exhales blissfully as Nico holds the cup in front of her mouth and she slurps through the straw Kat gave her.

We're standing on Main Street, surrounded by a sea of people in costumes. Every single store front is decorated to look like a haunted house with a different theme. There are motion-activated animatronic skeletons that keep making me jump out of my skin, thick spider webs stretching from awning to awning, and an entire plastic graveyard has sprouted along the lawns with names like IMA GONER and AL BEBACK on the tombstones.

On one side of the street a vintage-looking car has been pulled over, its bonnet popped open while several posed skeleton mechanics in high-vis jackets work on it. Rita is dressed as a witch and handing out her most horrifying ice cream flavours. It turns out Halloween is her time to shine.

I look around at the whole scene, delighted. Which is my predominant state of existence at the moment, by the way: delight. Kat had to switch me to decaf coffee because she was 'genuinely concerned' about my 'unnatural levels of perkiness'. I don't think anyone has ever accused me of being perky before so I can see why it might be unnerving. I actually think I could lift a car with the amount of endorphins flowing through my veins.

I might still be leaving in a few days, but I'm trying not to focus on that – it won't be for ever. There'll be FaceTime and phone calls and voice notes and flights booked in as soon as possible. It's not perfect, but it's more than I ever imagined would be possible, and more importantly Nico and I are in this together.

That fact still seems miraculous.

'Well, if it isn't the Hart family!' Art suddenly appears in front of us, pumping Nico's hand, while Annie stands beside him looking faintly confused by the entire world. Art is dressed as a scarecrow, Annie as Dorothy from *The Wizard of Oz*, and she carries Button, their sweater-wearing Yorkshire terrier, in a small basket. He doesn't look impressed.

'Nice to see you, Art,' Nico grins. 'Excellent costumes this year.'

'Thank you, thank you, you too.' He gives the three of us a long look. 'Are you . . .'

'We're from *Bringing Up Baby*,' Phoebe huffs.

We're having to explain our family costume quite a lot. Phoebe came up with it, and she and Nico organised the outfits, telling me it was a secret until the big day. Apparently they co-ordinated with the Roseport Players costume department, raiding their supplies. I'm wearing a long, shiny gold dress that was once part of a Cleopatra costume but has been repurposed as Katharine Hepburn's lamé evening gown. Phoebe wanted to rip the back off the skirt and have me walk around with my knickers on display like in the film, but I vetoed that pretty quickly, citing potential hypothermia and mortification.

'I got you a top hat for Dad to hold over your butt, like Cary Grant does in the movie,' Phoebe grumbled, outraged by the artistic compromises she was being forced to make.

'I *was* quite looking forward to that part,' Nico agreed.

Nico got off easy in a lab coat and a pair of round glasses, clean-shaven, his hair slicked back. Phoebe is the Brontosaurus that Cary Grant's character is trying to rebuild, and Taco is resplendent in a leopard-print jumper and a headband with a pair of leopard ears on over the top of his actual ears.

We look insane. It's perfect.

'I am the Brontosaurus with the missing intercostal clavicle,' Phoebe explains now, the small pale moon of her face the only part of her visible inside the bright blue inflatable dinosaur suit. 'Even though when I Googled it, it turns out there's no such thing as an intercostal clavicle. But it's a very old film. I guess they didn't have Google then.'

'No, I guess not,' Art agrees.

We chat for another minute or two and then they go on their way. Several more people stop us to say hello, and Phoebe grows increasingly irate about explaining our costume.

'This would never have happened if you had the hat over your butt,' she mutters darkly.

'Oh look,' I point to the other side of the street. 'There's Tara and Luke. Oh my god, she actually got him to dress as a cowboy!'

'*Bringing Up Baby!*' Tara squeals when she sees us.

'Yes!' Phoebe tries to punch the air but ends up bouncing off Tara and wobbling into several passers-by instead. 'Sorry,' she says. 'This thing's pretty hard to drive.'

'Nice costume,' Nico smirks at Luke, receiving a glare in return.

'Doesn't he look *so* hot?' Tara winds herself around Luke, staring up at him from under her pink hat, stars in her eyes. 'Finding leather chaps this close to Halloween was actually a lot tougher than you'd think.'

'Yet, still upsettingly possible,' Luke rumbles, but he smiles down at her, knocking the rim of his hat back so he can kiss her. Even I swoon at that, and Nico frowns.

'You said my costume was hot, too,' he grumbles.

'Are you kidding? Nerdy Cary Grant?' I fan myself with my hand. 'Yes, please.'

'Gross,' Phoebe says flatly. 'There's Maya and her mum – is it okay if I go and do some trick or treating with them before I meet up with Nana?'

'As long as it's okay with Sandra,' Nico nods. Phoebe ricochets her way over and then Nico and Maya's mum have one of those wordless parent conversations, through a series of hand gestures.

'Come on, Taco!' Phoebe calls, and the dog trots off, letting Maya pick up his lead before they head off to join the queues of hyperactive, sugar-filled kids outside every door.

'It's chilly,' Tara says. 'Let's go and stand by the bonfire.' She pulls a silver hip flask from the pocket of Luke's jeans and winks. 'We can warm up.'

'Sold,' I agree, thinking that there surely must have been a scene where Katharine Hepburn was wearing a big coat.

'Hi, Lee,' Stefano calls as we pass. He's wearing a Chewbacca costume and chasing his grandkids through the crowd.

'Hi, Lee,' Gerald and Carl say as they totter past hand in hand disguised as troll dolls.

'Hello, Nico. Hi, Lee,' Phil says. 'Dost thou like me costume?' He's dressed as Henry VIII and I think that's some sort of tribute to us.

'You look amazing,' I say honestly.

For a moment it's like I can zoom out on it all, this scene that I'm a part of. The bandstand holds the school orchestra – the students are dressed like zombies and playing a Halloween-themed playlist. Kat is set up next to them, selling her famous hot chocolate with Mei's assistance, surrounded by twinkling fairy lights. The funny thing is that, despite the crowds and the noise, I don't feel anxious at all.

I glance over to where a group of teenagers are huddled together by the bonfire; their mood is jubilant – helped along by the fact that the school's football team won their big match, or game, or showdown or whatever it's called, this afternoon and they're wearing those letter jackets, just like in the movies. When I mention this to Nico he grins.

'Now I wish I had a letter jacket to put around your shoulders. You'd be in small-town America, Hallmark movie heaven.'

'You're so right,' I agree. 'I bet they have prom, too, right? A proper one in a gymnasium with streamers and corsages and awkward photos?'

'I believe they do,' Nico nods.

'And one day that will be Phoebe,' I murmur, already smiling at the thought.

Nico, on the other hand, looks stricken. 'Christ, don't say that. She's already growing up way too fast. I'm going to be an emotional wreck when she goes to prom.'

I laugh, but I can picture it already. Phoebe in her dress . . . or maybe in a cool suit, and Nico taking pictures and blinking back foolishly happy tears while his daughter rolls her eyes, secretly loving it.

When I realise that I want to be there for it so badly it hurts I have to turn my head away and stare into the fire for several long breaths. Maybe I will be. Maybe I can be.

Suddenly it hits me, this thing Nico and I are talking about doing. It's a commitment, a real one, a long one. That's what we both agreed, but when I try and picture that future . . . one where I'm not here all the time, one where I might miss things big and small, it hurts in a way that takes me by surprise. It's not just Phoebe who might struggle.

And there's also the uncertainty about our marriage. We haven't spoken about it and I keep thinking I should bring it up. But how can I when the thought of signing divorce papers makes my stomach turn? How can I say, 'I know we've barely started dating, I know I'm leaving to live on the other side of the world, but do you think we could give this whole marriage thing a real shot?'

Way too much. We're not *actually* in a Regency romance novel.

'Darlings! There you are!' Claudia appears, interrupting my reverie. She's dressed like Marilyn Monroe in a blonde wig, a pink dress, a significant number of diamonds that are almost certainly real, and dragging Charles Saunders along after her. He's wearing his usual immaculate suit, but with a bowler hat as well, which I suppose makes it a costume of some sort.

I haven't seen him since the disastrous meeting on Saturday, despite the outrageous number of emails I sent begging for a face-to-face.

'Hi, Ma.' Nico kisses her on the cheek. 'You look great.'

'Oh, I know,' Claudia agrees. 'And to think, I just threw it together! Halloween completely slipped my mind this year, but this is *charming*, totally charming, isn't it, Charlie?'

'It is,' he agrees, and from the way he's beaming at Claudia, perhaps he's not as unhappy with me as I thought.

I am flooded with optimism. Maybe we're actually going to get away with this. All the situation requires is a heartfelt apology to seal the deal, and I am so ready to grovel.

'Mr Saunders,' I begin, 'I really need to—'

'Ophelia, baby!' a voice shouts from nearby, and I turn around to see a man pushing through the crowd towards us.

Oh, shit.

Chapter Forty-Three

Nico

'Is that . . .' I start, staring at the man coming towards us, wearing a powder blue velvet suit that I am ninety-eight per cent sure is not a costume.

'Frankie,' Lee agrees, her voice several octaves higher than usual.

Holy shit. This is bad. This is very, very bad.

'Who's Frankie?' Charles asks.

Yup, so bad. We are totally fucked. I do not think that introducing Charles to the notorious former head of a prominent crime family who has no idea about our fake back story is going to go down well.

'He's a friend from work,' Lee chokes out, just as Frankie reaches us.

'Frankie,' she manages, 'what on earth are you doing here?'

'What do you think?' Frankie exclaims, his eyes huge behind his enormous glasses. He plants a noisy kiss on Lee's cheek. 'I got guys everywhere so when I heard the news, I had to come and see for myself. After all,' he dusts off the wide lapels of his jacket, 'I think I had a little bit to do with it. Who do we have here?'

'Um, these are my friends Tara and Luke,' Lee says, 'Claudia and Charles. And of course you know . . . Nico.'

'Her *husband*,' my mum adds helpfully, because there's nothing she enjoys more than pouring petrol on a fire.

'Yeah, I know.' Frankie's expression flattens; he reaches into his jacket pocket and pulls out his cigar case. 'In fact, if it hadn't been for my high-priced champagne—'

'Mr Saunders!' Tara breaks in, clearly sensing things are about to go badly awry. 'Have you had a cup of hot chocolate yet? I know Kat was super excited for you *personally* to try it.'

'Oh, really?' Charles looks slightly bemused. 'I'm not actually much of a hot chocolate fan.'

'Don't tell Kat,' Luke puts in, following Tara's lead. 'She's been talking about it all week.'

'Well, I wouldn't want to be rude . . .' Charles murmurs.

'Let's all go!' Tara yelps with an insane amount of enthusiasm. For some reason she's waving her arms around a lot. 'Leave Lee and Nico to catch up with their friend.'

As Charles and Ma are swept away by Tara and Luke who are both talking loudly and at once, Frankie blinks.

'What did I say?' he asks, looking crestfallen.

Lee's face softens and she goes to hug him. 'It's not you, Frankie. It's complicated, but I'll explain everything. Honestly, I'm so happy to see you, it's just that you caught me by surprise. What *are* you doing here?'

'I told you, I heard the two of you got married.' He holds an unlit cigar to his mouth. 'When I looked into it, I realised it all went down when you were staying at my place. I wanted to make sure that everything was on the up and up, that you were being treated right.'

This time when he turns to me the affable old man falls away and I'm looking into the cold, hard eyes of The Shark.

'Oh,' Lee blinks. 'That's so sweet.'

Sure, that's one word for it.

'I love her,' I say, keeping my voice steady. I've stared down a predator or two in my line of work, so I'm not about to fall apart now.

An edge of approval creeps into Frankie's expression. 'Buddy, if I hadn't already figured that out a year ago we wouldn't be here having this conversation.'

He doesn't actually *say* I'd be sleeping with the fishes, but it is heavily implied.

'Frankie,' Lee scolds him. 'Stop playing the tough guy. You told me you liked Nico.'

Frankie and I both let out startled laughs at this, and maybe it's a bonding moment, because his expression softens a bit more. He reaches back in his pocket.

'And you'd better not even think about lighting that thing,' Lee frowns at him. 'You promised me you'd cut back.'

'Now, Lee . . .'

She lifts her chin. 'Don't you "now, Lee" me. You know Spuds and I chat on Instagram and he's rubbish at covering for you.'

'Wait,' I break in, 'you follow Spuds on Instagram?'

'We like to share ice skating videos.'

'Anyway,' Frankie picks up, and even though he keeps the cigar in his mouth, he doesn't light it. If I didn't know better I'd think he looked a little hurt. 'It looks like you're happy, so what I can't figure out is why you didn't tell me the two of you got married.'

'I'm sorry, the two of you got *what*?' a painfully familiar voice asks from behind me and I close my eyes for a second.

This cannot be happening.

When I open them, Lee is looking over my shoulder, stunned, so I know I'm not imagining things. I know exactly who I'll see even before I turn around.

'Jack,' I greet my best friend, who is staring open mouthed at the three of us. Beside him, Cynthie is all wrapped up in a winter coat and hat, wide-eyed and eating a giant bag of kettle corn. 'It's really not a great time,' I finish weakly.

'Yeah, I can see that.' Jack looks from me to Frankie to Lee. 'I'm guessing that has something to do with the fact that this guy just implied that you're married to my sister. Or did I mishear that part?'

'Oh, so I'm not the only one you didn't tell,' Frankie says, watching Jack from under lowered brows.

'Frankie,' Lee murmurs, putting her hand on his arm.

'Well?' Jack's arms are folded over his chest. 'Would anyone care to answer my question?' He's at his most sardonic, which means he's angry, but at this point he can get in line.

'You didn't mishear anything,' I grind out. 'I *am* married to your sister.'

'Oh my god, amazing,' Cynthie whispers, popping more kettle corn in her mouth. Her hazel eyes gleam with excitement.

'What are you two doing here?' I ask.

'After we spoke on Friday, it felt like something was up with you. I was worried,' Jack frowns. 'So we came as soon as we could make it work. Now I know why you were being so weird, I guess.'

I have no idea what's going on in his head, but he definitely doesn't look happy.

Cynthie comes forward, bundling first me and then Lee into a hug. 'I'm so pleased for you two!' she beams. 'It's about time!'

'What do you mean it's about time?' Jack asks her, his frown deepening.

Cynthie rolls her eyes. 'Please. I saw all this coming the second I met them.'

'You saw them secretly getting married in Maine and not telling anyone about it?' Jack's eyebrows arch sarcastically. He's going what Lee refers to as 'full-Darcy' now. Definitely angry.

Cynthie crunches thoughtfully on more kettle corn. 'Fine, that part was a surprise.'

'Hey!' Someone grins at Cynthie as he walks past. 'Nice costume, you look just like her!'

Cynthie smiles back at him, adopting a flawless Southern drawl. 'Thank you so much!' She holds the bag of kettle corn out to me. 'Want some? It's really good. I'm obsessed with this place, by the way. Did you know there's a woman selling banana and broccoli ice cream?'

'Can we get back to important matters?' Jack continues to look furious.

'Yeah, like why didn't your brother know you were married, Lee?' Frankie turns to her. 'I knew something wasn't right.' Then he turns to me. 'If you've tricked her into anything, you'll have me to deal with.'

'Who is this guy?' Jack growls, and then he takes a small step back when Frankie fixes him with a glare.

I can't help smirking at him, *yeah, you weren't expecting that.* 'Jack, this is Frankie Martelli,' I say, and Jack's eyes widen. 'He's your sister's friend, and the head of the Martelli family.'

'Retired,' Frankie says around his cigar, in a way that makes it clear he's still active enough to break Jack's kneecaps should the whim take him.

'Okay,' Lee says, and I realise it's the first time she's spoken since Jack and Cynthie arrived. Her calm voice is back, the serene mask falling into place, and nobody but me seems to even notice anything is wrong. To anyone actually paying attention it's clear she's feeling overwhelmed. It's all too confrontational, and I'm not helping by winding Jack and Frankie up.

'I'm going to take Frankie and fill him in on what's happened,' she continues smoothly, as I watch the pulse hammer in her throat, 'while you catch Jack and Cynthie up. Then I'll find Charles and the others to make sure everything's okay.'

'Who the fuck is Charles? I don't understand any of this.' Jack sounds annoyed again, clearly deciding Frankie's presence isn't going to deter him, and he's radiating tension. Lee's shoulders tighten more. She looks between me and her brother and presses her lips together.

'I'll explain it in a second,' I say to Jack, but my attention is on Lee. I reach out and pull her towards me, wrapping her in my arms. Her body is still tense, and I gently pinch her chin between my thumb and forefinger, tilting her face up to mine. Her big, blue eyes swim with anxiety.

'Nico—' she starts helplessly, but I drop my mouth to hers. I hear Jack make a huff of surprise at the same time as Cynthie squeals.

When I pull back some of the strain has left Lee's face. I smile, brush her hair back.

'It's fine,' I say softly, and I take off the white lab coat I'm wearing and pull it around her shoulders. 'I'll take care of it, you go and handle Frankie. We're good, Daisy. I promise.'

'What the fuck was *that*?' Jack asks when Lee and Frankie leave.

'That was you stressing your sister out,' I say. 'Next time you see her you could at least say hello, for fuck's sake.'

Jack blinks. 'I thought I did say hello.'

I shake my head in disgust.

'Look, there was a lot going on and I'm trying to process it all.' There's some colour in his cheeks now. 'I didn't even know the two of you *spoke* to each other, and now it turns out you're *married*? Excuse me for being a bit thrown.'

I exhale. 'Fair enough,' I agree. 'I should have told you. I'm sorry about that.'

'I'm sorry too.' Jack tucks his hands in his pockets. 'And I didn't mean to upset Lee. I'll talk to her about it.'

'I'd appreciate that.'

'So now you two have had that moving heart-to-heart *are* you going to explain what's going on?' Cynthie asks, taking Jack's hand in hers.

'Yeah, and why we're fine with Lee disappearing off with an actual mobster,' Jack puts in.

'Frankie loves Lee,' I say absently.

It's a good job there's a big crowd and everyone's wearing ridiculous costumes because for once Jack and Cynthie are flying under the radar, but who knows how long that will last. I glance nervously around to make sure we're not about to be mobbed.

'Let's find somewhere quiet to talk. Come with me.' I lead them through the crowd towards Scoops. Miss Rita is still handing out ice cream from her little trolley in the doorway and this is potentially a huge risk, but I have no choice.

'Nico!' she beams. 'Finally come to try . . .' Her gaze moves over my shoulder and her eyes widen. 'Oh em gee,' she whispers. She's already humming the *Blood/Lust* theme tune and I need to snap her out of this immediately before she causes a riot.

'Rita,' I say firmly. 'Look at me. Focus. We have a Code Red Wedding.'

Her eyes snap to my face. 'What?' she barks, and I'm relieved that her commitment to the plan has temporarily outweighed her need to read my best friend the fan fiction she's definitely written about him. 'When?'

'Charles is here. And you know who else has turned up? Lee's ex-mob-boss friend, her famous brother *and* his Oscar-winning fiancée. They all arrived about five minutes ago and none of them have a clue what's going on.' I wince, unable to believe I'm saying this. 'The crumpet is in the wind.'

Her phone is already in her hand. 'Say no more,' she says, 'I've got this.'

'We need a place to lie low for a bit.' I gesture past her and she nods, moving aside so that we can slip into the empty shop. I watch as Rita smashes down on the red alarm emoji. Soon the phones of everyone in town will be lighting up like there's an earthquake warning.

I hustle Cynthie and Jack inside and we sit at a table away from the windows.

'This is adorable,' Cynthie sighs. 'You know, Jack, it reminds me of that place in LA . . .' The two of them share another one of their secret couple smiles.

When Jack turns back to me his expression is definitely a lot more wintery. 'Now, enough fucking about . . . spill it, Hart.'

I rub my forehead. 'Okay, long story short, Lee and I got married in Las Vegas.'

'When?' Jack asks, and he leans back, his arms crossed over his chest.

'A year ago.'

There's a long, baffled silence.

'I think I need another bag of kettle corn,' Cynthie murmurs.

'You've been married for a year?' Jack explodes. 'And neither of you told us? What the fuck, man?'

Of course he's hurt. I knew he would be, and it feels bloody terrible.

'It's not that simple,' I sigh. 'We didn't actually know about it.'

'Okay, whatever this story is, bagsy the movie rights,' Cynthie says and I manage a reluctant laugh; even Jack's mouth softens a little.

I fill them in on what they've missed, keeping the finer details to myself. I think we've already traumatised Jack enough.

'Jesus, your dad was such a bastard,' Jack says at the end, shaking his head. 'But this is the most insane story I've ever heard, and I'll remind you that I star in a TV series where I've been brought back from the dead three times.'

'Only twice,' Cynthie argues. 'You can't count the time you came back as Lucius – he *was* your evil great-great-great grandfather.'

'Still,' Jack doesn't look impressed. 'You're saying this all started out as a mistake and now . . . what? Suddenly it's real?'

'Not suddenly,' I protest, knowing it sounds weak. 'Lee and I . . . we have something special. We always have, but it's changed. I love her, Jack. You know me, I wouldn't say that if I didn't mean it.' I need him to believe me.

He holds my gaze for a long moment and then he gives a tight nod.

Cynthie, on the other hand, has hearts in her eyes. 'I think it's wonderful. The second most romantic story I've ever heard after ours.'

'Oh yeah,' I scoff. 'Really romantic when you signed him up to that penis enlargement supplement website. He was getting emails from them for years no matter how often he unsubscribed.'

Cynthie laughs, delighted. 'Oh my god, I'd forgotten about that one. We were *feral*,' she adds sunnily. 'I'd love to take the credit but I think that particular prank might have been Hannah. Pretty sure she was the one resubscribing you, too, although I *may* have encouraged it.'

'Monster,' Jack says fondly, and he drops a kiss on the corner of her mouth while she hums with pleasure.

I cough and Jack turns his attention back to me, his expression thoughtful. 'I don't know what I'm supposed to do about this. My best friend and my sister. I feel like I should be threatening you or something.'

'Look, I'd rather cut out my own heart than hurt her,' I say, then I sigh. 'Not that there are any guarantees. It's a complicated situation.'

Jack runs a hand over his jaw, and his mouth pulls down but he doesn't say anything. He's still processing, which is fair enough. It's a lot.

'Well, I for one think it's great,' Cynthie declares. 'You and Lee make so much sense. Everything else is just details. And we're here for you, one hundred per cent, okay?'

I look at Jack and he nods, his expression softening. 'Of course, man. Anything you need. You know that.'

I reach out and put my hand on his shoulder. 'I should have said before . . . I'm glad you're here. I can't believe you came.'

He shrugs, his mouth finally pulling up into a smile. 'My best friend senses were tingling. I could tell you were upset about something, and god knows you're not the best at asking for help.'

'Now,' Cynthie rubs her hands together, 'where's this Charles character? I think it's time to hit him with the professionals.'

Chapter Forty-Four

Lee

After explaining the situation to Frankie as briefly as possible, and agreeing that it would be best for him to beat a tactical retreat for now, I make my way towards the hot chocolate stand. Here Charles is being flanked by not only Luke, Tara and Claudia, but Mei and Kat as well. They have arranged themselves around him like a human shield, and it does not look casual. The poor man looks hunted.

'Hi!' I say brightly, and everyone sends me a relieved look when I am clearly Frankie-free.

'Lee! Darling!' Claudia practically throws herself on me. 'We were telling Charlie that you and Nico had probably snuck away just the two of you because you're so *happily* married and *deeply* in love!'

'Yep,' Kat nods eagerly. 'The most happily married. The most in love.'

'And so stable,' Tara chips in. 'That's what we always say. Wow, Lee and Nico. Couple goals. But in a responsible way.'

'Extremely responsible,' Mei agrees.

'Yes, I . . .' Charles looks like he's feeling dizzy.

'Oh!' Phil in his Henry VIII costume bounces up. 'Were you just talking about how happy and in love Lee and Nico are? Because boy, do I have some stories to share! Actually, there are four of us who tell them best. We like to act out the various parts, if you'll hang on for one minute . . .'

'That really isn't necessary,' Charles says weakly.

'Hey . . .' Nico's hand slips around my waist, and I sag back against him in relief. He's brought Jack and Cynthie with him.

'You must be Mr Saunders,' I hear Cynthie say, her hand outstretched as she glides towards him, her famous smile wide and sincere. 'I've heard so much about you. May I call you Charles?'

All the colour leaves Charles's face. He looks like he's seen a ghost. 'No!' he says. 'No! This is taking it *too* far.' He glances wildly around at the group of us, before pointing to Cynthie with a trembling finger. 'This woman won an Academy Award last year!'

Cynthie's smile falters. 'Did I say something wrong?'

Charles reaches into the pocket of his coat and pulls out an envelope, holding it out to Nico.

'I can't do this anymore,' he says. 'I was happy enough to go along with the charade in the beginning. Of course, I thought the people in this town were a bit overenthusiastic, but they're clearly very fond of you. And naturally, I hadn't anticipated what a pleasure it would be spending time with your lovely mother,' here his cheeks turn pink, 'but I told your brother that I'm concluding the investigation early, so there's *no need* for you to bring in further witnesses to this pretence of a marriage, especially not ones with an Oscar on their mantelpiece.' He gestures at Cynthie.

'I also won a Teen Choice Award,' I hear Jack protest.

'*Pretence* of a marriage?' I murmur, feeling all the blood leave my head as his words sink in. 'You mean . . . you knew?'

'Of course I knew,' Charles scowls. 'I *am* excellent at my job. There didn't seem any reason to bring it up when I came here with a specific remit.'

'So you were happy to let us tie ourselves in knots because you'd already decided we were going to fail the assessment?' Nico sounds furious.

'No, no,' Charles sighs. 'You misunderstand. I was under instructions to make sure you *passed* the assessment.'

There's a stunned silence.

'What?' Nico asks.

'I had to make sure all of the paperwork was in order, do my due diligence, but there was never any question of you failing,' Charles says.

'But why wouldn't you tell us that?' I ask, bewildered.

He looks offended. 'Because that would be deeply unethical! Which is what I told your grandmother when I spoke to her. Not that she seemed to appreciate the fact.'

'You ... what?' I'm glad Nico's arms come around me again, because I'm having trouble standing. 'When did you speak to my grandmother?'

'Yesterday.' Charles looks nettled. 'She's the other person listed as inhabiting your London address. Of course, at first she tried to go along with the story, even though she obviously had no clue what I was talking about. It was simply part of the consultation process, dotting every i, but eventually she asked me why I didn't just tell you the truth ... got quite angry in fact. And I'll tell you what I told her *and* His Grace ... we must be extremely careful to keep everything above board, in case any other beneficiaries ever challenge this decision in court. I have simply been trying to do my job to the best of my abilities while protecting your interests.' He removes his bowler hat, produces a handkerchief from his pocket and dabs at his forehead. 'This whole thing has been extremely stressful if you must know.'

'Oh, Charlie!' Claudia throws her arms around him, and he goes even pinker.

'Yes, well,' he blusters. 'If you could all forget that I told you any of this, that would probably be for the best. That envelope contains a letter from your brother that should hopefully explain things more fully. Now,' he draws himself up, 'Claudia, might I buy you a drink back at the hotel?'

'I'd be delighted,' Claudia purrs, and the two of them make a hasty retreat.

'Charlie's got game,' Luke whistles.

'So it's over?' Tara asks.

'Just like that?' Nico sounds dazed.

'But I didn't even get to do my bit,' Phil moans. I'd actually forgotten he was here, which just goes to show how wild the last few minutes have been because the man has several pillows strapped to his stomach and is wearing a codpiece.

'He told *Gran*,' I whisper, 'she knows I lied!'

'It'll be okay,' my brother says. 'We'll talk to her together.'

'Tomorrow. There's nothing we can do about it now,' Nico says gently.

I nod, knowing that letter must be burning a hole in his pocket. 'Magda's already picked up Phoebe and Taco. We should head off.' A thought strikes me and I turn to Jack and Cynthie. 'Where on earth are you two staying? Darlene's wig room is already taken.'

'I have no idea what that means,' Jack says, 'but we're staying at the inn. Magda organised it for us, she said the place is just about ready to open again, anyway.'

'Wow, Magda, a heads up might have been nice,' Nico grumbles.

Jack winces. 'I think she was under the impression we were invited.' He throws his hands up when Nico glares at him. 'It was supposed to be a surprise! A nice one! I didn't know we were walking into the middle of a French farce.'

'Don't worry, we'll look after them,' Kat says to me. 'Darlene's doing two-for-one cocktail hour so we can show these Hollywood types that Roseport knows how to party.'

'Come on, Daisy,' Nico throws his arm around my shoulder, 'let's go home.'

The house is quiet when we get back, and I feel wrung out. I change out of my gold dress and into my cosiest pyjamas and a pair of fluffy socks while Nico puts the kettle on.

In the bedroom I stare down at my hand for a moment, twisting the rings on my finger. The truth is out and Nico has what he needs. Our relationship might just be starting, but our marriage is about to come to an end. With a sigh, I slip the rings from my finger and leave them on the bedside table. Claudia will want them back.

Pushing my complicated feelings aside, I head back for the living room and Nico. 'How are you feeling?' I ask as we sit on the sofa. He pulls my feet into his lap, absently running his hand up and down my calf.

'Honestly, I'm not sure.' He shakes his head. 'Mostly confused, I think.'

I eye the envelope on the coffee table. 'What do you think it says?'

He shrugs. 'No idea. I haven't talked to Ward since Dad's funeral and that was only in passing. Before that it had been years.'

'I never liked to ask about them so I wasn't totally sure,' I admit. 'I assumed you were all estranged.'

'Yeah,' he sighs. 'I don't think anyone was exactly thrilled when Dad married my mum so soon after his first wife died. Ward and Rupert were only babies themselves, so we were all very young when my parents split – I guess there wasn't any reason for them to stay in touch. Harder for Mum than it was for me.'

I flinch at that. Knowing Claudia, she'd have bonded with her stepsons.

He nods at my expression. 'I doubt Dad would have let her have any contact. I don't know much about them, except that Rupert is married and he has two little boys. Dad had his heir, his spare, his line secure, so there wasn't much need for me. Honestly, I think Mum getting pregnant was the beginning of the end for them.'

He says the words without emotion, but I know that what I'm looking at is a very deep hurt, the kind that has impacted his life in a hundred different ways, big and small.

'You know,' I say carefully, 'whatever that letter says, it doesn't change anything. Your dad was a bad father, a bad husband, a bad man. And you're *nothing* like him. He might have made you feel like no one needed you, but that has never been true.' I scramble up, onto my knees beside him. 'You, Nico Hart, are loved.' I press my lips to the sharp line of his cheekbone. 'Deeply.' I kiss the hollow underneath his ear. 'Irrevocably.' My mouth finds the tiny scar above his top lip. 'For ever.'

His hand tightens around my waist and he pulls me into his lap, dragging me in for a long, slow kiss. Our marriage might be ending but his heart thumps under my splayed hand, each steady beat a promise.

'I love you,' he whispers against my skin, and I wonder if those words will ever feel ordinary or if it will be like this every time – an explosion of joy that feels too big for my body to hold.

'I love you, too.'

We sit for a moment, quiet and content. 'So,' I say finally, 'do you want to read it? Or are we doing some sort of ceremonial burning?'

'You read it,' Nico says, 'we can always do the ceremonial burning afterwards.' But he doesn't relinquish his hold on me, so I reach over and grab the letter, still settled across his lap.

When I rip open the envelope I pull out a sheet of thick, expensive-looking paper topped with an actual family crest. The handwriting that covers it is scrawled and untidy in bold blue ink.

'*Dear Nico,*' I start. '*If you are reading this then it means Charles has completed his assessment. I am sincerely sorry that you had to endure it at all. I spent a considerable amount of time trying to find a way around it, but our father managed to tie things up pretty tight. It was a vindictive thing to do, but perhaps that's not surprising – he was a vindictive man. The conditions of the trust have now been met, and I will ensure a swift transfer of the funds in their entirety. They should have been yours all along.*

'I regret that he kept us apart for all these years, but more than that I regret my own complicity in allowing him to do so. If you feel that you want nothing more to do with our family, I wouldn't blame you, but Rupert and I would both like the chance to get to know you and our niece if you were open to the idea.

'I leave it to you. In the meantime if I can ever offer any assistance, don't hesitate.

'*Ward.*'

I glance up from the letter to find Nico's expression thoughtful.

'Not what I expected,' he says finally.

I run my finger over the ink. 'He's very Jane Austen, isn't he? Very formal and full of honour. I bet he does a lot of *striding*.'

Nico's mouth kicks up. 'Yes, he does actually. He's always seemed like a serious sort of person.'

'What do you want to do about it?'

He glances down at the letter again, then he plucks it from my hand and throws it back on the table. 'I'll think about it,' he says. 'Right now I'm very happy to concentrate on the family I have.'

Then he turns the full force of his concentration on me and I find I have no complaints about this decision.

Chapter Forty-Five

Nico

The day after Halloween is Thursday and so rather than bringing her home, Magda takes Phoebe straight to school, which is good news because after the emotional upheaval of yesterday, I'm ready for a slower start. It was late by the time we got to sleep, and not just because I couldn't keep my hands off Lee, but because there was so much to talk about: this whole situation with Edward but also our surprise visitors, the fact that Gran knows what's been going on . . . and that she didn't hear it from us.

Lee's still asleep when I wake up, and I take a moment to look at her. The morning light filtering through the curtains casts her face in tantalising shadows. I linger over the kissable corner of her mouth, the gentle curve of her shoulder, the way the sheets are rumpled just so underneath her hand: there's art in every line of her.

Eventually, I tear myself away and head for the shower, leaving her to sleep. When I come out of the bathroom, one towel wrapped around my hips, another ruffling my still wet hair, Lee is kneeling up on the bed with a troubled look on her face.

'Here,' she says awkwardly. 'I think you'd better give these back to your mum.'

I look at the wedding rings in her palm, and frown.

Shit. I guess there's no need for them anymore, right? Charles knows the truth, the game we've been playing is over. I've known this was coming all along so I'm not sure why it feels like a horrible surprise.

Lee and I might be married on paper, but we're only just starting out as a couple. I don't have much experience with long-term relationships, but I'm guessing that four days in is too soon to tell the person who just agreed to be your girlfriend that you actually want them to be your wife. We're still something new and delicate. This situation calls for patience and maturity – not my natural strengths, but I've spent the last year working on them. I can do this.

'Right,' I say after a moment, like it's no big deal. 'I guess that makes sense. I'll give them back to her today.' I open the drawer on my bedside table and pull out the ring box, placing her set carefully inside. Then I look down at my own hand and twist the ring from my finger. I try to ignore the wrenching sensation in my gut as I do so.

'No more pretending,' Lee says, and maybe there's something wistful in her voice, too.

'We don't need to pretend anymore,' I say with a touch of desperation. 'Real is better, Daisy.'

She smiles at those words, and it chases any sadness from her expression. 'Yeah,' she says quietly. 'Real is definitely better.'

Then she fixes me with a look, as if seeing me for the first time, and her eyes widen. Her gaze trails over me and my body's response is instant. She watches, fascinated, as a bead of water falls from my damp hair, rolling down over my chest, and I watch her, a hectic flush rising on her cheeks.

'Your eyes are doing that thing again,' I huff out a laugh. 'I don't know why I ever thought you had any kind of poker face. I can tell the second you start thinking dirty thoughts.'

'Oh, yes?' she asks, and her voice is husky. 'So what am I thinking about right now?'

'Well, I could tell you ... or you could come over here and show me.'

Her head tilts, and a smile plays on her lips. 'If real is better,' she says, getting slowly to her feet, 'then I suppose a practical demonstration *is* in order.'

'You know I love it when you're practical,' I manage, as she trails her fingers over my stomach. She reaches for the knotted towel at my waist and loosens it so that it drops to the floor and I'm standing naked in front of her.

Her smile widens, her right hand travelling lower, until she wraps her fingers around my cock, and the air hisses out from between my teeth. With her other hand on the nape of my neck she pulls me in for a long, lingering kiss, her tongue sliding against mine as her fingers glide up and down over my dick, and I groan into her mouth.

In a minute I'm going to peel the pyjamas from her body and fuck her slowly in our bed, until some of this desperate haze dissipates, until I can breathe and think and talk again. Will I ever get enough of her? *Is* there such a thing as enough? I've never felt like this before.

The blood is rushing so loudly in my ears that it takes a moment for the rapid knocking sound to register.

'I'm going to wring that bird's neck,' I mutter, but Lee's busy fingers have paused.

'I don't think that's Russell,' she frowns. 'I think there's someone at the door.'

'Ignore them,' I breathe, capturing her mouth with my own. I don't care who it is, the house could be on fire and I wouldn't care.

It could be seconds or hours or days before Lee pulls away again. 'Nico,' she's panting, her lips pink and swollen. 'They're still there.'

In fact, the knocking is growing more impatient.

'For fuck's sake,' I growl, grabbing a pair of jeans and tugging them on as I make for the front door. 'Why is our house suddenly the middle of the goddamn universe?' I take a few deep steadying breaths, waiting for my body to calm down, while the knocking continues.

'What?' I snap as I finally pull the door open.

'Hello, Nicolas,' Gran says dryly. 'I hope I'm not interrupting.'

Chapter Forty-Six

Lee

'Who is it?' I ask, having hastily pulled one of Nico's jumpers on over my pyjamas. 'Is everything okay?'

'Um,' Nico steps back so that I can see the person standing in the doorway.

'Gran!' I gasp, my brain unable to make sense of the sight of my grandmother standing on the doorstep, immaculately elegant in a long camel-coloured coat and a vintage Hermès scarf.

'Hello, Ophelia,' she says. 'Are you going to invite me in?'

'I . . . of course, come in.'

She steps inside, looking around with interest, stripping off her soft, leather gloves, and I'm certain her keen eyes miss nothing.

Her posture is relaxed, but there's thick tension in the air. Nico blinks at me, looking dazed. To be fair, a couple of minutes ago he was naked with my tongue in his mouth so it's quite the turnaround.

Gran turns to him. 'Perhaps you'd like to put on a shirt?' There's a glint of mischief in her eyes, even as her voice remains placid.

Nico looks down at his naked torso like he'd forgotten his body even existed. 'Shit,' he mutters, running a hand through his already tousled hair. 'Sorry, yes, I'll just . . .' He gestures to the bedroom, casting me an apologetic look.

'Would you like a cup of tea?' I ask, taking charge of the situation while he disappears. We're all British here so there's not a single awkward situation that cannot be smoothed over with a cup of tea.

'That would be lovely,' Gran says, moving around and taking everything in. As I fuss around making three cups of tea I try to see it through her eyes, the way I saw it only a couple of weeks ago. With a start, I realise how comfortable I am here now, how at home.

I also notice that things have changed in the last three weeks. It's tidier for a start, and there are several pairs of perilously high heels lined up next to the door alongside Phoebe and Nico's shoes. There's a romance novel from the library on the coffee table. The calendar on the fridge has my name on it, noting when I'll pick Phoebe up from school. There's a shopping list in my handwriting consisting almost entirely of green vegetables. Underneath, in Phoebe's round hand are the additions: 'Marshmallows, candy bars, cereal (the GOOD kind!!!!)'. Nico has tried to add 'flax seed' multiple times and it has been viciously crossed out.

I place the cups of tea on the table, gesturing for Gran to take a seat. Nico hasn't reappeared, and I guess he's giving us a minute on our own.

'Are you feeling okay?' I ask anxiously. 'After the journey and everything?'

'I had several glasses of champagne and slept like a baby,' Gran says coolly. 'The journey was no trouble.'

Okay then, I probably shouldn't have *immediately* questioned her health when she looks absolutely fine, but I couldn't help myself. I take a deep breath.

'Can I say I'm sorry first?' I blurt. 'I hate that we fought. It's not like us.'

Gran's shoulders come down. 'I know. I'm sorry as well. I said some things I shouldn't have because I was frustrated and it was wrong of me.'

I look down at my mug. 'I needed to hear it.'

Gran tilts her head, studying me. 'Maybe, but I could have worded it differently. I hurt your feelings and that's the last thing I'd ever want to do.'

I shrug, fighting the urge to smooth things over without acknowledging just how hurt I've been.

Nico walks out, dressed in jeans and a button-down shirt that I think he's used my travel steamer on, and I bite back a smile.

'Everything okay out here?' he asks.

'I was just apologising,' Gran says.

'Good.' Nico takes the seat next to mine, cups his warm hand at the back of my neck before stroking my back. It's a casual touch of reassurance, and a claiming, and Gran's brows lift.

'I see,' she says archly, and Nico just sips his tea.

Now Gran really does smile. 'Well, it's about time.'

'So everyone keeps telling me,' Nico smiles back at her, and the easy affection that has always existed between them is obvious.

'I can't believe you're here,' I say, shaking my head.

'I can't believe you thought I'd miss the fun,' Gran looks miffed. 'After that officious little lawyer called me, I booked myself on the first flight. Even your brother's in on the game before me. You can imagine how surprised he was when I turned up at the inn this morning.'

'You're staying at the inn as well?' Nico asks.

'I am, Magda arranged it.'

'Is Magda in touch with my *entire* family?' I ask. 'Next thing you know Mum and Dad will be turning up.'

'God, I hope not.' Gran wrinkles her nose.

'I don't know,' Nico says thoughtfully, 'I have one or two things I'd like to say to them.'

Gran's eyes gleam with something like approval, and then she delicately clears her throat. 'It's beautiful work you've done at the inn, Nicolas. My room is delightful and Magda's thrilled. I want you to give me the full tour later.'

He ducks his chin, obviously pleased.

'Anyway,' Gran sets her mug down, 'are the two of you going to fill me in on the whole story now?'

So the two of us take it in turns, and as expected, Gran enjoys the whole saga a lot, only expressing disappointment that she wasn't here to take part in the ruse.

'The lawyer would have believed it if I'd been around,' she says. 'The occasion called for a level of gravitas you were clearly missing.'

'You *do* have a lot of gravitas,' Nico agrees.

'I think we had more than enough enthusiastic participants, actually,' I say.

Gran's glossy red lips form a pout. 'Amateurs at deception from the sounds of it.'

'God, you and Phoebe are going to love each other,' Nico sighs.

Gran's eyes light. 'My first great-granddaughter. I can't wait to finally meet her.'

I know that Gran would consider Nico's daughter part of her family regardless of our relationship, but the words still give me a thrill. We're really doing it, blending our worlds, our lives together. My family is Phoebe's family in an even more real and tangible way.

'How long are you planning to stay?' I ask. 'Now that you're here I guess I should change my flight . . . I was going to go back to London on Saturday.' I'm smiling wide as I look at Nico. It feels like a reprieve, a few more days together, and his eyes hold the same mix of relief and happiness that I'm experiencing, but when I look back at Gran her own face has frozen in a mask of disapproval.

'I don't understand,' Gran says, her voice clipped. 'If you and Nico are in love and if, as it's perfectly obvious is the case, you're so happy here, *why* were you planning your return to London so soon?' The sharp look in her eyes makes it pretty clear that she knows why and she's not happy about it.

I need to handle this carefully, but it's hard to find the right words. I take a deep breath. 'I understand why you were angry and frustrated before. I'm sorry if I was hovering or being too pushy, but I'm not going to apologise for caring about you or for worrying about your health.'

Her mouth flattens. 'This isn't about me. I don't want you to stop living your life because of me. I won't be the reason you're somewhere you don't want to be.'

'I'm not.' I glance at Nico and his hand squeezes my knee under the table. 'Nico and I have talked about it, and we're working it out.'

If anything, Gran looks more upset. 'You don't need to work it out,' she bursts out. 'I am perfectly capable of looking after myself, and I'm *sick* of being made to feel like a frail old lady.'

My adrenaline spikes at the anger in her voice.

'Hold up.' Nico's voice is low and firm. 'No one thinks of you that way, but last year you had a heart attack and from what I gather you've not been doing much to take care of yourself since.'

'I don't think that's any of your business,' Gran says petulantly.

'It is my business because I love you, and so does Lee.' His tone brooks no disagreement. 'Maybe you don't want to think about how scary last year was, but we were all there, too. No one wants that again.'

'So I'm the villain because I want to live my life to the fullest?' Gran looks between the two of us. 'Because I want that for you as well? I want your life to be your own, not one that revolves around me while I become some sort of burden.'

'Stop!' I'm surprised by the sharpness in my voice, and by the looks of it so are Nico and Gran. 'This is what it all comes down to, and I don't know how to make you understand. I *love* you. You're not a burden and you never could be. Can you really not see that I would *want* to be with you, to spend time with you, yes, to take care of you if and when you need it? Are you telling me you wouldn't do the same for me? You already did. Was *I* a burden?'

'Of course not,' she huffs, but I'm on a roll now.

'I'm not just making this choice for you,' I say. 'It's not selfless and it's not only about your health. You're one of the most important people in the world to me. I don't *want* us to live on the other side of the world from each other. Nico gets that, he understands that we have to find a way to make this work for all of us, because our family isn't just me and Nico, it's you and Magda. It's Jack and Cynthie. It's Phoebe most of all. We're going to have to figure this out *together.* You get to live where you want and how you want, but you don't get to tell me how to feel about any of it. You don't get to tell me that you shouldn't matter or be taken into consideration.'

Gran is quiet for a long moment.

'And,' I add finally, 'I *do* want you to take your health more seriously, not because I want to make your life smaller, but because I want there to be as much of it as possible. I want you here for all the milestones. I want you to know Phoebe, I want you to know Jack and Cynthie's kids, I want Christmases and birthdays and I want Nico to take pictures of all of it. I want an album full of photographs. I want a family, and how can I have that without you?'

Nico has gone very still beside me.

Silence pours through the room, broken only by the ticking of the clock on the wall.

Gran blinks. 'All right, Ophelia,' she says at last. 'Perhaps it's not as straightforward as I thought, and it's *possible* that my pride has been getting in the way a little bit . . .'

Her gaze moves from Nico to me and back again, her expression troubled. 'I'll have to think about it.'

'Sure,' I shrug. 'We all will. It's not a problem that needs an immediate solution. We have time to work this out.'

'For now, perhaps you can show me around this town of yours?' Gran suggests.

I smile. 'I'd love to.'

'I'll come too,' Nico says. 'I can give you a tour of the inn afterwards.'

There's a knock at the door.

Nico sighs. 'I swear we never used to have unannounced visitors before you turned up, Daisy.'

I hold up my hands. 'I don't see how it can possibly be my fault when I'm the most anti-social person on the planet.'

'Who could it be this time?' Nico mutters as he pushes his chair back. 'Your ex-boyfriend, perhaps? My high school nemesis? My father back from the dead?'

To our surprise, it's Frankie, looking extraordinary in a teal satin suit.

'If you've come by to threaten to feed me to the pigs, now is not the time,' Nico grumbles. 'We've got a guest.'

Frankie gives one of his booming laughs. 'Sure, pigs are efficient but there's the smell to consider. What you want to do is dump a body in the desert and let the vultures have at it.'

'Good to know.'

'Who,' Gran perks up, her eyes glued to Frankie as he sweeps inside, 'is that?'

I watch as his gaze lands on my grandmother and a wide smile breaks over his face.

Oh god, I think hopelessly.

'Yeah,' Nico mutters, clearly reading my mind and imagining the havoc these two combined could wreak. 'We should have seen that one coming.'

'Are we interrupting?' a voice asks, and Cynthie stands in the doorway, hand in hand with Jack.

'Of course we're not interrupting,' Jack jumps in before Nico can come back with a scathing response. 'We're their cherished visitors. My best friend, and my little sister.' The smile he gives Nico implies that he's still not sure if he should be making outdated threats to protect my honour.

I try not to roll my eyes. 'We're about to give Gran and Frankie a tour of Roseport. Why don't you join us?'

'We'd love that!' Cynthie's face lights up. 'I'm so into this place.'

'Cynthie made friends with half the town in Darlene's bar last night,' Jack says. 'Apparently they're having a bonus Dollyoke night before we go so we don't miss out.'

Nico groans. 'There's no possible way this ends without me having to sing "Jolene" in a bar full of camera phones, is there?'

'Shouldn't think so,' my brother the West End star grins, any animosity forgotten. 'This place is amazing. Think we'll be able to fit in a trip to Acadia? We haven't hiked together for ages.'

Nico perks up at the mention of the nearby National Park. 'Yeah, could do.' He's got that dreamy look in his eye that means he's thinking about taking photographs.

'Magda also sent us with some news.' Cynthie is practically dancing from foot to foot. 'She's throwing a party at the inn on Saturday night to celebrate the reopening!'

'A party?' Nico looks panicked. 'I haven't finished the place yet.'

'Don't be silly, Nico,' Gran chides. 'It all looks wonderful.'

'And Jack and I can only stay a couple more days,' Cynthie looks genuinely sad about it. 'We want to make sure we meet everyone.'

Nico has no defence against Cynthie's pleading gaze. It's literally Oscar worthy.

'Fine,' he sighs. 'I suppose it won't hurt. I can probably get to most things over the next couple of days anyway.'

'I can help you,' my brother who doesn't know one end of a screwdriver from the other pipes up.

'No, thanks,' Nico snorts. 'Remember when you asked me to

help you put up those shelves at your place?'

Jack huffs. 'In fairness, I had no idea that pipe was there.'

'I told you to use the wall scanner beforehand,' Nico grumbles. 'And you didn't even know a stopcock was a thing, let alone where it was.'

'I thought you were *joking*,' Jack appeals to the room. 'I mean, come on . . . *stopcock*?'

'As I was being sprayed in the face by a metric ton of water, I wasn't really in the mood for cracking wise. I'll get the jobs done myself, thanks,' Nico says firmly.

'Perfect,' Cynthie claps her hands together, 'that's settled then. Saturday night.' She exchanges a sly look with Gran that definitely makes me nervous. 'And don't worry, Nico. It'll just be a nice, simple affair.'

Chapter Forty-Seven

Nico

'What do you mean it's black tie?' I ask Jack as he thrusts a tuxedo at me.

We're standing in his and Cynthie's room at the inn. It's strange to see it full of stuff, lived in like this, strange but good.

'I don't know,' Jack shrugs, dusting off the cuff of his own immaculately tailored tux. 'Apparently Cynthie and Gran got involved in Magda's party planning process and things have . . . escalated.'

'Escalated to *black tie*?' I groan. 'Is this why you called me in here? When did this reopening party turn into such a big deal? I'm supposed to be making sure all the finishing touches are in place before people start arriving, and then I'm meant to be going back to pick up Lee. Has anyone told *her* it's black tie? I doubt she has an evening dress with her and you know how much she freaks out about dressing right.'

Jack presses his lips together and waves an airy hand in the air. 'That's all under control. Gran and Cynthie are getting ready with Lee, Tara and Phoebe, and they're all coming over together. It's a girl thing.'

'So where has this tuxedo come from? You had a spare? You travel with two tuxedos on the off chance you'll need them?' I grumble. 'Actually, don't answer that, it's exactly the sort of thing you'd do.'

'Hey, there's nothing wrong with looking sharp. You might want to rethink your current devotion to plaid.'

I smirk. It didn't take too many of the romance books Tara recommended before I worked out exactly why a plaid shirt could put that hungry look in Lee's eyes. I'm filling my entire wardrobe with the things.

'Your sister likes it,' is all I say, but it seems that's enough because Jack makes a brief retching sound.

'I'm still getting used to this,' he mutters.

'Seriously though,' I say, putting a hand on his arm to stop him as he turns away. 'We haven't had much of a chance to talk about it. Are we good?'

His eyes narrow. 'Would you care if I said no?'

I exhale. 'Yeah, I'd care. It just wouldn't change things between me and Lee.'

'There you go then,' Jack shrugs. 'Listen, I'm not in any position to play the overprotective brother part, even if I didn't think that was dick behaviour. It's not my business who Lee chooses to have a relationship with. For what it's worth I know she couldn't have chosen better.'

'Fuck,' I mutter. 'You know I can't cope with you when you're being sincere.'

He grins. 'Why do you think I do it? Now go and get ready. You're basically the guest of honour, seeing as you apparently built this whole place with your bare hands.' He looks moody for a second. 'It's giving Cynthie *ideas* and I know you're very down on my DIY skills but I'm going to need you to show me how to put up a curtain rail. Also where can I get one of those tool belts? Honestly, I think it's mostly about the tool belt.'

'Buddy, you gotta earn the tool belt.'

There's a knock on the door.

'Nico, there you are!' Magda appears. 'Why aren't you ready?'

'I only just found out about this black tie thing,' I huff. 'Don't you want me to check on things downstairs before people start arriving? You've had me up on the second floor all afternoon and I still needed to clean up after those final touch ups.'

'No, no,' Magda grips my arm and starts dragging me out the door, 'that's all been taken care of.' She marches me down the corridor and Jack's amused laughter follows us. 'But you really need to look your best. The whole town is turning out and people are very excited. Rita's wearing a tiara!'

Sounds drift up from downstairs. It sounds like a suspiciously large number of people running around. I'm sure that was Phil that was booming away, and if the Roseport Players are involved, things are almost certainly getting out of hand. Someone was bashing cymbals together earlier, and when I asked about it Magda said the school marching band wanted to play during the firework display.

My ominous 'What firework display?' had been met with silence.

'Bloody hell,' I mutter, looking down at myself, covered in dust and paint stains from all the last minute jobs I've been crawling around doing. 'I need to go home and have a shower.'

'Don't be silly,' Magda laughs. 'There are so many bathrooms here. I thought you and Lee would like to stay over tonight anyway.' She stops outside the door to the library room. 'What do you think?'

I smile. 'Yeah, Lee would probably love that, actually.'

'Excellent.' Magda opens the door and basically shoves me inside the room. 'Then you take your time, and make yourself presentable.'

When she shuts the door behind me I take a moment to look around. Lee's favourite room has turned out well, but it's not the quality of the work that catches my attention now. Magda has obviously been scheming because the bed is covered in red rose petals. There's a tall silver ice bucket next to the two armchairs that holds a bottle of seriously good champagne. On a table next to it are two champagne flutes and a plate of chocolate-covered strawberries.

Yeah, Lee is going to love this.

Not wanting to delay things further, I shower and change into the tuxedo Jack handed me. He's a bit broader than me these days, so I'm surprised to find that it fits like it was made for me. It's been such a long time since I wore one of these things that I'm still fiddling with the bow tie when there's a knock at the door.

'Come in,' I call, and Jack slips inside.

He runs an assessing eye over my suit. 'That looks good.'

'It's great. Perfect, in fact. Now I really am worried – are you travelling with tuxedos in a range of sizes?'

'Hey, all bodies fluctuate,' he smirks. 'Sorry if it's a bit loose in the crotch, though.'

I treat him to a withering look.

His eyes slide away from mine and he coughs before he reaches in his pocket. 'I figured you wouldn't have cufflinks.'

'Not all of us travel with cufflinks on their person, no. I thought I'd just roll up the sleeves or something.'

Jack's expression switches to one of outrage. 'This is an Armani tuxedo, Nico. Show some respect!'

'Fine, fine, sorry!'

'Anyway, I have a spare pair you can borrow.' Jack holds out his hand, a pair of simple black and gold cufflinks in his palm.

'Thanks, these are really nice,' I say, admiring them as I quickly twist them into place.

'Yeah,' Jack swallows. 'They were my grandpa's.'

I look up at him. 'Are you . . . crying?'

'What?' He blinks outraged. 'Obviously not. There must still be some sawdust or something floating around in here.'

'Okayyy.' I watch him, bemused, as he blinks again.

There's another knock at the door and this time my mum bursts in without waiting for an answer.

'Oh, *Nicolas*,' she murmurs, staring at me, and she definitely *is* crying. 'You look so handsome!'

'Thanks, you look lovely.' And she does, she's a knockout in a long blue velvet number. She's also clutching a large envelope in her hand. 'But why are you crying?'

'It's the sawdust in the air,' Jack jumps in. 'You're just immune to it because you have builder's lungs or whatever.'

'Yes,' Ma sniffles. 'Some of us have sensitive eyes.'

'Anyway,' Jack thumps a hand on my shoulder and gives a light squeeze, 'I'll see you down there, yeah?'

'Sure,' I agree while he and Claudia exchange a significant look.

Between the tux, Jack's sentimental non-outburst and Ma being unusually early to an event, something definitely feels off.

'Darling, I need to talk to you about a couple of things.' My mum drops down onto one of the armchairs and gestures for me to take the seat across from her. 'I asked Charles if he'd take a look at something for me, now that this whole mess has been sorted out.'

She hands me the envelope, and intrigued, I open it, pulling out the stack of documents inside. When I see what they are I almost fling them straight into the fireplace.

'Divorce papers? What the fuck, Ma?'

Her eyes widen innocently. 'Well, darling, I was only trying to be helpful. After all, better to do it as soon as possible, isn't it? I know you and Lee are planning on giving the relationship a go, but you're hardly going to stay married, are you?' She wrinkles her nose. 'It's always best to get the unpleasant paperwork out of the way.'

'But I don't want divorce papers.' My voice is too loud in the stillness of the room.

Her brows lift. 'Perhaps I misunderstood,' she says. 'When you gave me the rings back, I assumed—'

'Lee gave them to me. I could hardly tell her to keep wearing them, could I? She only agreed to this fake marriage thing to help me out.' I glare down at the papers in my hands. 'I was going to wait, to see if . . . I don't know. But I'm not signing these. I don't care if it's unreasonable. I'm not divorcing her.'

'Why not?'

'Because I'm in love with her. I want to be married to her. I want her to be my wife.' When I look up, my mother is beaming.

'I know, darling.' She reaches into the small purse she's carrying wrapped around her wrist, and extracts a ring box. 'But don't you think you'd better tell Lee that?'

I take the box and open it. Inside, the diamond daisy engagement ring sits alone.

'Where are the others?'

She stands, dusting off her dress, and looks down at me, her eyes full of affection. 'Jack has them, of course. Isn't that what the best man does?'

Chapter Forty-Eight

Lee

'I still can't believe Magda did this,' I say as Tara carefully curls the back of my hair. 'Who decides to throw a black tie event with less than twenty-four hours' notice? I mean, what were you doing travelling with a dress like that?'

Tara shrugs, stunning in a long, strappy dress of lilac silk. 'What can I say, I'm an overpacker.'

'But Gran and Cynthie, too!' I exclaim. 'Am I the only one not packing emergency evening wear?' As someone who takes a significant amount of pride in her ability to pull together a travel wardrobe, I'm shaken to my core by this revelation.

'You know that mine was because of a work thing,' Cynthie calls from the bathroom where I can see through the open door that she is applying her mascara. She looks gorgeous, too. Her dress is actually quite similar to Tara's but a darker shade of purple.

'I *do* always travel with evening wear,' Gran shrugs from where she's perched on the bed, elegant in a long, burgundy dress with a matching bolero jacket. She examines her fingernails. 'One never knows.'

'And you're sure this dress you have is going to fit me?' I call to Cynthie. 'You're taller than I am.'

'Not with the heels on,' Cynthie argues. 'Anyway, I don't see that you've got a lot of choice at the moment, do you?'

'No, I suppose not.' Whatever Cynthie has with her is going to be more suitable than anything in my wardrobe. Apparently the whole town is turning out in ball gowns and tuxedos.

There's a knock at the front door.

'I'll get it!' Phoebe yells from the front room.

'There, that will be Luke with the dress now.' Cynthie wanders through, her makeup flawless, her famous face almost dazzlingly perfect. 'I'm sorry I didn't tell you about the dress code switch earlier, or maybe we could have found you something in town.' She looks crestfallen.

'I wouldn't have been able to find anything in Roseport anyway,' I say quickly, feeling bad. 'I really appreciate you getting me an outfit for tonight.' As Cynthie's expression lightens I know I'd rather die than complain about it now; I'll wear whatever she's lending me with a smile, even if it's a bin bag.

'I'll go and grab it,' Tara says, putting the curling iron down. 'I want to perv on Luke in his tux.' She sends me a wink.

'You know I think your hair would look better up, Lee,' Gran muses.

'Do you think so?' I ask, turning my head back and forth in the mirror.

'Definitely,' Cynthie comments as she appears with a load of hair grips in her hand. 'Let me quickly pin these curls up. I spend most of my life getting my hair done so I'm practically a professional.' She holds the grips between her teeth as she deftly pins the curls in place forming a loose French twist. 'I wish we could have flown Patty in,' she mutters. 'I asked her for instructions, but she'd have done it much better.'

'A bit much for an inn reopening party, flying your hair stylist in,' I say with a grin.

Her eyes meet mine in the mirror and she squeezes my shoulders. 'I suppose so. Anyway, I haven't done too badly.'

'No, it looks perfect,' I say honestly.

'Okay!' Tara comes barging in with a dress bag over one arm. Phoebe is hot on her heels, dressed in a sparkly black and purple dress with a full tulle skirt that she and Gran picked out yesterday. Unbeknownst to us, Gran broke Phoebe out of school for the afternoon and the two went on a shopping spree. Needless to say, they're the best of friends now.

Taco trots in behind them, and even he is dressed for the occasion, a floral corsage pinned to his collar.

'Two pieces of news,' Tara declares. 'Luke in a tuxedo is the hottest thing I've ever seen, and the dress is here.'

'And the shoes!' Phoebe holds up a shoebox.

'Cynthie,' I gasp, opening the dress bag, 'this is gorgeous. Are you sure *you* don't want to wear it?'

She waves her hand. 'No, no. It was part of a photo shoot and the stylist said it washed me out. I wasn't sure at the time but I think he's right. It'll be much better with your colouring.'

'It's true,' Gran chimes in. 'Brings out the gold in your hair.'

I slip into the dress, which is a whisper of creamy silk. It's bias cut with a cowl neckline, and the back dips almost scandalously low.

'Oh, it is quite long,' I say regretfully.

'You're right,' Cynthie sighs, pulling out the shoes, which are high heeled and made of sapphire blue satin. When I slip them on the skirt of the gown still drags on the floor despite their height. 'I'm sorry,' she says sadly. 'I suppose I am taller.'

'It doesn't matter,' I rush to reassure her. 'I'll just hold the skirt up.'

'I guess that will work,' Cynthie agrees, and for a split second I could swear there's an unholy glee in her eyes, but even as I register it, it's gone.

'It's lucky we have the same size feet,' I say, admiring the shoes. 'And that they let you take these home, too.'

'Mmm,' Cynthie murmurs in agreement. 'Now,' she exchanges a quick look with Tara, 'didn't Luke need a hand with something in the car?'

'*Yes, and*,' Phoebe says, 'we should help him.'

'Why is Phoebe doing improv?' I ask.

'Because I told her that real actors improv all the time,' Cynthie says airily. 'She's doing a project for school.'

'Yes, and I am,' Phoebe says admiringly.

Tara chokes on a laugh. 'Anyway, let's go and help him.' The three of them leave and I'm alone with my grandmother.

'Are they being strange or is it just me?'

Gran shrugs. 'Ophelia, everyone in this town is slightly strange. Perhaps there's something in the water.'

'True,' I grin, 'but you like it, don't you?'

'I do.' Gran looks nervous for a second. 'Actually, there's something I wanted to talk to you about. I know we're due to head home next week, but I wondered how you'd feel about extending our stay?'

'Extending it?' I ask, bemused.

She lifts her hip, revealing a manilla envelope that she's been sitting on top of, and hands it to me.

I read the papers inside, then I stop and read them again slowly.

'What's an EB-5 visa?' I ask, my heart thumping.

'Basically, it's a way that people from the UK with plenty of money to throw at the problem can retire to the United States.' Gran examines her fingernails.

'But this is an application form,' I point out. My voice sounds very far away.

'Yes,' she agrees.

'Oh my god,' I whisper.

'It's not a done deal,' Gran warns. 'It'll be a while before we can get it all sorted. And before you start getting too excited, it's not exactly the solution you're hoping it might be.' She holds her hand up as if to stop me getting ahead of myself. 'I think Roseport is charming, but I'm not sure it's very me. Not at the moment anyway. Jack and I had a long conversation about it, and if everything goes according to plan, I'm going to split my time between here and California.'

'California,' I murmur, trying to take it in.

Gran's smile is slow and full of mischief. 'I think I'd enjoy Los Angeles, and of course, there are other attractions to visit nearby.'

The penny drops. 'Vegas?' I say with a laugh. 'Frankie doesn't waste any time.'

'Darling, we don't have the time to waste,' Gran chuckles. 'And you know my British beaus have been such a disappointment lately. I think it's time to broaden my horizons.' Her expression becomes thoughtful. 'But I hope you won't be upset about my decision not to live here full time. We'll still see plenty of each other, and who knows how things will work out later on, but for now this feels . . . right. And I promise that I'll try and take better care of myself. Jack says I won't have a choice in LA because he's hiring Cynthie's personal trainer to torment me and I'll be drowning in wheatgrass.' She wrinkles her nose. 'It was one of the few downsides.'

'And you're really happy about this?' I ask cautiously.

'Absolutely,' she nods. 'A new adventure for me, near all of my grandchildren. I think it's just what I've been looking for.'

'So . . . I can stay.' I say the words out loud and they sound dazed.

'You can stay,' Gran agrees. 'If that's what you want.'

In response I fling myself at her, making a strange sound that is somewhere between laughing and crying. 'I can't believe you'd do this for me.'

Gran's arms close around me, a rare and wonderful hug. 'For

both of us, my precious girl. Now stop crying or you'll ruin your makeup.' She whips out a handkerchief and starts dabbing at my eyes.

'I'm so happy, I don't even know what to do with myself,' I admit.

'Well, you look beautiful, and I know what will finish your outfit off perfectly,' Gran says, reaching for her purse. 'I accidentally packed these, but they don't go with my dress, no idea what I was thinking.'

She holds out a beautiful pair of sapphire earrings, a dazzling flash of blue.

'Wow. Are you sure?' I ask.

She nods. 'They're the same colour as your eyes.'

'As *your* eyes,' I laugh.

'Must be why your grandfather bought them for me,' she agrees, digging through her purse again so I can't catch her expression. 'Now, we'd better go. The others will be waiting for us. I think I heard Bud arrive.'

With that, we join the others and bundle into the cars, talking and laughing, and make the short drive to the inn. There are lots of cars in the car park, but everyone must already be inside.

'Are we late?' I ask.

Tara smiles. 'I think we're right on time. Nothing like making an entrance. Let me take your coat for you.'

When we step through the front door I come to a screeching halt. The entrance hall is empty, but the whole space is full of flowers and flickering candles.

There are wildflowers everywhere, banks of them spill across the edges of the floor, they climb up the banisters, as if growing half way up the stairs. Cornflowers and poppies and anemones and daisies. It's beautiful and magical and totally overboard.

'What?' I manage to get out in my confusion.

I hear a noise from the stairs and I glance up to find Nico standing there in a tuxedo.

'I think we'll all just go through to the other room,' Cynthie murmurs in my ear, and, distantly, I register that they're all leaving, but my eyes are glued to the man who is slowly walking down the staircase towards me.

'Hey, pretty girl,' he says softly.

'Nico,' I murmur, still trying to understand how any human being can be so handsome that they literally knock all the air out of you. 'What's going on?'

His mouth kicks up and he laughs. 'Okay, now I feel better. It's taking you even longer than it took me.'

'What are you talking about?' I look around at the flowers. 'Who did all this?'

'I believe Cynthie and Gran put their brains and their resources together for this one.' He shakes his head fondly.

'Well, it's gorgeous, but it's a bit much, isn't it?'

He smiles. 'We'll see.' He examines the flowers twined around the staircase and plucks a daisy free, coming towards me. Reaching up, he carefully tucks the flower into my hair.

'Perfect,' he says, and I melt.

I touch his arm. 'I have something to tell you,' I say and I'm bubbling over. I get to tell him that I can stay.

'Can I show you something first?' he asks, his tone strangely serious.

'Of course.' I expect him to take me through to the big drawing room where I can hear the murmur of voices, the gentle hum of string music, but instead he leads me back to the stairs. I hold up the hem of my dress, careful not to trip, and I think I see amusement flicker in his eyes again.

'I wanted to show you, before the party started. I put the finishing touches up this morning.' He gestures to the wall by the stairs, and that's when I realise that it's covered in dozens of framed photographs. Most people I don't recognise, but among them I spot photographs of Magda and a man who must have been her husband Tom. Pictures of Phoebe's mum Stacie, first as a child herself and then later holding a tiny, round-cheeked Phoebe in her lap.

We climb higher and there are pictures of Nico, Nico and Phoebe together, Phoebe and Magda, and then I spot it. There's a picture of me. It's from that night in Las Vegas, and I'm sitting with a huge pile of poker chips in front of me, laughing. It's a stunning photograph, and I recognise Nico's work straight away.

It's the first picture of me, but it's not the only one. There's one of me and Phoebe tucked up together reading on the sofa, there's a picture of all of us in our Halloween costumes, there's one of me leaning down to talk to Taco who is staring up at me like he loves me. There's the one Nico took that day on the overlook when I had been watching him and Phoebe with my heart in my eyes. The selfie of the three of us; Magda patiently bent over a pair of crochet hooks trying to teach me what to do while I sit surrounded by tangled wool. Me, looking out the window in our kitchen, a cup of tea cradled in my hand. The trees outside are a blaze of orange and golden light limns my profile. I look happy. Peaceful.

I didn't even know he had taken most of these, but each one is perfect, each one is a love letter. At the top of the stairs is a different kind of picture. It's a Polaroid. It's not beautifully shot or perfectly lit. It's slightly blurry. It's our wedding photo.

My eyes are tearing up. I look at the pictures of me, mixed in with all the others. He's letting me know that he sees me, that I'm a part of something. A family.

He links his fingers with mine and pulls me up the last couple of stairs and along the hall. When he opens a door I realise it's the library room. Only now it's finished and it's gorgeous and there are books everywhere and also rose petals for some reason.

'Oh my god.' I stop in my tracks. 'You did it!' I pick up my skirts and rush over. 'You built a ladder!'

I run my fingers over the handles and step up, my heels hooking over the rungs. I touch the shelf of books in front of my face. 'I love it!' I exclaim, but when I look back at Nico over my shoulder I almost break my neck.

Because he's down on one knee, my daisy-shaped engagement ring in his hand.

Chapter Forty-Nine

Lee

'What are you doing?' I gasp, and I flail about, until Nico jumps up and carefully lifts me down from the ladder, my overlong skirts tangled around us both.

'I thought it would be romantic,' he says ruefully. 'But I should have remembered you'd be wearing impractical shoes.'

'Forget my shoes!' I hiss. 'What . . . what were you just doing?'

He rubs a hand over his jaw. 'Well, I get the impression Cynthie planned for me to do it in the entrance hall, but I think this is a bit more us, don't you?'

'I honestly don't understand anything that's happening tonight,' I say slowly.

'Right,' he agrees, and he seems nervous. 'Let me start again.'

'Okay.'

He takes my hand in his and there's so much tenderness in his face that it almost hurts to look at it.

'Last year,' he says, 'when I met Phoebe, it changed me. I felt like all the molecules in my body had rearranged themselves and I was something different, something new. I was her dad, and I was scared but I'd never been happier about anything. It was like my entire world shifted in that moment and nothing would ever be the same.'

He takes a deep breath. 'And then three weeks ago it happened again ... when we stood outside this building and you fell into my arms. One moment, a single instant, and my life changed for ever. *I* changed for ever. I don't know what games the universe was playing when we got married in Vegas, but I know that you were meant to be my wife. That I was meant to be your husband. I know it with every fibre of my being.' He keeps hold of my hand, and in his other he holds the engagement ring, the diamonds glinting in the soft light. 'Marry me, Lee. Not by accident, do it on purpose. Marry me like you mean it.'

I think he's smiling, but honestly, it's hard to tell through my tears. He brushes his thumbs tenderly under my eyes, and I wonder if it's possible to experience so much happiness that you simply burst into a million shiny pieces.

He looks down at me, cradling my face in his hands as my whole body collapses against him. 'Well?' he says, and I can feel my ring in his hand, pressing against my skin. 'Are you going to keep me waiting for an answer?'

I laugh, a watery sound. 'You built me a book ladder,' I manage. 'Of course I'll marry you. Or stay married to you, or whatever we're doing.'

He slips the ring onto my finger and then he's kissing me, and I'm kissing him, and he lifts me up off the floor, his arm clasped around my waist, my feet kicked in the air like the romantic heroine I know I am.

'Okay,' I say when we eventually untangle ourselves, 'I actually have some news, too.'

His eyebrows lift. 'So you *did* figure it out?'

'Figure what out?' I ask, but I'm too impatient to wait for a reply. 'Gran's moving here,' I blurt.

He pauses. 'What?'

'Well, not here, or at least not all the time, but she's going to be here with us or in LA with Jack. I can stay.'

I watch him absorb the words, watch so many emotions pass across his face until he settles on one: joy. Fierce, absolute joy. 'You can stay,' he says, his forehead resting against mine. 'You can stay,' he breathes it like a mantra.

'If you want me to,' I tease.

The answer I get is another kiss, a soft kiss that melts into something deeper, sweeter. My hands press to his jaw and I pepper kisses everywhere I can reach and he laughs, a sound of such pure happiness that I want to get drunk on it.

'We'd better go downstairs,' Nico says when we finally break apart, attempting to straighten his bow tie. 'They'll all be wondering what's keeping us.'

I pout, play with one of the buttons on his shirt. 'No one will even notice we're missing. Let's stay up here for a bit longer.' I trail my lips across his jaw.

'I absolutely think they will notice,' he says, a strange note in his voice.

I step back so that I can look at him properly. 'What do you mean by that?' I ask, suspicious.

He grins down at me, his eyes sparkling with mischief. 'I mean that the whole town is downstairs waiting for us to get married.'

My mouth drops open. 'What?'

He laughs. 'Daisy,' he gestures towards me. 'You really didn't notice? You're wearing a wedding dress.'

I look down at the beautiful gown. 'No. It's not like it's a white dress. It's cream. Gran says it brings out the gold in my hair.'

'Baby,' he brushes the backs of his fingers across my cheek, his smile wide, 'it has a train.'

'It does not,' I say indignantly. 'It's just a bit too long because Cynthie is taller than me.' Although, now that he says it, I suppose the length is a bit train like. A very, very short train that a person could easily miss.

'I could be wrong,' he shrugs, 'but weren't Tara and Cynthie wearing matching bridesmaid's dresses when they arrived?'

'I—' I open my mouth. 'They were different colours. The necklines weren't the same.'

'I'm wearing your grandfather's cufflinks,' he says, pulling up his sleeves. 'Your brother cried when he gave them to me.'

'What?'

'Well, he said it was sawdust, but I think we all know there's not a speck of the stuff in here.'

'Oh my god.' My hands go to my earrings. 'Gran's earrings. Something borrowed, something blue.'

'And I don't know if you noticed but it's like a florist's shop exploded downstairs. I'm pretty sure there's a string quartet down there as well. Possibly some doves. They might have run away with things a bit . . . I can only assume there was a town meeting involved.'

They played me, I realise. They all played me like a fiddle. Especially Cynthie, making me feel like I'd be a monster not to wear her too-long, photo-shoot-reject dress, which I now realise is obviously couture bridal wear. I suppose the woman is one of the greatest actors of her generation so it was hardly a fair fight, but *still*.

'They threw us a secret wedding?' I murmur. It finally sinks in. 'The whole town threw us a *secret wedding*!'

'Welcome to where I was about an hour ago.' Nico nods. 'And you know, if this isn't what you want then I get it. It's a lot. I know about a dozen different ways we can sneak out of here and drive off into the sunset. We could head straight back to Vegas, the two of us.'

He grins, and every time I think I can't fall any more in love with him, it happens all over again.

'What do you think?' I ask.

'I think you look beautiful. I think everyone we love is

downstairs. I'd marry you right now, or any other day, anywhere, any way you want.'

'Okay,' I say, slipping my hand in his, the decision as easy as that. 'Let's do it.'

'Are you sure?'

'Oh yes,' I smile up at my husband, at the man I've loved for as long as I can remember, 'I'm sure.'

I wonder if there's ever an end to this, a floor or a ceiling to how much love I can hold for him, or if it's just something that spins on forever, infinite.

I suppose I have a whole lifetime to find out.

Epilogue: One Year Later

Nico

'It was nice of Frankie to give us the same room,' my wife says, standing by the enormous window that offers a spectacular view over Las Vegas.

'Well, you only get one second, first wedding anniversary.' I wrap my arms around her from behind, pulling her against me.

She trails her fingers over the tattoos on my forearm, the daisy and the bee inked in swirling black lines. A perfect set.

'As opposed to our first, second wedding anniversary in three weeks' time?' she laughs. 'This is going to get confusing.'

'Nah,' I kiss her cheek, 'we *should* be celebrating as much as possible. Want to get married a third time? Maybe we could have an anniversary in the spring, too.' I'd like that. I want to fill our house with daisies and promise her my whole life over and over again.

'I don't think we need any excuse to celebrate,' Lee murmurs, and I can't argue with that.

There's been plenty to celebrate over the last year: putting several stamps in Phoebe's passport, including a family trip to Norway to see the Northern Lights; Jack and Cynthie's wedding; Gran's continuing good health (who knew the woman would become best friends with Cynthie's terrifying personal trainer?); Phoebe's first ballet recital, with her entire family in the front row; Tara and Luke getting engaged after six months of long-distance dating; my photography exhibition at a local gallery; breaking ground on our house extension, complete with a separate granny flat for whenever Gran comes to stay, and – Lee is adamant – a library ladder of her very own.

But for all the big things there have been a million tiny, perfect inconsequential moments with my wife that matter even more. Cleaning up the kitchen the morning after we had our friends over for New Year's Eve, bickering over the grocery list, watching Lee teach Taco how to roll over on command and acting like they were ready to take Crufts by storm, pouring her a glass of wine when she stays up late working at her laptop, becoming a regular fixture at Darlene's line-dancing night.

A whole album full of family photographs already, with the promise of more to come.

I hold her for a moment, enjoying the feeling of her in my arms. It's been the best year of my life, but sometimes it still takes me by surprise – the way I feel, the happiness I didn't even know I was capable of.

'Tell me the truth,' Lee says after a moment. 'Should we be worried about Phoebe?'

'She's with Gran and Frankie.'

'Exactly,' Lee sighs. 'I'm fairly certain she said something about learning how to count cards on the internet. And she *is* very good at maths.'

She can't quite keep the pride from her voice. Boasting about Phoebe is one of Lee's favourite hobbies.

'Sounds like Frankie's problem to me.'

'You can be the one to bail our daughter out of jail,' Lee huffs.

'I've already got a savings account earmarked for that inevitable occasion,' I smile then, my teeth closing around her earlobe.

She shivers against me. 'You know I can't resist you when you're being fiscally responsible.'

'That's good news because last time we were in this room I wasn't allowed to touch you, and I have a lot of plans for that giant bed next door.'

Lee turns in my arms, her eyebrows raised. 'Interesting. I have some thoughts on the subject, too. Perhaps we should compare notes.'

I lean in, my nose nudging against hers. 'When you say compare notes . . . there's an actual notebook, right?'

She smiles, and the glimpse of her dimples has my heart racing. 'Of course. As you might remember, I have a lot of opinions about physical intimacy.'

'Maybe you should show me, Daisy.' My voice holds a challenge. 'Kiss me like you mean it.'

And she does.

Acknowledgements

As always I'm so grateful to my agent Louise who saw the slow-dancing-to-I-Will-Always-Love-you potential from my very first garbled explanation of this book, and my whole fantastic editorial team at Simon and Schuster – Molly, Mel and Misha, even though a copy editor would tell me that is too many M names close together! Thank you for believing in this book and helping to make it a reality.

Thanks of course Sabah, Harriett, Gen, Sarah, Kate and the rest of the S&S team – the absolute best in the business, and to Tamsin and Gillian for the immaculate copy edit and proofread. Thanks to Pip and Serene for literally the most beautiful cover I have ever seen.

I'm so thankful for my writer pals who truly kept me going when I was working on this one and are such constant, kind cheerleaders: Sarra Manning, Kirsty Greenwood, Cressida McLaughlin, Jane Casey, Hux, Lucy Powrie, Sarah Chamberlain, Rebecca Ryan, and especially Dr Laucy Vinewood.

It's so nice when writers you love and admire turn out to be the loveliest people, so thank you to Julia Quinn, Marian Keyes and Lynn Painter for proving I have excellent taste.

I am overwhelmed by all the support I get online and could pack another 400 pages with bookstagrammers who have filled my cup this last year, I'm so grateful to every single one of you. A few special shoutouts to: Katie @katieprouty, Lucy @lucyslumos, Shelby @whimsyreadswithshelby, Kayla @kayreadwhat,Emily @Authemmie, Diana @Lavaslibrary, Robin @Cozyinthenook, Kelly @nuclearfiction, Eva @evavastheworld, Sam @bookishsam71, Vero @themoonphoenix, Bethany Louise @escapebeyondpages, Jodi @more.time.2read, Becki @bookswithbecki, KLou @bookbeforeuleap, Tilly @tillylovesbooks, Emily @em_jacobs_reads, Diana @lavaslibrary, Isabella @isabellalolareads, Jen @oh.how.novel, and Cindy @thoughtsfromapage.

Thank you to every single reader who read *Let's Make a Scene* and reached out to ask for Lee and Nico's story. I hope it was worth the wait!

To the real life Reading Between the Wines – there was only ever going to be one name for Lee's book group! I promise I will make it to PEI soon – and then we'll drink pink squirrels together.

To ALL the incredible book groups who have been so kind. Book people truly are the best of all. Special thanks to my bffs at Found Family Book Hive – Jen, Cale and Danielle, and to the incredible Sarah Lamagna and the Prose Before Bros book club. Thanks to ALL the amazing booksellers who I know are out there literally hand selling my books, particularly to Hannah and my Mr B's family.

Thanks to Emily Dayton – I wrote that line dancing scene just for you! Justice for Twisters fans!

Thank you to my friends and family who have not seen me for the last 6–12 months! I still love you! And thank you to Peege and Bea – my whole entire heart.

Oh, and thanks again to Dolly Parton just because I think it's good practice for us all to thank her as loudly and as often as possible.

Discover more from Laura Wood

Available now

Simon & Schuster